A Previous Life

A Previous Life

Another Posthumous Novel

Edmund White

BLOOMSBURY PUBLISHING
NEW YORK · LONDON · OXFORD · NEW DELHI · SYDNEY

BLOOMSBURY PUBLISHING
Bloomsbury Publishing Inc.
1385 Broadway, New York, NY 10018, USA

BLOOMSBURY, BLOOMSBURY PUBLISHING, and the Diana logo are trademarks
of Bloomsbury Publishing Plc

First published in the United States 2021

ISBN: HB: 978-1-63557-727-3; EBOOK: 978-1-63557-728-0

LIBRARY OF CONGRESS CATALOGING-IN-PUBLICATION DATA IS AVAILABLE

2 4 6 8 10 9 7 5 3 1

Typeset by Westchester Publishing Services
Printed and bound in the U.S.A.

To find out more about our authors and books visit www.bloomsbury.com and sign up
for our newsletters.

Bloomsbury books may be purchased for business or promotional use. For information
on bulk purchases please contact Macmillan Corporate and Premium Sales Department at
specialmarkets@macmillan.com.

For Quinn, and to the memory of a great love

They both suffered at the idea of practicing a deception on her, but deception, to a quite unexpected extent, gets easier with practice.

—PENELOPE FITZGERALD, *INNOCENCE*

But me and my true love will never meet again.

—"LOCH LOMOND," SCOTTISH FOLK SONG

Ruggero was my muse. He always encouraged me as a writer, never gave me negative remarks. The only things he corrected were errors of fact or tone or inconsistencies. As a trained musician he could feel the structure of my work—and often improve on it. He always showed me respect. When I made suggestions about his writing, he always took them with gratitude and humility. Gertrude Stein said that writers need only praise, and Ruggero followed her advice without perhaps knowing it was hers. He read every word I wrote as soon as I wrote it—for an insecure egomaniac like me, that was the ideal response.

He left me probably because he was lonely. Everyone liked him but he didn't make friends easily.

I was the reckless suicidal bitch because I disturbed our "arrangement." I wanted to be the wife, not the other woman.

CHAPTER I

The year 2050

S he came back into the room where the fire was blazing and looked with admiration at the familiar face. Yes, he was in his seventies but still slender and handsome with his strong profile (big Italian nose, huge dark eyes, full lips still red).

She was laughing to herself as she sat on the taboret next to his high-backed tapestried chair.

"What's so funny?" he asked, looking at once wary and charmed; was she laughing at him (which she sometimes did) or had she noticed some new, never-remarked-on-before endearing trait?

"All evening I kept looking up from my book and wondering if you ever slept with anyone for money."

He stood, expressionless (this was how he showed indignation). "Have you forgotten I'm a lord from Sicily? Why do you ask?"

"Calm down. You've always been so handsome." She was smiling now but not laughing. "Surely someone must have offered you some money, if only to see your strong body. And you've always been—well, not amoral but a good sport. If you're so attractive now, you must have been irresistible at thirty or forty. I've seen the photos. I know."

With each flattering supposition, he relaxed. He sat back down. He looked at her as if verifying her degree of sophistication. At last he smiled. "Well, yes, once, when I was forty and still looked thirty, Edmund White, we were great friends but he was already in his eighties, paid me twenty symbolic dollars. I undressed though he kept his clothes on. He wrapped the bill around my member. The situation, unique in my experience, made us both laugh; he loved pretending. And I was, and am, as you know, such a narcissist that it made me hard."

"And?" she asked, after denying that he was a narcissist.

"Well, I don't need to spell it out. I kept the twenty dollars. He loved to play—that night he decided he was a naïve American tourist in shorts with a camera around his neck and I a wily, not very clean *scugnizzo*."

She'd heard the word but forgotten what it meant.

"A street boy in Naples, always cheerful, looking like Caravaggio's *Bacchus*, dirty feet, a hungover green color, who will do anything for a few lira. Of course I was the one who ended up with the expensive camera."

"I've performed fellatio on you," she said, a bit too blunt for his taste. "Did you like it when he did it? Did he?"

"Remember we were great friends, and though I knew he was an *invertito*, we usually talked books. Or baroque music. He didn't know as much about music as I did, but like most European writers he was widely cultured and a good conversationalist."

"But he was American," she objected.

"Yes, but he lived in France and Italy more than half his long life—so long, he told me, that he'd forgotten his Social Security number."

"Didn't submitting to his attentions make you a bit of an invert, too?"

"In those days, in that century, especially in the old Mediterranean world, our idea was that it was the part you played that determined your identity, not the gender of your partner."

She got up and poured them a bit of brandy, and while concentrating on her little task and not looking at him, she said, "And were you always the active one?"

He laughed. "Guess."

"You were always the active one."

He patted his crotch; the conversation was exciting him. "I don't mean to be crude, but with this I would never have been allowed to be

2

passive. By definition, I suppose, with a woman a man is usually active unless she wears a strap-on or ties him up, and undergoing penetration or bondage never appealed to me. The few men I granted happiness to, once they saw Bruce"—their nickname for his penis—"*ils ont voulu chaque fois en profiter.*" Like his ancestors who spoke Latin when they said dubious things in front of the ladies, Ruggero reverted to French, the language of his nursery and his grandfather's table, when he said anything off-color. She wasn't as at home in French as he was (although she'd spoken a patois as a girl), but she knew he meant all the pederasts and most of the ladies had been eager to submit to that hard, giant member.

He sipped his drink and slouched slightly back in his chair. She could see the outline of his penis, held by his trousers in a bent position, which made it look even thicker. He said, "But at the risk of being indiscreet, may I ask, did you ever take money for sex?"

He was forty years older. She'd been married twice and he once and they'd both agreed soon after they met never to talk about their past lives; transparency had destroyed their earlier marriages. He'd said he "detested nostalgia," but she thought that was just an indirect way of saying he wanted to avoid the penalties of frankness. Their avoid-the-past rule had led them into frustrating impasses. He'd begin, "I knew a woman who traveled all the way to Shanghai in search of the perfect orgasm—" and he broke off. Or she'd say "My cousin dated a woman I myself had seen for a while—" and again she had "to nail the beak shut," as the French said. They strode past each other clothed in great black capes of mystery. If Ruggero was in one of his possessive moods, he could turn what she reported as one of her innocent little vacation romps into a major orgy; she'd learned to avoid such reminiscences. We all model ourselves, trying to be more agreeable, on what one's partner praises or damns in a previous lover. In their case, they were flying blind, since they had none of the usual cues given by the other one's recollections. Now, though, they'd found such harmony together that, though by nature he was secretive and compartmentalized, she liked to think he could be bullied into confessing. Her love for him was so all-consuming and her respect so great that she assumed he'd be honest about himself and accepting of her avowals. Which of his impulses would win out? she wondered. The secretive or the frank, the honest (she dared not repeat the troublesome "transparent") or the retouched? He was too honorable to enter a contract he wouldn't remain faithful to. Then she remembered he'd cheated on Edmund and left him for the substitute teacher.

"You like to write," she said, touching his thigh, "and I'd like to try. You've always said my emails were entertaining, especially when we were apart and writing each other five times a day. You read my silly little novel about my ex . . . Even then, when we met, you were in your late sixties and I would have imagined you would have already sussed out all your emotions, but I always felt your urgency, your questions, your intensity—which made our correspondence exciting."

"Yes, well, I feel that way now, and though we're absurdly happy all the time I'm never bored. It turns out happiness isn't boring. We're always discovering new things."

"But once you said you were easily bored."

"By ideas—even musical ideas—that unfold in an obvious way, a way I can easily second-guess, but not by the emotions of the woman I love; I feel I hang on your every word, as if every word will determine my fate."

"But you must know by now," she smiled, "that with me your fate has long since been sealed in your favor." She noticed that whenever she said something to him that was deeply felt, she could feel tears welling up at the back of her eyes. Why? Perhaps she was just expressing her own ardor, or maybe honesty about such serious, unchanging matters suggested their opposite, the transience of all things human. Nothing could last forever, not even the life of a beloved man already on the near end of his seventies, despite his taking such good care of himself, as he did partly out of vanity, partly out of consideration for her, largely because he hated leaving the party. Since he didn't believe in the afterlife, he accepted that this was the only action in town. Like Achilles he thought it was better to be a living peasant than the lord of the underworld—and he was no peasant, but a Sicilian *magnifico* from Castelnuovo. His surname was Castelnuovo, his palazzo was called Castelnuovo, and he lived on Castelnuovo Street, something that the university registrar that time had thought must be a joke.

"But what should we write?" he asked with a slightly false respectful-ness, as one might ask a child which color one should paint a room.

"Our confessions," she said. "In an edition of one, for each other's eyes alone. To be burned after a single reading. The truth, the whole truth, and nothing but the truth. Of course we know the broad lines of each other's life, but we've never been able to put in the fine shading. Oh, come on, don't look so solemn. It will be fun."

"Let's shake on that." He extended his hand, which she grasped. "And when will the delivery date be? We must present our confessions to each other on the same date. And read them out loud. I have to see your reactions to what I read."

"In two months? At the New Year's?"

"It's a little unfair since I've lived so much longer."

"But you've forgotten more," she said, keeping up the bantering tone.

"Can we skip childhood? I find childhood so tedious and predictable."

"But that's the part I remember best," she objected, then said, afraid he'd back out if he had to write something that didn't amuse him, "All right. So we'll begin with early adolescence."

"*D'accord*," he said, which she knew meant he agreed.

CHAPTER 2

S ix months had gone by and the day was fast approaching when they'd agreed to read their memoirs in alternating chapters out loud to each other. They were in the Engadin, in the little town of Sils Maria. Around the corner, in a two-story house painted white with green trim, Nietzsche had lived briefly in the upstairs room. Now the Engadin was a costly ski resort, twice the site of the Winter Olympics, but in Nietzsche's time, it must have been one of the most remote places on earth, reachable from Italy only by a steep, perilous road through the Maloja Pass in a carriage, then a sleigh pulled by six lathered-up horses baring their big yellow teeth around the bits, their breath visible in the cold mountain air (a sleigh ride was disagreeably called a *Schlittenfahrt* in German). The most famous village in the area was St. Moritz.

They had no visible servants there, though an expensive service washed the sheets, shoveled the roof and walkway, watered the plants, ran the sweeper, aired the rooms (throwing back the heavy duvet), turned up the heat a day in advance of their return, dusted everything (though there was no dust so high up in the mountains). The simple priceless side tables inlaid with split reeds and designed in the 1920s, the overhead lamp from the 1950s made in Milan, sprouting multicolored metal cups of light, the matronly restuffed 1950s couch from Paris in green velvet, the polished wood zigzag chairs, the huge painting of the naked, dagger-wielding artist himself with Italian words spilling out of his mouth—all of it materialized before their eyes as Ruggero turned on the track lighting and disarmed the security system. The room looked glaring and guilty as a police photo of a murder scene. Not one thing in it had Constance chosen. She had put up a favorite Chagall poster of a red rooster, but it had mysteriously disappeared and found its way into the unused maid's room. She knew the house represented the high point of taste (she knew it because connoisseurs exclaimed over it and shelter magazines often asked to photograph it but were always turned down. Ruggero was worried about thieves and tax collectors).

This afternoon they'd arrived in their four-wheel drive, so suited for navigating through the snow. Ruggero had insisted on skiing right away. Constance didn't really ski. She'd taken lessons but was afraid of heights, and even the mountain lifts made her sick. The only reason to ski was to keep Ruggero company, and after she discovered he found her ineptness annoying she abandoned the unpleasant effort. Whereas he had gone on ski holidays with his distant cousins every January since he was six, she had never even put on a ski boot until she was twenty-eight—and had promptly broken her toe and had to sit slightly drunk by the fire with a lap robe and a brandy snifter (how delightful!), watching through the windows the dying light illuminate the downhill racers.

Ruggero liked to be in control and reveled in his superiority—athletic or intellectual or social. As long as his partner wasn't embarrassingly crude or dense, he seemed to think it normal that he'd outshine everyone around him. Of course he liked that his wife was beautiful and young enough to be his daughter, though he didn't like it when people thought she really was his daughter; it didn't matter she didn't speak proper French or Italian or Spanish (no one spoke Sicilian and almost everyone spoke English). She wore clothes well, never put on too much jewelry or weight or makeup or perfume, had the perfect laugh and an unaffected, unobtrusive American accent. She'd learned about entertaining from him but never tried to exaggerate her origins and was quick to acknowledge how humble they were. She knew that the only acceptable thing to give a host at a dinner party was a small box of chocolates, that after-dinner drinks were vulgar, and that a thermos of hot herbal tea should be prepared in advance and left in the study. She knew not to serve raw oysters to Midwesterners and to avoid red meat with guests from the coasts.

That there should be no music over drinks, that candlelight gave people headaches, that too many forks or glasses looked forbidding.

SHE TOOK A nap. In her dreams she was walking through a mysterious foreign city under windowed closed-in wooden balconies that protruded out over the sidewalks on either side (could it be a Turkish city?) when suddenly the telephone was ringing. It was like a huge black insect crouching beside the bed. She reached for the heavy Bakelite receiver and said hello, though she couldn't remember for a second which language was appropriate (*Pronto* or *J'écoute* or *Guten Tag*) but then to her relief it was Ruggero, speaking in English: "Don't panic, darling, but I'm in hospital. I broke my leg skiing. I'm a hundred percent okay." She was suddenly wide-awake and wished she had a cigarette, though she'd given them up ten years previously.

He explained that he'd broken his promise to her and hired a helicopter to fly to the very top of the mountain, where there were no pistes, in fact nothing he could see but a line of wolf tracks. Once he'd moved from the flurry and commotion of the helicopter and it had glided away, he was all alone with the purity of the mountaintop, this pristine unmarked snow, no other skier in sight, the only other living creature a huge eagle floating by on motionless, extended wings. He found the solitude and the windless cold exhilarating as he slalomed down across the treeless heights. The snow was firm and trackless and his feeling of entitlement—of his sole possession of these unblemished slopes, entirely imperial, his lungs burning with the thin, chilled air—provided him with the acme of excitement.

Now, after ten or twelve minutes of the unsullied pleasure of heli-skiing he could spot the first other skiers getting off the lift—and suddenly his right ski struck something and he was flying through the air and he landed on his back and felt a terrible shooting pain scorching his spine as if it were no longer fretted bone but a single bolt of lightning. He thought, Will I be paralyzed for life? Better to be dead, he told himself, he who'd always been the fittest, most attractive example of whatever age he was passing through. But he banished that thought. Now he looked down on his splayed body as an angel might loom above a recently abandoned corpse. Was his leg broken? Back? Was he bleeding?

Fortunately he'd fallen within sight of the other skiers, one of whom was already most likely phoning for help. The helicopter was back, whipping up clouds of snow and deafening the silent slopes as it lowered itself like a fat woman on a skinny man, except here the skinny man was him . . . Ruggero was floating into and out of consciousness, but amidst the falling, thickening veils he thought he could see someone picking his way carefully down through the air on a floating ladder, like an angel on the *scala paradisi*. Ruggero had a brief lapse of consciousness, as if several feet of celluloid were missing from a restored film—and suddenly the sepia register had abruptly switched to blue. Here was a bearded medical assistant with a young, handsome face bending over him and speaking Swiss German, which Ruggero could understand but didn't like to encourage. The medical assistant was listening to Ruggero's faint voice; he spoke in real German if with his Italian accent, not so unusual in the Ticino or among Italian-speaking executives working near here in Zürich.

The man said in English, "Don't worry. You've broken your leg, that's all. We can lower a stretcher from the helicopter and have you in a good Swiss hospital in minutes."

Ruggero whispered, "At the mere cost of twenty thousand dollars, I suppose. Pity it didn't happen on the Italian or German or French side of the country, where I would have been fully covered." He felt vexed again that Switzerland remained outside the European Union. Of course, he could afford it whatever it was, but the Swiss were so stubborn. And greedy (everything they did was primarily done to protect the independence of their banks). He'd rather buy a new Land Rover with the money—but at least he was alive and wouldn't be receiving medical treatment in Zimbabwe, say, and with any luck his leg would heal properly and Constance could make him *petits repas* and they'd be cozy in their chalet, though in reality he despised coziness and preferred magnificence. Comfort was for cowards. The way Americans sought out their comforts so zealously struck him as obese and sexless. He hated the Swiss and the Americans, besides Constance, of course—and suddenly he realized he was in a disastrously foul mood.

"I'm going to give you a pill so you'll feel less pain during the transfer."

"And be fooled into signing any document the hospital needs to bleed me dry."

"You're certainly being unpleasant and paranoid."

"This isn't the first time that the Swiss have drugged me and then asked me to sign documents to their advantage."

The medical assistant sat back on his haunches. "Do you prefer we leave you here in the snow?"

Bitterly Ruggero said, "I'm freezing."

The young man gave him fentanyl sublingual, which made him instantly confused. Within seconds Ruggero, smiling and stoned, was tilting and teetering through the air on an airlifted stretcher toward the racket of the helicopter and its maw.

CHAPTER 3

Yes," he said to Constance, "I'm fine except my leg will be out of commission for a month. Broken in two places. No pain . . . No, the ambulance will bring me—my leg wouldn't fit in our car. They're going to keep me here overnight so they can charge me another ten thousand euros . . . What?" Then he was talking to a nurse: "Schwester, when will I be going home tomorrow, do you know?" She said something and he said, "It will probably be in the afternoon. No, don't worry. No, stay at home. Stay cozy," he said sardonically. "I'm glad we bought those sausages for your dinner. And there's some rice. And that bottle of Liebfrauenmilch from Rheinhessen—not the best, but something at least. I'll go to sleep right away. They loaded me up on fentanyl. I'll call you in the morning. Please don't worry, darling."

She hung up and wondered how many men and women he'd called darling. She'd find out soon enough when he read his pages to her. Luckily they'd brought their memoirs along. Now they'd have plenty of time to read and absorb them. Tomorrow, after his morning phone call, she'd trudge the five hundred meters to the shop in the village and order lots of food and firewood to be delivered. Hot chocolate, too. And what he called *pécul* in French, as if toilet paper sounded too crude and *carta igenica* too pedantic. And lots of canned goods—and good rye bread.

After that moment of practicality she gave in to her emotions and began to sob and walk in circles in her stocking feet cross the polished wood floor, her hands stroking her flanks through her skirt. Luckily the floor was heated with, she supposed, miles of delicate wires under the surface. Everything here was up-to-date technologically but looked 1950s chic. Or seventeenth- or eighteenth-century rustic, like the oval primitive painting on the wall, one that shepherds would fix to their wagons when they led their flocks up to the high grazing fields in the summer and would cart back down and hang in their cabins in the winter—in this case a mountain scene of a waterfall and a grassy slope and two sheep with dirty haunches, a dog, and two lovers. She'd been told that Swiss collectors could pay half a million euros for one of these primitive paintings since, like rich Americans, they had nothing old and from their own country to buy except these daubs, the wood usually cracking, the colors fading (the Americans bought primitive portraits or eighteenth-century Pennsylvania copies of English furniture). This shepherd painting was rather sophisticated; a dealer had identified the lovers as the Persian princess Granida and the shepherd boy as Daifilo, characters in a seventeenth-century Dutch pastoral; how they had ended up in an Alpine village was a mystery no one was eager to explore lest it cast doubt on the panel's provenance.

Constance wept, crouching down and wedging her narrow hips into a handpainted child's chair, all tendrils and blossoms. Probably as Granida had wept until her old aristocratic fiancé released her from her vows and graciously let her marry the handsome, unsuitable young peasant Daifilo. The tragedy of age and youth in love was an image they lived with constantly. But the whole culture surrounded them with reminders of how absurd it was for someone old to expect love from someone young.

She was indeed panicking. Whenever the least thing befell Ruggero—an ingrown toenail or a bad cold or now a big thing, a broken leg—she immediately imagined his death and wondered how she could go on living without him. Oh, why had she ever fallen in love with a man in his seventies? As he pointed out, anyone could die at any age. Usually he was so witty and energetic and beautifully dressed, his memory so sharp, his body so lean, that she forgot their age difference unless they were among strangers. If they needed a cup or a knife from the kitchen, he was always the one to leap up.

Yes, that was her huge, latent fear, his death, his cruel abandonment of her. They had no children because he didn't want more. They still had lots of sex. He had two grown sons who didn't much like her and who were German businessmen; though they were called Gianni and Carlo, their mother was Bavarian. They were fiercely loyal to Brunnhilde (yes, she was actually named Brunnhilde!), and they had refused to attend Ruggero's second wedding. Carlo had pointed out that Constance was his age and would be a more appropriate bride for him. "Except," Ruggero said, "she'd never marry you at any age." "*Excuse . . . me*," Carlo said in English; he could be rather camp in English. Everyone laughed.

Constance and Ruggero had met at the French consulate in New York when a gay man she knew invited her to a dinner for ten. The consul was a charming young screenwriter with a satirical eye and his wife a Brazilian beauty who'd studied philosophy with Bourdieu. But the guest who fascinated her was an Italian seated next to her named Ruggero. He said he was a harpsichordist from Sicily; when she complimented him on his English, he said he'd studied music for years in London. He looked at her diamond ring and said, "Pity it's not real." She replied, "If it were real, I would have hocked it years ago."

Later in the conversation, after the cheese course, she was a little drunk on Bordeaux and whispered, "You're really good-looking," and he said, "And you haven't even seen the best part yet, the part below the belt." When she looked bewildered, he laughed and said, "That's something we say in Sicily." Under the heavy white damask tablecloth she took his hand but joined in on the conversation across the table. Ruggero said, "Why do you speak French?" She explained that she'd been raised by French speakers from Mauritius. When it turned out they both lived in Chelsea he asked if he could accompany her home in a taxi. In the car he started kissing her, and they went directly to his apartment ("Driver," he called out, "make that just one stop between Ninth and Tenth").

Constance thought it required a lot of courage to be in love—since, as someone said in that AIDS play *The Inheritance*, which she'd seen in a revival in London, "All love ends in heartbreak," which must be true unless you both died in a car crash at the same instant, as her lucky parents had done. Courage because you had to accept every day that you were obsessed with him, that the burn across your solar plexus was the fear of losing him, that your heavy sigh as you stepped out of the shower was the anguish of mortality, as if you were wringing out a washcloth heavy with mercury. Logically she should be fearing his death (crossing the street the wrong way in London, a splinter from the broken femur slowly working its way to his heart, a sunstroke on the treeless, stony streets of Florence), but what she was really afraid of was her own death. She knew that we're all alone at the moment of death—and Rilke wrote that you should embrace solitude, but she couldn't. It horrified her that she'd be alone to die. He called it her "fear of abandonment"—maybe that nice young therapist he'd seen thirty or forty times had supplied the phrase; it didn't sound like something Ruggero would have come up with on his own. It wasn't abandonment she feared, it was death. His death or hers. She winced with pain as if she'd been branded. She leaped up and circled the room again; she went to the mirror over the fireplace to see herself crying, as if she had to have visible proof of the pain she was feeling.

She couldn't bear the thought of his leaving her. Of course there was always the possibility he'd leave her for someone new, younger or prettier or just new, but she'd cried so hard on his beautiful chest as she confessed those fears and he'd reassured her so tenderly that now, at least on her sane days, she felt safe. She couldn't forget that, famously, he'd dumped Edmund without warning. Ruggero, however, really did love her, sometimes so much he accused her of being a witch. She wished she were a witch able to cast a daily love spell on him. She didn't think herself worthy of him—he was so much kinder, smarter, more cultured than her, sexier. And he ruled himself with such enormous self-discipline; he could account for every hour, every calorie, every word. He practiced his harpsichord for two hours every morning and two in the afternoon, though he could amp that up to seven unbroken hours if he was going to concertize. She loved the way he beat back the pages of the score as if they wouldn't stay put unless punched. She loved the look of his long, narrow feet expensively shod that had no pedals to push but that he, nevertheless, kept poised as if on invisible starting blocks for a sprint. She loved his long, expensively veined hands with the pink, perfect cabochon nails. She loved the way he tossed his head back and to one side for slow, expressive passages or scrunched it forward between his shoulders in a perfect storm of concentration when he raced through a fiendish presto, forked veins on his forehead standing out. Unless he was actually reading the score, his gaze was fixed on some inscrutable point in the middle distance, a target he would reel himself in from and look, a moment later, as dazed and surprised as Heidegger at merely existing in the world. Heidegger said all useful experience begins with amazement—and Ruggero always looked amazed. He took nothing for granted. All his experiences were useful then, QED. He'd written a noted article on Heidegger.

It was strange sleeping alone in their big bed and she awakened five times, alarmed each time that he wasn't breathing beside her, smelling of his delicate citrusy cologne, his breath like the abrasion of the finest cloth-backed diamond sandpaper on wood that was already smooth. All five times she was certain that she'd missed his arrival, that he'd rung the doorbell in vain, that he was hobbling around in the raincrusted snow, homeless, cold.

In bed she switched on the big TV, changed channels till she got CNN, thought guiltily that she should be watching France Inter to keep up her French, but finally settled for the warm bath of English over the cold shower of French. She let herself get absorbed in the catastrophes of the day (drought, floods, fires, mass shootings) but kept sensing that just behind the firewall of consciousness the blaze of panic was out of control over her absent Ruggero. If her grip on today's soothing disasters weakened for a moment, if her attention to the comforting horrors slipped, then once again she'd be engulfed by the silence shouting, *I'm alone. He's not here.*

Yes, it took courage to be in love. As if one were distractedly pretending to lead banal daily life, not tiptoeing out to the crater above the throat of the volcano and its boiling magma reservoir. Courage to call him sweet names, as if saying endearments to him were the most normal thing in the world, something taking place in a small dacha among aspens rather than in the throne room of the Kremlin. Weirdly, she believed she really was inside the onion-domed gaudy Kremlin, so intimidating and belittling was her intimate life.

Sometimes she longed to move out of this perilous zone, break off with him definitively, content herself with a dim gray life rather than one alternating between shadow and sunlight, ice and fire, fear and hope.

Lovers had to be cool, not frantic or operatic. They had to have ice in their veins, to be heroin addicts, not jittery like her, high on the crystal meth of passion. Why didn't he hold her all the time till her heart would finally slow down and she'd fall asleep? She took a Xanax—good thing she hadn't drunk any wine.

The phone rang. She would have said she'd suffered a sleepless night except now she'd been alarmed into wakefulness. She must have been asleep after all—but what time was it when she passed out?

Yes, he'd be discharged this afternoon, and the solid-gold ambulance, he said sarcastically, would deliver him home, its meter scrolling through thousands of euros plus the exorbitant salaries of the two heavy-duty nurses.

CHAPTER 4

Even on the stretcher, attended by his toothy aides, Ruggero could turn the smallest event into something festive. A joyful excitement was ushered in with him like the polar cold that might cling to someone's coat as he enters a warm house. He looked sheepish, though, with the happy smile of a boy who knows he's already been forgiven in advance, would always be forgiven. "Oh, my Constance, *c'est bête*! I've made a mess of it. Now you'll have to wait on me hand and foot."

"I can't think of anything I'd rather do," she said with a smile. "And now you can't run away—you're my prisoner. The only punishment for your accident is that you'll have to eat my food."

"But you're an excellent cook!" he protested.

The male nurses had meanwhile established him on the chaise longue by the window, next to his red Italian harpsichord with the pastoral scene painted on the inner lid—a sophisticated echo of the primitive Granida and Daifilo, but with fresher colors, finer brushwork, an uncracked wood support, and no sheep.

When they were alone she asked him, "A cup of tea?"

"Water. No ice," as if their long time together had not already taught her to forgo ice, that American, liver-destroying eccentricity. He added as she headed for the kitchen, "The only bad thing about liquids is that it will make me urinate, which will be an extra chore for you if I have to hobble to the toilet leaning on you."

"It will be worth it if I get to hold your penis," she said merrily.

He looked at her with a smile and a raised eyebrow.

She guessed she'd never get it through her thick head that he really did love her. He didn't seem to suffer from her absence as much as she did his when they were apart. But then his grandfather had always been there beside him, and though his parents had vanished, he didn't feel any separation anxiety. He'd lived in the same house in Castelnuovo his whole childhood and adolescence. A friend had once said to her that Ruggero and she were codependent. When the friend had explained what that meant, Constance had cocked her head to one side and said, "That sounds like my definition of love."

The friend objected, "But codependence is a constant torment."

"Yep."

"It means you're not self-sufficient, that you're horribly vulnerable."

"Yep."

"That you can't authenticate yourself but must scramble after his approval night and day."

"Yes, but I have my ways of disguising my neediness."

"Really?"

"No." She thought for an instant. "But he says I don't make him feel claustrophobic. Or oppressed."

"I wonder."

"I wonder, too. I live in constant fear of losing him."

She'd come to associate love with constant torment, the fear of losing him or boring him. She knew he'd dropped Edmund from one day to the next, and yet he'd pledged eternal love to Edmund, written to him his most intense love letters, sworn that Edmund had made him the man he was.

Now she had him here, his leg immobilized in fiberglass, incapable of running away. Not that that soothed her. He told her how much he loved her—and she smiled but waited for the other shoe to drop. Why were there tears in his eyes? Did he feel guilty about something he'd already done or was planning to do? Was there some terrible revelation about to be launched like an underwater torpedo traveling undetected rapidly, inexorably toward the vulnerable target?

Did his constant surveillance, his unremitting jealousy, suggest that he wasn't faithful? She knew how possessive with Edmund he'd been. Ruggero was in his seventies now, not in his forties—could he be trusted?

Could she? She had no desire to cheat, and how would she and with whom? Unlike the Italians, Swiss men scarcely looked at you. They were too polite.

Yet the pain of being so dependent on such a secretive man who seemed to need no one, certainly not to miss anyone—it was like being addicted to a drug and fearing the supply could be cut off at any moment.

It seemed safer to her to dry out and be free of him, to find a bed of wildflowers rather than a hothouse of rare orchids. They were more beautiful, the orchids, but fragile. They weren't hardy—less beauty she needed, but stronger support.

She wondered if they'd have sex. And then they did; she only sucked his cock, though he was groaning and telling her how good it felt and he was running his hands through her hair and pulling her up to kiss her on the lips. It was the moment he seemed most Sicilian to her, a classical god rising out of the river, his member erect and unsheathed, his hand strangling it, his stomach muscles gnarled under a generous treasure trail, his haunches strong and furry. Here was where myth met reality and transfigured it. Although she knew Sicily well, it glowed in her imagination mysteriously—the silhouette of Mount Etna where the hundred-headed monster Typhon was defeated and buried by Zeus. The fire and hissing smoke coming out of Typhon's eyes, whereas the clangor of the shifting rocks reverberated from Hephaestus's forge, just above the monster's head. She loved everything about Sicily. The outlying islands. In the summer the oppressive heat. The sacred Greek temples. The lavish Renaissance palaces with their dark green velvet-covered chairs stranded in seas of pink marble under giant crystal lusters.

After sex she moved more slowly, as if to get used to the constant blessing of his presence (or to pretend she was getting used to it). He had never caused her harm; why was she so afraid of him? As she came back toward him after setting herself to rights in the bathroom, he said, "Come here, little one." He patted his chest and she lay her head above his thudding heart, now beginning to slow down. "Why so worried looking? So frightened? I'm still here. I'm not going anywhere." When she raised her head to look at him, he brushed back her hair on one side and said, "I can read you like a book."

She had wrapped his legs in a wonderful tasseled plaid cashmere throw; she found his cast strangely erotic, especially because he was dressed only in a nightshirt. She'd pulled up a straw-backed chair from the kitchen so she wouldn't have to shout. He noticed that her hands were shaking so badly it was a miracle she could read at all. She seemed so ashamed of her nervousness that he made no comment on it (in Italy, sports fans, *tifosi*, were said to suffer from typhus fever and to tremble with the disease—or excitement. She was his beautiful *tifosa*).

CONSTANCE READ: I was born in 2020. My parents died in a car crash when I was twelve. I was an only child and treated as a frail treasure by my parents. I was always being told by my parents how special I was— until I wasn't. We were rich then, or as Americans said, "comfortable." We lived in a house on fields rolling down to the Ohio River. For at least a mile down from the house all the trees had been cleared and the land had been planted with lawn, pocked here and there with brown spots. The guy who mowed the lawn with a tractor was always scattering new grass seed, to no avail. It reminded me of a balding man who keeps doing treatments where his hair is thinning . . . My mother was just a veiled face and a splash of Shalimar as she bent down to kiss me on her way to a concert. My father for me was even vaguer, the smell of cherry-flavored pipe tobacco and a stubbly cheek.

Ruggero wondered how much longer this would go on. The room was too hot and he felt drowsy, but it would never do if he fell asleep during her confessions. Under his cast, just above his knee, he imagined he could feel sweat collecting; he had the strongest urge to reach under his cast with a narrow, long-handled back scratcher and rake it across his knee. He could guarantee she wouldn't doze off during *his* pages. He must remember to get some paper to take notes, things to praise, before her next session. Taking notes might keep him awake.

". . . awakened in the middle of the night. Marie-Louise, my mother's friend from Mauritius, was sobbing and wringing her hands, literally, as if shedding the heavy oil collecting on her wings. She had a strange white rag pulled tightly across her hair and a pink nightgown of a sleazy synthetic fabric that clung to my sheets and crackled when she pulled it away. I'd never seen her sleeping clothes before. They made her look like a priestess. But why was she crying?

"What is it, Marie-Louise?"

The little woman grabbed my face between her calloused hands. "Ah, *ma petite* . . ." and she shrieked and tore off her ragged headdress—and she was bald! I'd never before suspected she wore a wig, though I should have wondered at her perfectly combed smooth brass helmet. "What's wrong?" I asked gently, with a smile as if I was not involved.

"Your parents . . . Both of them *tous les deux* . . ."

"Yes. What? Is it serious? Don't tease me. Tell me!"

"*Ma chérie. Ma bien-aimée. Tous les deux* . . ."

"*Dites-moi!*"

"*La mort.* They are dead. *La voiture.* The car." She mimed with a straightened hand a smack against her other lower stationary open palm.

"An accident? Are they in the hospital? Are they all right? Where is the hospital? Do they need us?"

. . . Oh that's why she was so upset at my broken leg. For her, poor darling, the hospital spells death.

"They are dead. *Morts.*"

I grabbed the poor woman and shook her. "Speak English! English! I can't understand you. *L'amour?* Yes, they love each other. What on earth are you trying to say?" And I began to sob.

"They is dead. *Morts.* Not *l'amour.* Dead."

And we both began to cry harder and harder, wrapped around each other, a yang and yin of grief. She knew how to wail; I'd never learned how. It gave us something to do. Better than the silence that fell over us when we wore ourselves out, as we stuttered into a morbid silence. We looked at each other in amazement, a shocked, entirely inappropriate moment, as if weirdly smiling at the first spurt of blood.

Ruggero thought: She does write well, at least in her figurative language, which Aristotle said is the most important aspect of writing though the one that can't be learned. But she's breaking all the rules, going on like this about her childhood. Poor girl, she probably needs to make sure I under-stand it in its full grisliness . . . What a blow it must have been.

Constance read: Marie-Louise was very dear to me. My mother had met her on holiday in Mauritius. She'd been staying with us for three weeks; her plan was to join her relatives who'd resettled in Ohio, of all places. After their death she brought me little invalid's meals of rice and boiled carrots, of toast and honey and very hot, very mild tea made of dried rose hips.

We spent a few more days in the big house, skulking about, seldom getting out of our nightgowns, falling asleep on a couch or in an armchair. I was always exhausted, but when I awoke I never felt rested. It was as if I'd had to scrub the world's longest tile porch on my hands and knees and when I'd finished start all over again. Two dogs with dirty paws and wide grins in my dream kept trotting in circles after each other, happy guys oblivious to the work they were creating. There was no end to my labors.

Because I was just twelve, a part of me was excited by my uncertain future. Just yesterday all I had to look forward to was only another year in school—but now!? Where would we go? Marie-Louise didn't even know how to drive. My poor father had a younger brother, Ted, but he'd sounded and looked uninterested when we'd Skyped him. He only said he'd send flowers if we gave him an address for the ceremony (big deal! It could be done with the push of a button).

I heard Marie-Louise speaking in English to Mr. Brown, the family lawyer, and to her sister and her uncle in their language, a French dialect, an indecipherable bit of gabble, though occasionally they'd break into real French. Three words of patois then two of French. It seemed to me that most of their exasperation was expressed in French, which I'd already vaguely "studied" for five years at school, seldom getting further than the formal way of saying, "Sit down. *Asseyez-vous.* Make yourself comfortable. How are you?"

Marie-Louise ordered small quantities of food, which were delivered. Daddy had never permitted too many gadgets in the house; he wanted everything to look, he said, as if it were 2000, comfortable, unostentatious. He didn't mind how much we delved into the past, even into the eighteenth century (his favorite) as long as we never advanced beyond 2000. He had a modern gymnasium and fitness tracker in the basement and, on the ground floor, a modern kitchen with a hundred programmable devices, but those were the only concessions he permitted. Now that he's been dead for so long I've almost forgotten him except for these details, which I treasure. And the smell of his pipe.

Oh dear, she thought as she read to Ruggero in the chalet, he's going to think what every armchair psychologist says about me—that I have a father complex. Whereas, truth be told, I think of Ruggero more as my bold, brave, almost pure teenage twin, and when he makes love to me, it feels deliciously incestuous. Or as my husband. (Which he is! As if by magic.) Or my demon lover.

To keep him interested I should get soon to the part about sex, sordid though it was.

CONSTANCE GOT A glass of water and resumed her reading: With the inheritance and the insurance policy Marie-Louise and I had more than enough money. The lawyer, I seem to remember, doled it out to us month by month. Since my father was African American I was alert to any hint of racism, the fear of entrusting so much money to irresponsible people, especially given that my mother was from an old Castilian family who were extravagantly if naïvely—racist. They were relieved I could almost pass. They said so. No educated American could have committed their horrible gaffes (they even asked my father if he'd fallen down a chimney, thinking that a wonderful joke—luckily my father didn't know the Spanish word for "chimney" and my mother refused to translate).

We sold my parents' house partially furnished, though we had to clear out the basement and the attic; Marie-Louise found workers (she was resourceful) and arranged a dumpster to be parked in our driveway.

Soon we were living in Bowling Green, Ohio, with Marie-Louise's aunt and uncle. The town had just thirty thousand citizens, half of them from the university. Aunt Marie-France and Uncle Félix were among the twenty foreigners in town, though there were many in nearby Toledo, apparently, and Félix would travel there to an Indian grocery (we ate curries).

The house smelled of sandalwood incense from smoking sticks that someone would light before the oleograph of a saint. They'd also propitiate her with a tangerine, say. I never knew if this was a tradition of the Île Maurice or one they'd invented. They were very Catholic. They did everything to music. I had my own room in the big old wood house, but the music reached me through the heating vents and it was hard to concentrate on my homework. There was only one bathroom on the ground floor, for all of us, adults and the two teenage girls, Antoinette and Hélène. They were fascinated by me, by my silken hair, my pale skin, my tiny butt, that I was twelve and still didn't have my monthlies, that I seldom danced and sang even less often, that I didn't make the sign of the cross whenever I walked past a church, that I had this strange desire to be alone and would go on long walks by myself, that I didn't alternate like them between excitement and sullenness, that I didn't think it made you more grown-up to be always indignant about something, that I could read for pleasure and not just for school, that I was bored by all the local contests (best ice sculpture, biggest watermelon, best baked goods, fastest plow race, most thorough leaf-raking, biggest pumpkin) and that I could seldom be lured to the movies and had a bigger vocabulary than they in French (and English) but barely got by in their patois after months of total immersion, though I learned it later just by osmosis.

I felt alone and afraid. The only familiar person from my old life was Marie-Louise, and she'd changed subtly. She no longer treated me as a young lady but as just another annoying kid. Now she used the intimate instead of the informal form of *you* (*tu* not *vous*). In fact I never heard any Mauritian or any other African say *vous* except on formal (and awkward) occasions.

I didn't talk to anyone about my feelings. Because they weren't named, my feelings became atmospheric, large, heavy clouds of darkness slowly circulating, like sheets in a windowed drier. I would take a ride on my bike in good weather through the town, always ending up at the university. It was an ugly campus of boxy buildings; the oldest structure was the Prout Chapel. I felt a sort of unexplained compatibility with the students, and I liked the idea (which I'm sure I overestimated) that they were leading the life of the mind, cleverly disguised by their dopey, overheard conversations. The school colors were orange and brown.

If feelings are unexpressed, they're like big strangers mugging you in the dark. I missed my parents and our old life in our old house, where all the curtains were pleated, sand color, and made to order, where every silver cup was filled with cigarettes though no one in America had smoked for half a century, where my parents, though slim, were always dieting (half a melon with a sprig of mint for the first course). My father was both sentimental and nostalgic and had a big collection of twentieth-century automobiles, which he'd often drive. If he parked an antique 1990 Buick convertible in town, it would draw crowds. He was Black in a white world, though many "white" people were darker than he was. Maybe he felt uncomfortable in both worlds; maybe that was why he spent most of his time with Mother and me. He'd inherited a small fortune, Atlanta burial insurance, so he didn't have to work and we were always off on small adventures. We drove to Cambridge, Massachusetts, to see the glass flowers, for instance. We went to Pennsylvania to see Frank Lloyd Wright's house Fallingwater. My mother had gone to exotic places, such as Mauritius and the nearby Seychelles, for solo vacations (my father hated to fly). She had her own money (her father had been a judge).

We were always happy together and would sing songs in the car, though Mother, as a Spaniard, didn't always know the words. She taught us a wild song from her youth that sounded flamenco:

Yo me levanto temprano y me pongo a trabajar
Con mi guitarra en la mano, yo nunca paro de cantar.

It was called "El aire de la calle" and was about the carefree bohemian life. There was even a verse about "black blood in my veins," which my parents thought was funny. For the Spanish, I guess black blood was a sign of something wild and sexual.

Now I was learning a whole new patois vocabulary, which my "uncle" Félix was teaching me in his playful, chuckling way. He would be watching television when I came home from school every afternoon and want me to sit beside him on the old ripped couch. He was a roly-poly big man with a bald head he polished till it gleamed. He always smelled of witch hazel, which he used instead of aftershave—it was a brisk, bracing scent, so at odds with his gentle indolence, the spirited overture to a sleepy opera. He was neatly dressed in carefully pressed aubergine or light tan clothes, roomy enough for comfort and sprawl. His wife, Marie-France, was always ironing for him. It seemed to me he changed his shirt three times a day. No jewelry. When one of his daytime TV "shows" (as he called them) ended with interrogative, unresolved notes bleated by the Hammond organ, Félix would stir and consider making a red pepper-and-okra dish for supper to go with that rotisserie chicken Marie-Louise was going to bring back from the supermarket. Maybe the prospect of levering himself up from the couch seemed over-whelming or maybe he was drawn into the next soap opera, but his resolution to cook subsided and he placed a friendly hand on my knee. He liked to startle me by announcing he "was rude as a goat's beard," or something was not worth "a grandmother's fart," which he muttered in his strange French. He called me his little *toubab* (a toubab was a white person), though I pointed out my father was a person of color and he, Félix, was white. In fact the family, they said, were aristocrats in France and had emigrated during the Revolution first to Réunion, then to Île Maurice.

One afternoon when I came home he was cooking meat in peanut sauce, something I didn't like though I had a typical educated American's desire to embrace other cultures and spoke with scorn of our own cuisine, much as I liked it (hamburgers, baked potatoes). I stood on tiptoe to kiss his cheek as usual, but he wrapped an arm around my waist, which startled me. He was always kind to me and I felt slightly guilty for feeling reserved toward him.

"I've been stirring this pot for hours, and before that I was pounding a cassava in the mortar to make froufrou. I have a shooting pain through my shoulder. Would you give me a little massage?"

That rang all my alarms, but Félix was already headed for his bedroom and I didn't know what to say. At school in sex ed class they'd warned us against older men "grooming" us, but they hadn't exactly told us what to do to stop them. Anyway, I thought if older men showed an unearned interest in us young, unsophisticated girls, we should be kind to them for their interest. Even so, I was scared.

He had a single bed and a dark wood twentieth-century chest of drawers. I couldn't place the prevailing odor at first, then I saw a bottle of shiny thick sauce, a nearly black tamarind sauce. He pulled off his shirt, lay on his stomach, patted the mattress beside him, but no sooner had I perched there than he reached back, turned over and drew me into a deep embrace. He said, "My poor little orphan girl. I can see you need affection. Well, then, what is an uncle for unless it is to show his niece a little love? He touched my small breasts through my shirt then unbuttoned it. When he saw I wasn't wearing a bra he said, "Oh, no, the slut!"

I tried to explain that I'd never worn a bra, that I didn't even own one and that I wasn't a slut, I was just a little kid really—but he opened his trousers and revealed a short, stubby penis, almost as wide as it was long and of a dark marled color, a mudstone cylinder. He placed my hand on it and said, "What a greedy girl! She can't get enough dick."

Then he laughed it all away and said that now he saw it was true, Americans were all puritans. They didn't like normal affection or even jokes about sex. "What puritans!" he said, shaking his head. "Shall we make that our little secret and never tell the girls? Should that be a little secret between your uncle Félix and his puritanical niece with the heart of ice who can't even understand a joke?"

I bowed my head in miserable assent. Félix grabbed my chin and tilted my head back. "What?" he exclaimed. "No smiles for your uncle?" He thought for a moment. "You know, I'm lonely, too—here in this cold town where the sun never shines, so far from my childhood friends." Then he laughed and said, "We'll keep our little secret, won't we? Now, smile!"

I can hardly imagine the horrible rictus of a smile I produced.

Félix started preparing my favorite dishes and even pulling my chair out for me at the dinner table like an old-fashioned gentleman. When he'd come upon me in some unexpected corner of the house, he'd lay his big hand on my buttocks. "Don't look so panicked. I'm not hurting you. Remember our secret. We won't let anyone know you're a puritan, that you hate human contact, that you have ice in your veins. Here—I got you this little silver bracelet. Don't tell the other girls who gave it to you. Now, see, I'm not such a monster."

Oh, dear, Ruggero thought as he listened to her. I knew vaguely about her abusive uncle, but she'd never told me the exact words. I asked her now if she thought her abuse had made her turn toward women? She said angrily, "All normal people are polyamorous. You are! Were you traumatized?" I've accused her of being a greedy girl, hungry for sex, but a) that was true and b) it was light, playful, a game, not some horrid story of child abuse. Is she transposing our precious moments into her wretched past with this criminal colonialist? Or have I had the misfortune of unintentionally repeating in our lovemaking the most savage outrages of her past?

CONSTANCE: (I BEGAN reading again, full of misgivings that I was presenting myself in an unattractive light—powerless, perverted. But Ruggero smiled and nodded encouragingly, though with his usual reserve.)

I NEVER ENJOYED submitting to Félix though he was always saying I was "voracious" or "greedy" or (in English) "hot to trot." I tried to inventory all my words and gestures, striving to decipher which might have given him that impression, but I could never locate a single licentious thought or movement. "Oh, baby, she's so turned on! She just can't get enough." I would never embrace him back, I never opened my mouth when he kissed me, I never made a sound when he entered me, and I was so dry he had to use a lubricant, not to ease my pain but to facilitate his passage. The first time he hurt me and I bled. "Oh, the slut, the horny bitch, she's gotta have it," he'd say. Once I said, "No, I don't want it. Leave me alone."

He said, "You can't fool me. That's a hungry pussy. Which hole is the hungriest? Your cunt or your asshole or your mouth? Huh? Tell me, which is the hungriest? I know you're starving for my cock. I want to feed the hungriest hole."

Every day I rode my bike for hours after school and did my homework at the university library. I waited to go home at suppertime when I knew I wouldn't be alone with Félix. He didn't seem to mind my absence. He was watchful, alert; in the old creaky house he could tell which room I was in. Sometimes if he'd catch my eye, he'd wink obscenely, run his tongue over his lips and touch his crotch. In the afternoon sunlight I could see a spiderweb floating in the breeze just outside the window. It looked like a glass tissue that had been laid over an old 78 vinyl record then hung up to dry, every groove carefully registered. That was how I thought of Félix, waiting for a moment of vulnerability somewhere, lurking in the corner of his tightly strung web.

Once he grabbed me in the hallway and unscrolled a yard of tongue down my throat. He had grabbed me so tightly around the waist that I couldn't pull free. "I can tell you're hungry for it, right, baby? Never enough for you, right? You may pretend to be a puritan, but your uncle knows you're a slut."

Once a month until I was fifteen he'd sleep with me. He liked my breasts that were filling out. After dinner he'd get mellow with his third beer and start telling me about the village in Mauritius. "It's called Quatre Soeurs and it's twenty kilometers southeast of the capital, Port Louis. We used to live in Flic en Flac. I owned a little hotel, called La Bergerie—just fifteen suites with individual showers and local art on the wall. I was the chef for the outdoors bistro. Most of our guests were French."

"What did you cook?"

"African food, but also French. And I had an Indian sous-chef. Most of the people in Mauritius are of Indian descent—indentured servants. Lots of curries. The fruits and vegetables . . ." and he kissed his bunched fingers.

"Why did you ever leave that paradise for . . . Ohio?"

"We'd had years of drought and then the most terrible rains for weeks and weeks. Global warming. Ten meters of the beach were destroyed. Then the good weather came back and a young, rich American came to stay and he offered to buy La Bergerie at twice its value. Americans, rich young Americans, are so strange. They all dream of an island paradise and owning their own little restaurant, not realizing it's backbreaking labor every day. He paid us in euros. And we came here."

"Why Bowling Green?"

"A Mauritian friend of mine had a curry-in-a-hurry next to the campus and I cooked for him on weekends. But he went broke. These stupid Midwesterners don't like spicy foods. Anyway, we had enough money to live quietly."

He gradually lost interest in me as my breasts filled in and my pubic hair started coming in. He suggested the hair was a genetic mistake and "not at all esthetic" and urged me to shave it off; he even bought me a Lady Gillette. I refused, saying the other girls in the locker room would notice and think it weird.

Although I associated men with pain, I couldn't help noticing a reedy young student who always sat near me in the university library. He was tall with a very white face that called for sunscreen and rosy ears almost as if there were a light held up behind them. His ears stuck out and the lobes were attached to his jaw—pink handles to a big white Toby jug. Though he positioned himself so near me, he never looked my way. He had long black dashes on his long pale face—oh, he didn't even shave yet. I liked this bloodless, immature kid; I felt he was safe with his big lobeless red ears.

We never spoke for the first two weeks, or rather fifteen days. On the fifteenth day he picked up one of the books I was glancing through and asked, "Is this any good? What class are you reading it for?"

I must have turned red since I wasn't studying in any class—I was still in high school. I was blushing because he'd caught me, but as he later told me he ascribed it to my shyness, which he found so appealing. Much later, when he told me of his first impression, I felt a bit of a fraud, seeming shy when I'd repeatedly been assaulted by my uncle. I was no longer a virgin, and if a nice boy like Colby went to bed with me, he'd discover soon enough that I had a "past." Maybe I really was a "slut." Colby, obviously, was a virgin, or so I suspected.

He began to walk me home as I wheeled my bike. He told me that he was studying Mandarin and Chinese social structure and Buddhist art and Chinese linguistics ("Completely useless!"); mainly he was learning a technical and financial vocabulary. A Chinese corporation was underwriting his education because they needed on the payroll a few American *bi ren* ("nose people," as they called Caucasians for their big noses). The Chinese gave him a monthly salary for studying the useful aspects of the language—no Sung dynasty poetry, lots of thermodynamics. He seemed happy enough, though he was reedy. And listless as if he'd shot up a foot in the last six months and was exhausted from his growth spurt. As he walked along beside me, he didn't lift his feet and stared unemotionally at the ground, though that was just his resting state; whenever I'd ask him a question, he'd light up, and smile sweetly down at me from his great height. He smelled of unwashed flannel, a doggy smell I found comforting.

He accompanied me to what he thought was my door but was actually a block away from my house. I'd smile at him and scamper up the stairs and kill time until he trudged away and I could run over to my real destination. One day my "sister," Antoinette, saw me and shook her head in mock disgust, her hands on her hips, and said, "Girl, what kind of foolishness are you up to?"

"I thought he'd be more impressed by this house because it's bigger and looks richer."

"Shii . . . nothing wrong with our house."

My real reason was that I didn't want to run into Uncle Félix and add to his suspicions of my sluttiness or bring about a confrontation with Colby.

One day Colby invited me over to his parents' house to meet his mother and father. His father was smaller than Colby but more muscular. He lifted weights. He wore a graying mustache. He was a professor at Bowling Green State University who taught Milton but talked sports (tennis was his game). I wished he'd talk about Milton, whom I'd just read; I knew nothing about tennis.

Colby's mother was English (I'd never heard an English accent before except on TV). She collected strange-looking teapots (a battleship and an Eiffel Tower), which you could never imagine being used to pour tea. Colby had told me on the way that she was bipolar, which meant depressed or excitable—like your grandfather, Ruggero. She was in her excited phase, and she chattered nonstop while sizing up the books and rearranging them in the bookcase. Then she darted to the desk and scribbled something. The father scarcely seemed to notice her, as if she were a starling hopping along the sill.

I wondered if Colby's penis looked like Félix's; he was the only man I'd seen nude. I'd become addicted to Colby's wet-collie unwashed-flannel scent and honestly that's what drew me to him, nothing more. Did I smell like a slut? Could he tell I'd been used? Did that disgust him?

He'd never even put his arm around my waist—how long does it take for an ordinary man to warm up? Maybe I preferred we stay just friends—I'd had enough sex for one lifetime.

That very afternoon Colby's parents disappeared, the father guiding the mother off to the car. "We have chores to do, dear. Groceries."

Colby put on some quiet, slow pop music and asked me if I'd like to dance. He held me rather stiffly at some distance from his body as he might have learned to do in ballroom dance class. I was intoxicated by his musty smell. When I was a little girl, I'd bury my face in my collie's underbelly fur after he'd run into the lake. As he baked in the sun on his side at the end of the dock, the doggy, Timmy, became more and more fragrant. His stomach shone pink through the white hair. The freshwater smell of the lake joined the frankfurter smell of his hot pink flesh—and I was enraptured as I was now by Colby's dogginess.

Suddenly Colby swooped down and kissed me. I was so surprised—delighted that he wanted me, afraid he'd discover I was tarnished. Oh, I realize now my fears were foolish, but back then I had no women I could talk with; the only adult women I knew were related to Félix. I spent my days saying a mantra, "I mustn't tell, I mustn't tell," and eventually I heard that the teachers were concerned because I always seemed dazed or distracted or hypnotized.

But my grades remained good, the best in my year. I was determined to get a scholarship to an Ivy League school. That's what my real parents would have wanted for me. The house in Bowling Green was always too noisy for me to study, plus there was always the danger of Félix's attentions. The girls were singing nonstop and braiding each other's hair or playing basketball in the driveway and shouting. The grown-up women were also singing and pounding the curry leaves into the turmeric. Just to find some quiet and isolation I would stay after school in the university library, and there I'd usually see Colby. Without a word he'd move and sit beside me, usually squeeze my hand, seldom look at me. Sometimes he'd whisper in my ear and we'd get up and leave the library and walk downtown for coffee at a bookstore called Grounds for Thought.

But when it was already dark in the winter, he'd walk me home. He'd carry my computer and even real books, if I had any with me. Sometimes we'd stop by his house. He collected coins and had a new dime, mint fresh, from the late twentieth century he needed to show me. We sat beside each other on the couch. I wondered if he'd kiss me again or if he could smell the sluttiness seeping out of me and was repulsed.

There was a sudden flurry of knocks at the door and Félix burst in. "I knew I'd find you here, slut! I followed you here where you were about to spread your legs for this man."

Colby was standing up to him: "How dare you talk that way to my friend!" I could see he was shaking (from fear? From rage?). Colby had told me his father was in Champaign–Urbana giving a lecture on Milton's (metaphorical and actual) blindness and his mother was in bed, depressed. I wondered if I could say something in patois to make Félix leave the premises.

Félix railed against me some more as the world's greatest harlot who would give Colby syphilis, but Colby started edging him out the door, socking him in the chest periodically. Colby was taller if frailer than his adversary; Félix was a coward. As Félix was pushed out the door, he ordered me to come home with him.

Colby slammed the door shut and turned the dead bolt.

Spontaneously we hugged each other, still standing. We were both trembling. He patted my head. I felt he was cripplingly inexperienced but gallant. It seemed odd to think about gallantry after all the gender wars of twenty years ago, but there it was. It existed and it meant so much to me.

"Did he . . . hurt you?" Colby asked.

I thought I could vie for his sympathy but sully my reputation, or:

"No. He never touched me, though he said a lot of lewd things I just ignored. I'm sorry he broke into your house like this . . . I feel safe with you." I realized no woman had said that to a man in a century.

"You are safe with me. I respect you too much to hurt you in any way." Another first in a century. I wished he weren't quite so respectful. Ruggero thought: She wrote all this knowing I'd be her sole reader. So it's not just an objective account of her past but rather a message to me. What is she trying to tell me? That in spite of her adolescent trauma (do I really believe in the permanent effect of those traumas, or is that just more American sentimental nonsense, rather sickening factitious complaining?). She seems very at ease with a man. And with women. She's not afraid of sex, even kinky sex. When I fucked her in the ass the last time, I felt possessed by a god, and I said to her in a strong voice, "You are not my sweetheart. I am your master." She likes that kind of talk. She understands that we Sicilians are real men.

That excited her; in a second her vagina was sopping wet. The words had just sprung to my lips; I didn't think them out, then or earlier. I was an oracle speaking a god's words. I suppose I would have censored them or tried to if I'd thought of her as a sexually violated woman, but I never thought of her as a victim except of my imagination and hers. Maybe I slapped her ass unexpectedly because that made her vagina contract (though I didn't think out the hydraulics of passion; it's just that her thigh and ass called out for abuse, *cuisse de nymphe émue*).

I know I'm good at sex because I make love without irony, without quotation marks; self-consciousness is the curse of half-educated eunuchs. They would rather show off their sophistication than achieve transcendence. Only a *magnifico* like me can resemble a brute (without being brutish) and then express exquisite tenderness.

Ruggero started reading his first chapter but Constance interrupted him. "But you have to say what you think of my chapter."

Ruggero smiled and said, "It's very good. Your writing is very vivid. You evoke all the fearfulness of an orphan who lands in a traditional culture encysted in the flesh of the banal Midwest. A poor girl set upon by a ghoulish *soi-disant* uncle with, as her defense, a naïve, virginal boy, who is useless, gallant as his intentions might be. I'm so happy that my courageous Constance freed herself from that terrible milieu and won her way into Princeton. Only a brilliant survivor could do that."

Constance reacted as most people do when their evil relatives are bad-mouthed with a mixture of indignation and gratitude. She could damn them but other people couldn't. She felt warmed by his praise, though she knew she didn't entirely deserve it. Yes, she had studied late into the night every night, but it was pure chance God had given her bottomless wells of curiosity and a photographic memory (the photos only "developed" if she concentrated hard; just glancing at something didn't make it register permanently). Wasn't he, with his 200 IQ, being just a bit condescending? He had a doctorate in philosophy as well as one in music. And if she had (almost) a photographic memory, he had something much more rare and even more useful: total auditory recall. If he had to remember something, a date or a name or an opinion or a fact, his strange mnemonic device was to plug into a past conversation and listen to it in his mind. He could say to a friend who claimed never to have been ill that she had had pneumonia in March? No, April 2010, she'd told him so herself. He remembered every date in history if he'd heard it once on an audiobook. He slept only five hours a night; otherwise he was listening to books in bed; he'd listened to Aristotle's *Nicomachean Ethics* four times and Kant's *Prolegomena* twice. To fall asleep he'd listen to Wittgenstein's *Tractatus* though he actually believed in his quite different *Philosophical Investigations*. Ruggero was so strange that he could listen to one piece of music and hum a different one.

RUGGERO: LIKE YOU, I grew up without parents. In my case because my parents separated (divorce was forbidden then in Italy) and moved with their respective lovers to other countries, England for my father, who ran off with a saucy Sicilian minor, and the Netherlands for my mother, who'd met an extremely tall, pale Dutch invertebrate. They parked me with my grandfather in Castelnuovo, a small Norman-Sicilian village near Messina where my family had lived since the twelfth century.

Constance thought: I know all this. Who is he writing for? The ages? I thought our agreement was to write only for each other. Is he going to publish it? His sons wouldn't read it. Nor would Brunnhilde. His fans, I suppose. Maybe he thinks Deutsche Grammophon will print it as an insert with his lifetime recordings after his death—or post it somewhere.

RUGGERO: I WAS a good boy—a nerd, as you say in English. I went to the classical *liceo* and studied Latin and Greek; for us Sicilians the classics were a real part of our culture. I saw *Oedipus Rex* performed in the ancient Greek theater at Taormina—in Greek! The acoustics there aren't good for music, but for the spoken language they're ideal! Ancient Greek is full of aspiration and is a sweet sound, which really comes through. But everywhere in Sicily there are ruins of ancient buildings and places where myths supposedly took place or the sites of historic ancient battles. I had my genetic chart done and it was a summary of all the people who've swept through Sicily: 20 percent Turkish, 10 percent Greek, some Norman, North African, Roman, Sephardic Jewish from Spain. And then you know Sicilian was declared years ago to be an official language, not a dialect (and it's as different from Tuscan as Romanian); many of the loan words are derived from these conquests.

I wrote poems in Latin and translated from the Greek anthology into Italian—Tuscan, not Sicilian, but I'm not one of those fools who look down on Sicilian. Pirandello wrote some of his plays in Sicilian, after all. It's a very rich, deeply felt language, full of wise and cheeky idioms. Like Yiddish.

Just as I studied the classics, I wrote reams of music when I was an adolescent, before I knew that melody and harmony were *dépassé*. The village organist taught me composition and orchestration. He made me learn to play an instrument in each family of instruments—the violin, the oboe, the flute, timpani, trumpet, and of course the piano, the harpsichord, and eventually the organ. My grandfather loved music and was proud of my gifts, though he warned me that a gentleman couldn't ever be a musician—some sort of professional, doctor-lawyer, or military man *à la limite* or politician (Grandfather was mayor of our village and had even served under the Fascists, though we were supposed to deny that). But not a musician (the Esterházys had listed Haydn with the gardeners). I think it was even worse that I became a performer, a harpsichordist. Composer was bad enough.

When I was just thirteen, I became obsessed that I would meet an early death, like Pergolesi, who died from tuberculosis at the age of twenty-six. Despite the brevity of his life Pergolesi managed to compose many immortal works, such as his *Stabat Mater*, the most frequently reprinted score of the eighteenth century. My biggest fear was that I would be forgotten by posterity; this anguish haunted me and drove me through many precocious opus numbers. I was determined to make my mark before I was swallowed up by oblivion in just ten more years. As a late teenager I wrote many fugues for organ; I performed a new one almost every Sunday, usually following the church calendar, which had been reduced by Vatican II. I saw religion as merely a good excuse for music, whereas true believers saw music as a prayer to God.

Illogically, I also dreamed of becoming a model. To be sure, there is nothing as ephemeral as fashion, and posing for the camera is as substantial as confetti. My grandfather would never permit me to parade down the catwalk modeling strange new clothes nor to lend my face—so inescapably aristocratic—nor my slender, muscled body to a brand name in a full-page advertisement. But if talent in music was slowly acquired and somewhat less slowly demonstrated, photogenic physical beauty of the right sort came across in a flash. I knew it was beneath me but within my grasp.

As a teen, I became fretful over my health, avoiding drafts at all costs, making the family change tables three times in a restaurant to escape a plague-bearing breeze. When I was walking down a dark pathway, I would make my companion give me his arm, even someone not older or a close friend or a relative, someone I'd never normally walk with *a braccetto*; I was terrified of stumbling, cracking my skull open, and dying. When I got in bed, I made sure my body was clean and my underwear impeccable in case I died in my sleep (the Italian word for underwear is *mutande* and every time I changed pants, nerd that I was, I'd say, "Mutatis mutandis," in medieval Latin, "once the necessary changes have been made"). I wouldn't play soccer (concussion) and was reluctant to swim in the ocean (drowning) but I compensated for forgoing sports by doing a hundred push-ups and a hundred sit-ups every night (though I monitored my heartbeat). Sometimes I would dance in shorts, bare chested, around the library, half based on what I'd seen of ballet at the opera in Messina and half drawn from glimpses on TV of barefoot modern dance. I was often a faun, awakening to the maddening silvery taunts of hiding nymphs. My repertoire was huge—the butterfly wings of the scherzo in Mendelssohn's Octet, the langorous yearning of the "Méditation" in *Thaïs*, the stomping frenzy of the "Polovtsian Dances" from *Prince Igor*. Though I myself was an aristocrat, I loved impersonating the favorite slave from *Scheherazade*, all bracelets, plumes, abs, and a cunning smile. I would often dance in the nude after carefully locking the library doors. Sometimes I was an unsmiling model, one hand in his imaginary pants pocket. I'd position an antique mirror so that I might admire my slender body and thickening penis.

At a certain moment a chance remark by one of my grandfather's friends from Palermo revealed that the kind of music I was composing (inspired by Vivaldi) was impossibly old-fashioned. The only twentieth-century composers I liked were Debussy, Stravinsky, Shostakovich, and Bartók—all the rest were intolerable. The very sophisticated, Paris-educated man from Palermo said in my presence, talking of someone else, "The poor old thing is composing as if it were two centuries ago. No one wants to hear those silly pastiches, no matter how clever. You must make it new, as Ezra Pound said."

Those words threw me into a foul mood, then a serious depression—and changed my life. As people said (since they could no longer mention Asperger's—he was some sort of Nazi), I was definitely "on the spectrum," especially in my love of patterns, even in music (lots of double fugues).

My grandfather, who was a big red-faced man but had the most delicate soul, would talk to me by the hour about the aristocratic ideal—subtle but never frivolous, curious about everything but never pedantic, more witty than learned, as gentle with women as he was brave in fisticuffs, clever yet never acerbic, invariably polite though never sycophantic, spend-thrift, and debt-ridden, always generous and never cheeseparing. "But an aristocrat's best mode," my grandfather said, smiling, "is the art of living nobly in idleness, restless and reckless, with the manners of a Huron—that's the ideal, if the Hurons were very polite."

I think the remark about idleness was prompted by his concern about his manic depression, or bipolar cycles, as people say now (and have said for the last half century). When he was manic, he'd never sleep, he'd walk and ride his horse constantly, sing in the stairwell, wear his cape and deerstalker hat, write countless letters and fill the envelope surfaces with afterthoughts, write poems in Sicilian and instantly translate them into Italian, make long-distance calls to his brother in Rome or an uncle in Salò, play fetch for hours with his dog, try to snare anyone (including the two speechless maids, mother and daughter) into jocular conversations about our family priest, Father Piero, which would prompt them both into fits of signing the cross. When he was depressed, he wouldn't get out of bed, he wouldn't bathe or shave or read or even talk beyond a heavy sigh in answer to a question. He left his meal trays untouched, he wanted me to give him a shoulder to lean on when he made his way to the bathroom. If I'd read one of his poems out loud to cheer him up, his boneless hand would sketch an apology in the air dismissively. Then one day, for no discernible reason, he'd be up and about, suddenly curious about everything, joking, hungry, affectionate, and would even say, "What a wonderful life we have!"

I, who'd always been so diligent, hardworking and purposeful, took his recommendation of elegant sloth seriously. I became an energetic layabout; I couldn't resist throwing myself wholeheartedly into our aristocratic brand of laziness. Until then I had never in my life wasted more than a half day, and then only three times. I decided to become a genius at wasting time and took up drawing, though I had no evident ability, and collecting ancient Roman coins (most of the best ones were already in private collections). I did buy a rare coin of daggers and Phrygian caps and the inscription 'EID MAR' (Ides of March) commemorating Caesar's assassination and another one issued by Agrippa and Augustus after they killed Antony and Cleopatra and made Egypt a Roman province (hence the crocodile on the verso). And I thought I'd polish my manners till they outshone everyone else's, which meant anticipating a female servant's labors and performing them for her, deferring to a child's whims (as my grandfather had done for me) and inventing light verse and *mots* for every occasion (when a descendant of the last king of the Two Sicilies visited and asked me where I'd been "hatched," *covato*, I replied that alas I was born in the usual banal way, but that if I were an eagle like His Majesty, I might indeed have been born from an egg). I wrote the inscription under my grandfather's tinted photographic portrait: "In this image every hero shall see his rival, every sage his peer, every man his brother." My grandfather, though in reality, too heavy for a horse, was always out riding; once when I encountered him in the open country, which he endlessly traversed in his good moods, I said, "How nice to find you at home."

Fine manners, wit, and wasting time didn't suffice for me, as frightened as I was of dying mute and inglorious. I longed for posthumous fame (I preferred the more palatable word, *glory*), the only guarantee of my ultimate worth, the only dam against the flood tide of oblivion. I lay awake at night staring at the pale curtain that rose and fell in the spring wind and thought of the maw of anonymity I was about to fall into. I wanted my name, Ruggero Castelnuovo, to ring down through the ages, to become more and more huge and singular, like that of Shakespeare (whose father might have been Sicilian) or Bach or that undeserving Goethe or the *incontournable* Dante. I wanted to be foundational—but there was no way given the present disarray of modern music. I knew the kind of music I wanted to write, but everyone laughed at it and none one would perform it. My mind was programmed for detecting patterns and inventing forms, but no one wanted a theme and variations. I admired Busoni because he made up but seldom repeated patterns.

I saw patterns everywhere and they would torment me when they didn't soothe me. I'd look at the Trinacria symbol for Sicily with its three legs and Medusa head, and I'd picture the jointed legs racing in circles. I would arrange the bathroom tiles in my mind in endless configurations as I'd sit on the toilet and stare down. The flight of the starlings, expanding and contracting in clouds when the ancient towers of our village sank into sunset, aroused then calmed me; they were the orderly bursts of my anxiety.

I was so afraid of dying that I had trouble sleeping. Nothing could have been more comfortable than my grandfather's house nor his loving proximity, the idea that he was sleeping in the next room. Though Sicily can be defiantly hot in the summer, an imposition so great that just surviving it feels like a full-time job, our *casa* was wonderfully cool due to an ancient system of channeling cold, flowing spring water into the basement and an ingenious combination of thick walls, vents in the floors, airtight windows, and heavy shutters.

But I would become more and more anxious at bedtime. I was so afraid of dying in my sleep, a fear like creeping out on a ledge a hundred floors aboveground in a buffeting wind, that I'd read my dullest Latin text, the *Jugurthine War* by Sallust, in which he opines, "In my own case, who have spent my whole life in the practice of virtue, right conduct has gone from habit to second nature." He also thought a good man would rather suffer defeat by honest means than win by evil ones. But even he couldn't make me sleep. I'd steal some brandy from my grandfather's cupboard (I'd pocketed the key), but it only made me nauseous (I've never been drunk in my life).

In bed I'd lie in my lavender-scented sheets, stiff at the head end with the embroidered family crest, a silhouetted lion with one paw up, and I'd think of all possible paths to glory. Military? But how many generals do we remember? In Italy, Caesar and Garibaldi. Literature? Montale, Pavese, Moravia, all of them lucky enough to be anti-Fascist. Politics? Caesar, Mazzini, Mussolini.

I turned the pillow over and masturbated for the third time that day, though I'd promised Father Piero not to abuse myself ever again. Someone had told me each man had only five thousand times to come— wasn't I using up my lifetime supply at an alarming rate? I was so glad I wasn't Jewish and could enjoy my silky foreskin sliding over the sticky mushroom head. I scarcely paid attention, but when I was putting mental slides through my Imaginoscope, I lingered over and enlarged the picture of a man penetrating a woman though I saw only her long blond hair being gathered and swept by him from side to side and her surprisingly muscular legs wrapped around his waist; I dialed in on his wide shoulders and dimpling narrow buttocks. It took longer to climax if I left the male out of the picture.

At last, exhausted, my stomach cool and moist from the swipes of the washcloth, I'd fall asleep—but a second (or an hour) later I'd lunge up, gasping, terrified of dying. Sleep, not orgasm, was "the little death" for me. I could never remember what exactly had frightened me (the violence of waking worked against recollection), but it was death, I was certain it was death, swirling down the rusty drain of oblivion into the dark eventless ocean of being forgotten: death.

I'd of course heard of the power of the unconscious, but I didn't really believe in it. Now for the first time an idea that I'd invented and magnified, my fear of dying, had got out of control; it was no longer a whim I was scratching like a mosquito bite—it had become a big bloody lesion that smelled, that was rotting, that seemed incurable. I'd never lost my grip on my body or behavior before. Now I was suddenly gasping, I had the bends, my lungs were bursting, and though I'd courted this disaster, I'd never imagined it would go so far, take over, become irreversible. I was afraid to go to sleep now, afraid I'd wake (or not wake) in a panic. Never before had I felt powerless.

CONSTANCE WONDERED: DO I lavish enough praise on him? He's become one of the most famous performers in the world, although only cultured people recognize his name. He's won such awards as Best Artist, Best Baroque Recording, and Lifetime Achievement in the Gramophone Classical Music Awards. Year after year starting in 2020 though thirty years earlier he had won best Young Recording Artist. He's won the Choc de la Musique twice and the Diapason d'Or three times, the Pomo d'Oro once. But I think he needs encouragement every day or every other day. He no longer fears dying, having lost so many friends and family members; he's become a familiar to death. But he still wonders what he would be remembered for if he died today. For all those l'Oiseau-Lyre recordings, with the gold labels, of the baroque composer Bernardo Storace, the *vice-maestro di cappella* to the Senate in Messina in the 1660s. When Ruggero discovered—in his grandfather's library—a lost Storace manuscript, it made the news throughout Italy and was featured in many international music magazines. He also received massive (coterie) recognition for his astounding renditions of Jacques Duphly, the last great composer for the harpsichord. Duphly had studied the instrument with Jean-Jacques Rousseau and died during the French Revolution, penniless, forgotten—and without a harpsichord! Ruggero made Duphly's "La de Chamlay" a hit. Miles Davis said 20 percent of success was musical and 80 percent was self-presentation. Ruggero was a star on both counts. What he fears most is that he'll be remembered chiefly as the man who ruined Edmund White's life.

Ruggero needs praise the way birds need seed, not as addicts need heroin—in a constant but not an ever-increasing supply. Nor does he need reassurance from just anyone; I feel lucky that I've become someone he respects enough to want to please. But does he really care what I think? Am I just a suitable ornament to his life, just one possible portrait in the gilded frame?

RUGGERO READ: WAS I—am I—a narcissist? Enough to have told one of my partners I didn't want to be fucked, but I would like to be fucked by me! Not a narcissist in that I'd always imagined true self-involvement precluded curiosity about other people; though I seldom seem to be studying others, I observe and remember everything about them. Even years later, someone will say, "I've never been to Italy," and I'll say, "You were in Rome for three days in the summer of '28."

I was enough of a narcissist to be intrigued by my cousin, my father's brother's son, Giuseppe, exactly my age and resembling me like a brother, though he was an inch taller and looked hairier in a swimsuit (I felt confident I would soon overtake and exceed him). Our grandfather watched us carefully at dinner and couldn't help smiling—at these treasures of his table? At our uneasy straddling of the divide between childhood and manhood? In the way we looked like each other and resembled him? Our Cupid's bow mouths, our looming Adam's apples, our quick, dark eyes, our big Italian noses, our long, veined hands? Grandfather was red-faced and paunchy and had wild, beetling eyebrows; nevertheless we were obviously related to him. Although our grandfather made us speak in French at the dinner table, Giuseppe and I slipped into Sicilian when we were alone.

Was his cock as big as mine or even larger? I wondered. We were affectionate with each other, often roughhousing like cubs, walking down the beach with his arm slung over my shoulders, my arm around his waist. We were fourteen that summer in Castelnuovo. I had somehow rigged up a bare-bones gym in one room—two twenty kilo dumbbells and an eighty kilo barbell and bench. I'd dragged an old pier glass up the stairs and dipped it into the room. We had a door that closed and even locked and a tinny transistor radio we kept tuned to an Italian pop station, though I never listened to that kind of music otherwise. With our eyes studiously trained on the mirror we each pulled off our t-shirts as if our sole goal was to gauge our "progress."

Giuseppe kept stealing glances at me in the mirror, and I'd smile reflexively whenever I'd catch his eye. When I lifted the barbell, he stood, his legs spread wide, just above my head in order to spot me. He had to have a good solid stance to grab the weights in case I dropped them; it seemed to me he was getting hard unless that was just a fold in his silver gym shorts. Then I stood above him and I stiffened, too. Did he notice?

Soon after that we decided to run downstairs and get into the shower; we were already running late and would have to shower together. We couldn't disappoint grandfather. We had to be hovering seconds away when he rang the little silver bell to summon us to the table.

Giuseppe was even larger than I was, maybe by two centimeters. We were both hard. I was the bold one and said, "Here, let me wash your back." He reluctantly turned his back to me, as if he wasn't sure what he was supposed to do. His neck was red from the beach today. He was a mahogany brown from his neck down and his shoulders were broad, but the top of the shoulder blade, the acromion, was bony and protruding, as if he had not yet grown into it or as if were about to sprout wings. His buttocks were soccer round, luminously white, the crack beckoning and furry and unsuspecting. His hair was as black and curly as mine and I longed to run my hand through it. Just for fun.

When he turned back toward me, I revolved away, both of us still erect. He washed my back, his hands slippery with soap and warm with water. Tentatively, he washed my buttocks, which I hadn't done with him, much as I'd wanted to. My butt felt extra sensitive, though truth be told I wasn't used to being touched anywhere like that and everything felt exciting. I was shocked when he placed his swollen penis between my buttocks. He didn't move forward; I didn't back up. His right hand, long and narrow as mine, wrapped around my waist and then grazed my penis. The water was turning cold.

"We've got to get ready or we're going to be late," I said with a frog in my throat. Then I added, with a smile, "To be continued later."

"I've got a magazine of nude women."

"Oh, good."

We shared a room.

We were both happy at dinner with our wet ringlets and the fever blossoms traveling and darkening our tans, our smiles dazzling and nonstop and the overeager nodding and laughter we had to keep reining in. Everything Giuseppe said seemed to me brilliant. I could still feel his hands on my buttocks. Our grandfather, fighting off the effects of his prolonged afternoon *pisolino*, seemed a bit dazed if delighted by our overlapping comments, our carnivorous smiles, the way we leaned into the conversation, the way we lapped up the orange semolina cake and Chantilly cream, the way we wanted to know more about his own Sicilian verses but didn't wait to hear his answers. Our grandfather was in his manic phase and was as excited as we were, though for different reasons. He kept jumping up from the table to fetch another photo of some distant but suddenly essential great-aunt, leaving us impatient, sitting behind with erections, our expressions drained, though we'd squeeze out fleeting smiles whenever our vacant, lust-heavy glances would cross. They say people who listen with their mouths slightly open absorb more than those with their lips pinched shut; we were both drinking it all in.

Finally our grandfather was off and running into another pursuit (he wanted to look at the Morandi reproductions in a big art book, *un beau livre*, and write a sonnet to him), and we said we had our own "projects" and crept away. He was so absorbed in his Morandi frenzy he didn't even seem to notice our departure.

We felt formal and tragic the way overstimulated adolescents often feel when they know they are at last approaching the consummation of their long-delayed lust. I could hear one of my own cantatas in my mind, solemn and slow. I looked at Giuseppe as a parent might look at a son recalled from death, now strong and upright, just a few days ago pale and prostrate. At that time my feelings seldom were appropriate or made any sense.

As we went into our upstairs room, he trailed me and I became conscious, maybe for the first time in my life, of my ass as an object of desire. With one hand he touched my butt, and I seized up—oh, no, I thought, he doesn't hope to get in there, does he?

At the classical *liceo* I was studying Greek and had found in our library a volume of Theocritus, who was Sicilian, our instructor mentioned. My grandfather, who loved the classics, hired the instructor to teach me four mornings a week throughout the long summer holidays. I was eager to learn the intricacies of Theocritus's Greek in the *Idylls*. He wrote of "Priapus, the gracious one." I'd seen images of the rustic god with his enormous phallus. *Gracious* seemed an odd but endearing adjective to assign him, as if it compressed a precise personal memory of this uncouth Pan.

I felt Giuseppe's erection and he felt mine, though we didn't kiss, natural and tempting as it might have been. Would kissing suggest I was *frocio* ("gay") or he was? I rushed over to the door and locked it, then smiled at Giuseppe; I wanted to convey discretion, not shame. I pulled my shirt off over my head without undoing all the buttons. He did the same, and then we both bent over to untie our shoes and stepped out of them. Our belt buckles clanked on the bare floor. We were in our underpants now, his erection pointing to two o'clock, mine to one thirty under the white fabric. He was touching my ass again, which I didn't like; I grabbed for his. I think he got the idea that this was forbidden territory. "Don't touch the ass," we always jokingly said when another man became too friendly. We Sicilians like to do the penetrating.

I was fascinated by his body, which seemed so much like my own, though we weren't twins. His body, to be sure, had a will of its own, an independent sensorium, a unique motility based on a different history, even a tiny bright scar on his knee, unlike my faultless skin; his knee looked as if a long, arbitrary stitch in shiny silk thread had been pulled through the circular embroidery frame. I could see on his chest the short blond hairs that foretold the dense black growth I'd observed through his father's open-collared shirt; from his navel to his already-darkening pubic bush ran a slender treasure trail in silver, not yet the jet-black smudge it would become. My chest and stomach looked the same. His erection surpassed his belly button; mine just touched the lower circumference of my navel—both well-sewn outies.

At the same moment we had peeled down our *mutande*, releasing our hard Sicilian cocks like overeager hunting dogs. His hand gripped my mastiff just as I throttled his. I knew to add a drop of olive oil from the can lurking under my bed, just as I knew how to slide my hand up and down his *cannolo*, because his body was like mine. From the dirty photos and schoolyard wisdom I knew that female genitalia are hidden, convoluted, internal and wet, whereas the penis and gonads are external, frank, incapable of dissembling (either erect or flaccid) and dry, except for one trembling pearl of pre-cum.

We concentrated on manipulating our *cannoli* while looking at the semen-stiff pages of naked women, who excited us both, truth be told, though him possibly a little more than me. He kept up a running, mumbled narrative ("Look at those giant boobs with the big nipples wouldn't you love to slide your *cazzo* between them hold them pressed together and grease the chute oh yeah baby let your man fuck your tits that's right oh you slut you little slut feel a real Sicilian man"). Before my sessions with Giuseppe I hadn't realized being Sicilian meant you were permanently hot in the pants.

Feeling his hand on me felt so much more exciting than my own did. Why would that be? I wondered. He was a boy, not a girl . . . Our hands were the same size, they were equally dry (except for the drop of rancid olive oil that was being chafed into full stale life), they were pumping in the same way, but for some reason his hand on me felt more thrilling—was it because it was autonomous, unpredictable, so similar but so different, slightly more rapid than I liked, less pressure than I applied? Someone who desired or at least obliged me? Was it the gap between my anticipation and his performance? Was I supposed to imagine it was the chubby woman with inflated tits and a bad pageboy in the magazine who was jerking me off? I flipped that fantasy off and pretended it was Giuseppe helping me out (and he was!). In Tuscan a wank was a *sega*, but it didn't feel like a "saw" but like liver in a bottle—or a cousin's hand. His hips rose off the mattress and his member became fractionally bigger and harder and his breathing more rapid. He came first. I remembered how bored I'd become after I climaxed, casting aside the porno that had so titillated me a moment earlier, so I rushed to my copious conclusion. Giuseppe smiled, shook his head as if awakening from a dream, and said in Sicilian, "Great. Aren't these pictures *bonu*?"

"*Bonu*," I said, slightly disappointed that he didn't assign the greatness to me and my hand.

Out of nowhere he asked me what I wanted to do in life. I said "model." He frowned and said he would become a lawyer.

The following day (Giuseppe's last before he returned home) we visited the wild fields around Mount Etna (Castelnuovo was on the outskirts of Catania). For me, the Greek scholar and the reader of Theocritus, the grounds were sacred, haunted by the ancient gods and beautiful boys such as Hylas and his muscle-bound, besotted lover Heracles. The man went mad when the nymphs stole the boy from him—and I was careful, accordingly, not to lean too close to the cold spring feeding the placid pond lest the nymphs seize me as well. For an imaginative boy like me reality was a palimpsest, the countryside we were hiking through on the deepest layer but superscribed with myths from the distant past. I remembered that the ancients left ground they considered sacred unplowed and unhunted—and these fields looked suitably wild and holy.

Giuseppe gave me his hand to pull me up to the top of a knoll he'd already climbed. He smiled into my face and didn't release my hand. For a second I ran my free hand through his thick black curls as I'd been longing to do, just to know whether they felt like mine. They did.

I remembered that Hylas's hair was "unshorn"—was that a rite of passage, cutting a boy's hair? Giuseppe looked at me quickly and blushed under his tan—and I felt something tighten around my heart.

In a moment we'd sunk to our knees and then were sprawling on the long, unshorn grass. I was propped up on one elbow and occasionally glancing up over the grass to survey the surrounding fields, looking for shepherds or hikers, but we were alone, safe and alone except for a warm breeze, a zephyr. I touched Giuseppe between the legs and now understood that line in Theocritus: "His body rising like bread in warmth . . ." That part of his body, at least, was rising, and though now there were no surprises about what I would find when we were unclothed, I wanted to revisit the shrine, impure and brown and sticky and smelling of trapped moist flesh as it was ("Longing devours me to the very bones"). Was Theocritus right that falling in love with boys brings such pain? Yet I was sure I wasn't falling in love—far from it. He was just a "boy" (*un carusu*) who was "very handsome" (*trùoppu beddu*).

This time we didn't have his filthy pictures of slutty women as our alibi so we were more concentrated on the job to hand. He had a meandering, dull red seam running down the length of the underside of his shaft, from the foreskin to his large testicles, loose in their scrotum from the summer heat. My balls were loose, too, but I had no seam—these details loomed large for me: Freud's "narcissism of minor differences." His extra two centimeters, the clammy warmth of his penis, the bead of clear pre-cum, the thick blue artery from the bottom of his shaft into his sac . . . I wondered if I pulled his erection away from his body and toward his chest, would it snap back in place when I released it (mine would).

We didn't know what to do. A boyish rivalry and an unspoken etiquette of acceptable movements ruled us even as we were pleasuring each other in such an achingly intense way. I licked my right palm and he licked his before we returned to our "sawing." I knew through experience that that would feel better.

He lay back flat and groaned and raised his narrow hips and twisted to one side and shot all over the tall grass; cloudy, viscous drops of semen clung to the blades like a thicker, warmer dew. "*Annamu*," he said in

Sicilian (Let's go). I came and we pulled ourselves together and started trudging across the highlands, not looking at each other, ever so slightly embarrassed perhaps, but then, after twenty minutes of silence, walking side by side. He looked at me and smiled sardonically and even winked, and I put my arm around his waist and his arm lay across my shoulders. He was my *'mbaru*, my "buddy," and we were cousins after all. Nothing strange here, though we wouldn't announce it to the world.

When I visited him two weeks later at his parents' house, we sat through a three-course lunch and answered questions about our studies. I was a much stronger student than Giuseppe and had much wider interests including Greek and Latin, composition and the harpsichord, the latest advances in science, the chaotic politics of Italy and its well-dressed, buffoonish elected officials. I was outwardly pious though inwardly skeptical; I attended mass every Sunday but because the church in Castelnuovo had belonged to my family since the sixteenth century and I felt intimately connected to its fabric more than out of a strong belief in the efficacy of prayer. My piety was proprietorial not ardent. I also practiced on the organ.

I wondered if Giuseppe would have "outgrown" our way of fooling around in the two weeks since I'd seen him. We worked our way through the linguine with cherry tomatoes, pistachios, and mint, through the veal roast and peas, through the cold, delicious salad with orange segments, and then finally the homemade ice cream. Giuseppe's mother, my mother's older sister, was a famous cook, but she had many other interests including the study of Christian mysticism—like me, she was a brain, but unlike me she was a believer. I was virtually motherless, and enjoyed my aunt's attentions. As the English said, my mother had "bolted."

Just as I was despairing that Giuseppe, radiant and flourishing as he was, might have found a girlfriend and moved on from touching his cousin, his almost twin (he was two months older), he winked at me and said, "Ruggero has promised to help me with my Italian homework and to try to make some sense out of that Manzoni." His mother said, "What a good idea. Don't hang around us. Run along," and I was never so grateful to her.

As soon as we had locked ourselves into Giuseppe's stifling bedroom (it was on the attic floor), he said, "I've got something I just figured out during the veal roast."

"Boy, is it hot in here, " I said.

"Well," he said, "let's strip down. No need to be shy around each other, is there?" We both stripped down to our *mutande*, and Latinist as I was, I thought we were indeed "changing" or "molting" into our true, brighter bodies, and I remembered the line from Theocritus: "Under your skin the moon is alive."

"Don't you want to hear my idea?" Giuseppe asked, a childish trace of complaint about my incuriosity in his voice.

"Tell me."

"Well, I found these calipers in the tool chest." He held them up for me to see. "And at the tobacco store I bought this little notebook," he held it up, opened it, "and I've written Ruggero and today's date on the left-hand page and my name and the date on the right. My idea is that every time we get together we'll measure our *cazzi* and enter the figures and keep a record of our progress."

"*Bonu*," I said in Sicilian. "Great." Then I thought for a second. "But no cheating. We have to measure it the same way from the same place; it has to be scientific." I was already getting hard, and Giuseppe reached out to touch my erection through the two layers of white cloth at the fly level. "I'll leave the science up to you, Einstein. Better get to work before one of our uncles volunteers to help us with *The Betrothed*."

Bowing to his superior knowledge, I pulled down my pants and opened the calipers, applying its length to my shaft. "See, I'm pressing one end into the scrotum against the pelvic bone. Sixteen and a quarter centimeters." I entered the figure next to today's date. "Get yours ready." He did. Again I measured. "Almost eighteen."

"What?"

"Okay, okay. Eighteen."

"Put it in the book."

I did and then we each spit into our palms, peeled off our shorts and applied ourselves to our work. His hand felt so good on me and I only wished it were a girl's hand. I half-closed my eyes and imagined I was looking at a smaller hand with pink, varnished nails.

He said, "Wait!" He dove under the bed and pulled out a porno magazine and spread it flat on the bedspread. "This should help."

"Yeah," I said to the picture as we leaned across the mattress on our elbows, and I thought of the Greek word for "defiles," μολυει, which is sometimes used in ancient pornography for stimulant effect, as my tutor had explained. "Spread your legs, you filthy little slut, and show your big hairy slit," I grumbled. "Yeah," Giuseppe echoed, "you little whore, show your big boys your filthy hole," and everything felt right in the world, his hot wet hand on my sixteen-and-a-quarter-centimeter *cazzo* and mine on his ever so slightly larger one, which he was pumping into the circle I'd formed with my thumb and middle finger. We kept muttering dirty words with our eyes closed, when not opening them and immersing ourselves again in the muddy pond of the printed picture. He shot and then I finished myself off and though he didn't have running water he'd thoughtfully provided us with a cold wet cloth. Our sperm mingled in its folds. We dressed quickly and facing each other and breathing slightly on each other, we each patted and fiddled with the other one's curls until they looked right. "What crazy curls we have," he said. "Lamb's wool. But girls like them," he assured me, and I smiled.

Then we began to look at the Manzoni, sprawled out side by side on the bed. He's my cousin, I thought undramatically, just amazed at the simple fact. He's here. And I am here. He's my cousin. As I began to lecture on Renzo and Lucia and their great love, able to overcome every obstacle, Giuseppe's head slumped on my shoulder. I handed him down to his pillow and read the book late into the night, totally absorbed. When he awakened hours later, he wanted to have sex again. I was "game," as I learned to say in English years later.

CONSTANCE THOUGHT: RUGGERO quickly surpassed his cousin in dick size. I'll never forget a year into our relationship when he wanted to fuck that silken-haired, satin-skinned, twenty-year-old Colin while I watched. We smoked a joint and chattered politely with him, then I went into the bedroom. I looked down the long hallway at them embracing. They were both so tall and slender. I could hear their heavy breathing as you can hear ballet dancers breathing onstage when you're seated in the first row of the orchestra during curtain calls.

They undressed each other. The boy was wearing the Versace gold underpants we'd bought him for his birthday. They were kissing each other full on the mouth, twisting their heads from side to side. They had grabbed each other's penises through their underpants. Now they came down the hall and Ruggero pushed Colin down on the bed. They didn't look my way, but I knew they were aware of my presence. Did I inhibit them or excite them? Did they like that I was making an imaginary film of them, or were they self-conscious about my prying eyes? Ruggero always had to be hyper-masculine and dominant around me; was he downplaying his passivity with Colin so as not to disillusion me?

Ruggero's body, which he was always exercising by swimming or lifting weights, was something he fine-tuned like a professional driver working on his race car, as he himself adjusted his harpsichord before a concert—replacing a couple of strings, tightening them fractionally, putting new quills on certain jacks. His shoulders were alive with muscle like massive boulders streaked with shadows from overhead leaves. His lats looked as if the sculptor had squeezed the wet clay with both hands and left the grooves of his fingerprints on the fired pottery. His chest was hairy in a close-fitting emblem of an eagle's spread wings, whereas Colin's was pumiced smooth as if he were of a different species, not just a different age. Colin's buttocks were gleamingly white, rounded, pneumatic with youth, whereas Ruggero's were forceful, no less round but furry.

The two men were occasionally muttering to each other, again as ballet dancers might tease or reassure each other when their backs were turned to the audience and no one could hear them over the orchestra. Ruggero's penis was thick and hard, veins standing out in relief; for a few minutes Ruggero sucked Colin's erect bluish-white dick while his oily bunched fingers pushed into the boy's anus, opening it up. With my finger or fingers I had penetrated many women and some men (I kept my fingernails as trimmed as a full-time lesbian), so I could imagine that hot, muscled, wet grip—the idea excited me and I pulled my slip to one side and began to finger myself. Discreetly, because I didn't want to suggest they should attend to my needs. They were the spectacle.

The filtered daylight zebraed their bodies through the closed wooden blinds. I felt I was watching a living pornographic film directed by Caravaggio. Except it was a hologram, suspended in three dimensions that I could examine from different angles, a glittering mirage of two constantly moving bodies. I thought that if Caravaggio were working now, he'd paint these two, the fair man ravishing the dark, chiaroscuro. I knelt at the foot of the bed and watched up close as Ruggero entered the boy's pink welcoming hole. Colin groaned. From pleasure or pain? I wondered. But then he said out loud, "Yeah, fuck me!"

The boy was lying flat on the mattress, and as I dollied to the side of the bed and mentally filmed their bodies in profile against the striped daylight, Ruggero balanced his weight on his strong arms and lowered his body in punishing push-ups. Colin's long blond hair was spread out on the pillow, and his face, flushed red from passion, was buried into his raised and crooked arm, as slender as a girl's.

"I'd like to see Colin on his back," I said. They quickly, professionally, assumed their new positions, as if I really were the director. Ruggero looked at me over Colin's head, smiled, and raised an eyebrow.

Ruggero plowed into him rapidly and powerfully, Colin's long smooth legs hooked over Ruggero's shoulders. I went in for a close-up, studying the thick brown cock and the boy's receptive hole. It excited me how violent Ruggero had become; he was never like this with women, at least not with me. Now there was no trace of romance or mutuality or respect or courtship. Ruggero seemed swept away by his physical need, his intrusiveness. I had never seen him like this, all animal, pure desire, a nearly criminal domination. I thought—that must be the appeal of male-male sex. There's no social restraint, no pretense of delicate, domesticated passion. Two men, a top and a bottom, could surrender completely to each other without the institutional sanctions of marriage and its simulacra (dating, courtship, seduction). No "warming up." They were already hot, leaking pre-cum, kettles on the instant boil spitting moisture.

Colin splashed his come all over his stomach.

Ruggero said he didn't want to come but preferred recollection in virility. "Seriously. That was so wonderful I want to keep it in my loins and brain a bit longer."

He was still erect. A bit high from the joint, I sucked Ruggero for a while and liked the faint taste of Colin's ass and the lubricant. I was rubbing my clitoris and surrendered to a vast, oceanic orgasm.

We were all polite and kind as we ate our postcoital lunch at the table, back in our clothes. Ruggero served. Colin did most of the talking; Ruggero stroked my leg under the table—he seemed shattered. Was he falling in love with Colin? I didn't mind, since it wasn't with another woman. And I knew Colin liked me and wanted to please me. We were as formal as strangers at a funeral, mourners who've heard of one another but never met, our grief all that we shared.

Ruggero and his cousin hadn't had this kind of sex—they were both averse to kissing or being fucked. But I knew that Ruggero associated men with unbridled passion, instantaneous, unapologetic desire, and that he'd first felt that with Giuseppe. I was excited because I knew I'd benefit from Ruggero's delayed climax tonight.

CONSTANCE READ, SPEAKING of herself for some reason in the third person: When you're a teenager time passes by so slowly. When you've reached eighteen, you feel you've already lived a century. I've heard that it's neurophysiological since you experience duration, the sense not of clock time but of lived time, as it's registered against your metabolism, which is rapid when you're young (hence the sensation of time creeping by), and which is slow in old age (hence the impression of time rushing by—"It's Easter again?!"). Maybe it's also because you have so much free time as a teen, you don't keep an agenda, you don't rush home from work to shop and cook for six; as a student you can sleep in and skip a class if you've stayed up all night talking with a suitemate in a bull session, or you can get lost in a book and read till the bleak dawn, the blue-and-white reminder that other people are just getting up, that they have lives to lead, routines to obey, the boss's jokes to laugh at. So much of an adolescent's life is devoted to paying attention, since she can't categorize and dismiss anything—everything is happening for the first time. She can't file and forget things in alphabetized slots. If the present is all-absorbing, the future (which claims half her attention) is woven and torn up every day like the cloth on Penelope's loom. Her desires and fears get woven into the fabric of her imagination, ripped apart, and worked on all over again.

She had been admitted to Princeton because she had perfect grades, wrote a stellar essay, received sterling recommendations, came from an obscure town (under-represented in the Ivy League), and had scores in both math and language skills in the high 700s. She was fully funded, mainly because she played squash (Princeton had a bigger endowment than all of Canada).

Her suitemate was a gay guy from New Jersey called Edwin. Although both of his parents were from China, he was as American as hamburgers. He chewed gum, liked everyone, rowed for Princeton, ate with Ivy, the oldest and best eating club, had mastered the latest slang, and had revived upspeak from an earlier generation. He hugged everyone and pulled them in for a kiss on one cheek. He was majoring in American history and was researching Ronan Farrow and Rose McGowan. He loved everything about the early twenty-first century (which he was too young to have known), including its #MeToo movement; he thought he might write his JP (junior paper) on it. His sociology professor said it had instilled an atmosphere in America like that in the old Soviet Union. People would confide things in private, but in public they always adhered to the party line (powerful older men, especially ugly ones, in politics and the arts were all deemed rapists and had to be replaced by young women). Edwin disagreed and saw the movement as fascinating if unjustly forgotten and he linked it with the struggle for lesbian rights, though his professor said he was wrong and they were unrelated and the women's movement had come thirty years earlier.

Edwin had noisy sex every night with some other Princeton male athlete (his type were white wrestlers), but afterward they were urged out expeditiously (Edwin referred cynically to the trapdoor beside the bed). He would tap timidly on Constance's door and drunkenly ask if he could sleep with her (just sleep).

She usually let him, though she had to sleep with her back to him to avoid the whiskey fumes on his breath. She didn't mind his snoring. He would spoon with her, and when they switched sides and she became the big spoon, she liked feeling his beautiful skin and the muscles underneath like taut harp strings under a silk slipcover. One morning he got up to pee and gargle to freshen his breath. When he got back in bed, he asked if they could hook up and she said no. In a second he was asleep again.

The third time he asked a month later she said yes. She liked sucking his dick, sticking straight up out of his flossy and very black pubic hair, which looked like black grass. He told her that the *mao* in Mao Tse-tung's name meant the tiny hairs on an arm. She loved the bushels of straight, thick black hair on his head, which he wore shoulder length. She would run her hands through it when he was asleep and read his character from the bumps in his skull thanks to her personal version of phrenology. They usually fucked on their sides facing each other; she thought of that position as very fair, very "Princeton."

Her sports were squash, jogging, and cycling, but she ran a couple of miles a day, even in the winter when the cold air scorched her lungs. She liked running past the various faux-Gothic dorms and looking at the students watching TV, colors playing across their faces; or reading and throwing a textbook down in exasperation; or stepping out of the shower, bodies slick with water; or joking and laughing while sprawled in chairs or sitting on the floor, only their heads and talkative hands like sock puppets visible above the windowsill.

Edwin stayed home with her more and more. He seldom got drunk (the rowing team was forbidden to drink at all), stopped hooking up with boys, studied until late in the night, made her tasty stir-fries on a hot plate, massaged her shoulders every time he walked past her. He was always up for a chat. Whereas before he'd been so casual with her, almost indifferent, now he struck her rather as someone who was playing it cool. He would clam up and brood when she'd go out with someone from her arty eating club, Terrace. "No one in Terrace is a jock," he said once. "Maybe you like that. Maybe you think all jocks are dumb."

"I never said that, Edwin. You're not dumb. You're better informed than anyone I know about third-wave feminism."

"Big deal," he said bitterly. Then he lit up: "Say, my mom is coming down tomorrow with some goodies for us. She really wants to meet you."

"Why?"

Edwin didn't answer and became sullen, which was *maussade* in French, which also means bad weather. She felt the clouds closing in.

She finally figured out he was falling in love with her. She didn't know how to deal diplomatically with his infatuation. He was for her the kid brother she'd never had. He was funny and good company now that he'd given up his epic drunks. She was always happy to find him home and to have sex with him two or three times a week.

"We're so cross-cultural," she joked, "you making me Fukienese food and me cooking you little Indian curries." She smiled.

"I wonder what our kids would look like."

"At least they'd be well-fed."

That weekend his mother, a formidable lady in blue shantung slacks and a small red Jaguar, called them from the parking space near their dorm and asked them to help her carry in the "goodies." She was surprisingly young looking with the same wide face, high cheekbones, abundant black hair, and the same epicanthic fold as her son (after she left Edwin pointed out that she had a single-fold eyelid, to which Chinese astrology attributed a strong business sense—and sure enough, she was an accountant for a law firm). She talked constantly and loudly and smiled a lot but from time to time she darted a cold, appraising glance at Constance, who was aware of the curiosity. Why was she sizing her up? The mother, Tsu-Hsi, nodded enthusiastically when Constance spoke about her African American father, but after she left, Edwin confided that his mother thought black people were no better than apes.

"Edwin," Constance asked, "have you come out with your parents?"

He picked a twig off his shoes. "No. Chinese are very—"

"Traditional." He hung his head in shame. "I guess she wanted to get a gander at the ape you might marry."

"C'mon. Be nice." Then he smiled. "Do you think that's in the cards? Our getting married?"

"Seems unlikely. You gay. Me ape."

"As you know, I'm not a gold-star gay." She knew that meant he'd been with girls too. "And you're an ape who passes as human."

"So, what goodies did she bring the odd couple?"

"Braised-beef-and-scallion roll, bang-bang chicken, and spicy jelly-fish salad. These are all things that don't need to be heated."

"That was nice of her to make all that."

"She has a cook."

"Also a primate?"

"*Just let it go . . .*"

Edwin turned on the TV and looked at a basketball game.

It was especially awkward for her to have Edwin in love with her since she'd met a fascinating guy at Terrace, Fenimore. He was a tall, washed-out blond from an old family in Massachusetts, an art history major with a special interest in Pontormo. Fen was enraptured by Pontormo's *Deposition* in Florence and the earlier mannerist *Deposition* by Rosso Fiorentino placed into the rocky breast of Volterra. Whereas Pontormo's looked like a melting ice cream cone of odd, new flavors and lots of sprinkles, Rosso's was equally pastel but much more archi-tectural, the emphasis being on the actual unnailing of Our Lord from the cross by gaily dressed workmen on ladders. In both paintings the Virgin is shown fainting, though her *spasimo* was controversial theolog-ically, Fen explained. Some of the works that showed the fainting Holy Mother were censored by the Church, since several scholarly cardi-nals thought she should look calmly on at the Crucifixion in a state of grace.

"They didn't know much about motherhood," Constance observed. Fen thought it rather vulgar to subject theology to arguments about human nature—or so Constance concluded from his pained expression and embarrassed silence.

She began to make unnaturally cool remarks around Fen in order to impress him; she didn't succeed and ended up feeling awkward. He seemed to prefer laughing with a bushy-haired intellectual who stayed up all night and roamed the residential streets of Princeton. Named Josette, she was from Paris, but was not at all chic, no one's idea of a Parisienne. She was dowdy and overweight but extremely sharp and independent in her opinions. She was teaching herself Persian. She was an art history major, too, but her specialty was Moghul miniatures. Constance decided that art historians, trained to read symbols into the bric-a-brac of the everyday life of the past, knew everything—literally, *everything*. They could discuss ideas and why the blue Lord Krishna showed up in a painting by a Muslim. They understood why a gold scimitar was placed in a peaceful, geometric garden—or, alternatively, that the man nearly crushed under the dead savior's body was a self-portrait of the artist himself.

Constance would watch jealously as Fen and Josette chuckled over art department scandals, the reciprocal play of their smiles and laughs, the endless mention of first names unknown to her. She was only a freshman and didn't yet have a major; she was mired down in a general essay-writing course, a requirement for all first-year students. Then biology, which she hated, and French, almost too easy for her, then West African studies (she'd chosen these easy courses because she was afraid of feeling overwhelmed at Princeton). She always attributed superior intelligence to the people around her. In fact she had no outside activities except her various sports; she spent all her time at her desk. To qualify for Princeton she had had to list "activities," but none of them interested her. Back in Bowling Green, she'd volunteered at a reading center for the children of immigrants, she'd sung alto in a choir, she'd run on the high school track team—but that was all just window dressing to show she was "well-rounded." She'd dropped all that when she entered Princeton. As a result of her study habits she made the dean's list her first semester, and the other kids in Terrace thought of her as a "brain"— everyone except Fen and Josette, the only people she wanted to impress. They were lost in their world of subtle ironies.

She had a strange sense of rivalry with Edwin because he weighed no more than she and his beautiful feet were smaller than hers—and the disappointed jocks who showed up on their doorstep were more handsome than any man she'd ever hooked up with. She felt strange telling

Edwin about her infatuation with Fen. She'd always been transparent with Edwin about every detail of her daily life (though she'd never told him or anyone except Colby about her horrible rapist uncle). But since Fen showed no interest in her and she'd never even kissed him, there was little to tell except that she had a crush on him. End of story.

Then one evening over dinner at Terrace, Fen suggested they attend an African film festival Princeton was offering free. It was obvious he thought she might be interested, given her Mauritian (or was it Martian?) upbringing. She was thrilled that he had invited her to something.

"I WONDER WHY you write about yourself in the third person?" Ruggero asked.

She smiled. "I'm not sure I feel any connection with that girl I used to be."

"Or maybe you think the third person is closer to the storytelling mode?"

"A cautionary tale," she conceded.

Ruggero thought: That Chinese boy does sound delectable with his black grass pubes, his tiny feet, his trim, worked-out body, his smooth skin. Of course no one is more charming and attractive than my own Constance. She is so interested in the world around her, so infinitely adaptable, whether it's Pontormo or one of my baroque composers. Though I'm hardly an old man set in his ways who's bade adieu to Eros, nevertheless I am older than her father would be if he had lived—and she never showed an interest in older men before she met me. Age is obviously not *un goût exclusif* for her or even an occasional caprice; she must like me for myself. Well, I'm still virile and always interesting, rich, talented, and good-looking. Every day I'm rehearsing Fiocco's *Pièces de clavecin*, which "fit" so well to the hand—perfect, idiomatic music. It's awkward trying to sit at the harpsichord with a cast on my leg; my whole body is at an angle and now I have a permanent cramp in my side.

★ ★ ★

CONSTANCE READ: EDWIN chose to live with one of his Ivy pals the next semester because he thought as a bisexual it was unfair to monopolize my affections and mislead me; he had heard from me about Fen, who was white, tall, intelligent, from a rich family, and Edwin thought I should end up with him. Sure, Edwin was in love with me, but he feared he might revert to boys and, besides, what did he have to offer? A degree in American history with a concentration in lesbian feminism? Bigoted middle-income Presbyterian Taiwanese parents? No prospects?

What a postcolonial mistake the poor boy made. Fen married me for my money without loving me. Josette came along on our honeymoon to Polynesia on my dime. Josette and Fen sneered all the time at how tacky (*ringarde*) Bora Bora was and guffawed about the various arranged tours—of tropical fish, of parrots, of "gourmet" restaurants, of white-sand beaches beside turquoise bays, of some "ghastly" deceased artist's studio filled with gooey palette-knife views of lurid sunsets ("cheap slices of a cake left out in the rain," Fen said). Fen made love to me in our grass-covered hut suspended above water after many sticky rum drinks—that is, he let me suck him while he watched pregnancy porn (who would have guessed that would be his particular kink?).

I was so unprepared for this upper-middle-class WASP Ivy League life that I felt I must be doing something wrong. I always blamed myself—for not fitting in, for not getting it. White Americans confused me, especially their external friendliness and internal coldness. I'd been raised in a Mauritian household where there were real enmities and real alliances—not this strange American mixture of both. It was my first marriage and one of my first undisguised relationships with a man, a fellow student, someone clever and handsome. I felt I must be doing something wrong. It's a feeling I have with Ruggero, too. I struggled to make my marriage work.

Fen insisted on managing my money (the small fortune my parents had left me), and he lost it all. He never learned to have sex with me properly, which I regretted because I yearned to have children, if not immediately then eventually. Josette thought children were "tacky." He would buy expensive Renaissance gewgaws, fake gilt saltcellars, giant volumes of sixteenth-century world maps, that sort of thing, and he'd decorate our expensive Manhattan studio in saffron-yellow unlined curtains and walls painted the color of goose-shit (*caca d'oie*). On our American Express bill I found charges of thousands of dollars for Josette (air tickets to India, the best hotel in Udaipur): "She needed it for her Mughal miniature research, poor thing—just a little gift."

Within two years we were divorced, and I was broke. Now I wished I'd married little Edwin, who was a hundred times sweeter than Fen, more loving, more moral. I moved to be near Edwin. We had lunch once a week, always a joyful occasion. We felt so grown-up, eating out in Manhattan.

RUGGERO READ OUT loud to Constance: I was so proud to be Sicilian and my grandfather instilled in me an even greater patriotism. In the *liceo classico* I learned Latin and Greek and could translate from one dead language into the other. Of course even as a child I was addicted to music, though my grandfather wouldn't buy me a piano, maybe because he thought a gentleman isn't a performer or because he thought music would distract me from my classical studies. I cut a keyboard for myself out of black and white paper when I was six or seven and an aunt taught me how to read music. I remember the day I could decipher a simple piece by Kuhnau, Bach's predecessor at Leipzig. I was so elated; I felt a whole new world had opened to me. I played it on my soundless paper keyboard. The music, a prelude and fugue, appealed to me because it was formally strict—my wife knows how form appeals to my slightly deranged mind.

But the great joy of my youth occurred when a distant relative who lived in the north on Lago di Garda (where I'd never been and imagined as white turreted villas sprawling beside a misty lake) died and left me in her will a square wooden piano. My grandfather, who owned hundreds of acres worked by countless shoeless and dirty peasants, virtually serfs, had almost no cash, but he paid for the precious piano to be brought to Castelnuovo, a distance almost as great as from Turin to Copenhagen. I could scarcely sleep from my excitement. My grandfather said I should count on fourteen days before delivery, but to my

delight it was delivered after only ten days (he had deliberately overestimated the time so I wouldn't suffer too much from anticipation).

Four workmen in blue overalls walked the bulky square thing into
our house. It was wrapped in burlap and corseted in thick, hairy ropes.
It must have been very heavy. Every time the workmen advanced it
another meter into our house it emitted a hoarse clangor from its thickly
swaddled interior (the strings undoubtedly). Grandfather asked the men,
who were already dripping with sweat, to take it up one flight of high,
steep stairs to the *salotto*. They refused indignantly in a way no Sicilian
would have done (Grandpa said they were probably Communists from
Bologna, judging by their accents and manners). When Grandfather
gave them handsome tips, they finally agreed and struggled up every
perilous, backbreaking step.

When they left, grumbling all the way and wiping their faces theat-
rically, I stood in the middle of the room staring at my treasure, as
mysterious and haloed as a deity. My grandfather knew how deliriously
anxious I was and, chuckling, sent me out of the room. I left slowly,
reluctantly. When he called me back in, he'd revealed the instrument in
all its strength and beauty. It was housed in a rosewood box inlaid with
mother-of-pearl. Unwrapped, it looked much larger than before, by the
same logic as one way to tell if a painting is good is whether it looks
bigger from the painted side than it does from the blank-canvas side.

I was allowed to perch on a side chair with a carved wooden back and
a tapestried seat and play my Kuhnau prelude, which I'd memorized (my
Constance can vouch for my auditory memory). My grandfather, who
preferred Bellini (a Sicilian!) to these Germanic complications, eventually withdrew, a finger to his smiling lips.

I was alone with my great instrument, this immensely welcome
personage who'd come to live with us.

CONSTANCE THOUGHT: I certainly can vouch for his memory.

And I know how he loves his harpsichords! A modern copy of an
eighteenth-century Italian harpsichord with a brick-red lid with gold
flourishes, a single keyboard; and a big rattling French harpsichord with

two keyboards, the keys ebony and ivory and the whole magisterial like a notary's desk. He played tender little airs on the Italian harpsichord and big clangorous things like Duphly's "Médée" on the French instrument.

He was so impressive with his tight black curls, which his long sculpted hand kept fiddling with whenever it was idle. His big nutcracker nose, rosy lips, the seven-o'clock shadow of his beard, the quick, intelligent eyes with their sly humorous expression that the French call *espiègle*, their deformation of Till Eulenspiegel, the merry prankster.

RUGGERO READ OUT loud to her: I had a dangerously happy childhood and adolescence. Everyone is always complaining about how miserable they were as a kid, how the parents fought, there was never enough money, their siblings made fun of them, they had no friends. But I was the opposite—cultured, kind grandfather, only the one kissing cousin (Giuseppe), abundant food and sunlight, a fifteen-minute walk from the beach and the sea, a Broadwood box piano from the 1830s which someone from Messina came once a month to tune, and a wonderful large house. The Sicilian nobility disdained to call their mansions *palazzi* ("a word suitable only for Soviet-style council flats," my grandfather said) but referred to them as "houses" (*case*), just as the rich in Newport called their vast marble halls "cottages."

To be honest, I was lonely. Though my grandfather was always kind and respectful, he couldn't be that interested in me till I could discuss Latin and especially Greek poetry (Catullus and Theocritus, his favorites). In 1991, when I was thirteen, my grandfather gave me a computer. We were just getting the internet then (Italy was the first), and suddenly I was connected tenuously to the great world. Strangely enough the real world didn't interest me too much. There were only a few sites and the pictures were hard to download. I pretended it was "vulgar" but in fact it frightened me. I preferred staying in my utterly unreal world of privilege and dreams of glory. I even preferred researching the baroque from old books of the period. When my cousin tried to get me interested in manga I resisted that as well, just as I detested the teenybop music of the era.

Dangerously happy, according to my London shrink, because nothing would ever equal or even rival that sense of privilege and warmth, of beauty and sensuality, of learning deeply and feeling loved and secure—everything I knew in those glorious years in Castelnuovo. The shrink said I was always disappointed by my friends—never natural enough, never loving enough, never generous enough in a spontaneous over-flowing of good spirits, never refined enough without being self-conscious. Of course that continual disappointment all came before I met my wonderful Constance, so affectionate if groundlessly fearful of losing me. She has restored to me the happy days of my Sicilian youth. She cured me of my misanthropy, of the lingering suspicions a rich man has who frequents not other nabobs but poor artists, who feels used, "played" by men and women who are never disinterested and who desperately need patronage. It was Constance who suggested I start a foundation to give grants to people in the arts; that way I wasn't making handouts that would spoil my friendships. Even if I had the deciding vote, I could always claim the money had been given by the "board."

It was Constance who urged me to get back in touch with my biological mother, who'd abandoned me so many years earlier. The last address I had for her was Cannes; she had sent me Christmas presents for a few years but then forgotten about me. I knew nothing about her, whether she spoke French or remembered her Italian, whether she was rich or poor, still beautiful or old and wrinkled, alive or dead. I asked her sister, who lived nearby, Giuseppe's mother, if she had my mother's *coordonnées*, but my aunt Letitia said, frowning in the screen and muttering (she was slightly senile, but was still able to dress nicely and participate in the routines of polite society), "I haven't heard from that faithless bitch for years and never want to hear her name again in this life." My mother's name was Regina.

I didn't want to argue with Letitia and said, "I understand completely how you feel."

Her parting words were "Stay away from her! She's cursed (*maladetta*)."

The next morning I called my grandfather, over a hundred and alert only in the mornings, when he walked his dog and bought his paper. By the afternoon he was unable to walk or even to talk clearly, though he often sat in bed with an early book of Leonardo Sciascia's poems, *La Sicilia, il suo cuore*, propped up before him; he was usually dozing and pretended to read only when his old housekeeper brought him his afternoon tea and oven-warm fig cookies, *cuccidati*. I spoke to him about his little white dog and the latest "scandals and news" of Castelnuovo. Then, ever so casually, I asked if my grandfather had any news of his daughter-in-law, *la scomparsa* (the one who's gone missing).

"No. No. I never hear from her. Why?"

"I thought I might try to get in touch with her to see how she's doing."

"Why?"

"She feels like a loose thread in my otherwise—"

But then he breathed deeply and said in Sicilian, "Sciascia tells us that for the Sicilian, the state doesn't exist, only the family. The family is our state. Yes, you must find your mother. She's the ruler of your state. You can never know peace and order until you see your Regina," for that was not only my mother's name but the word in Tuscan for "queen."

My grandfather reminded me that my mother had a brother in Genoa named Max Bien-Aimé who would undoubtedly know how to get in touch with her. He pointed me to a bulky, messy address and phone book, bristling with yellowing insertions, old-fashioned Sicilian calling cards, and bits of torn paper; he'd been keeping it his whole life, and anyone writing his biography would do well to start with this old agenda, made by Venetians on heavy rough-cut pages sewn visibly with brown silk thread and now sun faded. The cover was sturdy cardboard stamped with blue and yellow lozenges. There I found Max's phone number but without the area code for Genoa (easily located).

"Hello, Max, it's your long-lost, dissolute nephew, Ruggero."

"Long-lost indeed," he said in a Genoese accent that had superseded his Sicilian accent after decades of living in the north, "though I thoroughly approve of the dissolute part. At least it sounds promising."

"So, what are you up to?"

"The usual *mondanités*, visits with the old families on the via Garibaldi as they call it now, though it was once the via Nuova—in any case the noblest street in Italy, the Grand Canal with better palaces and minus the smelly water."

When I asked him for my mother's details, he was amiable enough but he said in his boyish old man's way (left over from his racy youth), "I'm sure she'd love to hear from you but I'm always misjudging these things"—I'm known as the original *gaffeur*—"so I'd better get your phone number and give it to her. I'm sure she'll be delighted." Then he must have had a new idea: "If you come to see me, I may have it for you." I thought that "may" was outrageous, that I'd travel all the way to Genoa to see my uncle possibly on a fool's mission. I said I would come the following week on a Tuesday if I might.

When I arrived at the door of his palazzo, which looked seventeenth century and well maintained, I saw that his was only one of three apartments; the other floors weren't family members, at least I didn't recognize the names. Fair enough, I thought, to live on the *piano nobile* of a *casa* in the historic center, especially since he'd never worked that I knew of. I was wrong, he dealt in Renaissance paintings, but only vaguely and only because everyone he knew in Genoa, it seemed, had a "job"— winemaker, for instance, or investor, though that meant only that they sold extra bottles of each year's vintage or had inherited a few apartment blocks and collected rents. Max acted as an intermediary for his fancy friends who occasionally sold portraits by Cesare Corte, who despite his countless paintings of the Virgin was judged a heretic by the Inquisition for his Lutheran beliefs and put in prison, where he promptly died. Max had good connections with effeminate American curators because he was himself an *invertito* with excellent English from his years of living in London; apparently his small commissions were enough for him to survive in dreary, dirty Genoa, full of unemployed Arabs drifting around the port in faded djellabas. Max gave the Americans tasty Sicilian dinners and amused them by inviting them to the sumptuous houses of the odd marchese on via Garibaldi. Max smoothed over the linguistic complications and flatteringly allowed the curators to maintain their delusions of competence in speaking Italian.

Max lived with a flamboyant thing who wore makeup and lady's tops but normal male trousers. He never showed himself on the street as a flame queen, but at home he appeared to be just one more bottom on speed, never lighted, never ate a bite, was incapable of following the conversation. He was criminally young.

After dinner Pepito (he was Spanish) scrubbed his face clean and wrapped himself in a gray overcoat and said in his English, "I live the mens alone," and kissed Max full on the lips and scurried away through the blue lacquer entrance door.

I thought Max might apologize, but on the contrary he said, "I've never known such a deep soul as Pepito; the boy has the most exquisite manners and is so alert and curious and is the ideal companion. He's completely rejuvenated me. He's put himself in charge of my wardrobe." Max was swathed in a green cashmere shawl and was wearing bright yellow trousers, unusual for a Sicilian gentleman. "This is my *vestito di casa*," he said. "Outdoors I wear a dark blue suit, a gray silk tie, with a matching pochette."

"Matching?" I raised an eyebrow and immediately regretted it. I switched direction and smiled enthusiastically. "*Très chic.*"

"Yes, he has a great fashion sense but he's a truly deep thinker. His family is from Málaga, I think they might be Gypsies, in the hospitality business—waiters, you see—but frightfully traditional, and of course they tormented him as a boy every time they found him in his sisters' culottes or bolero skirts or sequined tops, much prettier than the denim he was expected to wear. I don't know how he got to Genoa, but I found him near the giant statue of the Madonna we have. You know we named her our queen so we would count as a kingdom instead of a republic and be placed above the salt, though our clever ancestors realized the Virgin would be easier to manage than a real queen. Forgive my excessive explanation, but I remember you always liked the past. History, *insomma.*"

"So you found him by the statue of the Madonna?" I asked, to steer the old man back to his story.

"Precisely." He said that he'd seldom known someone as enlightened and as pious as Pepito ("The Gypsies, you know, have a real cult of the Virgin"). "His sufferings made him wise beyond his years. There's not a drop of irony in his veins. But it's not just experience; he's wonderfully erudite, entirely self-taught. His natural elegance, however, makes him hide his vast learning. He never mentions it, and like all our fashionable friends he chatters only about clothes and encounters. Just as the *mondains* speak only of their schedules, their *emplois du temps*, so Pepito chats only about the men, usually Arabs, he's befriended around the harbor or in the narrow streets up towards Christopher Columbus's house. He reveres Columbus and hopes I'll take him to see the New World, though I've told him it has gone into a long, sad decline, but of course I will— imagine what a splash he'll make in what's left of New York!"

"A real sensation," I said to be agreeable.

He told me more about how Pepito had rehung all Max's paintings and would barely touch his food since he worried about keeping his figure. "Oh, that figure!" Max exclaimed, enraptured.

"He must be very good in bed."

Max instantly dropped his shawl. "I've never touched him. I swear! *Lo giuro! Jamais de la vie.* My doctor told me that I have such a bad heart that an orgasm would kill me. I haven't had an orgasm in three years. Fatal. Every time I kiss him I sing, '*O don fatale.*'"

"That must frustrate Pepito," I said gallantly.

Max grinned. "I think he finds plenty of men more suitable and willing. No, if I ever touched him, it would spoil everything. He explained it all to me. How he could never trust anyone in *toda mi vida*, as he says. How I am the first person he's ever trusted but that if he suspected I had any conditions to my love, it would spoil everything. He doesn't know of my delicate heart condition—and please don't tell him. Let him think my love is unconditional rather than that loving him would kill me."

I nodded solemnly.

"*Allora,*" he said. "I spoke to Regina and she's well and thriving. And she wants to see you. As you know, your father was always an unrepentant playboy with his English suits in black watch plaid and his club memberships and his royal relatives and his wit he said once, God must be so patient to be able to endure all the boring praise humans heap on him—so witty. So faithless. So your mother found it easy to divorce him. She called him one of the Black Sicilians, whereas she and I are both blond Sicilians and they never were well matched except in their frivolity. You, alas, are dark like your father, which of course can be sexy, I suppose. Anyway, Regina is living with a very distinguished Dutch millionaire called Aldo Kempe who makes bicycles and they're living at the Hotel Majestic in a rather cramped suite but with an ocean view. He worships her and has provided her with a small yacht, *The Naiad*, which they keep in Saint-Tropez, where everyone, even the waiters, speaks Arabic. Of course we Sicilians have a long history with the Arabs. They ruled us! I must say they were better at it than the Normans—cleaner. Better food. More tolerant. Less indolent. Better architecture."

"What does . . . Mother—" the word sat uncomfortably in my mouth—"do with her days?"

"What do any of us do? I look at paintings. And read about them. I've turned myself into a mannerist autodidact. Recently I've been attempting to sell more and have been entertaining all these American *invertiti* because I want to take Pepito to New York in style!"

Max rambled on about Pepito's wisdom and taste and *savoir de vivre*. I couldn't get him back on the subject of my mother.

IN CANNES, IN the Hotel Majestic, I had to make my way past all the horrible cardboard cutouts advertising what I imagined were the latest Romanian movies being sold on the market at the Cannes Film Festival. They were inevitably the story of a failed salesman of ladies' undergarments, no longer in fashion, not even in Transylvania. Or a delicate Japanese movie of a passionate geisha who loves a samurai so much she cuts off his penis and embalms it. Or a Czech allegory using puppets of a fascist government about honoring, then crushing, a jolly ordinary factory worker canning beans who becomes a champion long-distance runner with no style whatsoever. He just flops along the trail—and wins every time! When he turns into an anarchist spokesman for his mates, he must have his (woolly) legs broken (his puppet character is a bear). Or these were the plots I invented to go with the garish posters . . .

I asked for Frau Kempe's room and was sent up to a handsome suite on the second floor, not at all "cramped," as Max had suggested. The two male servants (Dutch, judging by their height, their yellow hair, big Adam's apples, comical smiles, and reddish complexions) seemed puzzled by the elegance of the Italian doctor their lady boss had summoned (Mother told me to say I was a doctor). They opened doors and suddenly I was in a big sunny salon, giving onto a flower-heavy balcony. The overstuffed furniture was so comfortable and covered with such subdued fabrics that I assumed the Kempes had provided it. They probably lived here except in the warm weather when they returned to his native Groningen.

Regina (I couldn't think of her as "Mother") was white haired, not too tall, a trim figure. I approached her and kissed her cold hand. She held my face between both her slowly warming hands and studied my features. At last she stepped away. "I knew you would be handsome—and you are!" She laughed a little laugh. "You must think I'm terribly frivolous, but I prefer you like that: beddu," which is Sicilian for *bello*, "handsome," and on her lips the word, pronounced almost under her breath, sounded unusually sweet. She went on in English, which I imagined was the language in which she spoke to her Dutch husband: "Of course I don't expect you to have any feelings for me, since I abandoned you when you were a baby. Nor do I feel any great maternal love for you. I know that very few women would speak this way—would permit themselves to—but when you were born, it was too late for an abortion and adoption was impossible in your father's family. It's not as if I ever had some great mission in life. I wasn't an actress or a scientist or a writer or even a philanthropist. I had no goal, no destiny. But I knew that, restless as I was, I could bring you nothing but misery. I'd be shouting at you all the time in frustration and anger."

She sat down with the sunlight behind her and the footlights of the reflecting sea playing on the neck and chin, a mature woman's most vulnerable points, but they held up well to Neptune's scrutiny. "So I provided you with a tranquil, respectable childhood and adolescence while your father and I ran about like mad things, gambling and dancing and swimming and flirting on Mediterranean beaches from San Remo to Saint-Tropez to the nudist colony at Cap d'Agde on the Baie des Cochons—pigs?—to the painters' favorite town of Collioure, across to

Ibiza and back down to Marbella. Bullfights, round pans of paella, a stroll along the Promenade des Anglais, big bowls of *pistou*, swimming off some Greek friends' yacht, a sexcapade with a French sailor—well, no reason to free-associate. Not a stable life for a child, as you can see—an unwanted child. Your father's father wanted you. Though I found him intolerably traditional, suffocating, really—for me, as a woman—"

"I can see what you mean."

"No, you can't, you're not a woman. A Sicilian man is one of the nicest things to be, especially a handsome, rich and titled man, but the rules for a woman are unrelenting, a good, pious, not-so-rich Catholic woman. I went to convent schools as a girl and I was kept stupid and stupidly innocent—we weren't even allowed to bathe naked or ever to see our naked bodies!"

"Is it true you bathed in water that had already washed a dozen girls and that you had to reach up under a plain muslin shift to cleanse your shameful parts?"

"Yes!" Regina nearly shouted, then adding in a near whisper, "I can see some terrible girlfriend once made you *au courant* with convent hygiene. And you no doubt found it perverse, erotic."

I tried not to smile.

Regina ruffled my curly hair. "All you men are disgusting," she said, and we both laughed.

"*Picuricchiu*," she called me. It means "little lamb."

She told me that when I was born, she had none of the usual warm maternal feelings. "We were living with your grandfather and grandmother in Castelnuovo and even if it's a big house we took all our meals together, which for me were torture. There was a restricted list of subjects to be discussed. The weather—which usually meant the heat in Sicily. The servants and their laziness and dirtiness. Relatives and their comings and goings. For weeks we talked about a scandal—everyone we visited spoke about the same scandal, something about a masked, aristocratic adultery and a duel."

"When I thought all this was being discussed in our day and age, I thought, Sicily will never catch up, certainly not the *perbene* people. We were living in the nineteenth century! I could see how much your grandfather was hovering over you, how ready he was to find fault with the way I changed your diaper or even lifted you out of the crib or bassinet that one day I simply handed you over to him and walked out of the room, saying, 'There, he belongs to you now.' And I never looked back. Your father was game. He made some arrangements at the bank—and the next day we took off. We never got in touch with your grandfather."

I appreciated her low voice, her clear English pronunciation, her ancient beauty, so hard to place as representing one nationality or another. I also admired the defiant way she admitted her absence of maternal feelings.

"Thank God," I said, "you left me with him. He was always kind to me. He never struck me. He always treated me with respect. We shared a love of the classics—"

"Ooh la la," she shook her hand as if she'd burned it, "the classics! You wouldn't have had much of that with me."

"We even shared a taste for the same poets, Catullus and Theocritus."

"Worse and worse. With me all you'd have learned was how to mix an American martini."

"I'm pretty frivolous now, or at least sufficiently frivolous not to bore people in the *monde*. But when I was a kid I was terribly serious and all I could think about were the classics and baroque music."

"We would have hated each other. I would have liked a scoundrel or star athlete as a son. But a prig? Never." She smiled sweetly.

"Looking back, would you say you've lived a happy life?"

She made a face. "It's not over yet. I'd say, 'It wasn't as bad as I feared.'"

I could see she was ready for a nap and I backed out of the room, as you might in leaving a queen, a regina.

Ruggero thinks: Later I realized Constance was disappointed that I hadn't had a dramatic reconciliation with my mother; she saw life in highly colored pictures, whereas I preferred it in *grisaille*. She was shocked that I hadn't observed Regina more closely or probed her with more questions. Constance had endless curiosity and like other Americans she thought personal questions were polite, "showed interest."

She was certain that eventually I'd reveal the "trauma" or, alternatively, the "closure" of our meeting in Cannes; she was disappointed that we hadn't wept and hugged. At least I was able to regale her with stories about Max and Pepito, who had made a deeper impression on me. Constance was only vexed that I hadn't believed Max's myth of Pepito's "depth." "You don't know," Constance insisted. "The boy might really be deep. I'm sure he's suffered plenty." Constance held it as axiomatic that suffering always ended in wisdom and sensitivity.

CONSTANCE'S THOUGHTS: OF course he knew he'd be reading these pages to me! What hypocrisy. He might as well address them to "you." I know we've agreed to write only for the other's eyes, but he's so vain he probably hopes his words will be preserved miraculously—in fact he's probably sending backup copies to friends. Like Virgil or Kafka, who left instructions that their manuscripts should be destroyed, but knew their last wishes would be ignored, Ruggero is hoping for literary immortality, whatever that means in these postpandemic days.

I can't believe he was so indifferent in seeing his own mother. I've always heard stories of the disappointment adopted children often feel in first meeting their birth mothers (an addled, toothless drug addict who lies about why she abandoned her child and is hoping to get money out of the adoptive parents), but even those children, God knows, aren't indifferent—bitter, inconsolable, perhaps, but not indifferent. If he wasn't indifferent, was he wounded by her studied coolness? What did he imagine would happen, what did he hope? That she would be incomparably clever and beautiful, that an instant sympathy between them would be established, a wordless understanding, an umbilical communication?

Constance says, "Do you really persist in seeing me as that naïve?"

Ruggero says, "I was not worrying about your reactions. But in any event if I'd be tiptoeing around your feelings all the time, I wouldn't be able to write a word."

"Far be it from me to inhibit you. Just let it rip!" Silence. "But I wonder who your ideal reader is. Just wondering. I don't want to be too female about it, taking everything personally, but in point of fact you are writing a long letter to me in truth. Aren't you?"

"I can't think of it that way. If it were really for your eyes alone, there would be no reason to explain everything. Or anything. You already know almost everything about me and I'd just need to hold up cards with number twelve anecdote, or number fourteen joke."

CONSTANCE READS: AFTER my divorce from Fen (our marriage lasted only two years), I needed a salary. I found a job as the Web manager of a venerable literary magazine. (I wore my hair in dreads for the interview and invented my "African" birth and childhood in Mauritius.) Since the review had been criticized for its lack of diversity and since I emphasized my father was Black and I was raised by Africans, I got the position. Imagine the raised eyebrows my first day when I showed up light skinned with straight hair and blond highlights; it's a miracle, given their impressionistic criteria, that I was competent at the job.

With some money coming in, I found an apartment to share on a quiet street in Bushwick. My roommate, Danielle, was African American; we had a floor-through in a 1910 graystone, three floors up with curved windows, bay windows, looking out at the cadmium yellow of the forsythia bush; it was late March. Danielle had the bigger bedroom closed off from the living room by sliding doors; mine was at the end of a corridor next to the kitchen, the old maid's room in the past, though the real original kitchen was downstairs, surely. When the building was broken up to three apartments, probably in the 1960s, our tiny kitchen was installed; the fixtures dated it. Everything was impeccably clean and the kitchen and the single bathroom smelled of harsh household products. Danielle was "correct" in her behavior but not friendly. She kept to herself and listened to old Johnny Mathis recordings on Spotify nonstop in her isolation; the music was saccharine not sugary, and Mathis sounded as if he were singing locked in an armoire. She had too many bright clothes, none of which fit her. The one time she left her doors cracked open by mistake I saw a pile of her gaudy dresses piled high on a Salvation Army armchair. She told me that Tuesdays would be my time to vacuum the public spaces and, she hoped, my own room. A condition to renting to me was no pets. She said she was allergic to cats, which people often say (especially clotheshorses) even when it's not true.

Danielle and I almost never hung out together. I could tell she was accustomed to paying roommates (in the bleakest way). She had her own shelf in the fridge where she'd marked her yogurts and her butter stick with a red Sharpie and her raspberry jelly and her English muffins; I just knew she'd go hysterical if I touched one of her purchases.

But one day we did venture out together for the first time to buy two small air conditioners, which were on a half-price sale. I remember that late-spring day only because we walked by two old ladies who were speaking my patois from Mauritius. With that impulsiveness that seems so eccentric to Europeans, including my Italian husband, I suddenly asked the women in patois if I could help them. They seemed astonished that I was addressing them in their own language—frightened at first, then delighted. One of them, smiling, said, "How ever—here in Brooklyn?" To save time I said my parents were from Quatre Soeurs though I'd been born in the States. They kept smiling and nodding as if I were a dragonfly forged in gold.

Danielle was equally surprised. "What was that? What language was that?"

"I was raised by a family from Mauritius. I couldn't resist saying something when I heard those ladies speaking my dialect."

Danielle looked at me as if I'd just metamorphosed into another, better person. "Girl, do you mean to say you're African?"

"My father was African American from outside Baltimore. My mother was white. They both died when I was twelve. Family friends raised me in a small Ohio town. They were from Mauritius but white."

"You've been holding out on me." It wasn't an accusation. I could see she was pleased. I didn't talk about my incestuous uncle or my lousy marriage. We talked often about my father, for hours and hours. I told her about my Black relatives in Baltimore, my father's family. Danielle told me that she'd suspected I was Black only at the beginning, at first glance. I told her that I never wanted to make a secret of my Black heritage, even though my white Mauritian "family" was pretty racist. I didn't want to affect Black speech, certainly not ghetto speech. It wasn't the world I'd known but it was one I was eager to explore.

Since I'd been in New York, I'd begun to question all my impulses. Why had I spoken in patois? Was it to show off, to impress Danielle, to appropriate someone else's culture? I decided I'd done it because I could. It would add to my mystery. And I liked pleasing other people, in momentarily seeing my reflection in a distorting mirror, even if only those women from Mauritius whom I didn't know.

TWO OR THREE times a week I had lunch with Edwin, who worked in SoHo like me. He was an administrator's assistant for a non-profit to do with affordable housing in the Bronx (the latest pioneering borough). He'd met a nice older man, Caucasian, on the new gender-fluid dating app, Sweetheart. Edwin had gone back to a Chinese name, Ai-de, which had something to do with wild grass and virtue but wasn't one of the original hundred Han names; he had complicated politically correct reasons for avoiding Chinese nationalism and embracing a Manchu-sounding name. The lover was balding, dramatically thin, and a millionaire who manufactured shoes. He seemed to be in his forties. Edwin told me over a two-martini lunch that he'd never been so adored by anyone, that the man, Hubert, worshipped him and never seemed to tire of him. "It's kind of fun being adored," Edwin said, with a lopsided grin. "Hubert kisses every inch of my body, and I mean every inch, including my very high instep. Very ticklish. And he's so rich. I keep having to play down my materialistic desires because otherwise Hubert would buy me everything in sight." I observed how proud Edwin was of Hubert's devotion. "You deserve to be worshipped if anyone ever did," I said with drunken bravado. "You're so kind. And so beautiful."

Edwin would have purred if he'd been a cat. I could smell the gin on his breath across the narrow New York table. He said, recklessly, "I'm sorry I thought you'd be happier with Fen than with me."

"It was my own fault. I should have seen he was really in love with Josette. They were happy only when they were together. Thank God you and I preserved our beautiful friendship." I reached across and squeezed his hand. "And I'm so happy you found your Hubert."

Edwin tried that comment on for size and ruffled his feathers to see if it fit. "Yeah, it worked out for the best, I guess. Anyway, I'm happy."

I must confess that when I returned to the office I put my head down on my desk for ten minutes. My boss was always walking past silently in stocking feet so I tried to stay alert in case he caught me napping on the job. But he knew perfectly well I often left the office after eleven at night. At least the first two months I was so uncertain, so inefficient, that I never felt the stories I was going to run online were good enough.

I became more confident, however. A few of the stories I edited went viral, never the best ones. The older writers, especially the older men, were mostly eager to please me. The good writers were usually appreciative of my efforts. I found I loved editing, getting into the DNA of sentences and finding the right conclusion of the essay, often hiding in plain sight. I reduced the number of pieces I ran every day from three to two. I got a few letters from writers telling me how much I'd improved their work. At first I thought the writers wouldn't respect me as a young woman. As it turned out, I rarely met them face-to-face and that problem didn't come up. In any event the writers invested me with an authority I didn't actually deserve, but I saw that the anonymity of my position and the aura of my title, online editor, played to my advantage.

A childhood friend of my mother's lived in a brownstone on Bedford Street in Greenwich Village; I met her purely by chance at a literary party for the launch of a woman writer's biography. We started chatting without much zest just because we found ourselves thrown together for a moment. Since Americans always feel it's safe to ask "Where are you from?"—because few cities are coded by class or prestige and anyway people are always moving about—I quickly discovered that the woman was Spanish and from my mother's town and that she had known my mother well and played with her every day after school. She'd heard about my mother's death in a letter from a relative.

An old woman neighbor upstairs on the third floor had just died after nearly fifty years at the address, and my mother's friend (who owned the brownstone) was looking for a "sympathetic" renter and I would be her first choice if I was interested. "Old girlhood associations," she said, which must have sounded too personal because she immediately corrected her sentiment by making it caricatural: "We Spanish girls must stick together!" I quickly registered my delight and scribbled down her name and phone number. I guessed from the high color that suddenly crept over her face that she figured she'd acted judiciously and benignly and congruent with her own happy childhood memories.

The rent was reasonable. The neighborhood was charming; two of Manhattan's oldest and skinniest houses were on my block. I had window boxes on the street side, which I planted with geraniums. At one end of my street was a legitimate theater and at the other an Episcopal church: sin and salvation. Next door was a bar-restaurant that had once been a speakeasy. Sixth Avenue was too far away to be noisy. I could walk to work.

Danielle was annoyed that I was moving out since it put her to the bother of finding a new roommate. Just when I'd become interesting I was abandoning her.

One Saturday in May I thought I'd like to take the C to Central Park from West Fourth Street to Columbus Circle. I felt uncomfortable in my t-shirt and shorts as I sat knock-kneed on the subway. When I got off, I ran through Central Park to the track around the reservoir. I noticed that an attractive man in his fifties, tall and lean with a beard more salt than pepper, was running beside me and occasionally smiling. When I'd done six circuits, I stopped to stretch near the Metropolitan Museum and thought I'd treat myself to a taxi home down Fifth. The man was stretching as well. "It's none of my business," he said, "but I could show you a way to run that would be much more . . . efficient."

I found his half smile and his self-confidence in mansplaining my jogging, something I did with unconscious gaiety, vaguely irritating. But I was too polite to ignore him. "Oh, what should I be doing in your opinion?"

I smiled to edulcorate my words.

The man stepped backwards and held up both hands in protest. "Sorry, lady, sorry. Do it your way."

I kept smiling. "No, tell me, I'm curious now."

"I can show you easier than tell you, which is a grave admission since I'm a famous writer."

"I'm a big reader. Would I know your name?"

"Only if you're cultured."

"Try me," I said.

"Howard Burch."

"Oh, I've seen your stories in the *New Yorker*."

"And?"

"Well, at least I finished them."

"That may be the most offensive thing anyone has ever said to me."

I looked in his eyes. He was serious. I smiled nervously.

"I'm generally considered by real readers as one of the best writers of the last hundred years."

"Forgive my ignorance. But isn't there pretty tough competition for that accolade?"

"If you're going to use a word like *accolade*, then, frankly, your opinion isn't of much value to me—or import, as you would say."

"To my ears *accolade* sounds like a perfectly good word."

He chuckled soundlessly. "You probably think *depict* is a perfectly good word."

"Back to my running style."

"Forget it. I doubt if you're going to change anything in your life."

Of course first thing I did when I got home was to look up Howard Burch. For someone who'd published just one book of stories (*First Love and Other Disasters*) and half a dozen in the *New Yorker*, he'd generated a tremendous amount of press. Apparently he was writing a huge novel and had received a million-dollar advance. He was already being called the American Proust.

He'd been both hostile and flirtatious. I remembered Noël Coward once mentioning "sex antagonism." That seemed to be what it was since he asked for my phone number before I walked away. I told him where I lived and he made a meal of it: "You know you can run around

Washington Square. There's no reason to come all this way—unless you thought the change of scene would bring you an exciting adventure."

I didn't like his tone and just shrugged with one shoulder as I walked to Fifth Avenue, where I hailed a taxi. Of course he didn't phone for three days, one more than I thought would be strategic. He immediately identified himself as Howard Burch, "the man who irritated you in Central Park."

"Oh," I said, "the American Proust."

"I wish they wouldn't keep saying that."

"I suppose it is a lot to live up to."

"Actually my writing is more interesting than Proust's."

"Oh?"

"I forgot you're not really a reader. But if you were, you'd notice that I don't indulge in Proust's longueurs, and unlike his, my prose is fresh, not an imitation of Ruskin's long-winded style. Nor do I destroy my anecdotes with distracting interpolations. And I never repeat myself."

"I can see you've thought about this a lot."

"Look, I was just making a friendly call because I have to pass by my editor's house on St. Luke's Place. But if you have to be unremittingly nasty . . ."

"I could meet you at that little pasta joint on the corner of Hudson and St. Luke's at seven and we could both grab a bite."

"Could you make that seven fifteen?" he asked.

"With pleasure." I hung up before he further problematized our meeting.

Soon I was embroiled in almost daily spider's-nest conversations with Howard, sometimes two or three calls, addenda to post scripta to erased final conclusions to further thoughts and clarifications to the formal withdrawal of a particular idea. I'd never known anyone so Hasidic in his interpretations, the hermeneutics of daily life. For him shul was held every day and often ran late. His literary style, it is true, was mesmerizing, especially in those stories he'd resisted overworking. It was halfway between meticulously detailed, autocorrected realism and orphic utterance, two extremes that strangely complemented each other and had never before been seen (maybe in Musil). Unlike a European writer he didn't show off his high-culture references, and unlike a "redskin" American writer he didn't swear or mainline emotion. He had a curiously hieratic regard for sex, never snickering, never less than reverential. Against this empyrean background of metaphysics and moral seriousness, he presented his unlovely Midwestern specimens, his characters (his mother and her old-biddy friends), pinning them through the thorax onto the spreading board. The contrast between his drab insects and his gold-spangled Prussian-blue backgrounds ennobled the bugs—his neurotic parents, to be precise. They were shown in all their Midwestern picturesque plainness, but they cast long, colorful shadows.

What about him attracted me? Did I think normal men would never understand me, I who had such a weird upbringing? I felt more comfortable with outsiders, though those who were self-confident, even arrogant. I who had hated myself as an abused adolescent and as a sort of charity case who'd been taken in just out of general goodwill but not because I had any rights with Marie-Louise's family, I was deeply insecure. I never felt at home in any world. I didn't understand other Americans' assumptions or everyday references. I didn't know how to behave. All of the men I fell for were self-centered.

RUGGERO THOUGHT: CONSTANCE has had terrible taste in men. Fortunately, she found me—third time lucky. She seemed to attract egomaniacs. Only that little Edwin sounds like a decent person, and he was gay. I remember meeting him several times and his uxorious Hubert. I guess Edwin is the male version of an Asian princess, the raven-haired beauty that all men, white and Asian, fall in love with, who thinks it's only natural to receive their tribute of sighs and diamonds. To be sure, he is a beauty with his small size and perfect butt, sticking out like a shelf, and that mop of hair and radiant smile and dimples. It must be the eighth wonder, that butt in tight white briefs. Sontag said that photos (or was it Roland Barthes?) always make us think of death. Why take it all the way back to photography? Of course Wallace Stevens reverses it: "Death is the mother of beauty, mystical." When I look at Edwin's perfect little hands, his smile that ignites the air, that inviting shelf, I can only think of his corpse in the grave, the worms threading the needles of his high cheekbones, the perfect hands fleshless, articulated, the tight scrotum balding, then blistering into decay, the shelf itself losing its precarious, heart-stopping angle of attack. I suppose death is the mother of beauty because only evanescent things move us, they alone tell us in confidence that they are sublime.

CONSTANCE READ: HOWARD Burch had a secure formula for seducing the minds of other men, especially heterosexual men. I heard him more than once mollify or disarm another writer, sent out to interview him by *Rolling Stone* or *Esquire*, by saying, "I've read your stuff. You're a damn good writer. You could be the greatest writer of your generation." Pause. "But you're too damn lazy." That one-two punch would level them every time. Even if they'd set out to take him down, Howard's unexpected praise had elevated him into an authority who saw their secret genius—but then he'd found the equally hidden fault of laziness in them and denounced it. That was right! Goddamn it, they'd betrayed their genius with their laziness. God (or whoever) had bestowed this sacred fire on them but they'd nearly snuffed it out by not trimming the wick. Get to work, you lazy pig—and they'd privately denigrate themselves for their failure to live up to their promise. They'd chosen mere pleasure over the holy mission of art conferred on them in childhood. As boys they'd felt the flames burn within as they stayed up all night composing their rhymed paean to Siddhartha or sketched out a study of Peter the Great—the first signs of that artistic talent (genius?) they'd wasted with drink and chasing after women and scribbling trivial journalism. And they'd alternate between self-hatred and a hope for redemption, the ghost without content of their Lutheran upbringing back in Dubuque.

Howard wasn't possessive or jealous (he was too canny for that), but his constant observations and revisions and evaluations were just as involving and consuming as jealousy, the successive acid baths of attention and criticism breaking down everything into their basic molecules. I tried to be lighthearted and insouciant around him, but I always felt assailed by his attention and vexed and more and more passive. He could turn a walk through the Village into an Inquisition. I would take his arm and be enjoying the glamour of my dress, its high bodice and tight waist and flowing skirts, and he'd be dissecting out loud why I was clinging to him.

"If it bothers you," I said, "I can stop." I knew from his fiction (or I thought I knew) that he liked women in dresses in light colors, "diaphanous in the sunlight," and I'd dressed to please him.

"Why would it bother me that you'd treat me like a prop—like a parasol?"

"And how would I indicate a more serious regard?" I asked. "Can't a gesture just mean what it happens to mean? When someone told Freud that his cigar was the maternal breast, he said, 'Sometimes a cigar is just a cigar.'"

"If you believe that, then you're beyond gullible. Freud was obviously undermining his whole system. Or playing possum. He didn't want others to interpret him."

"What do you talk to your shrink about five times a week if I might ask?"

"You."

"Me? Why ever me? What's there to say?"

"Don't pretend you don't trouble me."

RUGGERO THOUGHT: YES, it's true that Constance, despite her modesty and all her efforts at self-effacement, is, well, not troubling but absorbing. As soon as I met her at that dinner, I was fascinated by her. Not by her wit or beauty, which take a while to appreciate. No, by her integrity, if that means always being in character, of having character, of having the quiet certainty that people will come to see her value even if she doesn't often open the black velvet display case to show off her diamonds; she knows they're in there, burning with contained fire, ready to launch their hard mineral energy onto the world.

I don't know if I can bear her to spell out her abjection to yet another man. People say that women who always end up suffering must like to suffer, but maybe it's just that they love something (a trait, a social reflex) that usually ends up causing suffering. The woman who time and again pairs up with an alcoholic may simply be so insecure that only a drunk has the necessary bravado to break through the barriers of her shyness, to convince her he really fancies her.

I've never heard Constance dwell on her episode with Howard, though sometimes at parties people, knowing of their brief marriage, want to exchange funny stories about his chutzpah, his unmitigated effrontery, his absurd self-confidence. Constance never matches anecdotes, I suppose because she's heard them all, like the time he called the editor of a famous novelist and shouted, "Stop the presses! Your author has stolen my style!" or the time he was teaching in Rochester when he accused an elderly, mild-mannered novelist of crawling across suburban rooftops, sliding into an open window like a cat burglar, and reading Howard's top-secret pages on his computer and stealing them.

CONSTANCE READ: HE convinced me to marry him. Not right away but in his maddening now-you-see-it-now-you-don't way. His legend, based on his tiny known output, had grown to the point that he was a phenomenon, someone New Yorkers spoke about, or at least the hundred New Yorkers who mattered and shaped opinion. Accordingly one of those heterosexual male paladins who'd come out to joust and was now holding a broken lance wrote a worshipful profile for *New York* magazine and Burch's photographic profile was going to be on the cover with the headline: Burch—the most famous novelist you've never heard of. He invited me to pose with him. He wanted me to get a haircut just like his and to pose with him in three-quarter profile. When I objected that I was of no interest and was only mentioned in the article as his current Euterpe, he became very angry. I think he'd gotten the idea of the double portrait from reading Hemingway's posthumous *Garden of Eden*, in which the writer and his girlfriend live on the Riviera during what was then considered to be the wrong season (summer), get deep-bronze tans, dye their hair white, and have identical haircuts from his barber. Then she takes up with a local woman, who of course runs away with the writer. It's a beautiful polyamorous novel, much more sophisticated than anything else Hemingway ever wrote. And to think he worked on it every morning as only a five-finger exercise, just to get the blood flowing.

Why did I agree to marry Howard? Having been married and divorced, I didn't see the bond as unbreakable. The truth is, we'd started having sex and he was a wonderful, wise lover—the first I'd ever had to eat out my cunt, which drove me wild. I was having the first orgasms of my life. Whereas Howard was prickly and inquisitorial in everyday life, he was . . . well, dreamy in bed. That is, he went without transition or hesitation from one delight to another. He bit my nipples, then he had a tender finger on my clitoris, later spanked it, he kissed me lavishly, even tongued my nostrils, lifted me in his arms better to settle me on his average dick while I licked his neck with unconscious pleasure. He liked to look at his cock entering my lipsticked lips in a full-length mirror he held and angled until we could each see the other. I stole only glances at our reflection on the principle we despise our image as we never like the sound of our own voice on tape, that demeaning chipmunk chatter. I liked the look of his penis entering my mouth behind the veil of my long hair, which he grabbed and pushed back. His body was strangely perfect for a man in his fifties; of course I knew he jogged and he'd told me he swam a mile a day at the Fifty-seventh Street Y, that gay Valhalla.

And then his constant chiding, his mercurial mood swings had hypnotized me. I was always leaning forward to embrace him and, losing my balance, fell. He erased his grin, toggled a switch and as it were all the pluses flashed minus. Or it was like driving through a series of tunnels that keep interrupting the radio signal at the end of that Sibelius symphony, the one you really love, with the repetitious majestic horns and bassoons. He was unseizable.

Good, loving, adventurous sex, alternating and unpredictable fits of affection and hostility, riddling inquisitions—it was all as intense and involving as jealousy. In both cases, as the target of jealousy or constant inspection, one was center stage, the true luminary, drawing and holding a partner's spellbound attention or, as actors say, taking focus. But jealousy, once the spell was broken, could be rejected completely (why did

I ever care what he thought about me?), whereas Howard's sort of nuanced, ever-shifting evaluations were as binding as the snakes sent to strangle Laocoön and his sons. Jealousy could be banished by a word or a laugh but constant inspection wrapped its victim in ever-tighter coils.

We married. Later I realized that Howard married me only as an alibi. For the last fifteen years he'd been living in the big, underfurnished West Side apartment with two of his male lovers he'd met in the Y in the steam room. Although he'd never introduced those guys to friends or reporters, word had gotten out that Howard was a queer, in spite of his adult daughter from an early marriage. It wasn't congruent with Howard's literary persona to be homosexual; his giant novel was all about pussy (there was even a seventy-page sequence about the heroine's first orgasm). In that way it truly resembled Proust's book; by the end the narrator was virtually the only 100 percent heterosexual character left standing.

By accident I met the two lovers once when I dropped in on Howard unannounced; he'd never mentioned them. With great irritation Howard introduced them. One, Peter, was tall and wholesome, a high school biology teacher who took pictures of buffalo in winter with frozen whiskers. The other, Chuck, did something I never did grasp though his sexuality was rancid and aggressive. He had a distinct odor, ripe, nearly repulsive, definitely seductive. I suppose when Peter had become too familiar or old to be fuck-worthy, Chuck had been intro-duced into the "family." If Peter was a big, muscular, hygienic Ariel, Chuck was a toe-sucking Caliban. I was shocked, to the degree I could be shocked, that these two desirable men were living with Howard. He had the knack of involving people, if that was just another way of saying he made them fall in love with him. I think I'd fallen in love with him at first sight, his tired eyes, his ironic, disabused smile, the way he deployed sex antagonism.

Peter was a well-built blond with a strong well-articulated voice, as if he'd grown up with parents who were hard of hearing. He had slow responses that when they finally came on were strangely unemphatic. He was extremely if generally friendly, with a magnificent smile, a broad-focus deep laugh, as if most things other people said were meant to be funny, which they were in the Midwest, though he would occasionally catch himself and realize the other person was actually serious, whereupon he creased his face in a sympathetic frown. He was probably the least vain person I'd ever met; he was so handsome naturally that he'd surely never thought of (much less used) moisturizer or conditioner or expensive soap in fancy wrapping paper from Spain, and looking in the mirror for him was just a hasty moment of friendly recognition or of setting things aright and never of doubt or hope. He'd learned just to stare when Howard became too inquisitorial; he'd say half-reproachfully, half-jocularly, "Oh, Howard," as if Howard was just up to his old tricks again, amusing but annoying. Otherwise Peter could listen to Howard's rigmarole for hours with respectful interest. Howard was interesting and never said anything predictable. He was often wise, always thoughtful, unpredictably critical then tender.

Both young men were packing up after years of living with Howard, years of shopping, cleaning, peeling potatoes, and searing the whole chicken in butter and olive oil. Of lying in his arms and sipping kisses (Chuck's kisses, I imagined, were more intrusive, even anal). Apparently they had both been given an ultimatum. A big West Side rent-controlled prewar apartment was not so easily found, and the lease must have been in Howard's name. They were being kicked out so that the unblushing bride could be moved in, the publicity proof that Howard loved pussy, not dick. Knowing Howard, they'd undoubtedly gone over everything for hours and hours until all the coral meat had been sucked out of even the tiniest little walking legs.

I talk about Howard coldly now, which I suppose is easy since he's dead, his big Proustian novel ruined by rewriting, and he's the butt of so many jokes he would never have countenanced when he was alive. He was a granitic man, beautiful in his way, prepossessing, either God or the devil, I used to think. He would say things like, "If you're going to reduce everything to the commonsensical, you're no better than the English middle class" or "If you want to be my disciple, I can't be bothered. I have plenty of disciples and they bore me" or "It's a shame you're just an empty head and a hungry cunt" or he'd sing something about me being a material girl, which was a citation from a late twentieth-century pop song, I think. He would take me to strange places (a Zen teahouse on Staten Island, a mall in Poughkeepsie) because somehow they were supposed to be "edifying" or "illustrative," of what I was never sure.

I won't bore you with the long, painful dénouement of my second marriage. Many women were jealous of me, I hasten to add, since there were few single suitable, marriageable male New Yorkers on the ground for a woman over thirty—or, say, even twenty-five. In spite of all their feminist polemics most women wanted to get married, especially those who'd put off marriage for a career, as if marriage was always an option and then suddenly it wasn't; after thirty, her climacteric, a woman lost her dew and was just brown petals curling in the heat and eventually shattering.

Howard was maddeningly sure of himself until Publication (no wonder he kept putting off the date year to year, as if he knew he'd overworked the canvas, erased the defining lines and smudged the delicate colors). He even changed the title from "*The Fallen Angel*" to "*Prolegomena to the Rest*," which was typical of his process or bad luck; if First Thought, Best Thought, then it follows Last Revision, Disaster. In his early drafts, which he often published, his great talent was his constant burrowing, his restless digging into simple, perfectly natural ideas, which, if he turned them often enough and raked enough, began a second budding. That was also the great fault of his writing (and his mind): endless revisiting, tireless retouching. His perfectionism was perverse, destructive. He'd thrown a delicate golden structure across the ravine and then slowly, achingly dismantled it. "Thrown"? Maybe "cantilevered." "Golden?" Why not "gold"? "Structure"? "But what do you mean? A small building? A kiosk? Too exotic, too Turkish. Maybe 'edicule'? That's good. It's a small shrine, usually independent of the neighboring building." So: "He'd cantilevered a frail gold edicule across the vale." Much better. More precise.

It became a cliché of criticism to say the Master turned out to be a hapless amateur.

But I won't go through all the moments with Howard that I already recounted in my little novel, *Harold's Ghost*, which you've read and might remember. Though I changed lots of circumstances to satisfy the publisher's lawyer, even making Howard Black though it's obvious he was as Jewish as Abraham, and saying he came from Akron rather than Cincinnati, all to avoid being sued by his daughter, Dove, the emotions are photographically real, even the sequence of feelings and happenings is exact.

I don't think I could ever recreate the shame, the ecstasy, the fear and the intense love of those years, mainly because I neutralized them by narrating them. Writing really is the kiss-off. While I was composing those pages I kept daring myself to be more honest, more complete, more eloquent, as if I were a surgeon grabbing ever smaller, ever sharper knives to excise the stupendous tumor. I wanted to prove to Howard's ghost (I called the character Harold) that I'd learned all the lessons he'd taught me about how to live and how to write, including the rule about letting metaphors become real and tangible.

We had difficult times together. I became retrospectively jealous of Howard's male lovers and was constantly suspicious that he was in touch with them. I'd let myself silently into the apartment and if he was having one of his hour-long tempestuous, then soothing, phone calls I'd try to eavesdrop—but he was always too canny for me. As far as I knew he was never in touch with Peter, although once Peter came by to pick up a winter jacket. He was with a slim, attractive new boyfriend who, I discovered, lived with Peter at the top of the Ansonia. Peter and the new boyfriend, Gustav (whose mother was a concert flutist from Idaho who admired Mahler) seemed very suited to one another. They both got up at six A.M. (went to bed at ten thirty) and jogged around the reservoir when, in winter, it was still dark out. Dawn was just breaking as they stretched on the steps of the Museum of Natural History, an institution Peter as a high school biology teacher often visited with his students.

I was polite as Americans think of politeness. "Where are you from? Oh, you're a flutist! I thought you said futurist, Gustav! And where did you go to college? Geography, how interesting . . ."

I kept thinking Howard would come back any moment, but he didn't. He was out verifying something about Zabar's for his novel. He was a perfectionist, alas. On the way out with the smiling, joking Gustav, whose glasses were as gold as his hair and whose buttocks I imagined must be hairless, ceramic white, innocent but receptive, Peter touched my shoulder and said, in a soft, confiding voice, "How's it going?"

I said, expressionlessly, "Fine." Beat. "Wonderful." Quizzical smile. "Why do you ask?"

"Remember, I lived with Howard for fifteen years." Peter arched an eyebrow. I felt he was sympathetic and had wandered to the limits of his discretion. He wore his pained expression of understanding but immediately canceled it out with a hearty laugh. He tapped Gustav on the butt and they both moved down the shabby, sunless entrance hall to the thrice-bolted front door.

"No," I called out, acknowledging Peter's kindly concern. "Everything is fine."

Howard had submitted his thousand-page manuscript, which I'd read three times. Convinced by his growing reputation as the American Proust, I admired every daring transition, every smudged effect, although I was keeping another parallel ledger and in this equally extensive but entirely unauthorized version the sensible part of me, the part that had read hundreds of books, was totting up the dullness, the pedantry, the obscurity. I think Howard was aware of this secondary but relentless take on his work, a part in which I had no confidence since he'd subjected me to a daily bombardment, a relentless pounding of my taste, my intentions, my whole personality, a part which was staggering about like a punch-drunk prizefighter just before he collapses and is counted out.

Everyone in Howard's orbit could see the emperor's new clothes; the imagined clothes hovered around his body in graceful folds and with shimmering silk seams. He was clothed / He was naked. It would be a reckless betrayal not to see the clothes and to dwell on the vulnerable naked chest and loins that, in an alternate universe, were unmistakably there.

It was terrible, as I've already written, Howard's last months. Terrible and uplifting. He was teaching creative writing as an adjunct at Princeton. I won't say that Ivy League schools are particularly snobbish and whoring after fame, but they are. His book came out in the middle of the semester. The students, who are clueless and uninterested in any adults other than their parents, didn't seem to realize Howard had been reviewed so widely and savagely. The other writers in the department knew for sure and were vocal and ostentatious in their sympathy. Louise Smith, who'd been exalted and damned in the press for half a century, was as kind and tender as ever; she'd never been bothered by rumors of Howard's preposterous seven-figure advance nor the Pleiades of "profiles" and the reverential glimpses of the coming triumph of the *Prolegomena*. She liked Howard for his ambition and fertility, which matched her own. For her a novel was just another chapter in a lifelong novel she was patiently constructing. Lesser novelists in the department—who'd published only one of two slim volumes that had been workshopped to death by several fiction classes in various prestigious universities and by a whole army of editors and copyeditors with ant-like patience—and who'd always resented Howard's prepub acclaim and well-publicized advances, were visibly excited. They tried to pull long faces during their constant coffee breaks, but the halls were ringing with laughter and the reviewers' words "overweening" and "humiliating" and "crushing." If the run-of-the-mill student in creative writing, who was having a pleasant artistic break from her concentration in nuclear physics, took her professor for granted even though her parents had never heard of him, Howard's two thesis students, Gemma and Sara, had followed his debacle in detail. Tellingly, they started skipping their appointments with Howard. They'd never liked his teasing, arrogant tone, but when he was still considered the American Proust they'd submitted to his comments with respect; now that he'd been exposed as the American Françoise Sagan, they no longer had to take his irony seriously. They'd already sacked two of their professors with Title IX complaints of gender discrimination. Now they started lightly in on Howard by asserting they no longer felt "comfortable" in his mocking phallocratic presence.

Amidst this hostility Howard lost all heart. We'd rented a beautiful big sabbatical house for the semester, complete with a gym in the basement. The Princeton side streets were so ill-lit that driving was dangerous. The invitations dried up and Howard, who was always so dubious about suburban socializing, definitely noticed the absence; only Louise remained cheerful and attentive. He and I became closer and closer. I guess he could tell I loved him and he was grateful for that. All his "fame" and grandiosity had always seemed alienating to me. He wrote a set of sonnets for me; he'd never written a poem before. They were all about how good and sweet I was. They exalted me, but the praise felt as unearned as his previous reservations.

Then one afternoon Howard had his office hours (obligatory if unattended). He said he felt lousy and lay down on the floor covered with a thin, industrial carpet. Luckily I was with him, reading an old copy of the *Kenyon Review* someone had discarded on an overwhelmed table of scholarly trash outside his office. It was an exegesis of a minor work (a story? a sketch?) written by Lionel Trilling in the 1950s. I looked down and Howard was making strange gobbling sounds, writhing on the floor and foaming at the mouth.

I ran out into the hall and called, "Phyllis!" She was the department secretary, a wide-hipped white feminist who wore peasant blouses and ethnic skirts from Lagos and who had a handwritten sign on her office door saying "safe space here." She dropped everything and ran down the hall, saw Howard writhing and called an ambulance on her cell. I rode with him and a nurse in the back of the ambulance the thirty miles to a hospital next to Rutgers. The admitting nurse, a Black woman from the Antilles, hooked Howard up to a drip and took his blood pressure and then an EKG on a wheeled metal stand. She opened his shirt and taped the EKG leads to his chest. Weirdly I was proud of Howard's majestic torso as seen by this stranger. Finally I asked the woman why her hair was coiffed so elaborately. She said she was a Seventh-day Adventist and they weren't allowed to wear jewelry, so all her efforts went into her hairdo. But even hairdos were forbidden by Scripture, I learned later, and wondered how the nurse had won a dispensation.

At the hospital Howard was slid onto a gurney and rushed by two orderlies into the emergency room, where the patient, still unconscious, was measured and scanned. The masked surgeon, who I could see from his eyes was Asian and young, said Howard's blood pressure was low, "but that's normal." Then he told me that the next morning they'd operate and give my husband a double bypass if his pressure, as expected, normalized.

After he was checked in and his Princeton health insurance card had been xeroxed, he was installed in a double room (the insurance wouldn't pay for a single I was told after I complained). Howard never recovered and died that night from a second, more violent attack. The other patient, who wore a football helmet because the top of his head had been shorn off in a car accident, slept through all the lights and sirens and paddles and rush of white-uniformed attendants. I was told that guy would probably be blissfully unconscious till the end of the week.

RUGGERO THOUGHT: NO wonder Constance is so insecure around me. She may be young but she's already lived through so much exploitation and abandonment. She's been raped by an abusive "uncle," she's been robbed by her first husband and humiliated by the second. She must have trouble believing in my love for her. She's always interesting and original, beautiful and passionate in her "needy" way (an odd American phrase I learned only recently). I like being needed. I've always been an overachiever, practicing as a musician many hours a day and then lifting weights to stay in shape; and clothes shopping so much, because an important part of my myth as an Italian is being chic and well-groomed. I never feel oppressed by her love, as she fears. Perhaps I need to be reassured as well—not really, but love is never too much for a Sicilian, independent and self-sufficient as we may be. We're a wonderfully affectionate race, constantly kissing and hugging and falling in love.

RUGGERO READ: I finished my *liceo classico* in Messina at age eighteen with a shockingly deep knowledge of the classics. I'd even gone with my class of just five boys to see Euripides's *Iphigenia in Tauris* in an ancient Greek theater. It was early May but very hot on the stone steps (we'd been warned to bring pillows but my *culo* was pillowy enough—those were my ass's glory days). We all wore sun hats, pretending our skin was fair, indoor aristocratic skin, but we were swarthy with our distantly Turkish, Spanish, and North African blood and we never had enough pretentiousness to burn, just tan. The play was a revelation, the actors so tall on their *cothurni*, their voices muffled by their masks, their bodies simplified by their robes, everything glowing in the late-afternoon sun, the dashing hero, Orestes, and his loving friend (and brother by marriage) Pylades, the shy priestess of the temple to Artemis, Iphigenia, who turns out to be Orestes's long-lost sister, mistakenly imagined dead. Everyone's dead—their mother Clytemnestra murdered by Orestes, who slaughtered her in revenge for her murder of their father, Agamemnon.

The sound of the Greek language—so liquid, with its rising and falling intonations, its blurred pronunciation, its umlaut *ü*, its gentle *th*, its multisyllabic rhythms, the measured cadences of (in this case) the female chorus—exalted me because I could understand every word (I'd read the text three times before our field trip).

I loved the classics because it was a taste shared with my cultured grandfather (and as a rejection of my playboy featherbrained father as I imagined him). Not until my early twenties, when I was living in London, did I learn the word *nerd*, which I felt had perfectly described me as a teenager—bookish, well-mannered, talented in so many ways (languages, composing and performing music), a bit snobbish, my understanding rapid, and my memory vast and exact, not the usual narrow-focus culture nerd but a weightlifter and a whiz in math and physics. I was a nerd also because I hated pop music even though a cousin of mine sang in an Italian boy band, the Plastic Boys, and played to huge audiences of teenyboppers (their hit was "Mi Piace, Il Tuo Corpo"). I hated soccer. I avoided politics. I didn't know how to dance. I didn't have a car until I was twenty (a red, antique Cinquecento). I wasn't a beach rat. I could speak Sicilian of course but spoke Tuscan most of the time. I never sat around the cafés; in fact I had a horror of cafés beyond standing at the zinc bar and downing a quick espresso. The idea of sprawling at a table for hours and eating panini and reading the pink sports pages or debating loudly with friends about government corruption—that life seemed to me so squalid. You could say I was proud to be a nerd once I knew what it was.

As for sex, my only partner had been my cousin Giuseppe until I was eighteen. Our sessions had dwindled away, I suspect mainly because he had met a compliant, beautiful girl from the village—and then he fell in love with a little countess, pure as only the children of the rich can afford to be. My school was all boys, though I'd had a reciprocated crush on a young widow from Viterbo who tutored two of us in Aramaic, a language I suddenly found fascinating.

Then I was off to Rome, where my grandfather bought me a little two-room apartment in a towering yellow-brick building near the Vatican, and where I was enrolled in the famous ancient conservatory of Santa Cecilia, not the academy in Parioli but the music school near the Piazza di Spagna. I loved the whole Roman life, not as disciplined or industrious as Milan's, much closer to our life in Sicily. People in the north said everyone from Rome south was picking their nose. In fact with my new Roman school friends our life was *meridionale*. We'd start phoning each other around five or six to see who was free, and by ten we'd all meet (five or six or even ten to twelve) in a bar for a coffee, and then we'd go out in the warm weather and sit beside a fountain next to a spotlit church. Every monastic order, even those that had disappeared since, had once had to build a mother church in Rome (many of the churches were abandoned, the doors unhinged, moss on the façades). All of us were eventually seated at a big table under the stars. The waiters kept bringing chairs out from the emptying interior. As the tables and chairs moved outside, they revealed more and more of the black-and-white tile floor. Outside we passed around carafes of sour white wine; they were standardized by the city government, and the exact liter mark was scratched under the SPQR symbol. Everyone was talking at once, and since we were just kids and musicians, someone from time to time would break out into an ear-piercing scale out of high spirits, the solfeggio from hell.

The students on a budget would order just a pasta course, something copious and spicy like spaghetti alla puttanesca or pasta alla gricia, and fill up on the tasteless cottony bad Roman *cornetti*. I didn't want to show off but I usually asked for the bill and silently gave everyone a big discount and made up the difference out of my own pocket. I think the older, more sophisticated students knew I was augmenting my share, but the poorer ones thought it was still too expensive but didn't dare to insult me by checking my arithmetic, though their parents back in Pontassieve had warned them about dishonest Sicilians. I had never had much of a regional accent but now I lost mine completely. Sometimes I'd be embarrassed because I used a word I didn't know was Sicilian. Once I asked a waiter to put a wedge of wood or cardboard under the leg of a wobbly table and I called the wedge a *taccia*. He just shrugged and walked away. Those were the days when, to get service, you had to shout, "*Senta!*" (listen), and the waiter would shout back, "*Dica!*" (tell me). I doubt you could do that now. Maybe . . . A polite, soft-spoken upper-middle-class boy was entirely ignored in that loud, knockabout world obsessed with soccer. I was hopeless ordering something at the butcher's.

I'm always slow on the uptake and scarcely notice when people are flirting with me. The few friends from Rome or London days whom I still see tell me that everyone was in love with me back then, male and female. (In England one of them said, "You were the universal ball. Everyone wanted you, but you seemed oblivious to our nods and winks.") I certainly didn't notice that Lucia was always sitting next to me in composition class, though every time I'd look her way she'd smile. I scarcely registered her—a pretty girl my age with a real romano accent as if her parents sold eggplants from a stall in the *Campo de' Fiori*, though she didn't shout but murmured. She was terminally thin and had bad teeth—a bulimic, I thought. When I got to know her later, she had a way of scrambling her food about on the plate at a restaurant, to say she wasn't really hungry and wanted to split the pasta, which she'd barely taste, to hide the scaloppine under a lettuce leaf, to take what we Italians call "cake" (fruitcake), and then rush to the toilet for fifteen minutes (upchuck time). She'd come back smelling of a mint and cologne and be red in the face (from all that time bending over the toilet?). She'd then recklessly order a double espresso, hell on an empty stomach.

She told me that she'd trained to be a dancer in a small ballet class as a child and teen but then discovered she wanted to be a composer. "It was the music that fascinated me, the way musicians would stick a fist into the bell of a French horn, the mutes on trumpets, the way the timpanist would tune his drum by tapping lightly and bending close to hear the sound, the way the harpist would stamp those pedals and lean the instrument back to her body, the way flutists would shake the excess saliva out, the warm-up when the first violinist would give the others the correct tuning, or the dangling string from the damaged bow—you could say all the mechanics producing those ethereal sounds, just as I loved the clop-clop of toe shoes at the ballet when the orchestra paused. My favorite moment of a concert was when the instruments were tuning up."

I convinced her to compose a mock tuning-up.

When our assignment was to write a double fugue, she panicked and asked if I could help her. I invited her to an early dinner (which I made—I still recall the recipe, one of the few I knew then, in Sicilian *pasta cu finocchiu*, chopped fennel and anchovies in a tomato sauce). She barely touched her plate, pretending she was allergic to anchovies, which I'd carefully washed free of their salt. She wolfed down one of the big cannoli I'd bought at a neighborhood *pasticerria* though of course that led to another 20 minutes in the toilet (I hoped she wouldn't clog the drain).

We started to work side by side in little folding chairs at a desk I'd made of a door on a trestle. I'm good at explaining things. Everyone says so. I think it's because I can remember all the steps I went through in mastering a subject. I can see (I suppose many people can) from someone's eyes if they haven't understood and without complaining go back to the beginning. Pencil in hand hovering over score paper, I asked Lucia to play a subject on my upright piano. She sat down on the bench with a whoosh of her skirts and lingering looks. She played a dozen notes all of the same metrical value, though at one point she skipped an octave. I wrote the melody down quickly.

"Now let's have your second subject. The same number of notes at intervals of three or five notes above or below the original melody. Or perhaps one for every two you've decided on."

She was quick and after studying the piano as one might look at a chessboard before a move, she rapped out her second subject, which I instantly transcribed. Having finished with her inventions, she gathered up her skirts (were they so full to hide her emaciated legs?) and returned to the chair beside me. I was in full cry, criss-crossing the two themes, when suddenly I noticed she was no longer looking at the score but rather at my lips. I stopped filling in the bars and looked at her in surprise while she dove in expertly to kiss me on the mouth.

A moment later we were grappling on our chairs, then we moved to the couch, which pulled out to a bed. I'd seen enough straight porno with Giuseppe to know about nipples, the labia, the clitoris. I found her clitoris right away; it was no bigger than the tip of her little finger, just as my hard brown nipples were a reduced version of her small breasts. Oddly, I noticed that by chance we both had just one mouth and one anus, placed in the center of a symmetrical face or twin buttocks. Her body was bone thin, her breasts deflated, her hip bones prominent and razor sharp, almost dangerous, her pubic hair sparse and colorless. Her mouth if probed deeply enough was sour under the taste of mints. With Giuseppe I'd worried about trespassing over his moral or role-playing limits, of being too gay, but I hadn't been afraid of breaking him—he was as sturdy as I was. For the first time in my life I realized that this creature was smaller, weaker, able to open her legs much, much wider (no wonder women could do the splits), but delicate, her rhythms and appetites slower to ignite but burning at a higher temperature once they reached their combustion threshold. I was almost jealous of her wild passions, the way she moaned on a low note and yipped on dotted eighths, flinched under my invasive hands, looked up with pleading eyes like a drowning woman through her wet hair, bucked, turned her eyes back till they were all revulsed whites. She was obviously an experienced slut, not the innocent I'd imagined.

The odd thing is that the person I admired the most was myself. I perceived my own beauty through her eyes—my broad shoulders, my waist that could be encompassed by two hands, my erection which was also a two-hander, one beside the other, my big Sicilian nose, the smoothness of my skin where it wasn't hairy, the manly torero elegance of my slender body, my dazzling smile not dimmed by coffee or red wine (I was abstemious). Was it normal to find myself exciting if looked at through her eyes? Whereas I'd always felt competitive with Giuseppe, with Lucia I felt from the beginning I was the victor. Or rather I was both the perceiver and the perceived, but only if my glance was mediated by hers.

RUGGERO: I CAN read Constance's thoughts. She's wondering if that is how I experience her and myself.

Ruggero said: No. That's not how I feel around you, Constance. I can imagine what you're surmising. But you have to remember there are great differences between how an old man cherishes a young woman and how a young man creates himself in the mirror of a girl's consciousness. At eighteen I barely existed; I hadn't lived long enough with me to discover my own dimensions. Of course I didn't notice this unfinished work. In fact I would have strenuously denied that I didn't know myself. But what was I really? A mood that colored the world around me, as tea infuses hot water. A swooping, gliding mind that sees only the minor movements below that might be prey, something nourishing. I was looking for self-definition. Although my thought was concentrated in my eyes, I was unfamiliar with the rest of this baggy, shapeless monster of self, all this vague potentiality, and my conversation revealed this uncertainty, because I was nothing but paradox hiding behind an irony meant to disguise whether I was serious or not.

But an old man is tired of himself and is looking for renewal in someone young. He's lived too long in the small room of an identity he knows by heart, a stale little room that must be aired and explored by a newcomer. She should bring flowers into it, a new soft throw. The old man and the young woman don't share the same references, the same past, but they discover fresh, new similarities, for our real inner life is not only and not mainly historical, a matter of the events defining our perspective; our real life is unique, so private it is almost incommunicable, and if the old man chances to share something *a priori* with the young woman, he thinks it's miraculous.

I'd always had women in my young life, but they'd usually been older, relatives, friends of my grandfather's or women who came in to cook, clean, or iron, in other words people to whom I owed deference, no matter how ceremonial, or who were servants but had that same mixture of medieval, Sicilian respect and intimacy that Russian peasants in Chekhov's stories have ("Here, my little countess, come and cry in your old Anya's arms," the serf said to the young baroness).

Now I had this obliging woman my age living with me and she would buy apricots because she knew I loved them or I would come home to the smell of brewing coffee. If she walked past me, she'd touch my shoulder—between us there wasn't the same anxiety about showing fondness there might be between two men. Sex, okay between men. Passion, yes. But fondness, no—it was too "feminine" unless displayed by a woman to a man, too tender, too familial, too "cheesy. " Not masculine enough in the military sense. A woman's fondness doesn't endanger the man or make him fear she is corrupting him because men and women (even subtle, "liberated" ones), play reciprocal, not dupli-catng, roles. She put roses around his bayonet.

And I liked the social role as well. If I'd enter a restaurant first, the waiter, twice my age, would ask, "Is the signore dining alone or will the signora be joining him?" and despite the class differences there would be an instant complicity between two married men. We both knew the compromises of marital life, we'd both traded in the excite-ment of the chase for the comforts of domestic habit. Or so we could imagine . . .

Lucia was from an old family. Family seemed to be as important to her as my grandfather was to me, and we understood and permitted that in each other—the long, endearing phone calls home almost every day. Although Lucia seemed to have an agonistic relationship to her shallow, scornful, bossy mother, she adored her father and he adored her. For her father's sake of propriety she kept on her old apartment, which stood empty most days. I thought that was a silly waste of money.

I had five recipes. She had seven. Often we ate out. Her eating became more and more normal—almost normal—as she escaped the influence of her mother and felt more and more comfortable with me. At the time I simply thought my life, my inner life, my emotional life, was no one else's business. Lucia often complained, especially after a long, tearful account of a bad moment in her past, that I never matched anecdotes. She was a wounded, self-centered girl who'd stared at her own navel for years, especially—as she reported—in psychoanalysis, which was rare if fashionable in Italy in those days, but she did eventually notice my reticence. I proceeded with the usually correct theory that if I didn't match anecdotes the other person would go deeper and deeper into her misery. The only thing I had to restrain was how much I'd let her "spill." The more she confessed the stronger was her attachment to me.

CONSTANCE THOUGHT: I imagine Edmund was the one who got him to open up. I can sense Ruggero is almost deliberate and willed, *voulu*, in his confidences now, but at least he does confide, even if it's not entirely spontaneously. Or maybe he's more interested in his inner life now that he's become a success in his career; many men are like that. They consecrate themselves for years to becoming good, and known to be good, in their work; when they finally succeed they start to interest themselves in themselves and their intimates. For an artist like Ruggero, he was never out of touch with his feelings, but then his feelings were like a second keyboard he was playing, a doubling of his technique; now he's free to entertain his feelings in their pure form. He once told me he had never had sex in its "pure" form—that is, it was always mixed with love or at least with sentiment.

RUGGERO READ: . . . THEN I took Lucia to Castelnuovo for Christmas. We flew to Messina where we were met by Beppo from the village who always drove us about in his roomy old car which smelled of cigarettes. We had to park outside Castelnuovo because the streets were too narrow for automobiles. We walked the hundred meters to our house. We held hands. I knew she was nervous because she'd be entering the world of my childhood. Each family, when known in its intimacy, is a foreign land, with its own customs, its idiolect, its prehistoric references, its rhythms, its unspoken expectations, its private jokes, its individual understanding of what constitutes the unsayable, its sacred sites, its No Trespassing signs.

My grandfather greeted us at the entrance to our house. I knew that was a rare sign of politeness since the stairs were difficult for him; ascending them was a struggle, as he hoisted himself up by grabbing the banister hand over hand, nor would he want a stranger to see him winded. He kissed me and kissed Lucia's hand then shooed us up the stairs ahead of him; I knew the drill and pulled her with me though she wanted to chat politely with him on the way up.

I gave her a tour of the house, explaining who decorated which room in which century. I showed her her room and the bathroom.

"Won't you be sleeping with me?" she asked.

I held my forefinger to my lips and whispered in English, "Of course not. But I might visit you after lights out."

She smiled but looked pained. I showed her the adjoining bathroom with its new tiles fitted around the big nineteenth-century English fixtures and huge porcelain tub, which always reminded me of Dr. Frankenstein's laboratory. She kissed me and I looked around guiltily.

"Come down and join us in the blue salon when you're ready," and I hurried out, without looking back.

I asked my grandfather if I could make him a whiskey and soda. There on a tray in the corner were the dusty old Scotch bottles, the beveled glasses, the ice bucket, and the blue, translucent seltzer bottle in its netting and with its tarnished silver nozzle. The maid came in, for once in her uniform, and passed some olives and fragments of Parmesan and little chunky slices of prosciutto (a *délice* I hadn't tasted since I left). Once again she'd forgot the little paper napkins for our greasy fingers. I told my grandfather I had a special gift for him (a signed first edition of *The Day of the Owl* by Leonardo Sciascia, a sort of Sicilian murder mystery).

He said, "It's such a pleasure to have a lovely young lady under our roof once again." Then he asked me about my musical studies. "I hope you're not going to become a performer. A professor, that would be all right. A composer, maybe. But not a performer. I'd hate to see our family name on a poster, especially since you have my brother's Christian name. For a gentleman music can be a pastime but not a vocation."

"Times are changing," I said, telling myself to stay calm. "Anyway, no one knows our name except in this little Sicilian backwater."

I sat down to play something on the harpsichord I was practicing. In a certain rapid passage I stumbled where I always did and shouted "*Cazzo!*" in frustration.

"Why are you so irritated?" my grandfather asked.

"Because I can't play that up to the correct speed."

"Well, that's your speed. Who cares what the others do? No one would notice anyway."

"The other musicians would notice."

My grandfather made a dismissive sound and waved his hand. "You are you. You set the standard."

Just then, fortunately, Lucia came downstairs and joined us. When she responded to his question by telling my grandfather that she was studying to be a soprano, a soubrette, to be exact, he told her that his French grandmother had had a lovely voice but had naturally had to give up her operatic career when she married, since her new husband was destined to be a professor of mathematics in Catania.

"*Capisco*," Lucia said tonelessly, "I understand," though I'm sure she didn't. She was far from being a bra burner, but I could see she'd been rubbed the wrong way. It discountenanced me to have her think of my beloved grandfather as an oppressor. He was just old-fashioned and Sicilian and had to be understood and respected as such. Tyrannical "lifestyle trends" have always irritated me; they are the true oppressors. But then again I would think that, wouldn't I, since all doors have been opened to me all my life?

My grandfather spoke of all the celebrated singers he'd seen perform in Catania or Palermo, names which were vaguely familiar; when the maid brought in pasta alla Norma, we had another dissertation on Bellini, a Sicilian. The main course was tournedos Rossini, another gastronomic compliment, followed by pêche Melba. I thought it was dear of grandfather to have constructed this menu, though it was too subtle for Lucia to register. After dinner we exchanged presents. My grandfather gave me the very precious score to the opera, *Don Chisciotte della Mancia* (1726) by the Neopolitan composer Francesco Feo. I took his gift as a contradiction to his earlier words; the original score of a very great baroque composer from nearby Naples seemed to be a tacit recognition of my passion for music.

He gave Lucia a bottle of Sicilian perfume, Zagara di Sicilia, with its light notes of lemon and bergamot. I don't remember what she gave him.

When we were back upstairs at midnight, Lucia said, "How did you ever emerge out of this stuffy world, you who are so open, so curious, so compassionate, so . . . universal?"

Although her words were meant to be flattering, I was (I hope imperceptibly) vexed by them. I was proud of my family, our coat of arms of a lion and the French words *C'est mon plaisir.* (Our origins were Norman, though half-educated people thought that was an Americanism, "It's my pleasure.") That night was the first and only time I was impotent. Did I feel the inhibiting weight of my ancestors watching me make love to this woman I suddenly found unworthy? Or was I vexed by her failure to like my grandfather?

When we returned to Rome, I'm sure Lucia was hoping our life would return to normal. I hadn't touched her in the five days we'd been in Castelnuovo. I'd been polite and helpful to her at every step (she *was* my guest), but she'd lost all her appeal in my eyes; if I was bothered by anything, it was that I was so inconstant.

CONSTANCE THOUGHT: AT least with me he never visibly goes into those moods. He seems to like me all the time, always to be siding with me in the little disputes of daily life, always approving even my most extreme moods and prejudices. I suppose you could say he dotes on me, which I'm sure isn't good for my character, too permissive, but I'm so unsure of myself that any condition on his love would seem to me a rejection. Why is he more indulgent of me than he was to poor Lucia? Is it just that he's older now and is charmed even by my faults? Has he grown more temperate? Or maybe he knows that in my heart I love him entirely, that I admire everything about him. Is it merely that I'm a better catch than Lucia? But I mustn't be too "female" in referring everything back to myself. That's what men hate most about women.

RUGGERO READ: I came to resent Lucia's presence in my apartment in Rome. I was always conscious when she was at home, breathing my air, stealing my time for study with her chatter.

I didn't have sex with her but we continued to sleep on the pull-out bed. Usually I was in bed with my eyes wide open, sleepless, rigid with resentment. As the tension increased she began to elaborate plans for our marriage, though I'd never proposed to her. I buried myself in my work. I was composing a ballet for a friend, a choreographer. I rehearsed at the harpsichord several hours a day; since I had learned to play the piano first, I had picked up some bad habits. The piano is percussive and it doesn't matter where you strike the key, even close to the nameboard; the harpsichord, by contrast, is a plucked instrument and the correct place for the finger is closest to the performer, a position that lifts the entire lever and pulls the quill sharply against the string.

Lucia would embrace me from behind when I was composing or practicing and give my shoulders a rub, which I found annoying. The only time, oddly enough, I found her tolerable was when she was on the phone with a friend. She sounded more natural, more interesting, a less predictable personality than when she was addressing me alone. With me every remark seemed loaded, somehow calculated. I couldn't bear it when she was strategically cold, thinking that would trouble me (it didn't). I liked it even less when she'd decided to be lighthearted, since she was never truly insouciant. If she threw her arms around me, I couldn't bear her boniness and her bad breath because she'd stopped eating again. I knew her goal was to starve herself into stopping her periods; she despised her adult female body again because I didn't love it, didn't love her.

Often I felt sad and guilty that I made her suffer—but guilt has always angered me. My irritation grew and grew. I resolved that I'd never live with anyone again, that I would be an absolutely free agent. It wasn't that I was a libertine; I didn't want to be a sexual buccaneer. I liked the stability and order of domestic life—but not at the price of feeling stifled, oppressed. Maybe I should go back to men. I knew my grandfather approved of female partners more than male: children; continuity; dynasty; respectability (as an aristocrat that mattered less to him—he assumed our way of doing things was the right way, just as my tempi on the harpsichord were the right ones because they were mine. We set the standard, didn't follow it). He didn't want to know what happened in bed between two men; perhaps it was unimaginable to him, that he thought Patroclus and Achilles just held hands.

I liked the social acceptance of heterosexuality but not the expectations, the ways in which family men were slated to abnegate the fulfillment of their desires in favor of their duties to their children and their wives. The father as guide, as mentor, as authority—the whole economy of duty was based on the female's reluctance to have sex. The male hormone, testosterone, is *the* sex drive even in women.

CONSTANCE THOUGHT: THAT'S completely crazy. Women like sex. Women's orgasms are much noisier and cataclysmic than men's. We're not as promiscuous as men but only because sperm is cheap, eggs dear; sex for us leads to babies and years of the child's dependence.

Perhaps women take longer to be aroused, but they're slower to unwind sexually; ask any horny woman who's wide-awake beside her snoring, postcoital man. Unlike apes, human females are almost always estrous, perhaps to lure back the men off on a hunting expedition: Come home, come home with meat for us and get some nice pussy! Women damn well better like sex if they're going to please the men returning from the hunt.

Surely Ruggero can tell I like sex with him; he's heard me scream with delight, look up at him with swooning pleasure, observed how I've become sopping wet just at his touch.

★ ★ ★

RUGGERO READ: I had not been taught any social skills that could rid me of Lucia. Fortunately, alas, one day she started sobbing when I shrugged off her embrace. She sat in the chair beside me. I swiveled to look her in the eye.

"Don't you love me anymore?"

My impulse was to reassure her, but the Rubicon glowed red before me and begged me to cross it. "No," I said.

She seemed startled. "You don't?"

I said, still looking her in the eye, though I would have chopped off a hand (I, a harpsichordist!) to be anywhere else, "I did love you, but I don't any longer."

"But why?" she wailed.

I shrugged.

"You're so cruel. I told myself never to get involved with a man who couldn't reach the high ground, for whom there was no higher court of appeal."

I knew I *could* be reached by an ultimate appeal. In my short life (which suddenly felt very long) I'd responded to many difficult people with compassion, but I just wanted to be rid of Lucia. I stared at her now without smiling or showing the least sign of tenderness.

"Do you want me to move out?" she asked, slapping her last card on the table defiantly.

I breathed deeply. "Yes."

"Really?" Now she glanced away and looked like an abused child. It took all my resolve not to touch her or kiss her. I turned myself into basalt.

A day later she left. I never felt so free! I swept the house and washed down the white impression of toothpaste her toothbrush had left on the sink.

SOON I MET Cesare and lived with him for four years until he had a vision and became a priest.

He was a student at Santa Cecilia like me, and he was so tall and blond that everyone was aware of him. Like me he was Sicilian, which always led to comments—"Sicilian? So blond? So tall?" What was not said but understood: "So handsome?"

I suppose he was the most dramatic beauty in our school. He was always joking and roughhousing. To me he seemed to be just a big kid but an endearing one. You could tell, he wanted everyone to like him. I found out he was a bass and had a beautiful voice; there was a scarcity of basses at Santa Cecilia, plenty of tenors and baritones, but only one other genuine bass, and that added to his popularity. His speaking voice was also deep, a voice from the balls, which only made everyone picture his balls, big and pink and wrapped in fine gold hairs, or so we imagined. When he sang, he made us think of the Grand Inquisitor in Verdi's *Don Carlo*, making the chandelier lusters tremble. I think he had found out that I was Sicilian too, which showed he was curious enough about me to ask around about me. He always smiled at me whenever he saw me, which I found flattering. Everybody was aware of his friendliness since he stood out—literally, head and shoulders—above everyone else, his great blond head pivoting above a smaller, darker crowd in the hallways leading into a classroom or a practice hall.

Once he bumped into me, looked around, registered who I was, smiled that whole snowbank of a smile and said in Sicilian, *Pi piaciri* (please) which didn't make much sense in any language. I took it as a mild invitation.

Then the woman for whom I was writing the ballet invited me and Cesare and three other friends to a group dinner and a concert. I was seated next to Cesare (whose idea was that?). He'd brought the ice cream, saying he couldn't cook. I brought the pasta course, pasta alla Norma (fried eggplant), which we warmed up in a big skillet. Someone else brought bread and a girl made *polpettone* (meatballs). The choreographer, Barbara, provided the place settings, the water, the wine and a big salad. I asked Cesare where he was from in Sicily; several times he touched my shoulder and, once, even my face with the back of his huge, warm hand. It shocked me, that liberty, and I think it confused the other students. He was strangely daring and shy; perhaps his great height and beauty made him both aggressive and self-conscious. Maybe he was drunk. I remember once he was irritated that the man at the next table in a sidewalk café was smoking (Cesare was always protecting his voice) and the man pointed out testily that they were outside and smoking was perfectly legal. Cesare said nothing but simply stood up to his full six feet four inches and the man stubbed out his cigarette immediately. I don't think Cesare ever struck anyone, but strangers were frightened of him. Yet he was equally ashamed of his height and often slumped, walking or sitting, a useless precaution since he always stood out wherever he went; he would still draw notice even in the midst of a Norwegian high school basketball team.

The whole dinner was festive; Italians are party animals though they behave and drink sensibly. After we all washed up and set up the chairs and the audience was seated, I played my new ballet score while Barbara occasionally narrated the action (which irritated me, as though my score were incomplete; did Stravinsky have to narrate his scenes of pagan life in Russia as he played the first piano version of *The Rite of Spring*?). Then several others sang in groups (I sang countertenor in one ensemble) and somewhere Cesare sang with his warm, lustrous bass. Walking beside me on the way home, Cesare said, "Oh, I can see you're a real musician. Maybe you could help me. All I have is my voice."

"And your presence," I added.

"Yes, thanks, but I can't really read music and I can't accompany myself on the piano. I have to be taught every score by rote."

"As Pavarotti did," I said encouragingly.

"Yes, but his father had a beautiful voice as well, and he grew up in a family of singers. He sang from an early age. I didn't start until I was eighteen. My German and English pronunciation is good, my Russian nonexistent and my French lamentable."

Suddenly I found him so attractive with his big blue eyes, rosy skin, white-blond mop. He was so obviously impressed by my musicianship that I was no longer intimidated by his towering height. I realized he would always submit to me, to my advice, my superior knowledge, even my princely social status (that may sound odd to an American, since in America everyone assumes she or he is "middle-class," everyone from Homer Simpson to John Rockefeller). I liked the idea of this blond beast (who was eight years older than me) submitting to me. I found the idea of two men, one active and the other passive, among the most powerful, most beautiful pairings in existence, even more profound (forgive me) than the man-woman couple. Why? you ask. Precisely because it's not biological. You know I agree with Baudelaire that an artificial woman's face—starved, made-up—is more beautiful than that of a tan, big-toothed, athletic California gal. More beautiful precisely because it is artificial, willed into being, original, less healthy, more achieved through ingenuity. Give me a pallid, chartreuse-colored *Vogue* model any day over a broad-shouldered, square-jawed Olympic female athlete whose chromosones are routinely tested.

Two men, top and bottom, must invent themselves. They weren't brought up to play these roles. They're winging it at every moment. That's the beauty in it, the art—as in the art of the *onnagata* in Kabuki.

CONSTANCE THOUGHT: HE has such a vile idea of women. But I'm sure that's not his real opinion. He can be a poseur and I remember that he was so taken by Baudelaire's essay on cosmetics. But he likes tan, healthy women; he likes beautiful women *bonne en chair*. What a *poseur*! But I wish he wouldn't say things like that. At his age he should be sincere. And all that about tops and bottoms!

Of course people are a collection of opinions, often things said by lovers they overheard and borrowed at all different times of their life, like travel stickers—for many voyages over the years, some almost effaced, some recent—on an old steamer trunk. Unless challenged they don't try to reconcile all these contradictory opinions they've picked up during a long life. But he has a doctorate in philosophy and should try to be more consistent.

RUGGERO READ: OF course I had no reason to think Cesare was interested in men. In fact I'd heard he'd had several girlfriends, that he was a professional heartbreaker. But I could see the submission in his eyes, as a young mahout can see devotion in the eyes of what will someday be his elephant.

I invited him to practice with me. He said he'd come the next day at four.

When he came, he sat beside me on the piano bench. Within seconds we were embracing; to paraphrase what Dante wrote of Paolo and Francesca, they practiced no more that day.

I was astonished by his huge dick, though generally, even in the locker room, I was indifferent to dicks. But in this case, it was the biggest one I'd ever seen and I hoped he wouldn't think it gave him fucking rights. I wanted to do all the fucking; that was my birthright, I believed. Over the years I've learned most gay men (as my aunt would say) want to be the "wife." But some, especially one with such a huge dick, would assume every man would fall down and worship it (not me). Of course at that time we were both inexperienced and didn't know the ways of the sexual world. We were happy kissing and licking and indulging in mutual masturbation. We would lie side by side and jerk each other off while kissing. His body was so big, it was like hiking up the mountains—buttocks, each as big as a Christmas ham, shoulders pink with health like glaciers in the evening glow, a wet mouth and a huge muscular tongue like a giant snail's foot. He couldn't resist sucking me once he'd glided down to my waist, kissing me all the way. He held my erect penis fastidiously in one vast hand (he was my Polyphemus and I his rival, Acis, and in my head I started singing, "Ruddier is the berry, sweeter is the cherry"). If Polyphemus had but one eye, I'd discovered it as the piss hole of his massive dick. He frowned at my penis in his hand and, evaluating, then unresisting, he began to lick it. The urge was too strong, the experiment too exciting. I knew my body (disappointingly to some) had absolutely no odor, so he couldn't be put off by that. He licked me experimentally, as if he'd find out in a moment whether I tasted good or bad.

Unleashed, he set about his job in earnest. I had the feeling he'd never done this before but that he'd fantasized about doing it during hours and hours of savage masturbation. He looked me in the eye for a moment, as if to verify I wasn't shocked by his zeal. I nodded encouragingly and he turned wild, as if all his fantasies, now that they were permitted, had become cannibalistic.

When I ejaculated all over his face, he looked offended for a moment and dragged his hand disapprovingly through the gobs of spunk on his cheek, his hair, across his mouth, even in his eye. I jumped up and fetched a washcloth and swabbed his eye but left the rest of the cum on his face. Like a cat tiptoeing into a puddle of milk he raised his paw to his mouth, then started rubbing and licking his face clean. He must have liked the taste or at least the abjection.

I wasn't in the mood to jerk him off and thought anyway I'd be doing him a favor by leaving him horny, desiring. Inexperienced Catholic boys like us feel guilty after they come; I was saving him from that regret and keeping him frustrated and focused on me and my superb body.

I would never move him in—I'd made that mistake already. Cesare—beautiful as he was, endearing as his voice might be—was deeply insecure about his lack of musical training. I knew he'd cornered several piano students to accompany him in songs he was learning, since he couldn't read music (and, as I was to learn later, he had no sense of pitch). His voice was a beautiful instrument he didn't know how to play.

I found him dazzling because he was a star, a beauty, intelligent, wounded, complicated—and submissive (to me, but not by nature). Several times, as we walked down Vittorio Emanuele and crossed the bridge toward the Vatican and my apartment, we noticed that a spectrally thin girl was following us: it was Lucia. She would dart into doorways if we looked her way. I even hailed her once with a big smile but she'd vanished like the Fire Bird. Sometimes late at night, after I was already asleep in my Lilliputian pull-out bed with my Gulliver-huge Cesare by my side, the phone would ring. When I would pick up, no one replied, but I could hear breathing and once a high-pitched whimper. In the corridors at school she'd often be tailing us. In the cafeteria she'd sit, alone, near us but never look up, pretending to be deep in a score. The choreographer of my ballet told me that Lucia knew in her whole body that I wasn't gay, that I was just posing as a sodomite to baffle her, to be cruel, to make it clear to her we'd never reconcile, demonstrating I'd found my true self in the gigantic arms of another man. Lucia was pious and determined to save me from burning in hell for eternity. My friend said, "I've known tons of anorexic dancers, but Lucia is in the danger zone. Someone should notify her parents. She should be hospitalized and put on a feeding tube." My first instinct was to reach out and soothe Lucia, but all I had to do was recall how she'd suffocated me with her obsessive attentions and I would forgo my altruistic urges. I didn't want her back. Later she was confined for a year to a mental hospital.

I tutored Cesare for hours and hours, and though I was patient with him, almost as if I were dealing with a child, a beginner, he would become more and more resentful. That is, he always followed my advice to the best of his means and would thank me profusely since he knew he had a long way to go to catch up, specially since the school reduced the number of students each year; the graduating class was only half the size of the entering one, but he had the usual resentment of gratitude against a benefactor.

That he couldn't read music was a grave problem but one that could be repaired if he took piano lessons, say, every day during the summer break. But his real problem was a faulty sense of pitch. If he had to skip down over an octave, for instance, from a middle C to a low B-flat, he could never find the lower note, no matter how many times I traced the interval on the piano. He would land on the A or whatever but never the right note. If he had to sing a long phrase of half-note intervals with lots of flats and sharps, I would break it down into three- or four-note segments and make him work on each unit until we returned to the whole phrase, but I'd be left pounding on the mistaken note. He'd always flub the longer phrase even if the segments were good. And I'd correct his pronunciation even in Tuscan, which he spoke with a slight Sicilian accent (a doubled *bb* instead of the single Italian *b*, something one would never notice in conversation or would think charming, as when you, Constance, say *siempre* in Spanish instead of the Italian *sempre*).

After our long rehearsals he'd thank me humbly but then when we'd have sex he was an extremely aggressive botttom. His kisses were those of a vampire and more than once he actually drew blood. My nipples are little hard brown things without sensitivity as you know but he'd maul me on one side or the other, like a puppy rooting for a teat. The worst was when he started angling that huge cock toward my mouth, battering my closed lips. Unlike mine, his cock smelled, which can be thrilling if you've taken the right drugs but as a daily *après-répétition* meal, it was repulsive. We actually wrestled but in the end I won. I'd fuck him and he'd wince all through it. I never let him have a release. I wanted to keep him permanently horny.

Once during a concert at school he sang with a quartet. My grandfather had come up to Rome and I invited him, since my ballet was also on the program. Cesare was chosen because he was the only bass available but it was a disaster. He sang the opening note a third too high, he continued off tune though the other three singers sang on pitch. My grandfather, who knew we were friends, whispered to me, "He's *stornato*" (discordant). When we were alone at my place, Cesare was smiling and said, "I was pretty good, wasn't I?" I said he'd been good in the rehearsals but not so good during the performance. I'd taped it (I still have the tape somewhere) and I played it for him and he could tell what a disaster it had been. The other students avoided him for a few days. Our sex life became even more violent. Then nonexistent. He didn't want me to touch him.

CONSTANCE'S THOUGHTS: THAT must have been hell on such an oversexed man as Ruggero! I've been troubled over our sex life recently because I would like to get pregnant. I'm young and though he thinks I'll remarry after he dies, I doubt if I will. I want to have his child. In any event, who knows when anyone will die? Look at my parents . . . If he got me pregnant he'd be in me all the time, at least for nine months. But he wants me to stay on the pill.

"I couldn't bear for my son to have an old man for a father and not a man in his prime, someone he could admire. Nor would I want to be taken as his grandfather."

"Who said it will be a boy? I want to have a daughter, Adelasia."

"But that was King Ruggero's wife's name; I don't want my daughter to have my wife's name."

"It's a beautiful name. She's my daughter, too."

The next day he pulled me into a kiss and said, "If you promise to kill him if he's a boy, we can have a daughter, even with that incestuous name."

I'm not the brightest thing and it took me a minute to register that he was saying no. I pushed him away. It was the first time we'd ever quarreled. Except once over which direction to take at a crossroads.

RUGGERO READS: CESARE used to tease me for piously composing motets to the Virgin for our family church in Castelnuovo, just as he liked to pretend I was a snobbish aristocrat and he was a man of the people. What gave him ammunition was that I loved sacred music and did compose for our church, and the choir is still singing one or two of my adolescent compositions. And once, when he said he'd like to learn to be as diplomatic as I am, I replied, "I'm afraid it takes six centuries of breeding." In truth I was an atheist who despised the Vatican and a republican who took seriously only an elite of talent and intelligence.

Then Cesare's own family (who'd been typical smug Italian nonbelievers and heard mass only during weddings and funerals and the men smoked outside while their wives were kneeling in the cathedral for Christmas and Easter) were suddenly awakened by a charismatic priest. The whole family became fervent Christians and insisted Cesare come to mass with them while he was in Sicily for the weekend. One evening he was watching a gangster movie when suddenly Christ's face appeared on the screen (no one else, it seemed, could see Him) and asked him to give up his life of sin and to serve the Lord. This was immediately after his fiasco as a singer at the school concert.

The next day, back in Rome after his holiday, he told me he was dropping out of Santa Cecilia and entering a monastery school in Sicily with the intention of becoming a priest. I said, "But you've never shown the least interest before in religion," and he told me about his vision of Christ. I just held the back of my hand to his forehead as if he were feverish and delirious. He'd always liked to sit on my knee, though it was awkward given his size. When something upset him, I'd put him on my knee (my foot well braced) and kiss him and comfort him. Now I started to pull him down but he stiffened. "We can no longer do that; I promised Christ I would give up the sins of the flesh."

I said, "Don't be so silly, darling. There is no Christ. He doesn't exist. Just because you poisoned yourself with a bad kernel of sugared popcorn while watching James Cagney . . ."

He said he was leaving Rome that night and heading back to Sicily and to the priest who had converted him.

"Where does that leave us?"

"I'm not sure." Then he thought a bit. "We can be lovers in Christ."

"Oh, yeah? How will that work exactly?"

"I still love you. We'll be together forever in heaven."

"But no sex here on earth? And you'll be a priest?"

"We'll love each other in Christ."

"I think that's creepy."

"I've made up my mind."

"Me too. I don't want any part of it," I said.

He was gone that same evening on a late train toward Sicily. He embraced me at the door.

I had no gay friends and I certainly couldn't discuss it with my grandfather. I felt injured, physically, as if a vital organ had been removed. It was better to be angry (at Cesare's foolishness, at the Church's profiting from mental illness) than to be hurt, which wasn't my style.

We'd been together four years, the most difficult of my diploma in composition. Maybe I'd neglected Cesare, but I don't think so (my shrink says I'm always trying to please everyone). I'd been harsh or just honest about the fiasco of his concert, but his lack of musicianship, despite the remarkable luster of his voice, would keep him from having a career, even as a high school music teacher.

I went for a long walk up the Via della Conciliazione to St. Peter's. It was raining slightly and no one was about except three short, dark-skinned nuns; I imagined this was the first thing they wanted to see in Rome after their twenty-hour flight from Jakarta. The way Bernini's arcade opened up after its narrow entrance and embraced me in its marble arms supporting colossal statues of bishops and saints thrilled me with its theatricality as it framed the façade of St. Peter's. I felt there was no place in the world less spiritual, more an emblem of wealth and worldly power, than St. Peter's, but in the rain, without the crowds, with a gentle winter mist floating among the columns, the place seemed poetic if the poetry was epic, not lyrical, secular not devotional.

I thought bitterly how my joking giant of a lover with the big dick and the failed musical career had been stolen from me by this hoax, the Catholic Church, which seemed legitimate only because it was so old and rich and counted millions of adherents, all of them duped by the incense and the glittering overpolished white marble. Heart of stone: the Church, I said to myself.

Then another part of me, an earlier part, realized I'd once fervently believed, was once a familiar of the Holy Ghost, the Spirito Santo, and that at least for the two years of puberty I'd prayed at bedtime (fearful I'd die in my sleep before becoming famous), wept at the feet of the statue of the Virgin in our family chapel, and feverishly composed my sacred cantatas with verses from the Bible, Old and New Testaments. If I was honest with myself, that old me was slightly jealous of Cesare's conversion, his mystical glimpse of Christ's bleeding head on the screen. It was ridiculous, but then so was everything but incontestable positivism. Numbers, measurement, verification—that was something solid, not ridiculous, but everything that gave us a reason for living (love, poetry, Bach)—none of that could be justified or even explained. I felt that Cesare had fallen victim to the Marauder Church on the heels of his singing fiasco, that there was nothing naturally religious in his makeup, that soon he'd be one more petty wrist-slapping, basketball-coaching village curate, that he might lead the local choir (ineptly), that he might even pinch an underage boy's rosy bottom.

The next time I was in Sicily, Cesare begged me to see Father Ernesto. I agreed reluctantly. He lived only two villages over, in Castelforte. I drove over in my little red vintage Cinquecento, found the church easily enough. I was just in time for our appointment. Ernesto's office was "backstage" behind the altar. The dusty corridor was lined with banners used in the yearly Santa Febronia festival and a box of hosts and what I guessed was a jug of sour holy wine.

"Come in, my son," the white-skinned, blue-knuckled man in robes said. He was someone in his fifties, I imagined. The surplice revealed he was at once skinny and possessed of a little belly. I was already irked that such a plain man would have designs on my beautiful giant.

"I'm not your son. I'm a stranger, "I said.

He smiled a little ironic tilde of a smile. "Welcome, stranger." He stood and beckoned towards a leather armchair that was losing its stuffing. I sat on the wide, welcoming arm. I didn't want to get hay or whatever it was on my trousers.

"So," he said with a Milanese accent, "let's talk about your friend."

"I'll leave right now if you continue to call him my friend. He was my lover. And it wasn't just one night. We were together four years and we made love hundreds of times. We both were very randy. And he took to it very naturally."

Ernesto raised a skeptical eyebrow. "God loves the sinner but hates the sin."

"Then he must have hated our sin thousands of times because Cesare loved sucking my cock and getting fucked by it."

"People change," Ernesto said quietly. "You've heard of the Prodigal Son?"

"Don't condescend to me."

We both sat in silence. Finally the priest asked, "Why did you agree to come?"

"I consider you a criminal. Because you haven't sent him to a psychiatrist. It's obvious that Cesare has had a psychotic break and you've just taken unscrupulous advantage of a poor sick boy. He keeps hearing voices while he's praying, a voice who's sending messages to *me*. I told him he should ask the Ghost to communicate with me directly."

"I see it very differently." Ernesto started to clean the lenses of his glasses with a dirty gray handkerchief, working with a diligence that was designed to upstage our dispute. "For me it's a matter of redemption. The Holy Ghost has intervened."

I said, "But Cesare didn't see the Ghost but Christ on the movie screen."

"So you admit it was Our Lord at least?"

"I don't believe one bit of your superstitious nonsense."

He actually stroked his chin. "Oddly, Cesare told me that when you two met, you were the pious one."

"I wrote church music," I said, "that's all. He made fun of me for being a holy water frog, a *beghina*, a bigot, but I wasn't. I just liked the music, that's all. And for a kid in a village much like this one there weren't that many other opportunities for hearing your music."

"Too bad you didn't acknowledge the divine inspiration of your gift."

"Too bad," I said, "that you can't see you're a vicious con man recruiting crazed boys for your empty pulpits."

He stood and made the sign of the cross over me. I turned on my heel.

TWENTY YEARS LATER, during the coronavirus pandemic, I heard from both Cesare and Lucia through Facebook. I'd never heard a word from either of them in the interim. Lucia had married the year after our affair. She was living in Palermo with her husband, who repaired air conditioners, and with their two children, Letizia and Bruno (she included pictures of them: cute enough). She'd put on weight. She said she still had me in her prayers.

Father Cesare irritated me by saying he'd never touched another human being since our "great love." I protested that that was twenty years ago and that I hadn't missed him at all or even thought of him once except as a good after-dinner story.

He asked me if I'd slept with other men.

"Of course! Hundreds of them. It's been twenty fucking years!"

"I don't know if I can accept that." I bit my lip.

"Well, I can't."

"You have no say," I pointed out. "You left me twenty years ago."

"I never left you. We're still together."

"Not in my mind. And anyway homosexuality is a sin."

"I hope you don't think I am flirting with you. I have taken a vow of celibacy."

"Then why are you bothering me? Wait—you're in a little Sicilian village under lockdown and you can't bless babies or perform the mass. For the moment you're not a practicing priest and you're remembering the last time you were a human being—with me, twenty years ago!"

Suddenly he changed the subject. "I've been ill. A bladder infection. It's become a major problem. I use catheters."

"You're only fifty. You can't be using catheters the rest of your life. I'll ask around and find you a good urologist. I can ask a friend who's a famous doctor in Milan. And how many years has *this* doctor been treating you?"

"Three."

"Time to find a good doctor . . . And I care because you're a human being when you're not a priest, a human being I once knew twenty years ago."

CONSTANCE'S THOUGHTS: IRRITATING as he can be—effusive but undemonstrative, never one to make the first move unless he fears he's about to lose someone, self-involved in a childish, innocent way, always shamelessly inviting other people to praise him, his cooking, his charm, his looks, especially his body, though he deflects compliments on the things he is certain are exceptional, such as his intelligence, his talent, his loving nature (a highly conditional love to be sure)—he is obviously an exceptional person. He never misses me although I always miss him (I even learned how to say those crucial words in Italian: *Mi sento la tua mancanza*—so complicated that it's obvious Italians rarely miss anyone).

RUGGERO READ: THEN I married Brunnhilde. She was studying piano at Santa Cecilia and was considered one of the best musicians in school. I guess at each disappointment I was see-sawing back and forth from men to women, although by then I'd decided I'd stay with women. You'll hate me for saying this, but I felt I could control a woman better than a man. The complicity between a man and a woman felt more natural, or at least more solidly constructed culturally. Even if almost two centuries of feminism had burned down the house there were still distinct traces of the foundations in the scorched earth, the complete layout of the rooms, a ghost version of past habitation. Brunnhilde had, thankfully, a very primitive concept of women's rights. I can remember opening the car door for her as I'd been taught to do; she slammed the door shut and opened it again for herself. If I helped her into her coat, she'd help me into mine. She said, "I'm not opposed to these ancient rites as long as they can seem motivated by friendship, not gallantry." She looked around guiltily.

She was rich, from a family that had backed Hitler (they had, I think, made radios for cars). Every member of the family received a big allowance from the German government to stay out of the country. It seemed an odd reward for collaboration, but I guess it was less controversial to have the Wittelbergs out of the public eye. Her mother lived in Coral Gables with Brunhilde's heroin-addicted brother. He had spent years as a pedophile in Bangkok and still had two Thai servants, ex-boys. One was named Krishna. When they walked through Coral Gables, Tristan was always in bright saffron robes followed by his middle-aged minions holding aloft a gaudy umbrella with tassels—either to protect him from the Florida sun or to signify he was somehow holy or royal, at least a big shot of some kind. His mother adored him and would follow him in the middle of the night if he was seized by the folly to be flown in their jet to Mykonos or to Singapore. He would sit on the Morning Beach in his regulation blue-and-white cabana with *Mutti* in her simple day face with dark glasses; Krishna and his assistant (son?) would wait on them, stand the whole time, if the son wasn't running off for another bottle of chilled vintage champagne, the color of fresh, slightly diluted urine.

I met Brunnhilde under unusual circumstances. One night a Korean bassoonist at Santa Cecilia went crazy and started stabbing people in the corridors as we were coming back from a lovely Brahms string quintet. I'd never spoken to Brunnhilde before but she had singled me out in the panicked crowd. She came running over to me and grabbed me around the waist. "Will you take me back to my room?" "Of course. Where is it?"

She led the way. By then the bassoonist had been subdued; she was weeping hysterically and sobbing something in her language.

When we arrived in Brunnhilde's suite of rooms, she locked the door, raked her hands across her temples and into the golden glory of her hair. Just my luck, I thought, to be approached by another blond taller than me.

"Poor Hei-kyung," Brunnhilde said. "I guess they didn't give a green light—you say 'green light'?—to her two-hour solo bassoon graduation recital." We were speaking English. I just shrugged, to indicate my ignorance of the fine points of English and the politics of the academy.

"She sounds like a borderline," I said.

"They all are." I was surprised Brunhilde would go so far.

Like me she had a piano in her room. It was so unusual for students to have their own keyboard instrument, though I had my harpsichord. But I guess we were both "well-off," as Americans say. She was so nervous that she sat down to the concert grand, a late nineteenth-century Érard, I noticed, and she ripped through Prokofiev's hair-raising early Toccata. Not one note of it was easy on the ear though it felt like the music appropriate to the workings of a factory—written in 1912 during our own Italian obsession with the machine and futurism, a piece first performed by Prokofiev himself in 1916 in Petersburg. As I watched her fine forearms batter the D as she alternated the right hand with the left, I observed how firm her flesh was. I was mesmerized by her speed and percussive power. Always a bit competitive I wanted to perform for her one of the really difficult English Suites by Bach. But no sooner had she finished than she played through the Scriabin Fifth Sonata, which began fretfully, tiptoeing, then became a bit crazy like a psychotic jumping in puddles, with faint reminiscences of real piano music— scraps of waltzes, eerie progressions, sudden galloping; the real sickening part comes when you remember Scriabin programmed it all with dancing colored lights. For me, this was the perilous beginning of the unfortunate twentieth century, which brought us John Cage's amplified water drinking, the topless lady cellist, the Korean handing out five thousand coins and five thousand smiles, and a man in tails striking a spoon on a frying pan twenty-nine times—but also the incomparable Bartók and Stravinsky and Debussy.

I was lost in admiration of her strength and delicacy. Her hands flew and attacked always with deadly accuracy, the most tender pianissimi, the most violent fortes, the most languorous rubato, the most perilous but super-confident and well-articulated glissandi, like water pouring from a fountain after a day of rain. She was a real artist. Her understanding of the music was idiomatic, her technique advanced, blindingly virtuosic. I suddenly regretted that I'd been born Italian; her teachers in Germany must have been incomparable. (As you know, Constance, I'm a proud Sicilian, but for a moment I felt minor, marginal, totally outclassed: provincial!)

Except for the occasion she'd begged me to take her to her room, I hadn't seen a scintilla of vulnerability. After she stopped playing she made me a cup of an astonishingly bad thing called "instant" coffee, something I'd never before been subjected to. I took a sip to be polite and put it aside then ate a spoonful of sugar raw to chase away the flavor. She sat in an orange chair opposite me, her body as, let's say, retracted as possible.

Her conversation alternated between a very mild joshing, a kind of sleepy teasing, and lots of half-uttered complaints. Given how powerful her arms were I was surprised by her weak speaking voice and wondered if such sleepiness and such feeble plaintiveness, the sound of pigeons mewling in the next courtyard, was considered elegant in her country. I'd always thought Germans were harsh and guttural (the men? the poor?) and was not expecting this soft cooing. It was dull, elegantly dull, but curiously not boring. She never bored me. Yet I can say she never challenged me. I thought of elderly aristocratic females in our family who discussed the terrible heat because there was no other respectable topic in our village. There were plenty of bloody vendettas and crimes of passion all around us, unspeakable Mafia wars, severed limbs found in the drinking water—but those, precisely, couldn't be spoken about, which left the weather. A lady could fan herself and "play heat," as they say in the theater.

Brunnhilde had a fascinatingly troubled and tormented childhood, which she was studiously writing about and which I would read about over the years we were together. She wrote slowly, since she was besieged with hesitations and doubts, which she had to clear away in order to reveal the terrifying reality of her past.

I wasn't even sure she liked me, though instinctively she'd been drawn to me that first time . . . and who am I to distrust instincts?

Did I like her? So many years later after so much Sturm und Drang it's a bit difficult to resurrect my original impressions and desires. I remember I found her dull (though her piano performance was electrifying), but pleasantly dull, as I said, in a familiar, aristocratic way. The tedium radiated by people so sure of their right to hold the stage—no, that's wrong. Brunnhilde never felt confident. But she preferred talking about gardening or relatives or the weather (and later, her surgeries) to advancing an idea. Or even a reflection. Where someone else might reflect, she sighed.

But she was beautiful. Her name Brunnhilde suggested the warrior woman of her magnificent physique but cowering inside was a little Greta, a timorous girl with flaxed pigtails. She was never completely happy, though she could be content in a provisional way, as if happiness had been granted for an instant only and might be taken away at any moment.

You know I'm loving if sometimes inattentive. The girls in my life—Lucia, Brunnhilde, you—are always so needy and I am capable of forgetting your needs, especially how pressing and insatiable they can be. Although I'm sensitive and observant, I don't always see the huge hollowness in you lot. Do I want to ignore you in order to buy some time for my own obsessions (the harpsichord, physical training, reading, cooking, philosophizing)? No, I don't think so. I always feel guilty about not fulfilling all of you, but radiantly happy when I succeed, no matter how belatedly. I'm not afraid of being exhausted by other people's demands. I've come to recognize that's a rare quality in me, the way giving of myself refreshes me; the more I give the more I have to give.

Am I the only person on earth who had a happy childhood? My "girls" all suffered, Giuseppe didn't, Cesare did. I had all the makings for a miserable childhood and youth since my selfish parents skipped out on me and left me with a conservative old Sicilian who was manic-depressive. But my grandfather was loving, and he genuinely seemed to admire me even before I'd done anything admirable—it was tenderness on credit. Of course I played the organ in our cathedral; I was allowed to practice whenever I wanted in return for working the eight o'clock Sunday mass. I was always curious and found a score in my grandfather's library by Domenico Zipoli, a seventeenth-century Tuscan from Prato who lived in Rome and was the organist at the Gesù, became a Jesuit, found himself in Spain, shipped out to South America as a missionary among the Guaraní people, kept composing to the delight of the Indians ("Give me an orchestra and I'll convert the continent," one musician of the period said), died of a tropical disease. Anyway, I was playing this obscure Zipoli piece and this unshaved, dirty old man came up to me after the mass in Castelnuovo and said, "I loved your Zipoli but you used a few stops that didn't exist in his day." It was then and there I decided always to be perfect in everything since you never know who might be observing or listening to you or judging you.

It's not that I think I was of a stronger character and that's why I was happy; happiness is genetic. I jumped out of bed every morning with a smile on my face. Though I've spent so little time with my mother and can see all her flaws, nevertheless we resemble each other in that regard. Her default position is happiness. She expects things to work out. Like me she's an optimist. Unlike me, she doesn't mind living a messy life. I have to have everything tidy—my thoughts, my surroundings, my bills, my duties. My physical well-being, as you well know, must always be optimal.

I invited Brunnhilde to Sicily, more as a lark than anything else, as you might bring a giraffe home to your village. I knew my grandfather, if he was in his manic cycle, would be amused by her statuesque beauty.

I'd phoned him in advance and there he was at the *portone* grinning maniacally. When he discovered she didn't speak French (no one expected a foreigner to speak Italian) he made up his own German: "*Gibt mihr seine handt!*" he said, sticking out his own. "*Ich zie mostra sein zimmer.*"

Brunnhilde kept trying to switch the language to English but finally gave up with a smile. Later I found out that most of her relatives were mad and that she was expert at humoring them.

"*Meine herz ist warme zie ist hier in meine hause.*" He even touched her face and said, "*Süsse.*"

She could see how sweet and well-meaning he was but she didn't like him to struggle when they still had Italian available. She said in Italian, "Your German is excellent but remember I go to school at Santa Cecilia and must practice my Italian." At last he relented and switched over to Italian. This time he touched her face and said, "*Dolce.*"

When we were alone, Brunnhilde asked, "Why does he speak that pigeon German?"

"During the war he was an officer and in a German camp for two years. He loves the Germans and hates them almost as much."

"Me, too." She was wonderfully kind to my four-foot tall ancient nanny, who struggled to speak Tuscan (I translated into and out of Sicilian). I thought, This is half the fun, wrestling with the various languages, smiling all the while in the universal language of affable intentions. My grandfather fought his way up the stairs; he wanted to show his terrace to Brunnhilde, which he'd just outfitted with new blue-and-white-striped umbrellas and a whole plantation of new healthy plants (in Sicily all plants flourish if the servants remember to water them). "An old man should replace his furnishings as often as possible," he told Brunnhilde, "on the same principle that an old prostitute should never be seen walking an old dog."

That night when I came to Brunnhilde's room she said, "I love your opa. He's delicious. I never knew one of my grandfathers—Nuremberg—and the other one was feebleminded, though a perfect dear. But seriously limited."

"I'm so glad you like him. I can see he adores you. You're very good with him."

She tossed her head back. "He's good with me." She was sitting there on the bed in her slip, her crown of hair combed out, her breasts uncupped and immense. I thought, Every scrawny Italian man would be salivating over this Anita Ekberg, though only someone squinting or blinded by lust would take her as a sosie for Ekberg. She did have her own grace; I'd seen Brunnhilde in Rome surrounded by all those boys on Vespas slurping and hooting as she walked in her queenly way along the Corso, graciously smiling and accepting their fracas as homage.

CONSTANCE THOUGHT: MY bad luck was the one time I met his nonno, before he died, he was depressed and bedridden. I could see he wanted to be friendly but he . . . just . . . didn't have the energy. He was over a hundred. I sat beside his bed for hours and held his hand; I hope he could feel how grateful I was to him for all the kindness he'd showered on Ruggero. Or maybe when you're that depressed, any human contact is irritating.

That was riveting when Ruggero said, "You lot," grouping all three of the women in his life, including me, as being needy. He admitted he could be inattentive though eager to please. Well, I am needy. He can't really meet my needs.

RUGGERO READ: BRUNNHILDE, though not Italian, had passed the Castelnuovo test better than Lucia. My grandfather's approval wasn't crucial to me, but it certainly carried a lot of weight. Buoyed by the euphoria of our delightful evening and by our dual concert, she on our old box piano and I on the harpsichord, in Bach's Concerto for Two Harpsichords in C Major (she'd say "Two Pianos"), I found her familiar, endearing, not imposing as before. I don't know why, but we owned two scores and of course she could sight-read flawlessly. In the first movement she sped along despite a missed (but never wrong) note here and there. Musically she was a good sport, like an ice hockey star out for a skate with the little kids, of good cheer and amiable. Reckless and energetic in the presto, not dreamy and introspective enough in the poetic cross-examination of the largo, solid but fleet in the conclusion.

My grandfather was overwhelmed with proprietary pride. The house was an artistic salon again, as it had been in his grandmother's day (she who'd been an opera singer until she'd had to give up her career). They had invited other "amateur" musicians to their *soirées musicales*, some of them extremely talented or even ex-professionals like my grandfather's grandmother. I have a vintage photo of her with her hair up in her Redfern evening gown from Paris, severely tailored in what was described to me as green velvet with gold braid, standing in the loose embrace of the grand piano.

My manic grandfather talked us to death about Wagner's Tetralogy, which he'd seen on four long successive evenings with his grandmother in Palermo. I think he was inspired by Brunnhilde's unusual name, and there he wasn't far off the mark since she liked Wagner's meandering piano music and Bruckner's piano transcription of his own gloomy Seventh Symphony, and she invariably over the years, especially if she'd drunk that second brandy, returned to this repertoire which is called late Romantic, though I never picked up on the romance. The only Bruckner piano piece I could tolerate was "Stille Betrachtung an einem Herbstabend" (Quiet contemplation on an autumn evening) and I'd call for it often.

When Brunnhilde and I were alone in her bedroom, I had the strangest sensation. As you know, I feel well in my skin, as the French say, *bien dans ma peau,* and given the ancient history of my forebears and our centuries in Castelnuovo I have authentic roots as few people do today, but I distinctly remember a moment of alienation that nearly capsized me, not social but individual. It was not anomie but anguish. I had this elusive but strong feeling that we are supposed to resemble ourselves and that to establish an identity we must perform it and *become* it in time, whereas our "real" or potential self is disorganized and unpredictable and all over the place.

CONSTANCE SAID: "YOUR English is really remarkable! You are the best explainer in the world, even very slippery intuitions." (She hoped her compliments would suddenly upstage Brunnhilde in his mind).

She thought: He did study philosophy, including that enigmatic Heidegger.

(Ruggero lowered his eyes).

★ ★ ★

RUGGERO READ: I thought I'd "show interest" in my quizzing by asking about her name and her family's interest in Wagner.

"Not just my parents! I was so unhappy as a child, constantly bullied by the other girls at school; my only refuge was Wagner. The minute I heard his *Tristan* I could picture a slender knight in armor wending his way through an ancient forest and brushing aside the branches heavy with rain. Wagner was my only friend."

"Didn't you have a horse as well?"

She lit up. "You remembered! Yes, darling Sieglinde!"

"Wasn't Wagner an anti-Semite?"

"Oh, all that's so silly. The minute you hear the prelude to *Das Rheingold* you forget all that silliness. He liked fancy dress; he must have been just attitudinizing."

"Strange to hear you say that."

"You don't believe, do you, Ruggero, that the sins of the fathers . . ."

"Not at all. I had a great-uncle who fought in Abyssinia."

"See!"

"And I'm not at all racist and I have no sense of guilt for what that uncle did, if he did anything really terrible."

Given how aggressive I can be sexually, I hadn't done anything with Brunnhilde until now except kiss her but suddenly I wanted to fuck her. Maybe it was because we were in Castelnuovo, where I'd jerked off so many times and cried and cried with sexual frustration, rerun mental movies of Giuseppe in sharp detail with some shadowy girl in which I quietly, calmly replaced him because the *Schatten Fräulein* chose me over him since mine was two centimeters longer than his and considerably fatter.

I guess I'd always been slightly intimidated by Brunnhilde but now after our jolly evening and especially after our four-hand performance I felt drawn to her, as if in her playing I'd seen the dynamics of her mind and soul: the intelligence, the feeling, the discipline, the inter-pretation. I think sex should always start out calmly. Five frantic half-clothed seconds in the dark of *ejaculatio praecox* are not my idea of coitus.

As I embraced her and touched her breast, she whispered, "Unfortunately it's that time of the month."

"Then we don't have to worry about pregnancy. A little bit of blood never put off a Castelnuovo."

"I'm afraid, Ruggero, it's more a flood than a trickle."

I suddenly thought how her English was better than mine. "Let's see how it goes," I said. "Here, I'll grab a towel to put under you."

"This isn't a good idea, Ruggero." She used my proper name more often than another Italian would. It always drew me up short, as if she were about to make some horrible confidence, but it meant nothing more than as if an American woman would touch your lapel while securing your attention.

I took off her shirt and trousers tenderly but matter-of-factly if that can be imagined. Once her sumptuous body was revealed I pulled off her panties. She raised a hand and said, "No, can we take a raincheck on that?" Looking her in the eye and seeing her no meant mostly no, I moved my hand to her large, yielding breast and resumed kissing her, our tongues as quick and agile as dueling swords. All writing (even thinking-in-words) about sex sounds as if it's going for the Bad Sex Award, whereas a picture is liminally more acceptable, though still qualifying as cheesy if exaggerated or too explicit or too shadowy and discreet. Talk of sex makes us blush or snicker. We were kissing passionately when Brunnhilde began to touch my painfully erect penis and liberate it from my trousers. She sucked it. I immediately groaned and felt the anguished rapture of hot wet flesh on hot wet flesh. She sank to her knees on the floor, first placing delicately a cushion on the floor as a sort of devotion throw pillow.

I was worried that she was only giving me her mouth because her vagina was off-limits and I started to pull her to her feet but she insisted wordlessly on staying in the "cockpit," as she called it, and who was I to decline this delicious offer. This wasn't her first experiment in fellatio obviously; she pulled back the hood and lacquered the big red head, then swooped down to engulf my testicles, one after another, then licked her way back up the shaft to my exposed meatus.

★　★　★

CONSTANCE'S THOUGHTS: WHY is he writing/reading this stuff when he knows I'll be his first and only reader/auditor? I know and admire his virility, know his penis by heart, know that menstruation would never put him off, know his sexual courtesy matched by his sexual boldness, know that he loved Brunnhilde's zaftig shape and came to resent that it promised more passion than it delivered, as if the Italians had discovered Anita Ekberg was a lousy lay.

RUGGERO READ: ON the train back to Rome we sat side by side, kept pretending to be interested in the passing landscape of tiled ocher houses and scorched fields but periodically looked at each other, smiling simultaneously, as if the sweep of the lighthouse were timed. I was worried it was all too *mièvre*—"soppy," do you say?—especially after we started holding hands. Her hand was warm and dry. To look at us you'd think we'd had a roaring night of anal and vaginal intercourse instead of just a bit of innocent oral sex.

I realized I liked her. Very much. I'd overcome my provincial distaste for her Germanness (just as I was used to northern Italians disdaining me when they found out I was Sicilian). Her "beauty," which had at first struck me as melodramatic, had now softened into something familiar and on its way to being dear. Her pianistic prowess, which I'd dismissed as showmanship, now seemed genuine, thoughtful.

RUGGERO SPEAKS OFF-SCRIPT: "I'll save the inevitable ecstasy and decline till the next time."

Constance went to the toilet, came back, seated herself, drank some water and started reading without prelude. She knew Ruggero, unlike most Italians, disliked all transitions. Whereas Venetians, for instance, made a great to-do about arrivals and departures, Ruggero preferred a simple, silent French leave.

★ ★ ★

CONSTANCE READ: I'D always been attracted to women but never could quite find my role with them. I can remember once glancing down the open blouse of a braless young woman and longing to touch her tender white breasts—a shock made me tremble all over. I never saw her again (it was in a changing room on the dock beside the lake in Zürich) but that excitement, which ran all through me like a sudden trembling head to toe, marked me deeply and I often thought of it. I'd had a moment or two of same-sex desire when I was a teenager, but the shame of being with my "uncle" tormented me and made me frigid.

I was living in Manhattan on East Tenth street and working for Reuters in some mindless routine job, something that left only enough head space to think about sex. I elaborated a dozen scenarios, most of them brutal, though I would have hated anything violent in reality. I worked with a young woman who had only two winter outfits, but both glamorous designer rip-offs, which she alternated every two days. One, I remember, came with a bronze sunburst over her heart. It seemed too showy for her drab personality.

She was full of stories about the crowd she ran with—or rather limped after. She suspected she was only invited to the bigger gatherings when they needed extra women in semi-couture clothes and imitation Manolo Blahnik leopard-skin mules. One night they must have been running short of even drab interchangeable women like me because suddenly Becky invited me to go with her to an East Village loft party, a "throw-back" fifties cocktail party. I accepted though neither of us was properly disguised for the event's theme.

It was in someone's huge loft that was sixty perilous steps up. I saw now why Becky had worn sneakers until she stopped ten steps below our goal to catch her breath, change into her fake mules with the skinny spool heels and ask me to check that her hair looked "well." She in turn ran her fingers through my locks and fluffed them.

As each person entered the loft she or he was asked to slip into a little booth to have their picture snapped. I sensed what a disappointment I was; a bored "stylist" handed me a pearl cigarette holder as my only prop. When I passed through to the thunderously noisy, perfume-reeking loft (wasn't patchouli the emblem of the sixties?), a journalist taking notes on the arriving celebrities, I suppose, said dismissively, "*Thanks* for making an effort." By the time I understood his insult I was being shoved into the room by the next arrival, who must have been at least a minor Somebody, since she was being interviewed. "Yes," she said with an English accent, "for donkey's years . . . Why am I here? I adore his work *tout court*. Obviously that's why I'm here."

Becky was sticking close. The music was vintage Mabel Mercer and everyone seemed to be drinking martinis. "Yes," Becky was saying. "He always has theme parties, which *Vanity Fair* loves to celebrate. Last year he painted his new toilet and had a 'toilet evening' when everyone had to wear brown and toilet paper was festooned everywhere and we all had to eat chocolate pudding. Then he had a 'tacky evening' to which I wore a leopard-skin miniskirt to match my Blahniks and a fire-engine-red rayon blouse and the music was Princess Stéphanie of Monaco. He's very creative. Duh. He *is* a famous artist."

By now we'd pressed our way to the bar and received our martinis. Becky was standing in a much more expository way than I'd ever seen her assume before. She was chattering to me brightly, nonsensically, almost like an extra in a crowd scene who's told by the director to move her lips and "talk." Someone must have told her that men are more attracted to animated women; in a bar the trick is to laugh and scream until late then ditch your friends and be all alone and mysterious. That will reel in the lone, sullenly handsome admirer in the corner every time.

We were squeezed together like paramecia in a brackish pond; some gaudy, well-dressed people seemed so self-sufficient as to be able, one imagined, to reproduce unaided (autogamy) while others more typically required fusion, of which there was plenty.

A graying woman in boots but not fat, holding an unlit cigar, came swaggering up to us; I guess we looked to be apt targets for a predator. "It seems our Hal has a new ephebe; did you catch the tiny blond boy, winner of the Exquisite Twink Award?" Eliminating the introductions and cutting to the insider gossip seemed very stylish and we nodded foolishly, though we'd noticed nothing of the sort in the teeming, dimly-lit crowd. Now that I looked around no one was smoking, of course, but half the guests were holding unlit filtered cigarettes to fit the theme. The music anachronistically changed to Judy Garland singing "As Long as He Needs Me" followed by Blossom Dearie singing her camp hit "Et Tu Bruce" in her baby-doll voice, songs that reflected if were not originated in the fifties. Of course I didn't even know who our host, Hal, was.

The handsome lesbian with her curtain of graying hair and cinched-in waist led us by the hand into a back bedroom. She shouted right into my ear something like "can talk" and we just went along with her. Once we'd escaped the noisy crowd and were in the bedroom with its paint-ings, which the woman identified as "a Tsaroukis" and "a Brainard," we sat on the double bed and she on a muslin-shrouded armchair. Everything was stark—artist taste, I guess. The mattress was firm and swathed in a cotton cloth that was Tuareg blue, probably bought right off a veiled man.

"Maybe Hal or the twink will join us. The twink might look very young and helpless, but I heard he's the chief copywriter at Doyle Dane Bernbach. These fags can be so creative. Of course Hal doesn't flaunt his queerness, but no one is fooled. He is a bit light in the loafers."

"I wonder if there's anything to eat?"

"With these WASPs there never is but the martoonies are limitless. I often trade my martini at a WASP fundraiser for a second dinner, chicken breast or a slice of ham or chicken wrapped in ham. But I could go explore if you're starving."

"Don't bother," I said. "That is so kind of you."

"Well, we butch dykes are nothing if not gallant."

I smiled queasily.

She said, "I'm one of the last authentic diesels—they're all trans these days. I'm sure nice little femmes like you two don't want a real man or a trans man but a genuine bull."

We must have looked astonished. The martini was a depth charge in my stomach fired by the submarine my brain had become. I wondered if I was smiling idiotically or if my head was listing to the left as it did habitually (relatives photographing me always had to urge me to sit up straight). I said with rubbery lips, "Actually we're both swingers."

"From the 1970s? You look too young."

"We are young!" I shouted, then immediately winced and my head exploded.

"I think I better find you some crackers." She strode away majestically and made me think of a jungle animal.

"Now you've spoiled it," Becky said, putting her cocktail glass on the floor with great care next to the fabric-edged sisal rug.

"How?"

"She probably won't come back now you've shown we're not available."

"I'm available and how! . . . I think. Who is she?"

"An art historian from Columbia, another ABD."

"What?"

"All but dissertation. Her last name is Hepworth, I can't remember the first. Since she doesn't have her doctorate she can't teach but works as something at the American Academy of Arts and Letters. You mean to say you like the ladies?"

"Who doesn't?"

"I don't."

"Well, don't look as if I'm going to jump your bones."

"I think you should lay off the martinis."

I felt a rage of objection rushing to my lips like vomit but I swallowed it in time and smiled and said, "You're right," and placed my glass next to hers. She got up and staggered on her Manolas to the abandoned armchair just as the art historian, chomping on her unlit cigar, returned with a bag of potato chips.

"Oh, you lifesaver!" I yelped, blowing her a kiss and then ripping the bag in half.

Reader, I went home with her. When you opened her front door with the three locks you were instantly confronted by a Mapplethorpe photograph with a four-inch white mat and a polished narrow beech-wood frame on an impeccable white wall. It was a big erect aubergine-colored African American penis, floating in midnight-black space. We kissed under it.

That night our sex was digital and lingual—women are the best at eating pussy.

She was attentive to my sensual needs. How agreeable, I thought, to be made love to by another woman, someone who knew one's body by heart. Men read up about this strange gastropod, a woman's vagina, or study porn for clues or consult medical textbooks, but it always felt a bit remote like a robotic arm lifting uranium through a protective screen. Whereas women yelped through intercourse and men just beetled on with grim determination, here we both were muttering, "Yes, right there, right there," or letting rip a little bacchic cry. Whereas men could just cooly dot their i's, women shuffled all the alphabet in a great glossolalia of buckling bodies and broken sobs. We were exhausted and lay about like slain houris in Sardanapalus's harem on the ruby-red bedspread.

Adele just "happened" to have a whole chicken in her fridge and some fresh tarragon. We were gobbling it an hour and a half later with some trimmed green beans she also happened to have on hand. I didn't associate this degree of domesticity with butch lesbians, but Adele was not a classifiable phenomenon. We had a long chat while we gave each other foot massages. It turned out that she as suspected was an art historian, that most of her friends were male homosexuals she held in mild contempt and quietly ridiculed for being effeminate, that she "worked on" (as academics said) the WPA muralists of the 1930s, especially those who'd done mosaics for Midwestern train stations, and had written some groundbreaking essays on their pre-mural sketches, that her real passion was Italy and she spoke Italian fluently, that she had been the administrator of the North Dakota art history program in Padova and shepherded all twelve students through homesickness, pregnancy, language acquisition, museum visits, broken hearts and, in one case, suspected violent murder. Her last lover was a poet who'd written the award-winning *Heretic Clitoris* but had left her for a drab cis-man! Adele was in love with Italy, usually cooked Umbrian dishes (she'd learned to call Umbria the "green heart" of Italy), and spoke with a colorful repertory of hand gestures that Italians accepted as normal but that struck most Americans as embarrassingly affected. At home she actually lit and smoked cigars. I never got used to the smell, especially when we returned on a winter night from a wine-soaked dinner to a stuffy, overheated apartment. My slip stunk. "Stinky-poo," she said.

I found out she was a shameless Donna Juana, notorious in the Village dyke bars. If she'd had such a well-stocked fridge it was because every Thursday night she changed her sheets, bought groceries and flowers and lots and lots of red wine, picked up her impeccable clothes from the cleaner's, donned a new men's blue button-down shirt from Brooks Brothers, put on her good boots and set out for a weekend of conquests. She hadn't expected to score at the retro fifties cocktail party but had struck gold with little me; she'd spotted the scintilla of lust and inno-cence in my eye. She was quick to evaluate any vulnerable girl, though I wasn't as inexperienced as she imagined.

She was equally shameless in her pursuit of rich collectors, whose paintings she would describe rapturously in a "monograph" for a hand-some fee: "the Perlmusser Collection," a coffee-table paean. She often entertained these shy, stuttering scions whom she "advised" on their acquisitions; she mixed them with the artists themselves who were only too happy to unload their no-longer-fashionable daubs without having their galleries deduct their 50 percent commissions. Adele took her finder's fee (she found the buyers, not the sellers). At first she thought the artists were shooting themselves in the foot by being so rude to what they called "these buzwah philsteins" but soon she realized the collectors were even more awed by this mistreatment. She knew the artists them-selves were from families of immigrants from Rochester, usually intim-idated by almost everyone, but the kids had picked up arrogant manners in art school. Cleverly, she hoodwinked some of her collectors into financing her on a monthlong scouting expedition to Rome in search of an elusive Fontana or an atypical Burri. One collector was dismayed to see Burri's name in *Art News* on the "previously famous now neglected" list. Adele explained, "Reputations are like hem lengths—they rise and fall. Burri is having a major retrospective in Akron next year."

"But only the burlap Burris are selling," wailed the collector, only recently educated on the Italian twentieth-century market. "And my painting is from the pre–Material period. I have a friend of my son's who's a researcher for *Time*. A Harvard grad. She's gotten me up to speed."

"That makes it all the more interesting and formative. A new art history collective in Butte, Montana, is reexamining this very period from a neo-feminist perspective," Adele said smoothly, reassuringly. "Anyway . . . *Time* magazine . . . Ha, ha! You can't be serious."

As you know, I'm reasonably social. Most lesbians avoid other people and live in remote places in the country. They rusticate. Not Adele. She was compulsively *mondaine* and urban. At first I thought it was for her career. She did buy and sell twentieth-century art up to Warhol's Disaster paintings. She always said it was hard to find important paintings. They were all being hoarded by the Japanese, who kept them in vaults. That's what she claimed. Originally I thought she wanted me to go with her to all those parties, but quickly I learned that being half of a couple cut down on her main social strategy: flirting. She liked to fly solo. She was the only lesbian I ever met who flirted with boys! And she would rate boys as "cute" or "sexy" or "adorable" and say things like "Check out that ass!" or "Like all Poles he's probably got big uncut meat." Things like that she said sotto voce, of course. She told me she wanted to be a man, but not a straight one: "No, I want to be a gay boy. They work out and have beautiful bodies. And lots of sex. Raised eyebrows."

At first she was romantic, brought me flowers and champagne, asked me about my day but glazed over when I started narrating it, got me to wear Chanel No. 5 and let me spritz my usual floral little-girl perfume on only when I slept alone. She said, "It smells like bubble gum, which is cute but not right for a real woman." She bought me a green satin quilt and liked me to lie on it in the nude, my hair spread out, my lipstick fire-engine red, while she snapped nice pictures with her phone, my legs slightly spread, my hand cupping my privates like Venus on the half shell.

But I just didn't have the star power to keep her interested. A faceless employee at Reuters was hardly a suitable target for one of New York's most glamorous butches. I tried to be more and more depraved, handing her a plain business envelope full of my pubic hairs, buying her a magenta-red strap-on, luring other women to join us and once a stoned gay boy, a cute little bottom, but I quickly understood that sex could never compete in her heart with snobbism. She would flirt with other butch lesbians, going all girly on them, or straight men, to the point of wearing a skirt and pimping for them, even leer at a gay boy and pinch his ass (or pimp for *him*, lining up a hottie top)—all this effort to make her into a New York player. For her, wealth rivaled fame, though she definitely favored fame. Academic fame, Page 6 fame, infamy for trafficking prepubic boys or girls, political fame bordering on corruption, dynastic fame. She was horrified by the mute and the inglorious. Like you as an adolescent she was terrified she'd be forgotten, one more featureless corpse cremated or buried, her funerary niche or grave overgrown, broken into by grave robbers. Whereas you became celebrated among the *cognoscenti* as one of the paladins of the baroque revival, she had no outstanding talents; her only hope was to be a footnote in someone else's biography. Her "work on" the thirties muralists had evoked only contentious rebukes from other art historians. She'd written a few generic books on popular moments in art history (*The Pre-Raphaelites* or *The Post-Impressionists*) but these were stacked on the dollar pile by the door of the bookshop.

She wore cheap men's y-front underpants by Hanes (three for ten bucks) and when we were alone, scratched her invisible balls. She bought many of her clothes on sale in the boys' shop at Brooks though her breasts were too big for the shirts. As the date for her term in Italy approached, I wondered if she'd invite me to accompany her. She didn't. A bit tipsy, I asked her if she wanted me to book a ticket.

"Not really," she said. "The school wouldn't like that. They're very stuffy and I'm supposed to set an example. Anyway, you have a job here and I can't support you, God knows. Frowny face." She often punctuated her speech with verbal emoticons. "And you don't exactly speak Italian. Tiny gasp. What would you do? Eat pasta twice a day and get really fat? Befriend an anglophony you overhear in the trattoria? Ugly smile."

I realized that our "love" was very provisional and that she slightly despised me for not knowing Italian (now I'm sure I speak better Italian than she does, though I've forgone the embarrassing if correct hand gestures).

I introduced her to some unknown painters I liked but she shrugged them off. Her theory was that anyone talented would already be famous. She wasn't in the business of "discovering" new artists and "promoting" them. Despite her sexual bravado and noisy Italianizing and her shocking Mapplethorpe, she had no confidence in her taste. She knew who all the current winners were and talked knowingly about "Ross" or "Susan" or disdainfully of "Phillip," but she would never groom a new, unrepresented painter no matter how talented. How would she recognize their talent if it hadn't been already endorsed by the four publications and ten critics and twenty galleries who counted? It was crucial for something to be new because the Zeitgeist was still evolving, of course, but how could one know in which direction? There had already been so many new movements in the past decades—the New Figuration, Conceptual Art, Land Art, Arte Ricca, Grunge Art, Graffiti, Recycled Bits of Masterpieces. Each one had been inevitable, to be sure, and was in a rigid dialectic, but you'd have to be a real brain to predict with accuracy which movement would take off. Imagine Adele telling a top gallerist to look at some nobody's slides. That would be too great a risk to Adele's own standing. After four shows on the Continent (especially Berlin or Paris) the "new" painter (a Mayan from Mexico who glues glass jewels on his portraits of Chac Mool, the rain god, but don't talk too much about that, don't want to sound too "ethnic" better be "retinal"), this new best thing can be taken up by New York and sold to Greek shipowners for their yachts or Japanese investors for their vaults.

Adele had her ear to the ground and could detect the latest seismic shift in the art market. One day she picked up your wife, Brunnhilde, whom her faulty dykedar had mistakenly identified as a potentially compliant femme.

RUGGERO THOUGHT: HOW could it be Brunnhilde never told me this before? It must be after we parted. This Adele sounds like a real slimeball. Poor Constance was so naïve back then but Brunnhilde was a mature, worldly woman—she should have known better than to take up with such a low-life fraud. She never showed the least lesbian tendencies and with age she was becoming more and more respectable. She came to detest me because of my own polyamorous adventures. That's why I've nailed my beak shut with Constance until now. Are we making a horrible mistake by reading these confessions to each other? Will our couple survive?

CONSTANCE READ: BRUNNHILDE turned out to be very uptight and Adele complained that she couldn't make any headway with her, though usually she had great success with women who'd been sidelined by men, women who were over thirty-five or intimidating or divorced or overweight. Or nobodies like me. Adele liked Brunnhilde because she was soft-spoken and well-dressed and an aristocrat and could speak German, French, English, and Italian. She'd been sent to England every summer as a teenager and still had remnants of an English upbringing. She said "chemist" for drug store, "lift" for elevator, "flat" for apartment and would declare things to be "naff." She said "looking glass" and "writing paper"—but you know all this! You were married to her. I guess you were divorced by the time we met her. I recall she never mentioned you, but she seemed to preen herself over those wretched sons of yours, Gianni and Carlo. Whenever we had a meal with her she ordered sausage, I remember. She had fabulous diamonds!

RUGGERO SAID, "GIFTS from me."

Constance said, "You're the least greedy and most generous person I know. Or have ever known. Sometimes you can be uncharacteristically harsh about someone."

"Like who?"

"Poor Cesare. Or poor Lucia. Will you talk about me like that some day?"

"Are you planning to cheat on me with God, the way Cesare did? Or badmouth my family and vomit all your meals as Lucia did?"

"They were sick people. You could show them some compassion."

"I was really in love with Cesare until he dumped me for God. I don't think I ever loved Lucia. But read on . . ."

CONSTANCE READS: THERE'S not much more to say. Adele met a female opera director from Romania who could speak Italian; Adele's spoken emoticon was "Bingo!" The woman's English was perfectly good but Adele preferred Italian, of course. She once told me that speaking Italian was one of the greatest accomplishments of her adult life and that achievement was meaningless in America. Whereas everyone in Italy assured her they'd never met an American who was so adroit, so funny, in Italian as she, really perfectly at ease, you-have-a-slight-accent-but-I-might-have-thought-you-were-from-Bari-or-Gorizia-or-Friuli, some-where not here, but Italian to be sure. The woman, Vadoma, was famous in international opera circles, had even directed the Met's production of Bartók's *Bluebeard's Castle* (the Met knew he was Hungarian but guessed Romania was close enough and Vadoma had built a set that resembled the 1880 illustrations for "The Pea Emperor," a Romanian fairy tale). Lucinda Childs choreographed it all into rapid walking back and forth. It was a critical success. Lucretia Smith sang the roles of all seven slaughtered brides.

I'd become very attached to the little French guy, Jean-Pierre, whom Adele had fucked once with her bright red strap-on. He was very amusing, as the French say of almost everyone, was a nobody like me but knew all the names in the art world, even actually knew a few painters. He befriended me. At first we thought the other one must be important but once we discovered we were both imposters we had a good laugh and started hanging out. "I'm nobody. Who are you? Are you nobody too?" He was very cute but inept at cruising; we'd sometimes go to a gay bar, which I liked because no man would try to pick me up and I could relax, once I realized no one objected to my presence and that in fact I was invisible. Jean-Pierre would fall for a guy but had no idea of how to reel him in. I wondered if this ineptness had something to do with his being French; I'd heard that they had a hard time speaking to strangers (was that why Americans said they were aloof?). So if I could see the guy was looking at my friend I might say to him something like, "There sure are a lot of guys out here, aren't there? Everyone complains that gays avoid the bars now and all use the apps." And soon he'd be drawn into conversation once I'd broken the ice. Jean-Pierre said he'd never had such success until I helped him cruise. Whereas many gay guys would flounce away if addressed by another man, knowing they could always score later online, they wouldn't be so rude with a woman. In truth, some of them hadn't talked to a woman except at work for years and years and they reverted to their high school good manners for the unexpected occasion.

There was always the possibility that Jean-Pierre wasn't their type, that he was too boyish or white or not into leather nor into meth, but most of them liked his looks and his accent. The good thing about accents was that they always gave everyone a subject of conversation, though New Yorkers were used to foreigners and often preferred not to remark on them, just as they were usually good at not staring at celebrities.

If Jean-Pierre didn't finally go home with anyone that evening, we never felt we'd wasted our time. We talked "like real people" about what we'd done that day, about what we'd hesitated to buy online, what I'd cooked for dinner (sausages and yellow peppers), what he'd warmed up in the microwave (Lean Cuisine), how he got bored during his workout at Crunch but soldiered on, about his office (publicity for the Disney shows on Broadway), about the people furloughed at Reuters, about whether Adele was falling for Vadoma, whether Vadoma was falling for Adele, about how inhuman Adele was to her parents, about how Adele could only have sex when she was drunk and even so familiarity had killed off our sex life ("Lesbian crib death," I said, "but it doesn't bother me"). He told me about his cat, Mister Rogers, and how torpid she was. He filled me in on the upcoming Netflix series (*Dark Noon* sounded good). He asked me whether I liked having sex with men or women more ("Depends"). I asked him if he liked topping or bottoming more. "I think it's so tacky-American to know in advance. We Europeans like mystery and romance. It's so sexy to bottom for a big-dicked man—I mean the idea is sexy, but you're always worry for the caca problem and does it really, really feel good? You've been fucked in the ass, no? So pussy or ass—what's your opinion?"

"Men like the ass more. Tighter."

"Yes, they do. But *you?*"

"That man is staring holes through you."

"I prefer Black men. They have better skin and they're sweeter."

She thought how few Black men she had slept with. She wondered if she'd feel more at ease with them. She'd heard they were sweeter than other men. Jean-Pierre raised the question of dick size. "They're bigger on the average. But the biggest ones are on white men."

"I didn't know that. How did you know?"

Jean-Pierre laughed and said, "*Je me documente.* Research."

"HE SOUNDS CHARMING," Ruggero said

Constance said, "But you talked to him. He was the one who brought me to that dinner at the French consul's where I met you."

"Then we must feel eternal gratitude to him for introducing us if only by accident. I like 'real people's' conversation, too. When I call my cousin in Sicily he tells me about his daughter Alabama and the plants he bought and his desalination plans."

Constance said, laughing, "Let me look at the book you're reading. *Principles of Non-Philosophy* by François Laruelle. And let's read the paragraph that you've underlined with an exclamation point in the margin. "If Heidegger affirms that the meaning of being remains unelucidated in Descartes' 'radical beginning,' then for us it is the radicality of that 'radical beginning' that is in question, since by all accounts the 'cogito' is a philosophical beginning (commencement) of the Ego, its resumption (recommencement) or repetition, rather than a radical beginning for philosophy; a philosophical beginning of the Ego from which philosophy excepts itself, rather than a beginning of philosophy within the Ego of 'in-Ego.'"

Ruggero said (coldly), "Well, that means something, believe it or not."

"I believe it. But it's not what real people say or understand."

"I have a doctorate in philosophy, remember."

"Thank God it hasn't infected your style."

"I'll take that as a compliment. But read on!"

CONSTANCE READS: I suppose when Adele had fucked me in every position and seen how unproactive in bed I was and how null my position in the world was, she lost interest. Brunnhilde wanted to be Adele's friend but Adele said, "Practically anyone can be my lover but it's very hard to be my friend." That's mean but you have to admit it's funny.

RUGGERO SAYS, "IT is funny. Poor stuffy Brunnhilde."

CONSTANCE READS: ADELE kept pursuing Vadoma. One day I saw them across the street on West End and Adele pretended not to see me and was wildly gesticulating in her Italian way and, just to spite her, I called out gaily, "Yoo-hoo, ladies!" and waved inanely as if we were all friends. "Yoo-hoo!" Vadoma smiled vaguely, as if she should recognize me. Adele moved me out, saying she was going to sublet her apartment while she was in Italy, which wasn't true, but she didn't want me around anymore. She almost pushed me out the door. It sounds like you when you were trying to shed Lucia. Of course, she wanted to pretend to Vadoma that she was entirely available. I was no longer possessive of Adele but I was jealous that Vadoma had taken my place.

RUGGERO SAYS, "ARE you ever jealous?"

"Of you? Fiercely. When you worked with that pretty soprano day after day on that Sigismondo d'India CD I was beside myself."

"Little Michela? Pretty, but I never took her seriously. I didn't even like her looks. Too young. Nice voice."

"Is anyone ever too young?"

"As your seventy-year-old husband I hope that's not true for you at least."

"I know I should pretend indifference but I'm lousy as a strategist. I'm obsessively in love with you."

"Ditto, as you would say."

CONSTANCE READS: SO Adele won Vadoma over. Briefly. Now that I'd vacated the premises, she tried to get Vadoma to move in with her (Jean-Pierre kept me informed), but Vadoma had a very nice apartment in the Ansonia with wonderful windows and a beautiful parrot, high up, and she had no desire to give up a jewel box within walking distance from Lincoln Center. And she got visibly bored with Adele's italianismo and her social climbing and her donnajuanism. When she complained about her cheating, Adele, who had exhausted all her lies, actually said, "A woman can still love someone she deceives." Jean-Pierre was there when she said it.

RUGGERO SAYS, "IT'S amazing that with all the bad luck you've had, with the early death of your parents, your abusive uncle Félix, your horrible marriages, your rotten relationship with Adele, that you've remained as sweet and open and loving as you are. Maybe that's the American side—optimistic, innocent, affectionate, starved for approval."

Constance says, "You make me sound like an abandoned dog with a dirty ruff who's about to pup. But it's true that it doesn't take three years of happiness, say, to recover from three years or ten of misery. Human beings bounce back quickly, especially when they're loved the way you love—tenderly, completely, physically, spiritually."

Constance thinks: Yes, that's true enough. But I often look at other men with an evaluating eye. Would he, that man, make me happy? Would he give me children? With him would I feel less afraid, less inferior? Once at a party I'd kissed a much younger man with carefully parted hair and a red rose in his buttonhole. I pulled away from him, terrified that Ruggero might discover me in another man's arms. But I'd liked his ardor, his youth, his desire, and I'd imagined a whole alternative life with him, one in which I was more secure, more normal, more enviably *average*.

RUGGERO READS (EMBARRASSED but pleased): Brunnhilde took me to her family's castle in the Ticino in Switzerland, not far from here. As I mentioned they were Bavarian but had collaborated so were paid a large stipend by the new German government to stay away. It was a very ancient castle with crumbling walls and battlements but they had modernized ten rooms where they lived. The rest was a sort of museum subsidized by the Swiss state; I think it was a museum of buttons, every kind of button, ancient and modern. A loony grandfather (the collaborator) had collected buttons; he and his mother spent their days sorting them. Compared to the public rooms, glacial with tiny windows, the family's rooms were overheated, painted indigo, equipped with hidden lights that bobbed alive every time you came into a room. The kitchen was so up-to-date I couldn't figure out how to brew a cup of coffee. Above the complicated oxidized-steel stove there was a television that gave one instructions for every recipe. Outside there was a heliport, but no one ever came except Tristan from Coral Gables and his mother and his two Thai "boys" (now in their forties and fat); apparently they flew their jet to Milano then switched to the helicopter. Everyone in that family except the corpulent Thais was always distraught; at every meal someone was sure to leap up and rush off, sobbing. You'd find them crouched in a remote gallery trembling and you'd have to coax them off the psychological cliff. It could take a lot of time. By the time you herded the family member back to the table, the dessert (invariably apple strudel) would have been cleared.

I remember at my first meal with the Wittelbergs the mother said, "I hope you like the eel. It's from our moat."

They were good about not speaking German around me. Of course they didn't know Italian or Sicilian. We all settled on English; theirs was a colorless airport English, which meant no one could be witty but just plod along with banalities. Tristan did say one funny thing, intentional or not: "Don't be fooled by Brunnhilde; she's not as nice as she seems." Brunnhilde slapped his arm playfully. A minute later her adolescent sister Isolde had run out of the room sobbing, her long blond hair streaming behind her.

To fill the silence I said to Krishna, "I love Thai food. Do you cook?"

Tristan answered for him: "Why should he cook? We have cooks for that. Anyway we go out every evening the three of us after the heat to eat in a restaurant in Coral Gables."

Suddenly Krishna said with real hostility: "And you, principe? Do you cook Sicilian food?"

I replied, "I love to cook after a hard day at the harpsichord. The good thing about cooking is that it's creative and immediately rewarding. I make all kinds of Sicilian street food. But don't call me principe. Everyone here I imagine has a title anyway."

Brunnhilde's mother said, "And it's against the law in Austria and in Switzerland—and in Italy!—to use titles. Anyway I was born a commoner and hateful Germans used to call me Frau Princess."

Tristan said, "You're just a countess. Krishna is a Thai prince."

I bowed my head reverently but I could see from Krishna's bitter little mouth that he was not mollified.

I was so bored I insisted on seeing the button museum. Brunnhilde volunteered to be my guide.

The unheated galleries had thousands and thousands of buttons on display. The old Wittelberg was a lifelong insomniac and his mother would sit up with him till dawn gluing quite ordinary new manufactured buttons of all colors to an old Jaguar and to a useless electric guitar. There were also rooms and rooms of historic buttons—ancient Roman coins, medieval Sicilian ones inscribed in Greek, Latin and Arabic, two-headed eagles from Austria, all glued to buttons, sometimes clumsily (you could see the hardened transparent epoxy oozing out behind the coins and even masking and dimming them).

When we returned, Tristan had refreshed his powder and rouge. I thought all these Wittelbergs were very attached to their mothers. Tristan was squeezing his mother's hand and she was looking away, shyly, vacantly. The servant, very muscular and friendly, brought in the

mon. She had
misplaced, that
hat real music
s apogee with
s sounded like
kept worrying
sounded like a
ntire repertoire
here his hands

d Carlo, but in
or even Italian,
hey showed no
e obsessed with
g. Culture was
omething to be
lost by heart but
tour the Italian
They were rude
icily. When my
erman to them,
riggle free. They
uld pantomime
usage and pastry.
g Formula I cars
he Amalfi Coast,

and was always
erland. Since the
ned Swiss–Italian,

signed and instead
deo games. When
, the most perfect
eat and kept their

cooked with juniper berries in
a blue t-shirt saying "drei könige."
ian name of Albrecht, though he
I learned later that all the butlers
it simpler for the family members

drug must have kicked in).
e met this German businessman

German," which wasn't true—I

e table said, "You should teach

nt enough." She smiled sweetly.
ned, close to tears.
ncouragingly, "*Kurschatten*?" I
w wax in her ears; maybe that

'is a gigolo, a shadow, who
."

s Mutti's *Kurschatten*." Tristan
rned later that he used bella-
Isn't it very very funny?" He

e must-see in Cefalù, "Did
r in the cathedal?"
he hotel. We never do."
games room. Four women
started knitting.

ause they were stable but
rs I wasted with her. She
with me, not even about

music, which is the interest I had assumed we had in com
decided that my interest in the baroque was childish and r
it all sounded alike ("wallpaper music," she called it) and t
didn't begin until Beethoven's *Bagatelles* and reached it
Scriabin. I liked Beethoven but thought her late romantic
trucks struggling uphill in gear number eight or ten and I
they'd burn out before reaching the peaks. Or Scriabin
gifted child who sleepwalks to the piano and plays his er
in oneiric snatches without ever waking up or seeing w
are placed.

We had little blond boys, two years apart, Gianni an
spite of their Italian names they never learned Sicilian
just Plattdeutsch and Schwiezerdeutsch and English. T
interest in me or music or Sicily or history. They were
sports, girls and later business or at least moneymakin
something to impress dates with and later clients, not s
lived and enjoyed. They knew that windbag Goethe aln
ignored Petrarch, Dante and Leopardi. When we would
hill towns by car they'd read their comic books or sleep.
to my grandfather and complained of the heat in S
grandfather would make an effort to speak his pidgin C
they'd just laugh. When he'd try to hold them, they'd w
hated Sicilian food, especially aubergines, and wo
gagging in a silly way. The only thing they liked was sa
As adults they settled down to skiing in Kitzbühel, racir
with their slanted fat tires, and renting condos on tl
where they could host chicks from Salerno.

The problem was that Brunnhilde hated Londor
taking the boys back to her family's schloss in Switz
castle was in the Ticino they might at least have lear
but they never left the grounds.

In Sicily they'd never read a book if it hadn't been as
of going to the beach they'd sit inside and play endless v
we drove them to an ancient Greek temple in Segesta
in the world, they lay down on the floor of the back

delicate veal sausages and sauerkraut cooked with juniper berries in champagne. He was wearing shorts and a blue t-shirt saying "drei könige." The family had given him the Wagnerian name of Albrecht, though he couldn't have less resembled a dwarf. I learned later that all the butlers here were called Albrecht, which made it simpler for the family members to recall.

Tristan suddenly became voluble (a drug must have kicked in).

"When *Mutti* and I were in Cefalù we met this German businessman who thought I was *Mutti's Kurschatten*."

I said, "Forgive me, but I don't know German," which wasn't true—I just didn't know that word.

Isolde who'd been coaxed back to the table said, "You should teach him, Brunnhilde."

"He'd never learn it. He's not intelligent enough." She smiled sweetly.

"But listen to my story!" Tristan screamed, close to tears.

Brunnhilde's middle sister, Erda, said encouragingly, "*Kurschatten?*" I noticed she had quite the build-up of yellow wax in her ears; maybe that was the secret of her remoteness.

"A *Kurschatten*," Tristan said to me, "is a gigolo, a shadow, who follows a rich lady around the spa, the *Kur*."

"Of course," I said.

"Imagine, the businessman thought I was Mutti's *Kurschatten*." Tristan looked around with enormous pupils (I learned later that he used belladonna every day). "I laughed and laughed. Isn't it very very funny?" He pronounced *laugh* as "loff."

To be polite, I asked, mentioning the one must-see in Cefalù, "Did you see the mosaic of the Christ Pantocrator in the cathedal?"

Tristan replied morosely, "We never left the hotel. We never do."

After the apple strudel we all moved to the games room. Four women sat down to play bridge and two of the men started knitting.

MY YEARS WITH Brunnhilde were good because they were stable but now that I know you I realize how many years I wasted with her. She was intelligent but seldom shared her ideas with me, not even about music, which is the interest I had assumed we had in common. She had decided that my interest in the baroque was childish and misplaced, that it all sounded alike ("wallpaper music," she called it) and that real music didn't begin until Beethoven's *Bagatelles* and reached its apogee with Scriabin. I liked Beethoven but thought her late romantics sounded like trucks struggling uphill in gear number eight or ten and I kept worrying they'd burn out before reaching the peaks. Or Scriabin sounded like a gifted child who sleepwalks to the piano and plays his entire repertoire in oneiric snatches without ever waking up or seeing where his hands are placed.

We had little blond boys, two years apart, Gianni and Carlo, but in spite of their Italian names they never learned Sicilian or even Italian, just Plattdeutsch and Schwiezerdeutsch and English. They showed no interest in me or music or Sicily or history. They were obsessed with sports, girls and later business or at least moneymaking. Culture was something to impress dates with and later clients, not something to be lived and enjoyed. They knew that windbag Goethe almost by heart but ignored Petrarch, Dante and Leopardi. When we would tour the Italian hill towns by car they'd read their comic books or sleep. They were rude to my grandfather and complained of the heat in Sicily. When my grandfather would make an effort to speak his pidgin German to them, they'd just laugh. When he'd try to hold them, they'd wriggle free. They hated Sicilian food, especially aubergines, and would pantomime gagging in a silly way. The only thing they liked was sausage and pastry. As adults they settled down to skiing in Kitzbühel, racing Formula 1 cars with their slanted fat tires, and renting condos on the Amalfi Coast, where they could host chicks from Salerno.

The problem was that Brunnhilde hated London and was always taking the boys back to her family's schloss in Switzerland. Since the castle was in the Ticino they might at least have learned Swiss-Italian, but they never left the grounds.

In Sicily they'd never read a book if it hadn't been assigned and instead of going to the beach they'd sit inside and play endless video games. When we drove them to an ancient Greek temple in Segesta, the most perfect in the world, they lay down on the floor of the back seat and kept their hands over their eyes, just to provoke me. They thought anyone who didn't speak English was "retarded," including my grandfather.

I felt that Brunnhilde had turned our sons against me. I would look at their perfect little blond heads carved with clean, impeccable features, their eyelashes above and below their enormous eyes suprisingly full and black on their honey-tan faces, their lips geranium pink, their little bodies strong and athletic in their shorts and I'd think, beauty is so deceiving. Those flaxen heads are empty; to the degree they have thoughts they're banal and full of hate and selfish. Oh, all right, they're just normal kids—there's the tragedy. For any Sicilian, family is the source of all love and loyalty, but my denatured sons didn't respect me. They weren't even interested in the ancient Sicilian titles they'd inherited from me. Their mother had taught them to consider Sicilians, even me, as half-savage.

I tried to be faithful but Brunnhilde had turned against sex with me and if she'd see Bruce erect she'd make a tsk-tsking sound, as if an erection were a subhuman mistake. No Sicilian can live like that. We're not obsessed but we have an unneurotic relationship to pleasure. I would gasp with delight when I pushed into her on the rare occasion; she frowned on all noises made in bed. I tried everything with her, even oral sex which as you know I don't much like. She pulled me up and away and said, "Do stop slobbering." When I objected, she said, "We already have two children."

I was in the flower of age and I was unwilling to give up sex, though I knew how destabilizing promiscuity can be. At that time we were living in London and I was teaching the harpsichord at the Royal Academy of Music and studying philosophy at King's on the Strand. I met plenty of attractive young men and women and some of them were pervious to my charms it seemed, but I was determined to make my marriage "work," as if it were a job. Sometimes it felt laborious. One of my big published essays was on the subject of pleasure in the ancient world, looking particularly at the preSocratics; my fluency in ancient Greek made my task easier. I studied with a great German scholar of ancient philosophy, Herr Schmitt, but Brunnhilde thought my studies and the lessons I gave were pointless.

Just as Brunnhilde failed to respond to Bruce, in the same way she ridiculed the harpsichord. She complained of its plucked lack of resonance, its unpleasant sound of "old dentures chattering in the cold," its dryness and absence of color. In the same way I came to dislike how pushy the piano was, its imperialistic way of kidnapping all the earlier repertoire meant for the harpsichord, its blowsy way of smudging chords, its cloudy imprecision. I pointed out to her that all of Bach was composed for the clarity and bite of the harpsichord and the majesty of the organ, not the quivering Jell-O of the piano, and that Bach himself, the one time he'd played a piano, said he disliked it.

"What is a Bach?" she asked playfully. "Just a running brook of tireless invention. I prefer my own Bruckner and his gay Lancer-Quadrille!"

Then, in a rare moment of intimacy, I told her about my affair with Cesare and she was revolted. "Do you mean to say . . . you were sexual . . . with another man? And you fully participated?" She wiped her mouth, as if she'd been fouled by kissing me. "That is disgusting. I didn't realize you were a pervert." She looked at a picture of our boring sons. "I hope it's not hereditary." Then her eyes became beady: "I hope you're not going to molest them."

That was a turning point. She'd gone off me already, but my past as a bisexual was the pretext she'd been looking for to spend more and more time with her loony family. My life became lonely. Each time I've felt isolated I've wondered if this is what old age means; have I entered it with all its privations already?

Then I've had a stay of execution, as when I met you, my darling. You've made me young again. So many times I've faced the firing squad of irrelevance and hopelessness—and then I've been magically pardoned and granted another ten years.

Luckily Brunnhilde had just come home to London with the boys to get them ready for Westminster. The three of them were tan and a bit pudgy from all those sausages and spaetzle. She'd become defensive in discussing her family. Usually she pretended they were all thriving though she did say that Tristan and *Mutti* were visiting again on their way to Krishna's "princedom" in Thailand (forgive me but I pictured a tethered sampan in a malarial river where old women sewed giant size fourteen Nikes for American importers). "Tristan seemed a bit odd," Brunnhilde volunteered.

Just an hour later Albrecht the butler was on the line. Brunnhilde was sobbing convulsively when she hung up and long ropes of saliva were hanging from her open mouth. I held her tight and she dug her fingernails into me as if she were drowning, then she pushed me away forcefully and flung herself across the bed. It was raining feebly and the rolling thunder sounded like heavy artillery assailing Maida Vale. Or maybe it was a grand piano being rolled across the floor in the heavens above us, the wheels digging scars into the parquet. Suddenly a bolt of lightning struck something dangerously close to us, as if the tympanist had hit a giant drum with clownish unscored frenzy.

In my remote, aestheticizing way I was thinking this was all a particularly tacky show of the pathetic fallacy (all nature weeps) but I still didn't know what Albrecht had said. When I tried again to ask her she looked at me with veiled contempt that I didn't already know something so important: "Tristan shot them all dead with a semi-automatic."

"All?"

"Yes, *Mutti* and Tristan had come back the day before from Thailand. So yes, all. All." The word itself became a giant hook that pulled her grief out of her body and she collapsed into hysterics for a good ten minutes. I sat patiently on the bed beside her; I was afraid to touch her. I just wanted to offer silent witness to her suffering.

When she composed herself for an exhausted instant she said with a little smile: "Albrecht said that he'd been playing with his gun for days and they thought he'd never use it." She told me that Tristan had shot himself in the head but was still alive though in a coma. Technically he was now Graf Wittelberg; a family council gathered on Skype and decided to recognize the title as Tristan's. They also ruled that if he died the title (the equivalent to count) would pass to Uncle Wotan.

A new burst of sobbing. She looked so vulnerable with her sun-lightened hair, her tear-swollen eyes, her heaving Teutonic bosom that I grabbed her with tenderness. She looked down and saw Bruce was erect. She pushed me away in disgust and said, "You pervert!"

The next day she had scooped up our sons and fled to Wotan's *schloss* in Würzburg, where Tiepolo painted the staircase of the Prince-Bishop Carl Philipp von Greiffenclau, a distant ancestor of hers.

I felt very lonely and old, a dessicated failure. But then a chamber group who knew I taught harpsichord asked me if I'd perform in the harpsichord concerto by Manuel de Falla. It would be in six weeks at Wigmore Hall. I came alive again. I didn't much like the piece; I always wondered why we couldn't just play Vivaldi or Bach or Fiocco and be done with it. Baroque music was new to most modern listeners, as fresh and unfamiliar as Falla, yet much more seductive and fascinating and tuneful. But I was happy with the challenge of playing the strident chords of the Falla and rehearsing with an orchesta of flute, oboe, clarinet, violin, and cello.

The cellist was a merry, brilliant, attractive woman named Hermione who always was up for tea at Saynes on Marylebone High Street after the afternoon rehearsals though she had to wheel her big shrouded instrument up the curbs and down. Saynes was so crowded with shoppers on the High Street that they took a dim view of the bulky cello; Hermione was wonderfully indifferent to their frowns.

As we rehearsed more and more and had tea more and more often I realized how much I enjoyed her company. She was so intelligent but unpretentious, a very English combination. She'd grown up in London and knew all the bus routes, which no foreigner could ever master. She'd been to Sicily often and loved Messina for its wonderful site on the strait just across from Catania, though she knew that all its antiquities had been destroyed in the earthquake. She preferred it to its rival Palermo, which was more feudal. "Messina is like England," she said. "More mercantile." She liked our pistachios.

She knew everything and had been educated like me at King's. She would ask me questions about philosophy and truly listen to my answers, then follow them up with more questions. Her face became peaceful and beautiful as she listened. Her usual mode was jolly and she adored gossip about our old teachers at King's, but the minute the conversation turned serious that peaceful attentive look would wipe away all the humor and irony from her face; in an instant she'd lose years of knowingness and return to a blissful, absorbing innocence.

I thought how arrogant I'd been to think I was intelligent enough to sustain any couple, that the woman in my life just needed to be sexy and compliant. I know you're wondering, Constance, how I rate your mind. I rate it very high. Ever since my brief affair with Hermione I've never been able to love someone who isn't clever. They say the brain is the sexiest organ of the body; let's not exaggerate. But truthfully it was exciting to look into that face that became lovelier with passion, just as young women in old Hollywood movies instantly turn, when their glasses are taken off, from spinster schoolteachers to sumptuous coeds. It was a thrilling if mysterious moment of communication, as powerful if as nonspecific as music, when I could lay Bruce between those burgundy-nippled breasts and look at Hermione's face, radiant but inconclusive, emitting a powerful message but about what exactly? She, who was a voluble but always original London talker, never said anything during lovemaking though her face took on a myopic, self-absorbed glitter of pleasure. Knowing that she was totally conscious of everything we were doing, that we were both daring and admiring, made our union more genuine and piquant. I loved being held between her muscular cello-gripping legs.

When Brunnhilde came back for a lightning visit she found one of Hermione's gloves, held it up like a dead rat by its tail, and said, "I'm glad my successor will be what's undoubtedly a messy Englishwoman instead of a buggered, depilated boy." In passing I couldn't help but admire her resources of vitriolic English.

Hermione was only a passing affair since she was suddenly slated to marry a rich English shipowner who worshipped her, conveyed her about London with her cello in a chauffeured Daimler (no more buses) and installed her in a vast apartment next to the Globe theatre with a balcony over the Thames. Best of all this was her first marriage, a fairy-tale match, and no one knew how she'd pulled it off, which was rather insulting to her if you thought about it. Peter McAllen, the shipowner, was in his harmless seventies, a great patron of chamber music, eager to have a trophy wife, someone fun and brilliant (the only obvious problem I could imagine was the comedy of the alcove, though I've become more forebearing about it at my great age).

I decided to move to New York, though it was about as interesting as a Swiss village in those postpandemic days. I wondered what was holding me in London now that my marriage was disintegrating and my boring alienated sons were living with Wotan. I'd received my doctorate in philosophy and my little book on pleasure in the ancient world had been published by Chatto & Windus in their Broadside series (without tedious footnotes). I'd performed the Falla and received good notices and even a recording contract from Deutsche; at last I was going to interpret some of my beloved Fiocco.

I didn't want to be near Brunnhilde and her disapproval. I had begun corresponding with Edmund White after I read *Our Young Man*, not his best novel, perhaps, but one that keyed into my fantasies of eternal youth (my Dorian Gray complex) and the almost erotic desire to be seen and admired as a model, both on the catwalk and in photographs. I knew he was an old man and I'd never been a gerontophile, no more than he'd ever been one in his youth, so I didn't daydream about dominating an old, pudgy man with skin tags and diaper rash.

But I did feel a strange spiritual bond with him and somehow wanted to exist in his eyes (perhaps part of my old horror of being swallowed up by oblivion, as can be seen by my first letter to him):

> Dear Mr White,
>
> My name is Ruggero, I'm Italian (from Sicily, to be more precise), but I've been living in London for several years. I am a professional musician, a harpsichordist. I'm not totally sure why I'm writing to you, I suppose it's because I've just finished reading one of your books and I'd like to congratulate with you about it. But I should rather say that as soon as I finished reading, I've felt almost an inevitable urge to communicate with you. Initially I wanted to write a letter on a nice thick and slightly yellowish paper using my best fountain pen and to mail it to your publisher or agent, but then I realised that an email is probably going to cause much less hassle to everyone, albeit so less poetic. You probably receive so many emails like mine, so I hope

you excuse me for the intrusion and for taking up some of your time when you're going to read these lines.

I have to admit that, despite having been an avid reader all of my life, I first discovered your work only last year when I incidentally found a copy of A Boy's Own Story *(which I liked enormously) at my favourite bookstore in London. I then read a couple of other works of yours but I wasn't at all expecting to walk out of Barnes & Noble's in Chicago (where I was performing) with another one of your novels (actually, I was looking for an essay on Jane Austen) and to begin reading it at the airport and then not being able to drop it and to spend the whole eight hours of the night flight to London still reading and reading. I won't deny that your writing has made a deep, very deep impression on me. It's been even upsetting and unsettling, I should say.*

I've always thought that (good) literature exerts its effects on us by resonating in almost physical, or rather psychophysical, ways: a sort of "consonance" and "dissonance" phenomenon that everyone who loves reading must have experienced at least once in life. I compare that to the sensation I've had sometimes in places like Rome when, while walking through the narrow streets of the city, a number of bells begin tolling at the same time, all with their different voices so that they vibrate and their sounds resonate differently within ourselves. I believe that the vibrations generated by good writers through their works have the same effect when they resonate and reverberate in their readers. For some people that can establish a very deep, strong connection, whereas for others it is much more superficial, and there might be even no connection at all. Sometimes it's a consonance, sometimes it's a dissonance as the emotional effects of those vibrations depend on people's life, personality, previous and current emotions, different stages in life. That's the amazing power of literature! Our Young Man *has acted upon me exactly that way, by making something resonate deep within myself, something that still resonates and feels alive, unexpected and surprising like an achy muscle that hasn't been used for too long. Your writing deals with all the aspects of beauty and its powerful, almost devastating effects on people's lives in a sensible way but I felt a harsh dissonance with my own life, which is centred on all that's opposite of beauty: parental abandonment and failed personal relationships. And I can assure you that such contrast is painful, almost terrifying. I could go on writing on this but I won't do it, it'd be too much.*

I'm no literary critic so certainly I'm not going to write a review of your book. I could look at some technical aspects, at structure, language, and so on. However, that's not what I'm interested in: knowing if your books have some faults won't change in the least the effects they've had on me as an individual. And for all those emotions I am very grateful to you. I still can't forget the impression that E.M. Forster's Maurice *made on me when I read it in my late teens. When one of your readers walks through the streets of London and stares at people's faces wondering who would be more similar to this or that character in your books, that's quite a success for a writer!*

I wish to apologise, Mr White, for such a long and personal letter. I hope that you don't mind too much and that as a writer you might find some interest in knowing how your works can affect your readers and their emotions, their lives.

I'd be truly honoured to meet you, so if you happen to be sometimes in the future in Italy or UK for a literary event or a holiday I'd be more than delighted to shake your hands and congratulate you in person.

Respectfully and with all the best regards,
Ruggero Castelnuovo

Edmund wrote me an email back right away, saying he was in Tuscany at the moment and, alas, had just been in London at a literary conference. Pity we hadn't known each other and been able to meet. Then we kept exchanging politenesses. He asked to see a picture and I sent one that day I'd taken in the mirror at our house in Castelnuovo, where I'd returned for a two-week vacation. I was in shorts and a polo shirt and really did look very young, like Guy in *Our Young Man*. By return email he agreed that I did indeed look very young. I told him that I was a baroque music specialist/scholar/performer and he told me he'd ordered three of my recordings. I asked him if I could address him by his first name. He was quick to agree and sent a nice portrait but said he looked every minute his seventy-eight years (which was true).

I began to read his many other books, especially his several autobiographies. I found myself often thinking of him. I told him I was bisexual and was married but about to get a divorce. I said that I had lived with a man, an Italian singer, for several years and had been very much in love, that I was probably that *avis rara*, a genuine bisexual.

What I didn't tell him is that now in London, after Brunnhilde's departure, I had several (male) fuck buddies and that I had had three-ways and endless hookups, that I was always the top and invariably had safe sex, that four times I had participated in the "cuckold" scene, i.e. I'd fucked a man's wife while he was bound and gagged and "forced" to observe; once the wife and I both insulted the poor (happy, erect) husband.

Edmund replied that he found the idea of my sexuality very exciting. I told him that my singer had had a psychotic break, had seen visions of Their Lord (as I called Him), and had become a priest. I told him I'd lied by saying I was forty; I was actually about to become forty-one.

Then, joltingly, Edmund asked me if I had any X-rated pictures. I thought he must be slightly crazy or dangerous, but I took some in my sunny room in Castelnuovo—and suddenly our epistolary relationship became much more romantic. I even showed my erection in profile.

CONSTANCE THINKS: I never heard these details before. It is rather shocking, not the old man's lubricity but Ruggero's exhibitionism—but it also shows he's a good sport, open to any dare!

RUGGERO READS: SOON we were explaining everything about our lives to each other, narrating them, as new friends or potential lovers do. I told him about Lucia and her homophobia, but I played down her craziness because I didn't want to sound too crazy myself. I'd already told him about Cesare's holy visions. Eventually I planned to mention how Brunnhilde's brother Tristan had slaughtered her entire family, but I reserved that tale for another day.

He talked about his husband, Michael, and said he was a writer as well, sometimes angry and aggressive but most of the time sweet. Ed said he'd had two strokes and a major heart attack with double bypass surgery. After the heart attack and the second stroke he'd had to relearn to walk, talk, swallow, hold a pen to write and that Michael had been a great support during all these crises. He'd come to the hospital every day (after the heart attack it was an hour away from New York). He'd written all the worried friends and scheduled their daily visits. He'd brought books and forbidden edibles. He'd played with the therapy dog and listened to the volunteer guitarist. He'd relayed gossip and was (unprecedentedly) always cheerful.

Edmund and I had gone rather quickly to signing our emails "Love" and "Much love." I sent him two books in English translation about Greek pedophilia by Eva Cantarella. I also sent him two published articles I'd written in Italian about castrati in the eighteenth century. I'd researched the medical procedure, the body effects, the quality of the voice (we even have a recording of the last, very old Vatican castrato in which the true quality of his voice comes out in a few spoken words).

Edmund knew Italian, sort of.

I'd suggested I might be giving a concert in San Antonio in December and might be able to stop off in New York for a day.

Then I thought better of it.

I wrote him in October:

To prove that I really think of you all the time I'm sending a couple of quick pictures I took for you today at the gym. You're definitely one of the very few (very few!) persons with whom I can talk literature, music, Greek homosexual poetry, and at the same time send X-rated pics without any embarrassment.

Talking of embarrassment, I'm about to make you a cheeky proposal: What would you ever say if I had a chance to come to New York around mid-October for one or two nights? I could arrange a work trip for a recording session and come visit you at the same time (to be honest the work trip is merely an excuse). I'm still not totally sure about my plans in December and I might not be able to stop by in NY on my way to Texas (and I would never forgive myself if I didn't see you). Please tell me with total sincerity what you think.

I SENT HIM pictures of my harpsichord, which was a wonderful copy of a historic Italian instrument of the seventeenth century.

When he wrote back, he was very excited about meeting me in October. I was still having problems imagining us in bed, given our age difference and my invariable preference for younger men and women. I wrote him this email:

> I'm reading again parts of My Lives and I've been having this fantasy: I'm a couple of years older than you and we meet at a boarding school where we're both lonely and longing for love. And then I'd become your best friend, your confidant, and you'd be mine and I'd reassure and protect you and give you all the confidence you need and we would be inseparable. I still remember how deeply touched I was by a movie scene I watched when I was seventeen or eighteen. I was somehow attracted to boys at the time but I had never had sex with any of them—with the exception of some occasional "playing" with my cousin, a very handsome Sicilian boy around my age when we were thirteen to fifteen. I knew he was—and is—definitely straight so the fact that from time to time we were having sex together—although feeling so exciting and gratifying for me—was also reassuring in the sense that I too like him would turn into a perfectly straight man in just a few years. There's a sequence in that movie that I can still figure very well the younger boy escapes from his dorm room at dawn to meet his best friend (they weren't lovers yet) and when they lie one next to the other, he lets his head rest on the chest of the older guy who strokes his blond hair, talking softly without looking into the eyes. To me those couple of minutes of the movie were incredibly touching and I couldn't stop thinking of how much I wanted to be in the same situation myself. Holding a younger insecure pal and having him on my lap and looking after him and after all his needs was the dream of my life.

I suppose you could say that before we met I could fantasize Edmund was a frail kid in need of encouragement rather than a fat, famous slug.

He told me that he, too, had a fantasy of being nurtured by an upperclassman, me, and that in his imagination he went to sleep every night with his head on my "powerful chest."

We were in an ecstasy of correspondence, when the imagination is unobstructed by this too, too solid flesh, the unpleasant friends, the unforgiving wrinkles, the pill-dry mouth, the slight snore, the harsh American accent. I could still dwell in the warmth and convincing eloquence of his written words, in the purely verbal realm of becoming rather than in the unrevisable truth of being.

He asked me how I could bear being with an old man and I replied that this time I was in love with an imagination and a heart. I didn't want to sound rude but I knew I could love someone old if that someone was Edmund.

He had written that he only felt at ease with people who could appeal to their better selves, set aside their habits and preconceptions, who could overthrow their previous judgments, entertain a sudden, unexpected transcendence of compassion.

I wrote him:

> *I love very much your idea of a compassionate originality within ourselves. That's often perceived as unforgivable weakness by others—especially in our society so celebrative of successful "flawless" lives—but I don't think so at all, actually rather the opposite. Only stiff—and weak—brains are stuck to their ideas and conventions. I've always got a great interest in people's weaknesses, not in a morbid way, but in a sort of compassionate attitude that would make me feel part of a more universal family of troubled humanity.*
>
> *Lots of loving thoughts my dear Edmund, you're always, always in my heart.*
>
> *Ruggero*

RUGGERO SAYS, "UNTIL I'd actually seen him, until he'd come under my thrall, I was still just a bit uncertain of him."

Constance says, impatiently. "You always speak of love strategically, as if it were strictly a matter of making a conquest. Did you love him?"

Ruggero says, wounded, "But I did actually love him then." Reflects. "Maybe always (a new thought). More tactically than strategically. I knew

I'd win the war if I set out to be the victor, but I wanted to seduce him right away, in the very first skirmish. I know you're shocked that I would resort to that eighteenth-century metaphor of love as war, but you have to remember I need to win, that my main drive in life is to win."

"Paradoxically I'm very self-sufficient. I don't miss people. Once I'd finally broken with Edmund, I never thought of him. No more than I'd missed the priest. For someone like me on the spectrum, experience is a set of Rubik's cubes I keep fiddling with, studying, and imagining in new and newer combinations until the solution instantly stares me in the face and all the different colors unite. I like to figure things out—how to tune a harpsichord, how to repair an amplifier . . . and statistics! I'm the only person in our world who genuinely likes statistics. I can sit over a spreadsheet with utter concentration for four hours without taking a single toilet break. And yet I want to appear human and for a Sicilian that means seldom to be alone though one might crave solitude—or scarcely notice it. Here's an example of my protective coloring: I put the dining room chairs on a slight angle and even reposition the items in the medicine closet so they won't look too compulsive. No right angles, which come to me instinctively. I know how to imitate normality."

Pause.

"Yes, I was in love with him. Remember, Brunnhilde had just rejected me, and I could only look back on the ruins of my life—Lucia's anorexia homophobia, Cesare's madness, Brunnhilde's defection. And my endless hookups with handsome boys (usually drugged in London), and my few sadistic ventures into 'cucking.' His written words had fired my imagination and set it on its trajectory to Venus and there were no awkward asteroids to impede its flight. I could even hear his voice in a couple of recorded speeches, and his overly inflected 'gay' voice may have shocked me at first but soon I found it endearing. As you know, Sicilian men have low voices and an intonation that is simple and straightforward; they want to sound imperturbable and authoritative or at least irreproachable. Whereas White's voice was fruity.

"Being a writer—or rather, being *chosen* by a writer—appealed to me. Literature conveyed exact images and ideas though with less immediacy and strength than music. I knew music imparted the most intense significance imaginable, but no two people could agree as to what that meaning was. I was convinced by Schopenhauer and wished I'd written my dissertation on him. He argued that music lies outside the hierarchy of the other arts; it doesn't express ideas; music is, in parallel to ideas, an expression of the will itself. As he writes in the *The World as Will and Representation*, "Music is an exercise in unconscious metaphysics in which the spirit does not know it is doing philosophy." Elsewhere he claims that for us music is an exterior and empirical exercise which permits us to grasp, without any intermediary, large numbers and the complex relationships which unite them—and these relationships could not be understood immediately if music didn't exist—that is, without passing through abstraction. Brilliantly, he states, "In music there is something ineffable and intimate; it approaches us as the image of a paradise perfectly intelligible and entirely inexplicable."

"He ends with the reflection that esthetic pleasure, the consolation of art, the artistic enthusiasm that effaces the pains of life, this special privilege of genius which indemnifies suffering, which makes up for the fact that existence is a constant torment, sometimes lamentable and terrifying—that art throws off this horrible yoke from our shoulders and gives us a vision of peace.

"Edmund seemed to have a keen if uneducated enthusiasm for music and a bewilderingly wide range in his tastes—everything from Monteverdi to Sibelius, a love of Stravinsky matched by an equal passion for Vivaldi. He despised Cecilia Bartoli as much as I did and worshipped the purity of Tagliavini's voice. In fact he played on his little bedside component Tagliavini's "greatest hits," and Giuseppe Pietri's "Io conosco un giardino" with its syrupy operetta harmonies became the national anthem of our love (I would have preferred Couperin's "Les Barricades mystérieuses").

"He commented on my two articles in Italian on castrati and he repeated (like a very intelligent parrot) all my observations, medical and musical. I sent him more photos of my big dick, right after I came. He noticed our family coat of arms (the *stemma*) on my bedroom wall just beyond my cloudy liquid, which I decided meant he had studied the pictures repeatedly.

"I told him I'd tried to bottom a few times but that I didn't like it; bottoming wasn't for me.

"I persisted in those pre-encounter days to see him as a little boy. He told me he was having a long, costly massage to sort out his back; I emailed, 'Please fix it, my little one, before I arrive.' I knew what his face looked like but I hadn't the least curiosity about his body.

"I told him I'd only spent a few days in New York years before when I'd played at the Italian Academy in their big medallioned hall Mussolini had paid for. I said that New York would always be associated in my mind with him. We liked to pretend we could have (might have) met years before. My family had made a two-week visit to Paris when I was sixteen and he was fifty-two and we worked up a fantasy that he'd cruised me at the Café Beaubourg in the men's room (the famous urinal was a wall of water) or at the Italian Academy from the stage when I was twenty-two and he fifty-eight."

Constance says, "But a man of that age would never have interested you when you were twenty-two—or now. And how could you ever have imagined he was your 'little boy'? No matter how taken you were with prep school fantasies."

Ruggero says, "But he had a very powerful imagination, almost as good as mine. Ha! From the very beginning, when we were most in love, we both knew that age was our enemy. Old, impotent, fat, feeble—it was a testament to his witchy powers that I could find him desirable in spite of all these challenges to my natural tastes and experience. I who had loved my sexy cousin and the brilliantly beautiful Cesare, the *zaftig* Brunnhilde. I who had had decades of experience with the crème de la crème, three-ways, four-ways, who finally found my beau idéal in you, my darling, thirty years younger than me—only his imagination and sweetness, so *attachantes*, could have possibly held me that long."

★ ★ ★

I WROTE HIM:

Ed my love, good morning! You won't believe the happiness, the joy, the turmoil that reading your email gives me every single time. Nobody can believe it, not even myself! The more I think about it the more astonished I am. I, the super rational Ruggero, totally and madly in love with you living on the other shore of the Atlantic who, until no more than three months ago, were "only" a name and a face. I felt at the same time impossibly distant but incredibly close. I woke up in the middle of the night only thinking of you and how I wanted to be with you and when I saw your email I almost cried with joy! My Ed thinks of me and has written me again! What could ever make me happier?

Constance says, "Only the people you've completely subdued do you describe as 'sweet.'"

Ruggero says, "I may describe only the people I've subdued as sweet but there are many people I've subjugated whom not even I would regard as sweet."

He looks over the tops of his glasses at her, then continues reading.

I was in love with him and he with me. I emailed him when I returned from Sicily to London:

I'm back in London, it's late night, and my last thought of the day is for you. Such is the pleasure of seeing your name in the email box and then reading the words you've written me that I've been edging on that to prolong my bliss. I woke up at six a.m. today and my very first thought—even before feeling my almost painful morning hard-on!—was to check if there was an email from you. However I didn't do it immediately, instead I took the phone away from the bed so I couldn't reach it. I went to bed and began thinking of our first meeting, of what I'll be wearing, how I'll do my hair, which fragrance I'll choose. I want to make your first glance of me truly unforgettable. And I fell asleep again half-dreaming of all that and I saw you in my dreams, welcoming me at the doorstep, saying sweet words. Then I woke up again—my erection even harder now—and I saw the phone glaring on the shelf but still I didn't want to touch it. I was longing to read your email, but wanted to prolong the longing till the unbearable and when eventually I read it it was like orgasming after a very long edging. How wonderful! Your words are like air to my lungs, electricity to my body. I wanted to masturbate in bed but I did it in the shower instead.

We were both unreservedly open and passionate. He wrote me after I sent him a photo of my cock and cum:

Dear Ruggero,
I fall more and more in love with you every day if that is possible. I love it that miraculously somehow I've become important to you. I love to think of your morning erection and of your jerking off in the shower. Today in my imagination I thought of holding that big erection in my hand; I hope that doesn't freak you out. I love you, my Ruggero.

He told me he'd never known someone so virile, so tender, so romantic, so handsome but that he'd often dreamed of someone like that. Edmund said he was sorry that he wasn't much younger, even younger than I, since he knew we both wanted that. He said he'd been careless to grow so old. I'd taken to calling him my little boy.

I wrote him shortly before my departure:

My dearest Ed,
I may be the boy who has (almost) everything but I burn inside only thinking I might lose you. The idea of being loved by you makes me the happiest man on earth and the only thought of losing you the most desperate. How's it possible? I don't know. All I know is that I feel this burning desire of being loved forever by you and I won't need anything else in my whole life. Right now I feel my entire happiness depends only on you.

Ruggero

Edmund wrote back that he would love only me for the rest of my life (love makes us reckless). In truth he loved only me for the rest of his life.

★ ★ ★

I TOLD HIM that I was a bit uneasy meeting him, he who'd known so many extraordinary people over the years, the world's elite, but finally the day arrived and I flew to New York with joy and foreboding in my heart.

He was wearing shorts and a red t-shirt one size too small; I of course was in a dark suit and mauve tie. I took him (*all* of him) in my arms and kissed him. Then we broke apart and looked at each other, the way a fisherman who's struggled with a barracuda for hours might size it up once he's pulled it onto the deck.

Within seconds we were in his bedroom and undressed and I saw it was going to be easy: I would just admire myself through his eyes. His admiration was audible as well—he kept whispering praise of my tight stomach, huge uncut dick, hairy chest, rough beard, the perfect globes of my ass. He even praised my weak point—my big Italian nose, which he traced with his finger.

One could say I was a narcissist, but in fact I enjoyed the pleasure other people took in me. It was a strange form of generosity, handing myself out like flowers on Easter.

In Trump we'd seen the whole ugly import of that word, *narcissism*—a total lack of empathy, a need to aggrandize oneself, a foolish, limitless urge to praise oneself ("better for African Americans than Lincoln"). I wasn't that. I fed on praise, but I was conscious, even wary, of the shifting realities around me. I was almost cripplingly aware of the feelings of other people; ever since my affair with Cesare (whom my grandfather detested) I'd feared that I could disappoint and degrade my beloved family; and I was too intelligent not to see the comedy in every one of my excesses. If tragedy is defined as a close-up and comedy as a long shot, I was always quick to see myself in the absurdity of distance.

Edmund had a good face, which was alarmingly mobile. Later I realized he would often check out for entire minutes, but his face read as unflagging attention. Maybe as an academic he'd picked up the whole dumb show of appearing intellectual: the wry half-smile, the disapproving wrinkled nose, the squint of discernment, the discreet roll of the eyes. He mimed thinking even when he was in neutral, mindless.

Don't ask me to reconstruct my successive impressions of him, as delicate as layered onion skin, but after two days I understood that he was warmer and more passionate as a writer than as a man. I knew that I was a tremendous gift to a man his age but he seemed only moderately grateful. In fact he was hard to read if one stared directly at the page, as it were; he was best decrypted with peripheral vision. It was almost as if a sudden side-glance would surprise an untoward look on his face, bored or even hostile, sometimes pleased.

Officially he was a jolly old thing, always smiling and caressing and blowing kisses, but there was something deeply reserved about him. I thought it might have to do with his having been hurt or misled or disappointed too many times in his long life, but I knew we'd never have time enough to reverse all the ill fortune he'd known, not even with the happiness I might be bringing him. He wasn't by any means extinct (he was fiercely ambitious) but in a few days I could feel how he was already sliding toward a late death.

His apartment was large for Manhattan I learned but it was impossibly chaotic with books and books spilling over every shelf and his closets stuffed with clothes I never saw him wear. Even so the rooms were "cozy," if that meant lots of low lights, odd objects here and there (an ostrich's dangerous-looking foot, a piece of quartz, a painted child's toy from India, a photo of glowering grandparents that had faded almost into invisibility, eighteenth-century andirons of bewigged gentlemen, paintings hung care-lessly about of dubious quality, even an icon)—nothing orderly or impres-sive, mere curiosities. For me it became the Old Curiosity Shop. Strangely enough, given my love of order and restraint, I always felt comfortable there with its obligatory wall-to-wall carpet (landlord's orders) and weather-damaged windows. He had a real fireplace, which was astonishing to me, a recent Londoner; strangely in New York it was legal to burn wood.

I don't mean to suggest his actual presence dimmed my ardor. I had ginned myself up to be in love. I needed to be in love after Brunnhilde's rejection. But instantly I spotted some problems—his failure to be wowed by me, his sour, weird "husband," his senescence and lack of obvious physical appeal. Nothing was clear-cut, however, at the beginning. If Edmund had been swept away by me at first it would have embarrassed me. Michael was an original, in both the positive and negative sense of the word. Edmund's charm almost made up for his age and chubbiness, and his passion in bed was a real surprise. At first I thought an act of pure will, my will, might overcome what I recognized as defects. I had told my shrink that what I wanted most was to move to New York to be with Edmund and she had said, "Then why don't you do it?" I had done it and I was proud of the eccentricity of my choice, I who had buggered so many beautiful boys and fucked so many beautiful girls. And I had been bored with my London life, so free of surprise.

I even landed the first job I'd applied for—as a teacher of the harpsichord at Juilliard. The Englishman who'd held the position was retiring. He and the dean of faculty admired my recordings. I'd taught in an equivalent conservatory in London. My recording of Fiocco had made a stir in that tiny, nearly nerveless world; I'd just won another Diapason d'or. A friend had taught me to be a hard bargainer about my salary. Left to my own devices I'd wave off any discussion of money but I'd learned that Americans only take seriously what they have to overpay for.

I've always been a good sleeper (except when as a teen I was afraid of dying), so I slept well with him. Edmund was a good cook and rapid. He threw away too much food; I liked to recycle. He was a relaxed small talker, capable of occasional Big Talk, polite in an unostentatious European way, "famous as a *gaffeur*" as he himself admitted, as my uncle Max had admitted (neither man was; it must have been a characterization demanding an immediate refutation). I seldom observed any serious social mistakes in either of them. Ed was fascinated by the very idea of social mistakes and I taught him how to pour espresso bit by bit into each of two or three cups so as to equal out the different grades of caffeine strength—something that I remembered my grandmother had practiced but no one since. I said that my grandmother had deplored "ladies" who were stingy about sugar or grated Parmesan, which they rationed; she would never visit them a second time.

Edmund was so devoted to me that I feared he'd bore me (what I feared the most, boredom, now that I no longer thought about dying) but passing, unshowy references to his famous friends (Foucault, Sontag,

Philip Roth, royalty) kept me alert. In the bathroom he'd hung all his honors and even an invitation to the Queen's golden jubilee. He was lively and knew a lot but was mysteriously uninformed about politics and tiresomely forgetful of names (old age). In conversation he was bothered by interruptions; his anecdotes were rehearsed; the give-and-take of teenage talk was long in the past. But he was aware of his shortcomings. He told me once that his nephew who'd lived with him when the boy was in his teens and hung out with him again twenty years later told him that in the interim he'd gone from being painfully solicitous to unworriedly egotistical. Ed had remarked that the composer Virgil Thomson had once said he wouldn't go any place where he wasn't already known—and if Edmund had retained that comment it must have been because it rang a large, resonant bell in him.

His mouth looked as if he'd just said the word *plum*.

People often attributed things to him, smart, ironic attitudes, that he was entirely innocent of, even unaware of. A Parisian editor friend of his was always doubled up with laughter, even miming holding his sides, because Edmund had just made some evilly witty remark, but it would invariably turn out that Edmund was innocent of any evil ill will and quite content with his polite "social" chatter, bland, kind, and depthless.

Once when Edmund (this is just one of a thousand instances but the one I recall for some reason) suggested to a friend who was translating Colette's *La Fin de Chéri* that he render *cette sauvage délicatesse* not as "feral refinement" but as "this wild civility," the translator confessed that it had taken him a moment to recognize Edmund was citing Herrick's "Delight in Disorder"—whereas Edmund had no recollection of that poem. The translator was polite enough to attribute this lapse to something like the coded wisdom of the Fool in *King Lear*.

Edmund had the odd smell of a skin fungus, which he tried to disguise with cologne. He said that his doctor had said he'd never get rid of his fungus.

He liked kinky sex, which also interested me. He said that since his viral load was undetectable and since I was HIV-negative, we shouldn't bother with condoms (I'd mistakenly thought he'd insist on safe sex). He liked to have his tits pinched and would groan in ecstatic pain; I wasn't too keen on fingering those cold, swollen erasers. He liked to be pissed on, which I liked as well. In the tub, of course, where he sat in his invalid chair (hope for the handicapped). He wanted me to stand, sans panties, over him in a kilt and slowly crouch and sit on his face, his torso and face entirely shrouded in hot, airless plaid. He liked to be spanked. He liked verbal slut shaming and to be called a "bitch" (which with my accent came out as "beech," somehow less offensive). I would call him a greedy boy, greedy for my big brown Sicilian cock (it wasn't really brown but I chose to think so). He liked to be fucked on his back with his swollen legs hooked over my shoulders. We both talked a lot during sex. Sometimes I spit on him. At the beginning he could still get it up and even come but eventually he became impotent, which strangely enough didn't make him less passionate. Or less desirable. We would end up with him licking my armpit while I jerked off.

I had decided that I would never refuse him sexual access to me. I remembered that the sixteen-year-old heterosexual Raymond Radiguet had said he would never deny his body to the much older, bony Cocteau, whom he loved but couldn't possibly desire. Cocteau caressed the sleeping youngster all night and wrote his greatest collection of poems to him, *Plain Song*, although the times required he make him a girl, just as Proust made his chauffeur Alfred into Albertine.

At first my love was so great that I didn't have to prod myself at all. I was so happy to be with him, he was so easy to be with, we were never with other people or almost never. We just had our romantic days (sometimes only one or two) and saw Michael rarely. Anyway, Michael was turned on by me and adored me. I, who am not conventional, as you know, but also am not indifferent to public opinion, eventually had to recognize we were a strange and unsuitable couple. I think Edmund had no idea of my reservations nor did I. My doubts were just a whisper to myself at first. We were very much in love. But love is always tested by friends, by society. That's why summer romances in isolation in exotic places glisten and then lose their luster like beach glass when brought home.

★ ★ ★

CONSTANCE THOUGHT: WHEN Ruggero first started courting me in such extravagant romantic terms, I asked an Italian woman friend, "Should I believe him or is he just being Sicilian?" She said nothing but frowned and turned the edges of her mouth down. How naïve could I be!

Of course, Ruggero did remain faithful to Edmund in his strange way even if he did leave him for a young, handsome lover—faithful in seeing him every week and emailing him or skyping him three times a day. Edmund did try to break it off three times but Ruggero would never permit him to disappear.

Ruggero never put me through that. He was always constant in his adoration, unceasing in his sexual ardor, which usually cools off quickly even in the most loving couples. I was the frightened one, the one that feared rejection and could turn the slightest misunderstanding into an ultimate break. Most men want to assume their contract with a woman is unbroken unless he is notified otherwise, but Ruggero was patient and tender, could smile his way through all my sulks, no unstifled fear could rile him, he knew how to love even a great neurotic like me. And yet I worried, suspected I had a rival, could even clearly imagine him or her. Ruggero was like a genial, unflagging host whose patience after the third day of the visit is wearing thin but is too polite to show it. In relationships he was always judicious. I was in constant anguish around him, felt unworthy, too female, too American, less and less young and attractive. I wanted children and could hear my biological clock ticking—a time bomb, really. I knew that Ruggero shuddered at the thought of more children and once said he was far too old to bring anyone into this world. "Anyway, darling," he said, "I want to be your child; I couldn't bear a rival."

Once a young male friend asked, on the eve of his own wedding, "What is the secret to a long marriage?" Ruggero replied, "It's the ninety/ten principle. You make 90 percent of the effort and she makes ten percent. Of course, you each think you've gone more than halfway."

★ ★ ★

RUGGERO SAYS, "AFTER my first visit I received this email from Ed":

> *Dear Ruggero—mi sento un po giù.*
>
> *No, I'm really happy that we spent such an ecstatic 24 hours together! You are my husband, my big boy, my owner. How could we have had more fun, more intensity, more scalding pleasure? Sleep well tonight, my Dominion; you've earned it.*
>
> *Your devoted butt boy*

Constance says, "I guess it's clear what were your roles. Did you keep all your emails to and from him?"

Ruggero says, "Yes, we both thought it was a great correspondence.

"I was so in love with him. I wrote him reams every day. He was worried that he wasn't young and handsome enough for me. Here's just an excerpt of my response:

> *I've had many young and very beautiful lovers—super-sexy Juan from Madrid still writes me almost every day, which is very sweet of him and flattering—and you know that I've never had an older lover. You're also the great artist who moved me to tears with his writing and the truth of his words. So it's not actual physical beauty I'm looking for in you—I hope you understand what I mean to say, I don't want to sound rude! You've completely won both my heart and my mind through a totally different route, and my feelings are unique and totally unprecedented (perhaps you're more familiar with this situation, but that's not a problem, it's understandable). I'm so much in love with the idea that I can be loved and idolized by you that my only desire is to meet you and give you back that happiness that you've brought to me. For this idea I'm challenging all my beliefs, my rationality, my old self, and I'm doing it very eagerly. You're a wonderful person and the idea of being part of your life is for me something that words cannot describe adequately. I'm sorry I keep saying the same things, I must sound really silly if not frankly annoying. I want to be handsome, intelligent, successful, elegant, attractive, irresistible, only for you, only to make you proud of me before anyone else and to be worthy of your adoration. Are these feelings*

healthy? I'm not sure if anyone would have an answer, but I've decided not to ask myself or anyone else this question.

CONSTANCE THINKS: POOR Edmund should have been worried by so much egotism and so little reciprocal curiosity. Ruggero was never so unobservant of me, nor, I wager, was he really as incurious about Edmund as he sounds. He's a quick study, as alert as a robin; he could easily see how totally he was loved and after his privations with Brunnhilde that's all he wanted, to be adored and cherished by an expert lover of men.

Perhaps Edmund should have been wary that a younger, even more passionate lover could replace him. But for those first months Ruggero didn't give a single clue that he was dissatisfied.

In my daily wanderings around St. Moritz I had met an American named Jason and I was becoming dangerously close to him. For so long I'd been terrified of losing Ruggero; when he was in the hospital with his broken leg I had nearly gone mad with fear and loneliness. With Jason I never felt that insecurity. He loved me and did not keep me in suspense about his affection. It was an artesian well of love; Ruggero's devotion was an intermittent trickle. It was always provisional, no matter what he said. Of course Ruggero made constant protestations of love, maybe to convince himself. Jason's love was simple and evidential, like opening hands: "Here it is!"

Jason had kissed me often and we'd had sex many times and I kept feeling I should tell Ruggero but I knew he'd make a terrible fuss and I've have to promise never to see him again—and I didn't want to forego my dream of living a quiet life with Jason and children.

WHEN RUGGERO MOVED to New York, he found a glamorous apartment just a twenty-dollar cab ride away from Edmund he told me. He didn't even bother with a divorce from Brunnhilde but gave her a handsome allowance for the boys. Neither he nor she wanted to remarry. Edmund was already married to Michael and though there was considerable friction there they had no reason to part. Ruggero understood that if Edmund won the Nobel, say, it would be Michael who would accompany him to Stockholm.

And then the doorman in his new building would say, "Your father has already gone up."

RUGGERO READS: EVEN before I moved to New York I began to call Edmund "my wife" and he called me "my husband." I'd bought us identical vintage Omega watches inscribed in back RC and EW 2018, and I'd bought us identical wedding rings. Often he referred to me as his "straight Sicilian husband."

Edmund would stay over in my apartment and get up late after I'd already been at Juilliard for an hour practicing or teaching. I taught harpsichord but I also filled in for an elderly woman who taught music theory. At Santa Cecilia I'd attended many music theory classes and also, as a baroque specialist, could explain how a toccata differed from a passacaglia or from a chaconne or allemande. I knew what a cantus firmus was and a mordent. I could even coach organists after my experience playing and writing for the organ in Castelnuovo. I had nearly fifty opus numbers, including a one-act opera, two full-length ballets, three string quartets, a series of impresssions of Taormina for the piano, four pieces for the harpsichord each based on women of different nationalities (the Frenchwoman, the German, *l'italiana*, the Spanish Gypsy)—not musical caricatures but subtle tonal explorations (the Frenchwoman was in the minor and slow, for instance, and the Italian brisk and in the major). I did variations on a theme by Hindemith from his opera *Mathis der Maler*.

Of course, I was never so much in love as I was before we were living in the same city. I had begun a novel about a French baroque musician and Edmund read every page, cheered me on, and corrected my mistakes (not so many!) in English. I read the novel he'd begun, *A Saint from Texas*, and praised it sincerely and rapturously. I felt he needed my encouragement, which surprised and gratified me.

I wrote him:

I believe that the two of us are the best couple ever!
I'm always so proud of you! And what would take me even up to the moon is the idea of making you proud of me. All becomes easy and gratifying with that in mind. I feel I can do anything.

From the first time I met him I'd bring a quart of freshly squeezed orange juice from the emporium across the street. He'd try to dose it out but within a day he'd drunk it all—cold, sweet, tangy. I often brought him sweets as well; big, flaky croissants or braided rolls of dark chocolate and pastry. Edmund had no self-discipline, whereas I could go fourteen or sixteen hours fasting; I was an adept of "intermittent fasting." I joked about wanting to get rid of my love handles, though I didn't have any.

We had people to dinner, mostly his friends, and I liked seeing them. I'd make a pasta course or maybe a dessert or I'd buy one, the wine as well (Edmund was a teetotaler) and I'd clean up and load the dishwasher. Americans teased me for my English accent and for using English expressions ("chemist" for *pharmacy* or "pudding" for *dessert*). I'm very social like most Sicilians and like a dinner of six or eight. I awakened most days frightfully early but if I stayed at Edmund's he made me coffee and toast, sat groggily with me and then went back to bed. His doctor told him to take two naps a day.

There were politics to navigate at Juilliard but I was both extraordinarily diplomatic and totally without ambition as an academic. I had my fortune and my career and never ever wanted to be the department chair or to be awarded tenure (though the school granted it to me after a year). We were already into the thorny years of political correctness and cancel culture. I had to administer to myself a "sensitivity" course online as to how to respect women and never flirt on the job. I had to leave my office door open whenever I met with a student. I pretended to be exclusively homosexual. That way I had my own pathetic minority status. No American believed in bisexuality in any event and I was no longer seen as a predator of women though quite a few male students saw me as prey.

I championed the work of a composer who was both Black and female and who'd attended Juilliard, Margaret Bonds. She'd studied with Roy Harris and collaborated on many vocal works with the poet Langston Hughes and wasn't half-bad. Bright. Cheerful. Unobjectionable.

I was occasionally on the road giving concerts. My biggest fear was that Edmund would not be faithful to me. I knew that he thought that was being "old-fashioned" of me, but I explained that he was a gay New Yorker of the promiscuous 1960s and I was a heterosexual nineteenth-century Sicilian—possessive and murderously jealous. Secretly, he confessed that he was proud that I was so possessive. I knew that so many younger gay men—writers, singers, scholars and just young lawyers, bankers and doctors in search of famous friends—paid court to him, but I soon observed that they weren't attracted physically to such an old man. A few of them he met on an age-discordant site, SilverDaddies, were genuine gerontophiles, but most just sought the prestige of his friendship. Most gay New Yorkers wanted to pair up with a muscular professional of the same age and degree of wealth. They wanted to be enviable. And then there was the whole top-bottom problem. Almost all experienced New Yorkers wanted to be the catcher not the pitcher, the minus not the plus, the penetrated not the penetrator. I was a real find, that rare thing: a rich, handsome top with a big uncut dick, a title and an accent, a musical career and a teacher in a famous school. I liked everyone and everyone liked me. I had the trim, manly, muscular body of someone who worked out every day, never smoked or drank, who was a Turk from the waist down and a Greek god from the waist up. My nose was too big for ideal beauty but gays read it as a promise of outsize genitalia. Stripped of my position in the world, as a mere body, I was attractive to all the gay men who stared at me at the gym.

I declared in an early email to him after I'd moved to New York that Edmund and I were the ultimate "power couple." I alternated between calling him "my darling wife" and "boy," as in "I'll be home soon, boy."

Good night, my sweetheart. Whatever I do is for you. I go to the gym for you, I write my book for you, I buy my clothes for you, even my job is for you, to make you proud of me. Nonetheless, I think that ours is a healthy relationship, that we have our own personalities and we are not codependent. I feel happy with you but I'm not desperate without you as long as I know that you love me (I know I love you, boy). As a friend said the other day, "I think yours is love, just strong, powerful love between two people who've found each other through a mysterious way." A cute Indian guy at the gym's changing rooms wasn't lifting his eyes from me while I was getting dressed after the shower and I felt so happy thinking that I was yours and nobody else could have me!

I knew that it excited him to be called my "wife." He didn't have to pretend to be macho nor to take turns being the aggressor, not that he could have. He had a tiny penis and was almost always impotent. It pleased both of us to consider his inadequacy as a reality of role-playing rather than as an age-related insufficiency. His heart wasn't strong enough for him to have testosterone shots.

Edmund's friends were often older (although there were lots of pretty boys in his circle), about a third were heterosexual. For me it was a relief not constantly crossing verbal swords with bitchy queens or to be au courant with contemporary gay culture. I scandalized everyone at one gay showbiz table when I didn't know who Patti LuPone was but Edmund defended me by asking if any of those Americans knew who Dalida was, the European equivalent. I was shocked they'd never heard of her: the Atlantic was wide indeed. Americans assumed their miserable parochial fads constituted world culture. I realized America was the richest third-world country.

I suppose Edmund wanted to demonstrate he was fearless about exposing me to all the great young beauties, to hold their young lean profiles scribbled over with stylish scruff next to his lined, puffy, smooth-shaved face, jagged asteroids beside the full moon, while keeping it all within the bounds of high culture (Bach on the sound system, no drugs, literary chat, good bourgeois cooking, no rancid sex bragging).

I was amused by American kitsch, its throwaway pop culture (the latest cable series, the blockbuster teen action movies, though never the bubblegum music); I wasn't stuffy and not a guard protecting the heights of Mount Parnassus. If I was a grown-up in my career, my education, my international culture, I was also a "good joe"—fit, handsome, virile, happy to be still young and the one crested cock in a flock of pullets. It was fun to be "one of the boys" while knowing I was actually a Sicilian grandee with relatives in castles all over Europe. I wanted Edmund to be proud of me and I knew he was. Or hoped he was. He'd had such a wild and well-documented past that I was constantly jealous.

When I slept in my apartment and not his I wrote:

> *I miss you but I know that we'll be seeing each other very often and that we'll put our lives together.*
>
> *Remember that I am very jealous and that you've to reassure me that you're not sucking or not even lusting after God knows how many boys. I am the O-O (double-O) man, the Only One.*

CONSTANCE SAYS, "I feel a bit cheated that you were never that jealous over me."

Ruggero says, "Did I ever have cause?"

"No, absolutely not."

"Women are more trustworthy than gay men. Gays think it's a part of their liberation struggle to be promiscuous. Once AIDS came along, of course, the stakes were higher; survival meant fidelity. But so many men cheated even so, got sick and infected their partners and blamed it on an ancient indiscretion resurfacing only now or said the doctor had stabbed them with a dirty needle, or the unfaithful lied and said they'd experimented with intravenous drugs—anything was better than admitting they got fucked by a trick. Possessive lovers demanded their partners give up marijuana and booze and cocaine, which could weaken resolution and lead to a misadventure. Edmund had slept with thousands of men and his sexual curiosity remained as high as ever, even if he'd lost his erections. When he was young and desirable he could permit himself periods of chastity, but now with age he needed to prove himself constantly. I know that he blinded his wandering eye for me."

"We had a nice domestic life. He named my apartment the Domus, an allusion to Nero's Domus Aurea in Rome, though mine was a bit less luxurious. Sometimes I made Sicilian recipes for dinner or more likely we went out to a restaurant (Mexican, Italian, Japanese, Indian) or he made dinner at his place. He invited me often to the ballet and I took him to the opera or to Carnegie Hall or the movies. It was strange at the ballet to sit beside this old chubby lover on a cane while watching the real gods and goddesses dancing onstage. I couldn't help desiring these long-legged men in tights with their perfect butts and the bulge of their codpieces and wondering how to meet them, where and through whom, but I gallantly accompanied my old man to the impressive lobby upstairs (did people think he might be my grandfather or that I was his gigolo?). We never ran out of things to talk about—music, English and Milanese friends who came to visit, Italian politics (I read the *Corriere della Sera* and listened to RAI on the radio), his sister, his novel, mine. I translated three of his stories, which were published in the *Cultura* supplement of the *Corriere*. I loved seeing our names printed side by side. When they break up, couples often wonder what they ever had to say to each other; of course what they discussed were their plans, their schedules—and in the case of a new couple like us, their love. I would often say my heart was about to burst because I was so much in love. Or I'd say I feared that Edmund would never love me as much as I loved him. But we had real subjects as well.

Sometimes he'd talk about his age and how he'd be dead before long, just after he'd found true love. I told him that no human being knows how long he'll live, that I, so much younger, could be dead of an aneurysm tomorrow or he could live to be a hundred (which I'm sure we both rather dreaded).

Or we discussed the psychological or moral aspects of our novels, because those dimensions are quite real in fiction and give it its animation. It's what readers compute and critics debate. People who say fiction is abstract like music, is nothing but pattern and development, or who insist it is sound and repetition as Gertrude Stein argued, are clearly wrong. No one ever read *The Making of Americans* twice—or for pleasure. The only problem with reading fiction is that it doesn't prepare us for the opacity of real life nor its tedium. The thrill of fiction is that it gives us the illusion that life is legible, character integral, cause and effect logical, love central, and the pace breakneck.

Edmund thought it strange that I, the image of Sicilian virility, would be writing about an eighteenth-century castrato. I told him that yes, superficially, it was an odd choice, but my novel was really autobiographical because both my hero and I had such mood swings about art, either elated or tormented, and we both pursued the absolute in art and love. I'd told Edmund how miserable I was as a teenager imagining that I might die before I'd become immortal as a composer. Now I knew that my recordings would be played forever by admirers of the baroque. And he thought my novel might be published.

I also thought the innocent, defenseless boy was Edmund himself, the boy I wanted to protect, even if that meant "unmanning" him. Just as the Duke's daughter, when abandoned, becomes mad, my abandoned exes went crazy.

He rarely smoked marijuana but once when we were high he confessed that he would make me immortal by writing about me, that I was the handsome and devoted Ranieri to his melancholy, deformed Leopardi. I wasn't happy with this pairing since I wanted to be the creative genius, though I was happy to be thought of as the handsome young aristocrat who saw to it that his friend's work was published and his grave honored.

It was all absurd since there would be no immortality and the world was hurtling to an early destruction.

He told someone else (who repeated it—Americans always repeat it, feeling tattling is their moral obligation)—that I was a true Romantic and an aristocrat. Of course I couldn't object to that characterization; I certainly held Romantic values, and I couldn't claim to be among the world's disinherited.

RUGGERO AND CONSTANCE were sitting comfortably by the fire. Hobbling on his cane, he'd just prepared them baked swordfish under a layer of olive oil, bread crumbs, and capers preceded by *bucatini all'ama-triciana* (pasta with a sauce of tomatoes, pork cheek, red pepper flakes, and olive oil cooked over a slow flame for two hours). Yes, the store in their town had pork cheeks (*guanciale*). He was keeping a diary of the dishes he served and the accompanying conversational topics, which Constance thought was an unnecessary strain to be "brilliant."

Suddenly the phone rang. Ruggero answered in four languages (not Sicilian, which nobody spoke). "Who should I tell her is calling?" To Constance he said, "It's Jason for you."

She turned a lobster red and said, "Yes? No, no problem. What's up?" Her question provoked some angry curses Ruggero could hear from where he was sitting. "No," she said, "this is not really a good moment." She snapped the phone off.

There was a long silence like a strong silk thread Ruggero was slowly exhaling, which floated across the room and began to tighten around her neck. She looked at her hands in her lap, which weren't writhing only because she'd commanded them to be still. Every time she looked up she met his dark eyes which he'd scrubbed clean of all significance. Was he furious? Intrigued? Impatient?

They'd been living far from friends here in the Engadin, making their little meals, reading their memoirs to each other. There were daily food deliveries from a shy, mole-like teen and visits from the boisterously cheerful doctor whose Swiss-German she couldn't understand and who always left behind an anesthetic odor as if he had vinegar not blood in his veins and who would scrub his big blue hands on arrival and hold them up like freshly skinned rabbits.

Their lives were so invariable and eventless that this horrible phone call from "Jason" had made their time together suddenly intolerably boring. Ruggero hated being a prisoner of a cast, which itched constantly. Worse, suddenly he *hated* being confined with this faithless bitch with her American twang, her moods, her lack of culture, her *vulgar* American admirer. He no longer loved her. He hated her. He'd been a fool, imagining a young woman of such beauty could love an old man. She'd put up a good show, but as an Italian "friend" had remarked, "If you made only 20,000 dollars more than her every year, her love would be believable—but you have *millions* more." He'd thought he'd been rich enough, virile enough, interesting enough to keep Miss Inconstance mesmerized in spite of their age difference, but now he saw there was no fool like an old fool, that in his vanity he'd been deceiving himself that she truly loved him, and perhaps she did intermittently as an only daughter looks up to her father. Foolishly he'd thought in his fury she'd want him to marry her out of romantic emotion but now he suspected she knew that by Italian law his immediate relatives would inherit everything unless he made her his wife. Boiling over, he thought of her as a greedy, materialistic whore; he'd *never* trusted her and she bored him as well with her bubble-gum culture. Now he knew why she went out every day for such long walks.

At last she said, "Jason is a bored, lonely American I met at the store."

"Slut!" Pause. "Why did you give him your phone number?"

"I thought you might like to meet him if you were getting tired of me."

"Good idea. Phone him. Would we have lots in common? Is he a banker from Idaho? Or did I get that wrong—a farmer from Iowa? Handsome? Young? Totally heterosexual? Phone him! I'd like to meet him." Ruggero angrily thrust the phone at her.

She broke into tears. "Have you gone crazy?" After she'd wiped her eyes and blown her nose, she smiled a little smile. "I spoke too soon about wishing you'd be as jealous over me as you were over Edmund."

When Jason came to dinner, after Constance's objections and Ruggero's tiresome insistence, Ruggero could see he was a contender. He was tall, blond, smiling with perfect teeth. His gestures were too broad and his voice too loud as if no one had ever pointed out to him the difference between indoors and outdoors. He was the kind of American man everyone used to admire—trusting, optimistic, friendly, masculine, the kind who shouts across open fields.

Ruggero asked him if he wanted a drink and Jason said "Scotch, neat." As he took a seat uninvited, Jason smiled guilelessly at Ruggero and said. "So nice of you and your daughter to invite me for a drink. I don't know anyone here. I'd love to invite you for dinner though I'm not much of a cook."

Ruggero said, "What chalet are you in?"

"The old Weisweiller place."

"Oh. Nearby. It's a lovely chalet. Big. Very old." Ruggero smiled, thinking that's where Inconstance went every day for her "walk," which never seemed to leave her with the pink cheeks or cold ears being outdoors in the cold should produce. "Are you here with your wife and children? Is that why you need such a big place?"

"No, I'm alone. I've been divorced for a few years. No children. Honestly, I just rented it sight unseen through an agent because I'd heard it was very good skiing here . . ." He lowered his voice. "And I wanted to try something new."

"How nice that you met my daughter, something new for you to try out," Ruggero said with a crazed smile. "She tells me you've been seeing a great deal of each other."

Constance was in the kitchen making the hot chocolate but she suddenly stopped moving and listened. Ruggero could hear her silence and attentiveness.

"Oh, yeah, it's been great. How long have we been seeing each other, sweetheart?"

When she didn't answer Jason looked puzzled and said in a soft voice, "Two weeks?"

She came in and handed them their hot chocolate and she said, "Ruggero is my husband not my father."

CHAPTER 5

Jason didn't know where to put his eyes. They kept moving around the room with the purposeless energy of newly struck metallic balls, not yet settled in holes or in range of the flippers, just idly speeding here and there. Finally he stood up and said in a new little voice, the one he must have had as a nine-year-old, "Should I just leave now?"

"Not at all," Ruggero roared. "It's not your fault you were lied to. Anyway, Constance, as she's called, will undoubtedly see you tomorrow during her afternoon walk. But it's unfair to you, Jason, that she gives you only an hour of her time. Surely you deserve more time to enjoy fully such a magnificent piece of tail."

"Okay," Jason muttered, "I'm out of here."

"Wait!" Constance ordered sharply.

Both men looked at her.

Constance said, "Ruggero, you've always insisted on your sexual freedom."

Ruggero muttered, "Here it comes."

"And you always told me that I was perfectly free."

"Yes, to walk out the door . . ."

"But I don't want to leave you."

"Keep me as your capon?"

"I'd say you're the cock of the walk."

"Greedy girl, you want two cocks."

Jason said, "Is he insulting you? I won't let another man insult my girl."

"Shall we have a duel? Pistols at dawn?"

"C'mon, guys . . ."

"I may not want to share you with this lothario from Winnetka."

"My name is Jason. And I'm from Akron."

"And how do you feel about sharing? When I'm out of this cast, I'll be rogering her hard and long twice a day. I've kept you well fucked even with the cast on, right, sweetheart?"

"What's happened to you, Ruggero?"

"No man likes to be cuckolded. Especially not an old man. Right, Jason?"

"I wouldn't know, Rog, old man. I've never been cuckolded."

"Just stick around, Constance. Wait till she gets restless and is on the lookout for new merchandise. She'll cuck you."

"This is intolerable," Constance said.

"For you or me? Or for all three of us?" Ruggero asked. "What's the name of that French bedroom farce—*Nous divorçons?*"

"Is that what you want?" Constance asked. "A divorce? Really? All that talk about how much you love me? Unto eternity?" Constance had somehow thought she could keep both of them in her life. She loved both of them.

Ruggero looked at his motionless hands. "I thought we were happy together."

"We were. We are."

"Then what's the problem?"

"There is no problem."

"Except?"

"You're old."

"And what? Aren't I able to keep up with you?"

"Of course."

"But you want a back-up plan?"

"No. I just like Jason." She looked at Jason. "Very much."

She thought, Ruggero is getting older. The main problem with older lovers is that, statistically, they die before you. They don't catch your references. They haven't heard the same pop songs, seen the same movies. If Ruggero gave me a child, at least I'd have him. Or her.

Maybe Jason will still be around when Ruggero dies. Of course in my momentous life I've learned to count on no one. All is maya. Whereas the Buddhists think transience is the best argument for giving up all desires, we pagan Christians know that we can enjoy the exquisite passing moment but recognize that it will be surprisingly brief. She looked at Jason as if she'd known him and loved him feverishly in a previous life, one that she was remembering only now.

"How do you like that worn-out old pussy?" Ruggero asked.

Jason said calmly and unsmilingly, "I found out I liked it fine once I got beyond the worn-out part."

Ruggero crowed as if to say touché: "Constance, so which of us has the bigger dick?"

She looked away and thought, At least Jason is wonderfully attentive and doesn't expect constant praise of his body and manliness. Strange to say he seems much more sure of himself, less egotistical than the Sicilian prince but no less vulnerable. Jason makes me feel more desired, more desirable. I always feared Ruggero, as if at any moment in a vortex of self-absorption he might push me away. And his rages, if he feels his authority is being challenged or his character is being questioned . . . Jason has that rare quality—rare, at least in my experience—of being not stingy in his quiet love, not even aware that he's dosing it out. I wonder if Ruggero's hostility will scare him off?

Jason and Constance smiled at each other at the same moment, a tender complicity that Ruggero noticed and that frightened him.

Ruggero, putting aside his irony, asked, "You may not have thought this out, but what are your plans? I don't want to pressure you, Constance, into choosing, since I'm afraid you might choose him. By mistake. But I'm sure neither Jason nor I want to share you, the way Tibetan women take several husbands. You're as far from Lhasa as you might be from Rosario, Argentina."

Constance looked to Jason for a reaction, and this impulse froze Ruggero's heart.

Jason said, "I would like to live forever with Constance."

Ruggero said, "And you, Constance?

Constance felt she was bungee jumping into a chasm. "I love Jason. I want to live with him."

Ruggero said, "Two weeks ago you were desperate to have reassurances from me. You sensed I was no longer in love with you. *Magari*," he added, using the Italian that meant would that it might be so. Then he looked at Jason and said, "*La donna è mobile.*"

"He means women are fickle—but I'm not."

"Will this be your third or fourth marriage, Constance? Someone said to Liz Taylor, 'You don't have to marry them to sleep with them.'"

Jason said to Constance, "I can't think of you living with such an acerbic man."

Constance: "He's not usually like this."

Jason: "I think I should be going to let you two hash this out. Maybe it's too soon to decide. But you know what I hope, Constance." Jason rose and moved swiftly to the door, pursed his lips at her in a long-distance kiss, let himself out and was gone. Ruggero made an exasperated sound.

After a pause Ruggero dragged himself on a rollator to the bathroom but then tipped over on the threshold. Constance shrieked, "For God's sake let me help you!" and rushed to his side.

"Leave me alone!" Ruggero barked. "You've humiliated me enough today."

Constance withdrew her extended hands as if burned and shook them in the air.

She went back to her chair and watched Ruggero struggle to his feet, urinate, roll back to his chaise longue, pull himself down, sit there bleakly, and begin to cry. Surprisingly, she didn't cry. She felt she could do nothing and bit the inside of one cheek. She wanted to kneel beside him but thought she couldn't have it both ways—betray him and keep him as a loving friend.

Her thoughts went to Jason. He wasn't arrogant but he was normally proud, no more. When she said he had a beautiful body his penis shot up and he said in a mucus-muted voice, "No woman ever said that to me before." She realized Ruggero expected praise and barely noticed when it was rendered to him.

She felt guilty thinking of Jason when Ruggero was crying. But she couldn't help but think of Jason's hairless torso, the golden filaments under his arms, his reddish scruffy beard when he went down on her, his touchingly small white buttocks when he crossed the room to bring her more wine, small and almost blue, boyish but muscular, that blend of boy and man. She remembered that's what Lady Chatterley liked when she saw the gamekeeper in the shower.

But it wasn't his body alone or mainly that she liked. It was his goodness, the sweetness of his smile, the American boyish friendliness. He was obviously loving, unreserved, unafraid to give of himself. She remembered those last lines of Herbert's poem "Love":

> "You must sit down," says Love, "and taste my meat."
> So I did sit and eat.

That was the generosity Jason always showed her, the hospitality of his love. With Ruggero she longed—painfully longed—for his affection, but he measured it out absentmindedly. Jason gave it freely.

But now that he knew she was married and married to a difficult old man, would he sense she was too complicated, suspect she was a gold digger, think she evidenced bad judgment? Was she more than he bargained for? There must be some reason he hadn't remarried in the last eight years. He must be suspicious of women or easily spooked.

She thought she must stay with Ruggero tonight. Would he do that for her if he was the one leaving?

Maybe. Maybe not. He would be worried about leaving his new nest unfeathered. That first night he'd returned from Sicily, as he told me once, he'd rushed to the substitute teacher's side, not to Edmund's. If he was breaking up with Edmund, he didn't want the teacher to suspect that Edmund was anything more than a friend. He even told

Edmund later, "I knew you. You held no secrets for me. I didn't have the same hold over him yet. I knew he liked my big dick, my wealth, that I was a confirmed top, that we were very cozy together, watching old episodes of *Golden Girls* together in bed, but he'd had several other lovers before me. He swore he loved me but everyone says that, or almost everyone. I couldn't be sure. We didn't live together yet—that took six months before I convinced him. We didn't even see each other every night. He had so many friends. And he was younger than me and handsome. If you, Edmund, feel lonely you can always hire a hustler. I think you can even make them go to the movies with you for a fee."

Of course that was thirty years ago and he, Ruggero, had surely mellowed in the interim. And now she was the young one and she was leaving *him*.

Was she leaving him? That thought had surprised her. She hadn't been plotting it nor chafing under Ruggero's dominion over her. She loved him. She was familiar with all his quirks, with the white spikes in his beard like tusks, his vanity, his exquisite manners, his high-voltage energy, swooping around doing ten things while she, stupefied, did one if she was lucky. He was curious about everyone and everything, a curiosity that often took a turn into jealousy.

She liked the freshness of Jason's body, the gold of his hair not touched yet with white, the tight fit of his skin on his arms and legs and torso. The skin on his elbows had not thickened yet, become a pad like the bottom of a dog's foot. Yes, Ruggero worked out constantly at his home gym, careful not to let his forearms become muscle-bound so as not to interfere with his harpsichord playing. She liked the pinkness of Jason's nipples, his hairless chest, in contrast with Ruggero's hard brown functionless tits and the gray and white thatch on his chest.

She hated the harpsichord.

But more than that Jason was young and American and plebeian enough to have grown up with democratic values toward women and African Americans and even *hoi polloi*, the rabble. His political correctness was innate, not a concession. To go from Ruggero to Jason was like passing from the barometric pressure of the valley to that of the mountaintop, a freeing, a lightening of the atmosphere though a challenge to the hiker's lungs. Would she burst with relief, with joy?

Ruggero was intelligent, not easily outraged but outrageable nonetheless, whereas she couldn't picture Jason ever angry or even disapproving. Maybe if pressed too far he could be indignant. Who knew? Maybe he could be an ax murderer. She'd met him only two weeks ago. She knew she could cuddle with him without having sex. If he cooked it was nourishment not performance. If he looked at her it was admiration not competition. Ruggero was competitive. Once when they'd Skyped from different cities (he was on tour) he'd leaned in to his miniature image on the screen and said something. She thought he was giving her a compliment but when she asked him to repeat it, he said, "I look wonderful today, don't I?" and she hastily agreed.

Ruggero had stopped crying and they were holding each other in the dying light of the short winter day. There was a part of her (a large part) that wanted to run over to Jason's chalet and fall into his arms, to secure her life to come, but she couldn't leave Ruggero in the dark, in his cast, in doubt. She had to console him. That's what women do. Console him . . . But what sort of consolation could she bring Ruggero if she was going to leave him for another man? A younger, richer, fonder man?

She'd been disappointed so often in love and been so happy with Ruggero that she wondered if she was making a terrible mistake now. Would Jason turn out to be a short-tempered philistine? A cruel egotist? It was grotesque to weigh one man against another, but Ruggero was the happy narcissist, and his good manners, his courtly tradition, inhibited any unpleasantness that threatened to escape him except when he was truly angry. He might behead her but he would never be rude. Wasn't she better off with a coldness she knew than a warmth she couldn't guarantee?

Yet when she thought of Jason's welcoming arms and smile, the American overwarmth of his chalet that immediately suggested shedding clothes, when she thought of his tenderness and his appreciation of her as a woman, the calm radiance of his face as he looked at her with nothing as abnormal as awe but with something as companionable as complicity, the look of a man who preferred women to men (not all that common), who understood other men mainly as fellow communicants at the altar of the feminine, liked them well enough if they weren't serious rivals (few were), then she melted, felt herself drawn to him. He liked all women and could flirt with someone's grandmother and bring out the coquette in her, or turn a conversation with a faceless telephone saleswoman ten hundred miles away into a moment of light seduction, who never ran afoul of twenty-first-century feminism because his respect for—but more importantly his fascination with—women was always obvious. Men of his sort just liked women, couldn't do without them, preferred a daughter to a son, felt an intimacy that remained reciprocal and never (she was sure of it) led to merging, not even in old age, which neuters most couples.

Ruggero smiled sardonically, "You have that faraway look in your eyes. Go to him. Eat the funeral meats at your wedding banquet."

She stood, reached a hand out but didn't touch him and rushed away. Jason was standing just inside his front door and took her in his arms and kissed her till her lips hurt.

She felt dizzy as if she were a child being passionately whirled about by the arms. They sat on the edge of the couch with its flamboyant red flowers woven into a mustard yellow background; they looked and looked at each other as if it were a game of who would look away first.

They talked late into the night about her relationship with Ruggero. Jason was very sympathetic about Ruggero and the only aspect he exaggerated was the age difference, which he pitied unnecessarily; admittedly it was great but they scarcely noticed it. No daddy issues. No incest. No condescension other than the "normal" aristocratic superiority shown to *Amerloques* (as the rude French call Americans, something Ruggero thought was funny and had adopted).

Just as she'd worried over Jason in Ruggero's house, she fretted over Ruggero now. It wasn't as if she'd outgrown Ruggero or that he'd come to annoy her. She loved him and knew she would agonize with jealousy if he found someone new (a woman would be worse than a man—she wanted to be the only woman in his life). When he was in hospital with his leg broken she'd suffered constantly. Was she overestimating her independence by imagining she could leave Ruggero with impunity? Had she acquired a false serenity because he'd been with her constantly during his convalescence? Because he couldn't hobble away?

Then she dwelled on Ruggero's brusque refusal to father a child with her. "You'd bring a human being into *this* world. She—or he—would never forgive you."

What would she feel if she could see another woman over there? A tall blonde with tiny features, the only appeal Brunnhilde had had for him during the last two years of their marriage?

To be sure he was the most enduringly enigmatic man she'd ever known. We never love someone we can understand. Only a mystery remains fascinating. His knowledge in so many disciplines and his curiosity about most of the other ones, his almost autocratic sureness of taste, his inexhaustibly social nature, his patience and wonderful diplomatic skills—in all those ways he was incomparable. But she knew that under his warm, sunny Sicilian ways there was a blue Martian heart. She'd seen from the email correspondence with Edmund that despite Edmund's lamentations Ruggero never veered a millimeter from his self-interests as he understood them. He'd once said that what he admired the most about his best friend, a Roman, is that the friend never did anything, not a single thing, that he didn't want to do—not a single walk on a hot day, not a single coffee with an unappetizing old uncle. This single-minded inflexibility was chalked up to the outrageous eccentricity of the friend (who was a parentless millionaire and unburdened by obligations), but Constance knew that Ruggero had gradually, over a long life, become similarly egocentric.

Oh, he was a nice person, indisputably, everyone agreed, kind to animals (though he didn't own one), partial to children (though his own, to hear him, were shallow, smug materialists and philistines whom he barely tolerated), a cheerful but reserved host, proud of his ancient family. But under his unreadable amiability Ruggero radiated disapproval. Few people, however, ever felt its evil rays. He had some childhood friends, lots of musician colleagues—but few adult friends, just two or three.

She could see his shadow as he stood and sat back down—their houses were that close. She tried to scrub him from her consciousness but she knew him so well. And, yes, cared so much for him.

Jason and she made love, she grappling him, he steady and serene. Not superior. Attentive.

The next day after their cozy breakfast he caught her at the window looking at Ruggero's chalet. Ruggero knew how to order food from the store, he wouldn't starve, but she imagined him falling and ending up in broken fiberglass on the floor.

Someone such as her who has been over years the constant object of jealousy (and the subject of an equal but opposite fear of being abandoned) feels an enormous relief when she's finally released. But also feels she has lost status. She's like the analysand who's proud that her case has been terminated, she is finally well—but has no one who cares about her dreams anymore.

Jason stood behind her and held her close by the waist. He didn't say anything but she felt his silence was interrogatory. At last she shrugged and said, "It will take a while." He went into their room and made the bed. He came back into the sitting room and brooded over his cell. Then he turned on the radio and settled next to her with a sigh on the couch holding a book. After a while she touched his thigh with a noncommittal hand.

Ten minutes later he jumped up and said, "Let's go for a walk down to Nietzsche's house." They both bundled up and put on boots. His were laced and took a moment; hers slipped on.

The sun was brilliant on the crisp snow. She felt the moisture in her nostrils freeze and the sun lay a cold, hostile hand across her forehead. Her ears were warm inside her fur-lined hood. She rather liked that Jason and she were both nearly anonymous and sexless in their coats, though she was a foot shorter. She looked back at their boot prints in the snow; her feet were half the size of his.

Being outside and with a goal made her less sad. Moods were such delicate things and she thought she must strategize hers before they defeated her. What were you supposed to do? Feed yourself positive messages. "You're with a handsome, sweet man who adores you." Why would adore have to rhyme with bore? "Remember, you left Ruggero, he didn't leave you." Years ago a shrink had said to her, "The unconscious can't distinguish between leaving and being left." Was the unconscious really that stupid? Is that why she felt abandoned?

She took Jason's arm with her gloved hand. A German-speaking couple with an apparent age difference as great as hers and Ruggero's passed them and nodded guardedly; she found the age disparity innocuous. Endearing. Jason seemed happy that she was holding on to him; it made her optimistic that he appreciated her affection.

If she were Sicilian she would sob or laugh, but she was only a tepid, confused American and she'd have to wait to see what she felt.

If she could "act ahead of her feelings," as the same shrink advised blithely, she would smile at and snuggle with Jason until he became a habit and Ruggero a memory. He phoned and spoke to Jason and asked him to pick up two suitcases for Constance; Ruggero said a driver was meeting him very early in the morning. Jason agreed and volunteered to come now.

"Alone, if you please."

"Of course," Jason said, as if it were obvious.

"I wonder where he's going?" Constance said, feigning nonchalance, a bit wounded he wanted Jason to come alone. "Probably Sicily."

"Why do you say that?"

"That's his safe space. He's like Antaeus; he draws nourishment from the ground."

Jason frowned and said, "I'm sorry. I don't know who he is."

Constance crossed the room and hugged him. "I didn't know either until a week ago when I googled his name." She kissed him and felt her eyes fill with tears, as they always did when she knew more than the man, any man. "He was some sort of ancient Greek myth, the son of Poseidon and Mother Earth. He drew all his strength from the earth. When they were wrestling, Hercules lifted him off the ground. Antaeus became weak and lost the battle. Anyway, Ruggero draws his strength from Sicily. He's always reminding us that Scarlatti was Sicilian, the father not the son."

Jason kissed her and whispered, "I draw my strength from you."

He suited and booted up and soon enough returned with two big suitcases. He put them on the bed and she opened them. So many half-attempted identities, failed aspirations, memories—it was a sort of diary of hopes and disappointments, like most diaries. She looked at him and finally said, "Uh . . . forget it."

"C'mon, what were you going to say?"

She laughed unspontaneously and said, "I don't remember—how embarrassing."

He seemed slightly miffed. "As you wish," went to the kitchen and poured himself more coffee from the thermos. Talking loudly from a room away, "He barely said hello. He'd cut off a leg of his jeans to accommodate his cast."

"He did?"

"Yes, and he was all packed. He must have been in a hurry. The house was a mess."

She thought, "Ruggero is resourceful. And stubborn." Almost guiltily, she smiled at Jason. He smiled right back, which she wasn't used to. Maybe that was an American thing. Reassuring smiles.

Automatic smiles.

When she saw a uniformed chauffeur take Ruggero's luggage out to the car and help him on his crutch over the unshoveled snow, anxiety gripped her and she imagined running out and throwing herself at his feet, one in fiberglass with his bare toes blue with cold. She'd beg him to take her back.

Hold on, she told herself. Don't forget the constant anguish he generated in you. The hard part is over—leaving him. You were in daily anguish that he'd leave you without warning. He didn't want children with you because he couldn't be entangled with you to that degree. Now your only job is to settle into happiness.

She woke up in a panic after several missing-the-train dreams but her flailings and mutterings awakened Jason too and he spooned her. He insisted they sleep in the same bed and in the nude (she'd always worn an oversize t-shirt and panties with Ruggero and he'd slept bare-chested in boxers). Nudity at first felt invasive and, when she was having her period, even obcene, but there were moments like this when she could feel him getting hard against her buttocks. She fell back into sleep and dreamed she was in an eighteenth-century painting, a Fragonard, blue silk ribbons against white rump, a terrier tugging at one end of the sash and a naked pretty boy with wings and a smile holding up a round mirror, which reflected her tiny features and raspberry and crème fraîche complexion.

With his strong arm circling her waist and his erection wilting against her, she lay still in the enchantment of his love as he breathed sleepily on her neck. She saw a five hundred-euro-an-hour shrink for three times who had a terminal-nurse, super-sympathetic manner that irritated Constance. Dr. Blumenfeld had that raddled, bony look of a woman who ate nut cutlets, drove a Mercedes four-door, had been abandoned at the altar of her local Zwingli church by a Bulgarian psychiatric intern—and had refused to take on new male clients for two years after. Dr. Alice Blumenfeld worked in a historic village peasant house that had been gutted and modernized inside leaving its wattle and thatch exterior intact (if fireproofed). She sat in an engulfing black leather Barcalounger. Her austere waiting room had faded plant prints on the wall and was intimidatingly underfurnished. She could dimly hear the previous patient being let out through an adjoining corridor. Then the doctor waited five minutes before admitting Constance—what was Alice doing in the interval? Checking her messages? Tidying the used kleenexes? Reading her notes from the last session? Preparing her bill?

Constance resented the compassionate look on Alice's face and the absence of advice. Constance jabbered relentlessly about Ruggero, cataloguing all his faults, starting with his show of fake concern and his lack of genuine empathy.

Alice said in her absurdly faint voice, "If I might hazard an interpretation, I would ascribe his indifference to his great age. Jung established that the old man facing death withdraws his psychic energy into his failing body in preparation for the great adventure: death."

"Well, that's silly," Constance said. To which the sadness on the doctor's face only deepened. Constance explained, "Ruggero is the most vigorous man you could meet. He's a famous baroque performer and tours one hundred and fifty days a year. He likes to have sex every day. He can wear the jeans he wore when he was twenty."

"I can feel your resistence but might we say he's a narcissist?"

"If you were a Sicilian prince growing up in a village that shared your last name and if you were famous throughout the cultured world—"

"Why did you leave him?"

Dr. Blumenfeld gave her a prescription of alprazolam for anxiety.

Why did she leave him? she kept asking herself. Good question.

Did she want to feel her partner's equal, which she certainly did with Jason? Was she tired of constantly scrambling to keep up, like a little girl rushing to match her daddy's long stride? Did she want her love to be repatriated—to know her lover's references and he know hers?

The real reason was that she wanted to have children. Ruggero quite rightly said he was too old to go through all that again. And he would be ancient by the time they were teens, dead when they were graduated from university. His sons who by Italian law expected to inherit would be very unpleasant if they had to share the pie, outsize as it might be. Nor was she sure he'd be a good father. His sons hadn't turned out well and now, as he faded into his seventies, he was more and more irritable. With guests he was wry and funny and had impeccable manners; her women friends thought he was matchless. But recently when they were alone he was morose or he snapped at her. He hated her taste in music (long ago she'd given away her Rachmaninoff recordings); nor could he bear her tiny art collection. He'd declared Chagall was the worst painter of the twentieth century and that flying blue cows were suitable only for an opera lobby built for the good burghers of Paris or Manhattan. He didn't like the obviousness, the predictability, of her conversation and recently compared her unfavorably to Edmund.

She had said, "But he was eighty and a famous writer who'd known everyone; I can't and don't want to compete with him. Maybe I'll compete with your other lovers, male and female."

Perhaps he was just stir-crazy from sitting inside that chalet and having no one else to talk to, though she went into raptures about his "life writing" and encouraged him to stay in touch with his few friends and cousins throughout the world. If the Skype conversation was in

English, the only language she thoroughly understood, she'd go for a walk so he wouldn't feel inhibited. She feared she bored him (was Edmund the only constant in his life who didn't bore him?) and when she'd return he'd always share a bit of gossip with her.

Briefly after a virtual conversation with a "member of the Great World" Ruggero would be glowing, and she could hear little bursts of intermittent chuckles coming from him like the aftershocks of an earthquake. He'd give her a full report of what he said, she said, they said and for a few minutes he might try to talk in the paradoxical, goofy style he and his friends shared, full of radical shifts in register from hieratic to demotic, serious to frivolous, flipping lightly from a big subject (the Czech baroque) to a small one (the best way to cook perfectly round potatoes fondant in the oven). Sometimes she could parrot back to him something he'd said on another occasion, but she wasn't as cultured as he or as inventive (or as *old*), and the conversation would necessarily deflate, the lightest, brightest silvery dirigible collapsing into a gray little burnt agonized relic of itself.

She couldn't keep it aloft. She drew blanks, she didn't catch references, she didn't laugh at the right places, she didn't even know that Vivaldi had been a red-haired Venetian priest. She was more suited to Jason. With him she could play the sophisticated Europeanized American. She knew he was the darling of a large, rich Midwestern family. Whereas Ruggero didn't see his parents, his beloved grandfather had died and he had no siblings, only coroneted cousins, Jason seemed to be in constant touch with his family, so numerous that she couldn't keep them straight.

She wondered if they'd like her. They sounded . . . well, "puritanical," as Europeans mistakenly said of Americans in general. They didn't smoke, they drank Diet Coke not wine with dinner, skipped desserts, said grace before meals, tried to look clean and anonymous but never fashionable. And each member of the famously rich family had a "cause." Constance didn't know much about these causes, only what she'd gathered from Jason's pillow talk. One sister, Tamasin, devoted all her energies and money to the wild white horses of the Camargue in France. Another, Erica, was a devotee of the Armenian American composer

Alan Hovhaness, a sort of mystic-ecologist enthusiast of "world music," who'd become an early disciple of Sibelius. Erica, working with Hovhaness's Japanese widow, the last wife of six, tried to bring the late composer's vast output into print; he'd written sixty-seven symphonies and had over four hundred opus numbers (not counting the hundreds of early works he'd destroyed). Jason's mother had mounted a campaign against alcohol, which had destroyed *her* mother; in their circle people looked at you strangely if you invited them over "for a drink" (better to say "pop," the Midwestern word for soft drinks). The father had invented some small but essential part of every computer, made a vast fortune, retired and taken up fly-fishing in Montana. He'd become a sort of monk of the outdoors. He was so grizzled and slight he looked years older than his age, seventy. Another son photographed wild lilies; he traveled the world but spent most of his time in Turkey with a handsome Kurdish pal near Lake Van.

That was so American, Constance thought—to have millions of dollars and become an indefatigable worker for some strange cause. Only gradually did she discover Jason's cause, which was composting garbage or something—it involved filling drawers in the house with worms and scrapings from the dinner plate. She supposed he knew that sounded weird, which must be why he seldom mentioned it and didn't practice it in the Engadin, though occasionally he did get the odd call from another cultist. She looked up worm composting online and could ask informed questions over dinner. She investigated the best diet for worms:

> The ideal diet for composting worms is nonacidic fruit and vegetable scraps. Grains, bread, coffee grounds, tea bags, and pasta are also fair game. Aged grass clippings, hair, and herbivore animal manure are compostable. Add shredded black-ink newsprint in moderation. Torn or shredded brown corrugated cardboard is acceptable. Clean, crushed eggshells add grit and calcium. All items should be small. Larger items should be cut up or run through a food processor. Smaller pieces break down faster. This reduces odor and discourages pests.

She teased herself for being like the Darling in that tale by Chekhov, the impressionable woman who takes up the enthusiasms of each of her three husbands—first the theater, then the timber trade, finally medical treatment for animals. Had she made a bad trade of Vivaldi for worms?

And yet he was so sweet. When she told him that she'd bored Ruggero, he put a note beside her coffee cup the next morning: *You could never bore me.* She'd smashed one of her toes riding her bike back in Ohio and she'd always kept it in a sock and out of sight around Ruggero, who disliked anything ugly; Jason made a point of kissing it.

CHAPTER 6

Ruggero never felt sad. Sometimes anxious, but that usually had to do with an upcoming concert. Now he felt disoriented. He'd always had the theory that women were more reliable than men, that they could remain faithful when one was away on tour, that they could be pacified for neglect during days of practice or musical research by little "romantic" attentions (jewelry, dinners in three-star restaurants, compliments). Women provided company but didn't demand companionship. He thought of them as accessories, like gloves.

Now he didn't understand anything. He'd treated Constance with courtly consideration, made love to her almost daily, reassured her during her crises of faith in the durability of their relationship, listened with patience to her memoirs, elevated her taste—and allowed her to put her pretty nose into every aspect of his life. When a baby cousin was christened in a Renaissance cathedral in Umbria and various cousins had attended the event via Zoom, he'd allowed Constance to stand beside him though she couldn't speak a word of Italian beyond *auguri*.

He'd outlived so many of his friends, who'd died of AIDs, COVID, or just the ordinary ailments (cancer, heart disease, pneumonia) of old age. With Constance, she'd kept him company, admired his body, been fascinated by his musical lore, loved his hours of practicing the harpsichord, "the very sound of home," she'd averred though Brunnhilde had hated the "arthritic jabbering." Constance had always been there when he fell asleep or woke up in the middle of the night. She kept herself busy somehow during the day and didn't disturb his parsing of the original Vivaldi manuscripts (which were all online now); he thought she read "women's" heartfelt books about "problems" by Jodi Picoult. Thankfully, she never discussed them.

Now, after Constance's abrupt decamping, he thought of visiting Sicily for a month and relaxing by speaking his own langue and talking to his tiny ancient nanny and eating his own cuisine (he missed Sicilian desserts). He went but stayed only two weeks. He visited his mother's tomb in their sixteenth-century family church. The stonecutter had added a delicate little intaglio crown over her name, Regina, and her dates. His nanny, who was blind, hugged him and didn't approve of his slender body. In Sicilian she said, "*Faccitta muriu, facciazza campau*," which meant "Little face (timid) died, Big face (brash) lived." Then he'd headed to New York. He was in constant touch with that amazingly beautiful boy Colin, who kept Ruggero intrigued with daily attachments and videos of himself dancing around his studio apartment (which Ruggero had subsidized for years) or working out with an older man who insisted on being called African American, though his skin was lighter than Ruggero's. Everyone in America needed an interesting identity. Of course the mainland Italians call the Sicilians *gli africani*.

When Ruggero Skyped Colin (they'd arranged to talk) the boy was bare-chested and wearing a blue-and-red jock strap. The self-described African American had kept Colin on a rigorous workout schedule and now he was still lean but his shoulders were broader, his legs more muscular.

Ruggero had tried his luck on Tinder and not been very successful. Everyone was looking for an employed top, someone aggressive in bed; so far, so good. But people were turned off by Ruggero's age and slim body and ethnic look. Men who were looking for daddies wanted them overweight, WASP, and wealthy. Ruggero wanted to be liked for his talent, charm, looks, not for his money. New York was unbearably transactional! Nor was Ruggero turned on by these simpering "boys" of thirty with their bad, confident taste in music, their expectations of being taken on shopping sprees and eventually put up in a little bijou studio in Brooklyn, their pretended sheepishness when they presented him with their eleven-thousand dollar American Express bill. He didn't mind *paying* for the shopping sprees, he just didn't want to sit on a gray velvet sofa like an old man and admire the gigolo's endless *essayages* of overcoats, one more sweeping and cashmere than the last. When he dropped one particular gym-rat airhead, the would-be "kid" snarled, "You're getting old, Ruggero, you're getting old."

Though the "boy" himself was well past his sell-by date. Colin was really young, sweet, and genuinely affectionate.

Ruggero was aggrieved that everything on these "dating" sites was quantified—age, dollars, degrees, inches, amount of hair, address. He knew he was a real catch but was frustrated that these trashy New Yorkers couldn't detect his worth. They didn't even know where Sicily was and confused it with Sweden or Switzerland. He carried in his brain and body the reflexes bred by centuries of refinement, class confidence, culture, and wisdom. Unlike these factitious bodybuilder New York males, he was genuinely masculine. Whereas these locals were parodies of working-class stereotypes, as if in America only firemen, cops, and construction workers could be active in bed; for Americans the exception was the concept of the masculine gentleman, which seemed to be a fantasy about James Bond or the Playboy Mansion, a "gentleman" only in name, his signs of gentility his shoes, marksmanship, and swift seduction techniques with women. No knowledge of the classics, history, modern languages, entertaining, the art of conversation, and the way to walk, sit, and moderate the speaking voice were required. The idea that a reserved gentleman in the salon could fuck the shit out of them seemed to elude these gay bros.

He didn't dare let his women friends at the Museum of Modern Art or at the Colony Club or the rich Italian expatriates or all those girls working for the UN or WHO or at the Italian Academy at Columbia—didn't dare let them know he was single, since he was rich, heterosexual, sexual, cultured, an Italian aristocrat. Whereas boys were "slim pickings" as he'd learned to say (he was compiling a list of Americanisms), women of a certain age were "thick on the ground." The last thing in the world he wanted was an arthritic seventy-year-old heiress with a face-lift and a Chanel suit. Let the real gay men with their laughter and serious social aspirations serve as their capons.

He'd met Colin through Constance, who'd picked him up at a Connecticut pool party. She'd never seen such a beautiful young man— lean, exercised body, radiant smile, eyes to match the pool, long straight hair (blond and bronze and platinum that you wanted to sift from hand to hand like treasure), strong legs covered with gold dust, hairless chest and, paradoxically, no treasure trail, a confiding but less than confident manner, something about him on the spectrum but at the most beguiling end of it.

He was talkative and insecure, not like the usual beauty, not like a model, say, who knows his face is his free pass anywhere, who knows his very presence is conferring a favor on you, who knows best not to say anything. Most beauties, like royalty, ask you bland questions about yourself and let you chatter on as their eyes, unfocused, scan the room and their smiles randomly punctuate your monologue. Colin talked about himself and his writing. As Ruggero was to discover, he was the most incoherent conversationalist and the most lucid essayist, as though tons of gravel had to be sifted to reveal a few grains of gold. He tried out a million ideas, interrupted himself, told shaggy-dog stories, wiped the saliva from his rosy, sculpted lips and plunged into a new cacophony, as if all the tunes on a disc were being played at once. There was no way of sorting out his meaning, though it was crystal clear once he typed on paper, as if that act sequenced out all the competing melodies.

Ruggero remembered Colin as the best sex of his life and who was strangely savage in bed, so in contrast with his sweet manners and kind, Christian thoughts. Sexually he wanted to slap or be slapped, to abuse or to be dominated. He liked to kiss deep and long and dramatically, leaping up from his chair and seizing his partner by the lapels, lavishing enough tongue on him to moisten every orifice and organ. Two big hairy male hands could encircle his narrow white waist, a neck to be choked. Like a great dancer he was always slightly off-balance, dipping perilously close to the floor, nodding submissively into a muscled clavicle, leaning back suddenly and precariously out of a steadying embrace.

Ruggero found him bewitching. Whereas with some of these depilated over exercised thirty-five-year-olds with their smart repartee learned over sodden dinners on Fire Island, Ruggero could stay hard only by imagining another man or woman, the instant he touched Colin's rump he was erect and leaking pre-cum. The boy had the most wondrous, silky-smooth, rubbery *culo*. And to penetrate it, millimeter by millimeter, was to achingly enter a terrestrial paradise. Pleasure was the most ephemeral thing in the world but also the most memorable. Every fiber of his body remembered this wonderful boy.

"What do you think of the existentialists?" Colin asked while they were still stewing in their own juices. "Have you ever read Sartre's *Being and Nothingness*? I talked to my friend Karen about Sartre today. We were sharing the world's best omelette with caramelized onions. We were in this wonderful little café on Tompkins Square. Of course you've eaten the best food in the world in Sicily. I'll have to take you to this café. Did you ever see an existentialist in Paris? Did they really wear all black? Did they forget to bathe? Of course you can speak French. . . . I want to learn German in order to read Husserl in the original. Those philosophical words like *Begriff* or *Ding an sich* are so hard to translate. Do you think one can have pure concepts which you keep trying to approximate with words? Or do words always precede ideas?"

Ruggero scarcely knew what to make of this stew in which the most improbable vegetables floated up to the surface—a radish, say, or an artichoke. He asked Colin if he remembered that he, Ruggero, had a doctorate in philosophy with a dissertation on the reception of Heidegger in France and the francophone world. He felt a fraud invoking a system of thought he'd nearly forgotten, one that intimidated the uninitiated, the way Wagner did the musically naïve. "Of course Heidegger was inspired by your man Husserl."

"Would you like to see a short story I wrote? It's about a gay massage parlor. You would? Sincerely?"

"Yes, of course, if we could lie just like this and you would read it to me."

For Ruggero it was only a ploy to keep the boy naked and to be able to admire his body for the half hour of the reading, but he was suddenly snapped out of his drowsy delectation by the brilliance of the prose. Everything Colin wrote was visual and steeped in feeling, different feelings distributed over the four main characters—a nagging sister, her brother, the owner of the massage parlor, in love with one of his masseurs but unable to name his passion, and two of the boys, one a grifter who pretends to be a good boy, wise and devoted, and his cynical successor who has no illusions about the object of the boss's desires. Ruggero admired the stereoscopic perspectives, the force and economy of the writing, the mystery hanging over everyone's motives, the way everyone was either deceived or deceiving, the economical manner in which the boss's pathetic past was brushed in.

Ruggero asked himself for a moment if he could fall for Colin. He knew that a thing of beauty isn't usually a joy forever and that Colin was wonderfully convulsed with confusion, too beautiful to remain faithful, with too many options for him to be controlled. Ruggero thought he'd do better with someone like a penniless substitute teacher, kind and devoted, pretty but not too pretty, 100 percent passive, conventional, not too clever, someone in awe of Ruggero's pedigree, big dick, wealth, fame, who would be a good little wife parodying all his ideas but with enough papers to grade to stay out of his hair.

And then Colin said the shocking words, that he was writing a thesis on Edmund White, the forgotten gay novelist of the twentieth century, ever heard of him, and the way his failed novel, *Caracole*, embodied the ideas of Michel Foucault.

"Oh," Ruggero said, "I knew him for a while. He was a member of my artistic salon."

"What really happened?"

"We just drifted apart."

"That seems unlikely. I heard White was madly in love with you. Why would he drift away from you? *You* must have done the drifting."

Ruggero didn't like the direction this conversation was taking. "It was much more complicated than that."

"How was it complicated?"

Ruggero had noticed that Colin had a conversational tic of challenging everything one said. Was it his revenge for being the one who was fucked, or his unpleasant manner of asserting himself in adult conversation? Ruggero revised those theories—Colin must be in his midtwenties and it was old-fashioned to assign social roles to sexual ones, wasn't it? Now people were "power bottoms" or "twink tops" or given to "flipping." More importantly they felt no shame (or thought they shouldn't feel any shame) for any consensual sex act, no matter how abject or feminized. In Ruggero's day aggressiveness had been prized, as were "straight-acting" men *hors du ghetto* and "non-scene." The bigger your dick, the stronger your fucking privileges. Little dicks were conditioned to take it as normal they'd get fucked. But now that hierarchy too seemed to be crumbling.

All well and good as humane principles for advanced people to subscribe to, but everyone still wanted to go home with the tall, silent young man with the big arms and big crotch who spit periodically on the pavement.

"Edmund knew from the beginning that he wasn't my type. I'd never been with an older man and though I revered my grandfather I'd never had a moment of sexual curiosity about him."

"You knew what he looked like from the beginning."

"Yes," Ruggero said, "but people change their minds."

"They do? After swearing eternal fidelity? And constantly suspecting their partner of cheating?"

Colin went off on a long tangent about what his friend Karen thought of Sartre; she believed that he'd actually stolen all his ideas from de Beauvoir. Ruggero was used to this sort of American third-generation feminism. To him it was a sign of Colin's craziness that he assumed everyone would know who this Karen was, but he just said diplomatically, "*The Second Sex* was such a brilliant book. My foundation financed the second translation, the good one."

On cue Colin smiled then, snuggled, "You have a foundation?"

"A very modest one. Luckily I'm no longer on the board."

"But I'm very sure your recommendations must weigh heavily," he whispered as he touched Ruggero's cock. In a moment he had it hard again. Ruggero himself was astonished that his refractory period was so short.

After Ruggero had another soul-destroying climax, Colin stretched like a cat, grinned and said, "But really, why did you leave poor Edmund?"

"He was too old for me. You can't imagine—the rolls of fat, the tiny, functionless penis, the sagging breasts and the giant nipples with a history, the bizarre odor of skin fungus, his lack of basic hygiene, the rotting teeth and horrible breath, his leaking bladder leaving dark droplets on the pale carpet . . ."

"You're still in remarkable shape."

"I can still wear the same jeans I wore at age twenty."

"Yes, but you're only a stroke away from the same bodily disgrace."

Ruggero smiled. "I won't have a stroke."

"My father died of a stroke and he was five years younger than you and ran a mile a day."

"Why did you choose to work on White?"

"I should have chosen the great Sedaris or Garth What's his name. But I didn't want to go to Romania or Bulgaria or whatever. But White wrote too much! I like reading theory but not fiction. Scholars have worked more on Sedaris than White, who was too prolific, though Karen likes two of his books, *The Joy of Gay Sex* and the *Flâneur*, his masterpieces. People are tired of all that gay stuff. I'm working just on *A Previous Life*; I haven't read any of the others. It's old-fashioned metafiction and White himself is only a minor character."

"There's always the biography."

"In which you come off as the villain. How shocking to pay court so romantically and assiduously to an eighty-year-old and then heartlessly betray him." Colin spanked him playfully, "Naughty, naughty."

"Don't believe everything you read. You're the first person I've ever met who's even heard of White."

"It's true he's forgotten. If only I'd chosen Sedaris." Just as playfully Colin slowly pretended to soothe the place on Ruggero's shaggy buttocks where he'd spanked him. Then a new thought lit him up: "But didn't you like having such a so-called great writer emailing you three times a day and proofreading your own fiction and listening to you practice Fiocco on the harpsichord?"

"It was oppressive, especially when I thought I'd have to have sex with him—it was like being betrothed to an eel—all teeth and slime, except the teeth were falling out. And then he betrayed me. I was living with—"

"—the substitute teacher?"

"Actually he was a very distinguished drama professor who'd studied in Moscow. That's just what Edmund called him."

"That and Butt Boy."

"Anyway, one night after a congenial dinner White announced to my lover that he was still having sex with me. We left immediately and I sent White back his keys and we never saw each other again."

"It was true wasn't it?"

"Yes, but I'm not sure Butt Boy—now you have me doing it—ever trusted me again."

"Americans believe in honesty."

"Alas . . ."

"You *were* sleeping with White."

"Not really. Every once in a while I'd let him rim me or suck my cock."

"That's sex." After a silence Colin said, "Didn't you ever miss White? You had a lot in common."

Ruggero said, "Never. I never missed him. I'm very self-sufficient. I don't miss people."

CHAPTER 7

Constance had been living for five years in a twelve-room house on
Beechwood in the best neighborhood, Point Breeze, in Pittsburgh.
She would have been ashamed to show the house to Ruggero; he was
used to Renaissance palaces whereas her mansion had been built in 1905,
which Americans thought was old. Guests were impressed by the sumptuous marble bathrooms, the large, totally up-to-date kitchen with its
two dishwashers and two ovens (the previous owners had kept kosher),
its many "built-in" fireplaces, its imperial master bedroom with a copy
of a Byzantine cross over the bed. All the window treatments were color
coordinated with the bedspreads and upholstery and paint on the walls
and cornices with their hidden, indirect lighting. Everyone was wowed
by the basement with its media room, gym, and wine cellar. Upstairs, as
part of the original house plan, there was a billiard table in its own
wood-paneled room. The grounds were 1.4 acres and there was a fountain with a small marble boy hoisting aloft a marble dolphin. In the basin
there were three goldfish which were brought inside during the long
winter.

She and Jason had had two children. She was the proud mother of a
five-year-old boy named Mark and a one-year-old girl, Nora. Constance
loved Jason for giving her children, for letting her have children (the

other men in her life had forbidden her). Now she was glad she'd waited because they were beautiful to look at, perfect specimens like their father, bright and sweet. Mark was musical and taking piano lessons, staking out hours of practice on the baby grand tucked under the staircase. Secretly she'd insisted on a name that could be Italian—Marco. She was also thrilled he was musical. In her most private musings she imagined he was like Ruggero. She'd learned to steer her thoughts away from Ruggero but, yes, she was probably still a bit in love with him. Once you've seen the northern lights sweeping across the heavens, how can you be satisfied with mere stars?

Jason made her feel safe. She was smarter than him and most of his Pittsburgh friends, all those couples who came to dinner, ate the food the German male cook so expertly turned out, swooned over every dish and even applauded when he came out at the end of the meal in his white toque to greet them. Ruggero had taught her not to compliment the food—of course one had a great chef! The Pittsburgh executives and their young wives were all gone by ten thirty, the men to sleep before their seven o'clock arrivals at the office, still snoring in the back of the limousine, the women to be ready to get the children off to school. In the winter Constance got up when it was still dark outside; Mark loved his kindergarten and gladly let his father drive him to school. When Jason returned he sometimes went back to bed; Nora slept between them or babbled and laughed and Constance was so happy with her handsome, dull husband and her merry little girl with the violet eyes.

CONSTANCE'S THOUGHTS: I tried to get interested in the so-called cultural life of Pittsburgh, but I could look at the Marilyns only so many times in the Warhol Museum or study only so long the Japanese prints in the museum (bad ones by Hiroshige in aniline dyes) or look at the Stan Brakhage films or listen to the wonderful orchestra with all its chairs endowed by United Steel (the bassoons) or Wheaties (the flutes) or Allegheny Electric (the first violins). My husband and I commissioned a piano concerto from Conrad Tao. It was widely and admiringly reviewed and the orchestra took it on tour to Ljubljana, Łódź, and Graz.

But I was bored. I jogged for hours every day and ran (and won) marathons until I was so thin my breasts had disappeared (poor Jason). Pittsburgh was so hilly I developed monster calves. I served only the healthiest possible food, which frustrated our cook, who quit, lured away by some "friends" of ours. I never let my children taste sugar. I varied food groups, made us pescatarian. And Jason stayed as slender as the day I met him. He also played squash at the club.

His real cause, as I'd known from the beginning, was garbage and worms, which I prettied up by calling "ecology" or "greening the planet," though in fact he was browning it. I became a docent two afternoons a week at the museum. I attended the dress rehearsals of the symphony and soon became the president, which just meant I had to give more money. One day our Viennese conductor broke his baton in a rage. Such behavior wasn't very acceptable, especially when he wounded with a shard the harpist who sat in the Monongahela Manufacturing endowed chair. I gathered both halves of the broken baton and asked the maestro to autograph them. He was as embarrassed as I intended him to be.

I took Mark with me to the rehearsals; for a little boy he was so patient and attentive, curious about every instrument and which instruments went together. He loved his piano lessons and could already play "Für Elise" and the "Berceuse" of Benjamin Godard. He wanted to have oboe lessons. I wondered if he'd take to the harpsichord.

Though he was so young, he seemed sort of gay to me; his walls were plastered with photos of me. He didn't want to play sports because he feared hand injuries that would impede his piano playing. He'd made a cult out of Princess Diana though she'd been dead for decades. He was unusually fussy about his clothes and especially his nails. He let them grow long and pointy. I paid him twenty dollars for every nail I clipped. He had only one other friend, a fat, taciturn boy from school who could play the piano much better than Mark. When Mark was playing, the other kid, Horace, stood right behind him and pressed his crotch between Mark's shoulder blades. I caught them at it twice though I didn't say anything.

I had the most unscientific suspicion that Mark was actually Ruggero's son—fastidious, beautiful, a dandy, musical. As if some of Ruggero's sperm had been held captive for years in a remote cavern of my body. That was a theory, telegony, Aristotle had and that the Soviets backed into the middle of the twentieth century. Of course, I knew that couldn't be scientifically true. Ruggero had always made sure I was on the pill; it was irritating the way he'd monitored my birth control measures. And sperm couldn't live that long. Of course I was being silly. Jason was even more beautiful than Ruggero, and Mark was clearly his son. I amused myself, however, with this fantasy. I told Mark that he had an African American inheritance, but he didn't seem to register what I was saying.

The worst part of the week was Sunday morning when we were obliged to attend the Presbyterian church; I had read about Andrew Carnegie's lack of faith and firm belief in evolution. He refused to believe in a God who'd predetermined humanity would be sinful and then crucified his innocent son in order to win forgiveness of the very sin he'd thought up and willed into existence. God was a tyrant, obviously, and Carnegie refused to embrace him; eventually he believed in the Bahá'í faith since it encompassed the best in all the world's major religions. But even though Carnegie was the presiding spirit of Pittsburgh, the *Bildungsbürger* were grimly and uniformly Protestant.

ALTHOUGH I WAS not a believer, I thought that if I ever believed I'd be a fanatic. Going to church couldn't be a mild little social ritual for a believer; it would be as radical and painful as childbirth, I was convinced. I didn't share my views with anyone, not even my husband. After the many different lives I'd led, I found this one reassuringly tranquil and predictable. No reason to rock the boat. My husband was still hard-bodied and his beautiful face was the same as the one I'd first encountered in Switzerland, except it looked as if Jason had wept and the lines had come off his hands onto his face. Nora couldn't talk yet but she kept peeping her only word, "Hi!" Even in the crib she'd be babbling her merry little "Hi!" Mark was doggedly playing scales and, at least to my ear, getting markedly better. Jason and I would sit and watch PBS with earbuds but guiltily take them out and hide them if Mark ran in to check on us. "That sounds wonderful, darling," we'd both exclaim, though Jason omitted the *darling*.

I read the big biography of Edmund White and complained out loud about it to myself. Jason could hear me grumbling—sometimes my complaints erupted into speech. "Edmund, I'm sure, would have hated this Freudian approach to homosexuality! It's scandalous in this day and age. Typical of a heterosexual. Aren't people straight or gay from birth?"

Jason: "I doubt it. How do you know what he would have felt? Anyway, the last time I checked you were heterosexual."

"But at least not a heterosexual man. And I hate the way he abbreviates Edmund's *affaire* with Ruggero and pictures Ruggero just as a villain, whereas for a while he was Edmund's greatest love. And he broadened Edmund's musical culture and he always encouraged Edmund's writing. We owe Edmund's last two novels, his best novels, to Ruggero—well, to Edmund himself, but Ruggero injected him with energy and creativity. There are few men who do their best work in their eighties. Ruggero was like the young Nureyev rejuvenating the much older Margot Fonteyn . . ."

"Why don't you write a better biography, maybe just one about their *affaire*?"

"I don't know how to write. Would anyone take me seriously since I was once married to Ruggero?"

"You wrote a novel."

"A bad novel. A flop novel. Well, it was widely read, then was completely forgotten and now it's out of print."

"You're always looking for a project. You're always so bored and complain about how unproductive your life is. Why not have a real project? And don't you—well, maybe I shouldn't say this—but don't you feel just a little guilty about leaving Ruggero so suddenly? Not that I'm complaining. You left him for me. But isn't that all still a bit unresolved? It's none of my business. But it would give you a sense of accomplishment. Of course I wouldn't want you interviewing Ruggero if he's still alive. I'd be jealous. You could make clear from the beginning that it's a personal memoir, based on your own experience as well. It would fill your days. It might even clarify your own feelings. You've always identified with Edmund. You're the only person I ever heard of who's read all his many books. I can't bear them. All that purple prose."

"We don't even know where Ruggero is."

"Some of his cronies must still be alive. You could interview them. Not Edmund's—they would all have passed away."

"Don't say 'passed away.' Say 'dead.'"

"Why?"

"I can't bear to think my husband would say 'passed away.'"

Jason scowled. "I'll learn to say 'dead.'"

"It's like women who refer to 'the husband' instead of Stan or Henry."

"Vulgar, you mean?"

She just bit her lip.

The more she read the old biography, the more she thought of writing her own. She tracked down the biographer through Facebook and he couldn't have been nicer. She told him she wanted to write something about the Ruggero-White *affaire* because it might be of interest to scholars and she had . . . secondhand knowledge. The man assured her that at least in academic circles there was a growing interest in White, partly because he was riding the coattails of the gender fluidity movement (genflu, as it was called) and the Maupin groundswell. The man said, "There have been several scholarly essays unpacking his story, 'An Oracle.' But poor White, he wrote too much and no one is interested in the gay movement, though I'm convinced twentieth-century studies will come back."

"Well, you're doing your part. Your biography is a revelation."

"I'm so glad you're doing something about that Ruggero business. The Random House lawyer wouldn't let me touch that; we were all afraid of being sued."

"Really?"

"In America everyone sues everyone for fabulous sums. Anyway, I'm glad you're doing this because White gave me all their emails and wanted me to use them. He was afraid Ruggero would deny everything and just say White made it all up: 'He's a writer of fiction, you know.' White wanted me to substantiate his version; I promised him. Now you can do it and I'll sleep more easily."

"Could you send me the emails?"

"Oh, God, they must be in a file on my computer or in the cloud. Right now I'm too busy but remind me in a month after I've graded all these genflu essays. Soon they should decide if they'll give me tenure or not. I've been tenure track for seven years. If they give it I'll never have to write another book and at last I can be done with White and won't need my research materials. My wife and children and I will have a guaranteed income for life."

"Oh, I'm sure you'll get tenure. Your book is really excellent. Once you've put White behind you, what will you work on?"

"Nothing! I'll watch college football. That's what I really like. Maybe I'll review a genflu book a year, or make that every two years. Just to stay current."

Constance began to reread White's entire oeuvre. Her church friends thought it odd she was studying this obscure sinner, though they paid lip service to the notion that God condemns the sin, not the sinner.

She found the books, especially after the eighties, easy to read and conversational. Of course she concentrated on *A Saint from Texas* and *A Previous Life* and the late short stories he'd written in the Ruggero era. She said to Jason, "I've become the world's leading expert on a writer no one's ever heard of except for a few old queens, the last of the gays who were twinks when White died."

At last, after endless prodding, the biographer pushed the button and sent the archived emails between Ruggero and Edmund. Constance took a look at the email from Ruggero in the January when he moved to New York: "Anyway, I'm happy, very happy with my life that is centered on you and that gives me enough joy for everything. You will always be part of everything in my life because you *are* my life."

It was hard to imagine just six months later Ruggero would have ended his *histoire* with Edmund and moved on to the substitute teacher. Ruggero constantly assured Edmund how much in love he was; they had dinner almost every night, Edmund cooking. A few times they'd go to the movies or the ballet or opera. Often they had dinner with Edmund's famous writer friends. Maybe Ruggero was so amorous (and even jealous when Edmund would have dinner with an old student) because he was trying to convince himself that he truly was in love with Edmund. Dealing with the always thorny issue of Edmund's age, Ruggero started pretending in bed apparently and in emails that he was the father and Edmund the "boy." Sometimes Ruggero would be the sixth-former and Ed his fag.

They exchanged pages all the time. Edmund was writing one of his countless autobiographies. Ruggero gave him the constant praise and reassurance Edmund needed so badly. He also gave him ideas and provided him with details from his own years on the road. Edmund had never had a lover before with a 200 IQ; in fact, like Ruggero, Edmund had usually chosen lovers who were beautiful but of average intelligence. They were easier to control, especially if they didn't work and were supported or at least heavily subsidized. Michael was brilliant but proud to present himself as a redneck, impatient with Edmund's fussy manners, tender suscepti-bilities and cultural pretensions. But Michael also lived on the allowance Edmund gave him, which made him more dependable but no less irascible.

Edmund appreciated Ruggero's brilliance as a scholar of the baroque, as a musician, as a widely cultured man who knew everything about history (and remembered all the dates!) and of course philosophy (with a concentration in twentieth-century German thought, especially the Frankfurt School). Ruggero was a genius at explaining difficult, murky subjects. He had been immersed in the classics and could translate by sight passages from the ancient Greek. He wasn't snobbish about his knowledge; he wanted to share it with everyone. He handed over every-thing he knew to everyone without the least condescension or propri-etorship or fear that others wouldn't be interested or wouldn't profit from his research.

Oddly enough, in May 2019, as Edmund later learned, Ruggero had first encountered the substitute teacher, and Edmund had noticed that Ruggero was buying lots of new clothes. He asked, "Why the new wardrobe? One would guess you had a secret lover. I'm afraid I might have bored you after all this time—which would be normal. You told me you're easily bored."

Ruggero had replied immediately, "Of course not. No secret lovers. I hope you're as faithful as I am! And you could never bore me. Tell me how I could reassure you."

They made love less often, she gathered from their emails, though when they did, Ruggero would pretend Edmund was a cock-hungry slut who would do anything to get fucked, that he was a "greedy bitch" who was bewitched by his big Sicilian uncut cock. Later, Edmund thought Ruggero needed this pornographic soundtrack in order to stay interested at all. Ruggero had always been turned on by dirty words and by imagining Edmund was a desperate old queen who couldn't believe her luck in lining up this beautiful Sicilian fisherman (the old queen part was true enough, but it sounded less wounding if it remained a pornographic cue rather than a realistic description).

I had heard about the break-up from Ruggero, especially once, when he'd had too much brandy. He said, "Really, Constance. I wish I had never met that vicious old queen. I feel like that poor guy on Fire Island who ran over Frank O'Hara in his sand taxi in the Pines. O'Hara was drunk, the driver didn't see him sprawled asleep behind a hillock on the beach, the driver was just an innocent straight man, a working man— and for the rest of his life people whispered, 'That's the guy who killed Frank O'Hara.' A few knowing queens in New York, especially now that the biography is coming out, point to me and say, 'That's the Italian who broke Edmund White's heart. Who? You mean to say you never heard of the ridiculously prolific gay writer Edmund White? His French used-book translations are the stars of the bouquinistes.' Luckily my lawyers scared the biographer off from dealing with me in detail.

"I want to say, 'White, White, White! I've had it with White. What about me? I'm a famous musician.' I realize I sound like the Baron d'Anthès, who killed Pushkin, Russia's greatest poet, in a duel. Years later, when Russian journalists would come to Paris to interview Anthès, he'd say, 'Pushkin! Pushkin! Pushkin! What about me? I'm a French senator.'" Ruggero never took himself too seriously. He said, "The real story about Anthès is that he was always dueling over women to throw the court off the rumor—perfectly true—that he was having sex with the Dutch ambassador, who was keeping him in luxury and had bought him a lieutenancy in the Imperial army." Ruggero always had wonderful anecdotes since his memory was impeccable.

I said to Ruggero, "Don't worry. At least with the people who count you're more famous than he is. Nobody wants to think about that horrible old gay liberation movement. It's as passé as feminism—ugh!"

"But what if it comes back?"

"Don't worry. It had its moment in the sun and now it's been eclipsed."

She realized that her book would be a new thorn in his side. She had loved him—she probably still loved him. But he'd been too old for her, too easily bored, potentially unfaithful. Her handsome American husband was almost tiresomely faithful, but she'd rather be bored than constantly afraid. And she'd wanted children and he'd given them to her. That was a Victorian way of putting it, but it's what she felt. Few of her real feelings were politically correct.

She took a dive into Ruggero's and Edmund's emails for the summer and fall of 2019. They were passionate, sometimes with love passion and sometimes with hate passion. In July Ruggero had announced in person that he would no longer be Edmund's lover, that he'd met a more appropriate man, his age, at the park.

Edmund had feared some sort of rupture. He and Ruggero had gone to Fire Island for a long weekend in June. It was Ruggero's first time. As he later said, one of his most tormenting inner tensions was between his longing on one side for stability and fidelity—a solid home—and on the other his constant desire for adventure, his perpetual horniness. "It's agony; I treasure the security of a committed relationship and I'm constantly tempted by passing strangers."

Edmund could feel how conflicted and embarrassed and confused Ruggero was. Edmund's disabilities—his overweight, his age, his reliance on a cane—could be overlooked in the warmth of his apartment, the charm of his (often flattering) conversation, the taste of his delicious but seemingly effortless dinners, their utter solitude. But here, on the island, he was just a fat, lame old man. When Ruggero wanted to go on a moonlit walk on the miles and miles of boardwalks through the whispering pines, White couldn't go on after half a block. "I can't even take a walk with you!" Ruggero said angrily, and immediately apologized.

In her notes Constance wrote: I should point out how beautiful The Pines was (were): how better than to quote this fragment White himself wrote and that I found in his papers at Yale:

> Everything there was seductive. The little houselights winking through the pine branches like fireflies; the deer in a dark clearing, suddenly surprised as if they were clandestine lovers; the clandestine lovers, suddenly surprised, tentative and delicate as deer, boys who'd stopped in a puddle of jeans on the boardwalk; the passing boom and hiss of big New York gay male voices, endlessly joking and laughing; the breezes gently trailing like the sleeves of a kimono; the distant tympani of the surf pounding on the beach; the musky, spicy herbal smell of joints piercing through the scent of pines and pines and pines, unmistakable as the adolescent voice of a single resinous oboe amidst the adult conversation of cellos and basses.

After the drunken dinner on the porch, wine and chicken and candlelight and mosquitoes, Ruggero went off for a long walk. He didn't come back for hours. They were supposed to share a double bed. Edmund got under the sheets; it was cold enough out here for a blanket. The knotty pine walls were all beseeching eyes. Edmund hoped he wouldn't snore or fart or flail about in his sleep—that would undoubtedly be too much reality for the already disappointed Ruggero. Edmund examined his diaper rash, the huge dugs, his undisguisable stomach, cupped his hand to inhale his sour breath, glared at his micro-dick. In the midst of so much self-hatred—the first night of that sort out of many—he took his valium and fell to sleep.

He knew from the exaltation of his own youth in the Pines how exciting and depressing it could be. Everyone was as masculine and muscular (masc-musc) as a gigolo on the Riviera but here they were lawyers and doctors or real estate scions. From twenty-eight on he'd never felt young enough or beautiful enough or celebrated enough—that was the curse of the Island. To bring all these interchangeable Princes Charming together, each of whom had thought he was unique before and each of whom longed to be the chosen one, the Cinderella, and to show them they were all alike or even interchangeable members of the chorus. It was just like assembling all the summa cum laude students from public high schools across the country and putting them in one Ivy League university freshman meet and greet. Now everyone else was just as smart or smarter—their only claim to fame had been dashed.

"I stood on the Botel balcony for hours last night," Ruggero said, "looking down at the dance floor. Some guys noticed me, but no one came up to chat me up. I felt old and ugly and unwanted."

"Fire Island is a race nobody wins," Edmund said. "No matter how much facial surgery you have, no matter how much weight you lift or lose, no matter how great a fortune you earn, you'll always be one year older than you were the year before."

"At least you're famous—that's the best aphrodisiac."

"No writer is famous. And no one recognizes a writer's face. If you're a rock star, maybe, even as chubby and lined as Elton John."

"It seems you chose the wrong racket." Ruggero squirreled away these Americanisms.

"Tell me about it."

Edmund always thought that visit together to the Pines had been a disastrous misstep. Ruggero had seen all those hot young couples together and didn't want to be chained any more to Grandpa. White was a catch if you knew who he was, but people didn't recognize him, the way they would a porn star.

But the real dark or twilit night of the soul Ruggero went through was that he knew you couldn't build a life with an eighty-year-old. You couldn't adopt children, put together an exquisite house, build a circle of friends, share a life. "I'm jealous of your past!" Ruggero would say. "I entered your life too late." He liked to look at photos of Edmund when he was young and muscled and black-haired and handsome. He was still handsome if you liked that sort of thing. Ruggero didn't.

Edmund constantly praised Ruggero's looks—his pale olive skin, the big dick lolling like a river god between the smooth boulders of his testicles, nestled in the soft reeds of his pubic hair, a classical scene only Picasso the draftsman could have done justice to; his hairy chest, his torso a hard cuirass; his stomach as muscular as a tumbler's and as flat as a mesa; his blindingly white smile, the burnt-honey eyes, the heraldic nose, the Brillo hair; the overall look, alert and self-satisfied, of intelligence and virility joined, the mischievous scintilla in his glance and smile; the pink health of his full lips.

But Ruggero never praised Edmund's looks now, only of the past. Maybe he didn't like them. He surely disapproved of his overweight, which he pretended he deplored strictly on health grounds, though everyone knew that excessive weight in the seriously elderly posed no danger once one was past late middle age. Even their sexual behavior, Constance suspected, consisted of Ruggero admiring himself through what he fancied were Edmund's yearning eyes. "You love that big Sicilian dick, you greedy bitch! You can't believe your good luck to have that monster in your cunt. How do you like your young Sicilian husband? How does it feel to have a real man fucking your hole?" That's what he wrote he'd most enjoyed in sex with Lucia—admiring himself through her eyes.

In July for two weeks Edmund went to Berlin for several gay events. When he returned Ruggero came to his house and announced he was leaving Edmund for a younger man he'd just met at the park. Ruggero claimed proudly that he'd never lied to Edmund, though in fact Ruggero had met the substitute teacher in May on a gay dating line. Edmund gave him back his wedding ring and they both burst into torrents of tears and held each other for a long time, rubbing their hot, wet faces together. Ruggero pocketed the ring and left, his face marbled with sobbing.

Edmund wrote in his pacifying way that he thought Ruggero's only mistake was not to have indicated sooner that he was losing interest.

Ruggero replied:

You're right that there were no early warning signs—or, in retrospect, that if there were any I refused to see them since they would have been too painful for you and me to face.

It's also true that wounding others is something for me almost intolerable, even physically intolerable, I mean. I recognize that as my biggest and worst flaw. It's probably the single most significant thing I worked on with my psychotherapist in London—the fact that it was so totally unacceptable to hurt those who are so dear to me that for years I could go strongly and heavily against my own feelings.

In retrospect perhaps I should have been "softer" with you and tell you something like, "I feel that things are changing a bit and that I should not think anymore of exclusivity and begin seeing people my age and see what happens, etc" but I wonder whether it would have been any better really. More thoughtful perhaps (and certainly more scheming). I don't know. So often with good intentions we make the most horrible mistakes.

What I'm certain of though is the absolute truth and sincerity of my feelings towards you all the time, and not one second only I ever pretended or schemed or studied anything. You remain one of the most important persons in my life and I want to be absolutely sure that you know this.

I'm pretty sure I was in competition with all the great people you are friends with, all the young writers and talented people you know, with Michael himself, I felt so insignificant compared to them and craved your attention. I still do, every day . . . Am I running away from that race perhaps?"

The understanding between them was that they would remain steadfast friends but no longer have sex. When Edmund complained to an Italian girlfriend that Ruggero was secretive and compartmentalized and included that email by mistake in one he sent Ruggero, Ruggero was full of rage and indignation. To his mind he was above reproach; his fits of anger were rare but always excessive. The ultimate betrayal, he thought, was to be bad-mouthed by two friends. And of course he was transparent and said everything! Or so he claimed.

In August Ruggero went back to his family home in Sicily, though his parents and beloved grandfather were dead now. Ruggero wrote ecstatically about swimming in the nearby ocean, about the elegant restoration of the house he had been overseeing, about his discovery of *two* family trees, one that said in the thirteenth century one of his ancestors had been made a *magnifico* by the Sicilian king ("that's equivalent to *lord*—of course I'd never tell an American that. Also, we have always been lawyers, doctors, property owners, never warriors").

Ruggero said he knew that Edmund was married to Michael and that they had spent twenty-plus years of history together. Even if they got divorced and Edmund married Ruggero, Ruggero would still be jealous of that shared past. Ruggero said if he could take twenty years off his life and give them to Edmund he would (that way they'd both be sixty), but since that was impossible Ruggero could only resent all those years he'd missed with Edmund. Edmund's age turned out to be the major problem, though that should have been obvious from the beginning. Edmund was so literal-minded that he'd believed in all of Ruggero's avowals of eternal love. Ruggero said that in the first part of a relationship one didn't know what one would come to feel later; no one could be consistent. Edmund admired the way Ruggero esteemed his own ability not to hurt anyone— that was his biggest "fault." Edmund felt he himself was like Giselle the peasant girl in the ballet who naïvely believes in the love of the young lord and who dies when she realizes he's deceived her. He wasn't sure he'd have Giselle's generosity of spirit when she vows to save her lover from the spirits of angry virgins (the Wilis).

And then Ruggero wanted to "build" a life with someone, to have children with a young partner ("We could name our son Edmund, would you like that?")

Ruggero insisted that he was not rejecting Edmund. Edmund admitted that he couldn't help being jealous of the substitute teacher. Ruggero hastened to say, "Jealousy is human and understandable but my feelings for you are *sovra human*," by which Edmund understood "superhuman."

Edmund felt suicidal, but when he mentioned he had saved up a cache of fifty valiums, Ruggero laughed and said, "Valium never killed anyone but all those pills might give you a terrible headache." The readiness of Ruggero's response and his mocking, deflating tone made Edmund suspect he'd weathered similar threats before and had decided always to take a hard line against that kind of melodrama. Edmund felt chagrined but he couldn't help but admire Ruggero's calm refusal to be blackmailed emotionally.

In his masochistic way Edmund insisted that Ruggero take the new lover out to Fire Island for the Labor Day weekend. "I'll never go there again," Edmund said. "You might as well enjoy the last big weekend of our share." Later Edmund called a housemate to ask for his impression of Ruggero's "boy."

The housemate, who played the crazy queen but was really thoughtful and discreet, said, "He's no Edmund White but he was perfectly nice."

Edmund asked himself if anyone anywhere might love him. Then he thought of a young man in Rome, Silvio, who was a gerontophile, a movie star, the author of five novels, a millionaire—and someone who'd always said he was in love with Edmund. Now Edmund got in touch with him and Silvio said he was hopping on the next plane and would stay with Edmund for two weeks, that they'd rent a car and drive to Maine, see friends of Edmund's and also of Silvio's (since Silvio liked old men he knew rich and famous ones all over the world).

Edmund, all innocently, told Ruggero that Silvio was coming to stay with him and that they might start an *affaire* and that Edmund would at last be able to get out of Ruggero's hair. Edmund might even move to Rome. In that way Edmund would stop annoying Ruggero and Ruggero could devote himself completely to his marriage with the substitute teacher and to their little son, Edmund.

Ruggero was so wounded, jealous, and angry. He said he'd never been so anguished. Whereas he'd taken up with someone who was completely different from Edmund (young, beautiful, fresh), Edmund had just *replaced* Ruggero with a rich young handsome talented Italian who *also* liked old men (how unfair!).

Ruggero couldn't sleep. He didn't sleep for three nights. He had never suffered like this. He felt so jealous, so obsessed, so possessive: "You are mine and I could never be more possessive of anyone else than with you." Edmund really was a witch, a sorcerer. Just as Ruggero was about to put Edmund in the freezer, here he was again, bubbling on the front burner. Oddly enough his greatest worry was that Edmund would find Silvio to be better sex than Ruggero. Ruggero even reported that a Sicilian friend had asked him, "How would you feel if Edmund preferred that Roman guy in bed?" Ruggero: "I'd feel terrible. Miserable." Edmund thought that this sexual competition sounded strange. Lots of people in the world were good sex, a very few of them lovable, most of them hateful or boring. To Edmund being good sex was neither a necessary nor sufficient condition for being lovable, though God knew it helped.

When Edmund mentioned that he and Silvio were planning on a car trip through Maine, Ruggero wrote, "Why did I never think of that? That sounds wonderful. You and I must go on a little car trip." Later Edmund realized that was impossible because Ruggero didn't have an American license and was afraid for immigration reasons to be caught driving in the States with his international license. And Edmund no longer had a license (could never have passed the eye test).

Ruggero thought of coming back early from Sicily to plead with Edmund not to move to Rome. "It would be dangerous for your health! What if you had another heart attack over there? Do you think Silvio would help you? The moment you were no longer the famous, brilliant novelist, he'd drop you. I've asked around about him. His 'husband,' that old aristocrat, he's bled for his fortune and parked him far away in a village. The old man will die soon and Silvio will inherit everything. He's already picked up two or three fortunes from old men. He pretends he likes old men because he knows he can dispatch them off and no one will suspect. I've done my research; everyone in Rome knows about his schemes. Rome is a village. You know that. You've lived there."

Later Ruggero would say after they'd quarreled, "I saved you from a famous liar. He told you he supported his old lover, who's one of the richest men in Italy, who lives in a castle! I won't make that mistake twice—I won't stop you the next time."

Edmund didn't believe anything Ruggero said about Silvio. Ruggero in his agony wrote that he loved Edmund more than the substitute teacher. "There now, I've said it. I love you more than him."

When Ruggero returned from Italy he didn't arrange to see Edmund that first night but only the second (perhaps he'd reserved his homecoming for the substitute teacher). He did admit, shamefacedly but proudly, that when he arrived at JFK, he'd tried unsuccessfully to force his way into the departure lounge for the evening plane to Rome because he knew Silvio was leaving New York then. "I didn't want to kill him, honestly I didn't, I just wanted to see him, but security wouldn't let me in."

Edmund was a bit flattered that a Sicilian man would think of murdering someone out of passion for him.

Edmund and Ruggero sat together in the same leather chair and wept for two hours, holding hands and looking into each other's eyes. "My darling, my little boy," said Ruggero, "don't ever leave me again. Promise you'll never leave your Big Boy."

Edmund didn't point out that it was Ruggero who'd left him for the substitute teacher. Nor (big mistake) did he ask Ruggero now if he'd leave the other guy. Edmund didn't want to set conditions, partly because he thought Ruggero wouldn't meet them and would angrily hold out for his freedom of choice. And mainly because he didn't want to spoil this charged moment of passionate reconciliation. And he recognized that Ruggero wanted a future with a man his age.

Then Ruggero led Edmund into the bedroom and made angry love to him.

Edmund was totally surprised since Ruggero had decided to be faithful to his new lover. In the calm after the storm of passion, as they were lying in bed and smiling in astonishment, Ruggero said, "Since I've already been having sex with you for years, it's not really cheating for us to go to bed."

Edmund thought the substitute teacher might not see it that way, but, hey! He remembered that when years ago his French lover had left him for a richer man, he'd come back to Edmund for sex. His best friend in Paris, the Mme de Merteuil to his Valmont, had congratulated him: "Now you're the other women, *la seconde*, a much stronger position." What deplorable morals they all had!

The next day Ruggero wrote in his fluent but not always accurate English: "You are mine and I could never be more possessive of anyone else than with you."

Ruggero spent more and more time with the substitute teacher—planning their little family, Edmund supposed. Certainly whenever Ruggero was around a little child, boy or girl, he would melt with pleasure, though he appeared to be reluctant to commit himself to a dog, much less a child. Nor did he seem eager to get married, though marriage would be advantageous for visa reasons and the substitute teacher was very, very keen; a lawyer had advised Ruggero that even a common-law marriage, if it went on long enough, could end up costing him dearly. Almost in passing, Ruggero had warned Edmund that a spurned Michael as a divorcé could fleece him—yet another reason for not getting married or divorced. Ruggero was the least materialistic of all men, but he was aware of practicalities, it seemed.

CHAPTER 8

They entered one of the most passionate periods of their affair. It was perhaps the last real blaze of the fire they'd built and unmade, the sudden flames released by the collapsed structure of the half-charred logs.

They decided they were master and slave, which stylized, and provided pith to, their roles of submission and domination. Ruggero would call Edmund "slave" and spit in his face, martyrize his nipples, slap his ass, fuck him brutally. Ruggero would keep up his monologue: "Give me that pussy, you whore! She loves that big brown dick, doesn't she? You lucky bitch, you're really getting fucked by that big uncut Sicilian dick. Slave, get on your knees and suck that cock that smells of your ass."

It was then that Edmund wrapped twenty-dollar bills around Ruggero's dick and pretended he was the hapless American tourist who'd stumbled on the fisherman asleep on a beach in Catania. Ruggero-the-fisherman caught the nerdy American—wearing his toy clothes (Izod shirt and mustard-yellow shorts)—staring at his huge penis and the Sicilian wagged it mockingly in the tourist's hypnotized eyes, stunned with desire by the snake-charmer.

Edmund felt comfortable in this role because it excused him for being so old: a slave was ageless, his submission more important than his desirability. A slave was desirable because he was property. Ruggero exulted in his role. He proudly wore the leather harness that Edmund buckled around his chest. He wielded the cat-o'-nine-tails Edmund pressed into his fist. He fastened the studded black leather collar Edmund provided around Edmund's neck. Edmund knew he had never betrayed Ruggero by thinking of someone else in sex, and he was sure Ruggero was faithful in that way at least, no matter how unappetizing Edmund's body was. Their encounters were too momentous, their identities too strong, to permit any infidelity in thought. They were two souls communicating, even if there was sometimes static on the line.

In the evenings Edmund kept mooning around the phone and checking his emails. Would Ruggero wake up at midnight and declare, "It was all a terrible mistake. I love you. Come back to me." Edmund had written that in a letter to Alfred Corn, his oldest friend.

One day Michael shouted at Edmund, "He's not coming back! Get that into your head!"

Ruggero had never felt so handsome and virile. He would look at himself in the mirror beside the bed and say with astonishment, "I'm so handsome!" Or he would look down at his erection and say, "I love my cock! I'm so proud."

Edmund would praise Ruggero for his overflowing testosterone and Ruggero felt he'd never been so slim or well coiffed or so lustful. He would jerk off three times a day. He sent photos of his beautiful erection from the toilet stall at Juilliard; Edmund said it was a "two hander" because it took two fists to hold when erect. Ruggero would say that Edmund and the substitute teacher were "lucky bitches" because they both got to feast on his perfect masculine body. Edmund said, "I guess I'm just a slave in your harem." Ruggero exclaimed, "Not just another slave. You're my empress."

Rather comically Edmund would sit on his invalid chair and be pissed on. Quick shower, a big bath towel, and they'd rejoin each other in the bedroom, Edmund kneeling on all fours, presenting his ass to his young or at least younger lover. After a few minutes Ruggero would collapse back on the myriad white pillows, their whiteness matched only by his brilliant smile and the cloudless whites of his eyes. Edmund would suck the dungy dick; the taste didn't frighten him off at all. He augmented his mouth with his hand. Love makes us all ludicrous.

Ruggero seemed happy with these new roles. Sometimes he'd put Edmund's heavy kilt around his naked waist. Edmund would lie flat on the floor and Ruggero would stand hovering over him. Edmund would look up into the shadowy depths and see his testicles and the violent liftoff of his penis. Ruggero would then kneel over Edmund's face and plant his asshole right on Edmund's mouth. The suffocating wamth and dark- ness and moisture of the heavy wool fabric isolated and fetishized Ruggero's ass, balls, and dick. Edmund would prop himself up on his elbows so he would be at the right angle for sucking cock. Both of them thought it was a sign of their superior intelligence and sensual powers of seriousness and concentration that they didn't joke or make marginal comments or remind each other of their real social identities. Ruggero was no longer this charming Sicilian prince with the 200 IQ but this big dick sheathing and unsheathing itself into a mouth too generic to be just Edmund's.

Afterward Edmund would lie with his head on Ruggero's chest and Ruggero would suddenly sit bolt upright to check the time so he wouldn't be late for his coffee date with the substitute teacher at Eataly. He would wash ass and cock carefully (avoiding telltale scented soap). He was careful.

Many times Edmund would say that Ruggero must tell the substitute teacher that they were still having sex. Ruggero said, "I know you so well. I know you better than myself—honestly I do. I can read your mind. But I can't be sure of him. I don't really know him that well."

"You still should warn him. He can take it; he's a gay man almost forty, a New Yorker; knowing that you were deceiving him in secret would break his heart."

The next day Edmund emailed Ruggero and said he, Ruggero, was at the height of his powers, passionate and so horny all the time. Ruggero wrote back, "I'm so glad that we can enjoy that together, the flowing testosterone I mean. You lucky greedy boy caught me at the right time . . . I'm almost jealous of your good luck! I've never been in better physical and mental shape and never so sensual and sexual."

Ruggero repeated that the substitute teacher and Edmund were both "lucky bitches" feasting on his virility and beauty.

At this time Ruggero commissioned a professional photographer to make nudes of himself, but he was disappointed by how tired he looked in the photos and he didn't like his skin color. Edmund pretended he liked them but finally said they made Ruggero look Peruvian.

Edmund wrote him an email saying, "Yours is the best tasting butt in Christendom."

Edmund's beloved sister, Margaret, decided to have a family reunion, attended by some of her adopted Black and Asian and possibly Italian children and by their beautiful, sweet Texas cousin, a retired lawyer. They dined out at a "nice" restaurant, Margaret made a fancy dinner, they went on a boat trip up the Chicago River, looking at Marina City, the corncob-shaped towers where their mother had lived on the fifty-eighth floor (she who was afraid of heights but was always up for a challenge).

The three adults were all in their seventies or eighties and had played together as children in Dallas. Naturally the talk in that meandering, relaxed Southern way kept turning to distant memories and the present pains of old age. Finally, Edmund burst into a rage. "I just lost the love of my life because I was too old. For me it's not a laughing matter." He didn't want to dye his hair or follow youthful fashions or have cosmetic surgery. But he wasn't yet reconciled to being old, certainly not to sharing this tragedy with other wry, rueful, genial, guffawing seniors.

When Edmund returned to New York he raised the S&M stakes with Ruggero: "Now I'm obsessed with the thought of living in a cage in your guest room. Intermittent fasting, kept nude, let out to do chores for you, sometimes permitted a legal pad for scribbling, listening all day for my master's footsteps, frequently flogged (he'll know why I deserve it), drink out of a dog bowl, led on a leash to the Master bedroom, positioned for a blowjob or fuck. As a Christmas present it would be fucked on its back so it can look in its master's eyes."

Ruggero responded: "That's so hot, such a big turn-on. Nobody could see you or talk to you without my approval and I'd control everything, decide everything. You'd be totally my property, totally submitted."

IN THE NEXT year and a half they had sex once a week with diminishing ardor though always with the pornographic muttering Ruggero had first learned to like with his cousin. Ruggero moved in with the substitute teacher. Ruggero would email Edmund twice during the day without fail and Skype him every evening at seven. He would keep Edmund abreast of their social life with the teacher's theatrical friends (Ruggero had no American friends). Once a week Ruggero saw a gay psychotherapist Edmund had found for him but at least according to Ruggero they mostly chatted about American politics. Ruggero listened to the Italian news every day and read *La Repubblica* and the *Corriere della Sera*. With the teacher he was picking up more and more American slang (the teacher didn't speak other languages). Their loft was sixty steps straight up, obviously not chosen to accommodate the eighty-year-old obese crippled White on his cane. He would gamely pull himself up the stairs just as Ruggero's grandfather had years ago reportedly ascended the steep steps in his *casa*.

Ruggero had exquisite taste and had furnished the ballroom-size living room with a mixture of antiques and fifties-modern pieces. Edmund had contributed a silver lamp and nice pictures—certainly Ruggero after their final breakup must have looked at those gifts with unrelieved hostility. He must have been tempted to bundle up those presents and ship them back—but then perhaps he reasoned he'd given Edmund gifts every bit as precious. It was a fair exchange. The teacher had hung three banal theatrical posters from his days as a chorus boy.

Every time Edmund infuriated Ruggero it was over the subject of the substitute teacher's constant fawning over Ruggero. "Teach" would call him "Bello," which Ruggero had once called Edmund; surely the teacher had learned the word from Ruggero. The teacher would constantly fondle Ruggero in front of Edmund (Ruggero *never* touched the teacher). When Edmund complained, Ruggero said, "He does it mostly in front of strangers. He's very insecure. And maternal."

"He'll make a nice mother to your children."

"He will!" Ruggero agreed with a big, unironic smile.

When Edmund invited three of his famous writer friends to dinner at the loft, Edmund tried to "draw the teacher out," as his Texas mother had taught him to do, but the teacher was too busy caressing Ruggero and calling him "Bello" to be able to respond (or to help get the meal on the table). He was shy in front of new people.

When they were all alone on the sidewalk the famous friends said, "Do you think he knows?" meaning, "Does the teacher know you and he are still lovers?"

Two of the three said surely he knows but Edmund and the French novelist said, "I'm sure he doesn't."

Edmund said, "Ruggero promised to tell him but I'll bet he didn't."

"And what about all that stroking and kissing?"

"Ruggero says he does it because he's maternal."

Ruggero emailed that he had so enjoyed the evening and wasn't his food delicious?

Edmund couldn't wait to tell him that the famous guests had thought the teacher was dull and middle-class with all his fondling. Edmund wasn't sure the others had mentioned "middle class." Maybe Edmund had invented that. Ruggero was immediately in a rage: "The idea that you vicious queens couldn't wait to say those bitchy things! And your French friend was virtually having sex with *his* trick—surely you saw him playing with the boy's cock under the table. You of all people should know that hospitality is sacred to a Sicilian. I rushed home from Juilliard to throw myself into cooking for you lot and you couldn't wait to get to the corner to bad-mouth me."

Edmund pointed out it was the teacher not Ruggero they were bad-mouthing.

"It's an outrage! Over my dinner in our loft you queens attacked my charming lover. And you were so happy to report on their treachery and yours! And François dares to call *me* middle class—I an aristocrat and he the son of an unemployed alcoholic bully? We've read his books."

The friends had all agreed that the substitute teacher was a pretty piece of ass. That's when Edmund started to call him "Butt Boy." In a ghastly bit of "reaching out," Butt Boy had smiled at Edmund one night and said, "We must have some bottom solidarity!" Edmund in a bitter excess of comedy often made his friends refer to Butt Boy and to "bottom solidarity." Of course he knew the teacher was infinitely more handsome and sweet than he was.

The next rupture came when Edmund took Ruggero and the teacher to a hit gay movie. The audience was mostly made up of well-tailored, well-scented older gay men and their equally upholstered longtime lovers or their skinny new young tricks in jeans. Ruggero sat between both his wives, the old one and the young one like a pasha who's stayed loyal to his original bride but now has a delicious young piece on the side. He held their hands but in such a way that the other one couldn't see. The new one was always simpering and kissing his cheek and wrapping her hand around the potentate's shoulder. Edmund was in a jealous rage and wanted to bite the hand.

When Butt Boy excused himself to go to the loo, Ruggero asked why Edmund was in such an uncharacteristically bad mood. "Because he keeps fawning on you. It's embarrassing."

Ruggero said, "For Christ's sake it's a gay movie. Everyone in the audience is gay. Everyone is crying and consoling one another."

"Well, I hate it. It hurts me. You promised to tell him, obviously you were too cowardly to do it. He's not cruel—he's kind and intelligent. He wouldn't do it if he knew how much it hurts me."

"You're being unreasonable."

"It's because I'm in a jealous rage. And it's all your damn fault!"

Ruggero was seething with anger. As he said later, "I've never spent a more painful hour. I wanted to run away but I didn't want to make a scene."

Edmund had dared to remind Ruggero he was still lying to the teacher about his sexual activity with his ex-lover. In his fury Ruggero emailed Edmund, "I suggest we start all over and not use words to wound each other. Let's just start with the obvious facts: I'm Sicilian and I play the harpsichord. I'm forty-one. You're American. A well-known writer. You are seventy-nine. We wrote each other thousands of words before we ever met and words have been our undoing. Let's get back to the raw facts. And, by the way, I'm going to tell the truth, the whole truth, to my new lover. That way we won't have to be afraid. No one will have to be afraid of the truth."

Perhaps he did tell the substitute teacher that he and Edmund had "overlapped" as sex partners with Ruggero. But he certainly didn't admit he was still fucking Edmund and would continue to do so for the next year and a half.

Edmund stopped wearing his wedding ring and it took two weeks for the flesh to fill in. Ruggero never said anything if he noticed the change at all.

Edmund didn't really care except he didn't want to watch the teacher constantly mauling Ruggero and hear him calling him Bello. Edmund didn't say that but Ruggero said, "You'll never see him again. I wanted to make you part of our life. But it didn't work out. You're the easiest person I know and the most difficult." That really rankled—to make you part of *our* life. Their life together was the only solid reality.

Edmund thought it was obvious that Ruggero, who knew he was in his prime—what the French call "the flower of age" (*la fleur de l'âge*)—and had seen in Edmund how destructive time would be, wanted to enjoy his peak physical condition with another fit, mature man, not an old wreck. By analogy, people work hard to enjoy themselves with the rewards of their labor—not just to be charitable to the needy. Ruggero didn't fast and lift weights just to humor an old queen. He'd always been aware of how fleeting time is and he surely didn't want to waste his prime on Edmund.

They didn't speak for a month, but Ruggero had promised to escort Edmund the night when he would be presented with a gay award for his AIDS work. Ruggero met him at the vast ornate former bank on Forty-second Street. Edmund was thrilled to see him looking so elegant in his tuxedo. They were both wearing their gold watches that commemorated their first meeting (maybe Ruggero had chosen his only because the black strap matched his black tie). Edmund seated him between himself and the presenter. At their table were gathered Edmund's beloved sister and her son Luca. They'd bought evening clothes for the occasion and flown in from Chicago.

Ruggero was charmed by Luca. The boy was adopted, and Ruggero imagined despite his red hair that his birth parents were Italian (in fact his mother was from Brescia). When Ruggero noticed the boy hadn't eaten his first course, prosciutto, he asked him why. Luca said, "I didn't know what it was," which touched Ruggero deeply. He told Edmund that he would gladly pay the boy's college tuition; luckily that offer was never taken seriously.

The whole evening seemed to pacify them both, though Ruggero wrote, "I know I promised to take you to Castelnuovo one day. But now I can't—our relationship is too conflictual. I wanted to do it so much, but you've ruined all that." Soon they were back to daily emails and Skypes, but Ruggero never wrote with passion or love again, just casual affection and admiration. Edmund speculated that his feelings had changed or that he was afraid Edmund would betray their sex arrangement and in a pique forward their emails to Butt Boy. They continued to have weekly lunches (every Friday when the teacher was away giving lessons) and sex, but the sex was no longer sadistic nor very intense. Their affair was like a crashed car that rolls off the road and slowly loses a wheel, a door, the roof. When Edmund noticed one of Ruggero's climaxes had been unusually copious, Edmund said, "Wow! You must not have had sex recently," and Ruggero thought about it and replied, "I didn't yesterday but we did two days ago."

Ruggero invited the teacher to London and then on to Milan. Even from Europe, Ruggero kept up his daily Skypes. They came back on New Year's Eve and Edmund invited them for caviar, blini, and champagne. At midnight they all three embraced.

So it rolled painfully, noiselessly, sometimes pleasantly on for the next year and a half. Ruggero did sweet things such as giving a huge publishing party for Edmund at the same Forty-second Street bank. It was the last big get-together for them before the COVID pandemic. Ruggero reported that the teacher had cried after the party and said, "You and Edmund know all these fancy people but I'm just an average guy." Another time he said to Edmund, "I don't know what you and Ruggero find to talk about so long. I can never think of what to say to him." Gleeful as a gargoyle, Edmund chortled evilly.

The teacher could read music (he'd sung in operettas, after all) and he very proudly acted as a page-turner when Ruggero played a new piece on the harpsichord. Ruggero, who had almost too much energy (though it was concentrated, not scattered), found a beautiful chaconne for orchestra by one of his obscure baroque composers and transcribed it brilliantly for the harpsichord. Bach had made similar transcriptions of Vivaldi, and Ruggero imitated Bach's method of adapting orchestral effects to his instrument. Ruggero was resolved to record his transcription. The teacher turned the pages and whispered later to Edmund, "Good thing that you requested that."

Once Ruggero had asked Edmund if he found the teacher dull and when Edmund hesitated Ruggero answered for him, "A little dull."

"But very sweet," Edmund said.

"Very sweet," Ruggero agreed quickly.

Edmund got tired of being unhappy but every night, around two or three in the morning while, alone, he watched old video clips on a university channel, saw the great dancers and heard the great singers of the twentieth century. He looked at Claudio Arrau in his late seventies playing Debussy and Edmund thought no twenty-year-old could play that as well. Despite his liver-spotted hands and his head retracted between his shoulders, the bags beneath his eyes and his dyed mustache, his playing is incomparably athletic and delicate, accurate and moving. Dancers and most singers shouldn't continue past forty, writers long in the tooth started repeating themselves or talking in shorthand, but painters and choreographers and composers could continue flourishing into old age (Titian, Balanchine, and Bach sprang to mind). Somewhere (not in his Nobel speech) Yeats said that when he was a youth his verse was feeble but it was vigorous and young in his old age.

Edmund was obsessed with old age, this curse that had befallen him. On the other hand he knew that so many of his age cohorts had died young from AIDS and he had been spared (or had they?).

During the pandemic the teacher and Ruggero and Edmund and Michael had many Sunday dinners together. As Ruggero said, "You and Michael are my New York parents. You've both stayed safe and we have too. We don't see anyone and we both have tested negative. All four of us are in the same pod." When Ruggero and the teachers would come to dinner, Ruggero would bring the first course, usually pasta but sometimes a rice bake, and the dessert (often a light steamed pudding, lemon scented). Edmund would prepare the main course and set the table. Ruggero would wash the dishes and prepare the electric coffee maker so it could just be switched on in the morning (or at noon in these pandemic days).

Ruggero had discovered a nineteenth-century Italian writer who'd written *The Science of the Table*. Ruggero liked him because he wasn't subservient to French cuisine and maintained the integrity of his own country's recipes, which Ruggero was slowly working his way through. Every night Ruggero entered into a notebook his remarks on a particular dish and what the guests had talked about and thought of the chicken cutlets in the *passata*.

Edmund even said to the teacher, "Ruggero used to write me about how much he loved me, but now he only emails me about what he ate!"

"Aw! He still loves you."

"I wonder . . ."

It seemed a hazardous conversation for Edmund to be having with his replacement.

Ruggero and his partner were taking daily Zoom classes from their trainer. They were daily developing their biceps and shoulders—without neglecting their legs. All too many gays splice a massive torso to chicken legs. They both looked wonderfully fit and healthy, also because Ruggero monitored their food intake down to the last calorie.

Edmund would lie awake at night hating this ancient body that had betrayed him. First one tooth then another fell out. He would look in the bathroom mirror at his massive, sagging man boobs, which, if he lifted things, were invariably pressing down on a red (and smelly) skin rash. His big belly, muscled from a life of sit-ups but still "thundering" (*tonitruant* as the French would say). And what was this new horror? Black hair that should be under his arms but had somehow drifted down his side. The micro-penis, so small it was hard to aim when pissing. The grotesque buttocks like something dreamed up by a vengefully realistic painter portraying his grandmother in the nude (Larry Rivers's *Berdie*). The heavy shoulders like a fighter's copied in lard.

He would weep over his poor sad anatomy. He thought of how Jean Genet had said of Rembrandt's *Woman Bathing in a Stream*, a fat woman lifting her shift and exposing her legs—"That's me. That's how I look without clothes." If Edmund would fart in bed he'd burst into sobs. He thought, "No wonder Ruggero moved on from this shipwreck to a spirited smack under sail." It was a miracle that Ruggero had been able to kiss this foul mouth, fuck this crepey ass, hold this obese carcass. He hoped Ruggero and the teacher would live long enough to know the humiliation of being old and ugly—but of course they wouldn't, they'd be as slim and stylish as the elder Rothschilds, Marie-Hélène and the Baron Guy, whom he'd see on his island in Paris, the Île Saint Louis, as they entered their gallant last years. He, too, could starve himself into slenderness if he had the will, but that was precisely what he didn't have. He needed the little comforts of life since he no longer had the great one.

Edmund would send a basket of fresh peaches or a pound of pecans, ingredients for Ruggero now that he was a serious chef. Ruggero bought Edmund a whole new sound system when the previous one died of old age. He was always darting about town; if Edmund said he was yearning for black pasta Ruggero would rush to buy it at Eataly.

They edited each other's manuscripts and Ruggero translated a few of Edmund's. Nothing for Ruggero was a bother—he was infinitely obliging. He was always good company, even-tempered when he wasn't in a rage, eager to empty the garbage, indulgent of Michael's moods and potty mouth, brisk, amused and amusing—the best kind of Italian: formal but warm. He was always beautifully dressed, a designation (*ben vestito*) that he thought was an obligatory part of his Italian identity. He could pretend he took an American's *faux pas* as a perfectly reasonable observation; his conversational maneuvers were like those black-clad, conventionally invisible scene-changers in the Bunraku.

CHAPTER 9

Constance sent some of her pages about the Ruggero–Edmund affair to the original biographer. He wrote back praising her ability to quote effectively, to summarize, to move the narrative along, to use metaphor in a way that enriched the text. But he had serious reservations:

I wonder why you don't speak more clearly about Ruggero's evident narcissism and cruelty, his determination to do exactly as he pleases at every moment, despite the veil of modesty and thoughtfulness thrown over his terrible egotism. And then Edmund's tiresomely low self-esteem, his eagerness to accept crumbs. I think you quite rightly mention his psychological and sexual masochism and also his secret, inner reserve, something he shared with Ruggero and, in both cases, made real intimacy impossible.

This is just an off-the-cuff response (not, I hasten to point out, an academically thought-out judgment), but why must Edmund always be unhappy in love? He seems to have suffered in every decade of his life. Was it the fate of his generation of gay men? Was he drawn to Ruggero like a tired old moth to a bright new flame? Are all thinking people unhappy in love?

Was Ruggero bewitched, like the troubadours of yore, by an impossible love (in their case a chaste love for their lord's wife, in his by a young man's love for an old man?). Was Ruggero the sleek, brilliant Alcibiades in love with decrepit, onion-nosed Socrates? The Ranieri to White's Leopardi? In each of these cases the unlikely, unnatural love was proof of the young lover's refinement, of how he could obey his spiritual love above his instinctive physical distaste. If Socrates and Leopardi had lived, would their beautiful young admirers have abandoned them eventually as Ruggero did for the beautiful Butt Boy? Would nature have taken its revenge on the spirit?

I think you have avoided these basic philosophical and psychoanalytic issues. Worse, you seem afraid to speculate beyond a certain point about the thoughts and intentions of your characters. I know it's considered improper to say, "Undoubtedly White was feeling . . ." or "Most likely Ruggero was thinking . . ." but in my opinion a smooth, convincing "life narrative" must take these liberties. We all theorize about our friends' motives; why should the biographer be uniquely deprived of this possibility?

Of course as the man who wrote White's life (I wish I had chosen a more colorful, commercial, and felicitous and talented Violet Quill, like Felice Picano, whose posthumous fame grows every year), I recognize that his three years with Castelnuovo were the most fertile and inspired of his life, that he'd finally evolved, at least in his fiction if not his life, out of the "gay" swamps onto the terra firma of polyamory, the happily adapted genital stage beyond his fixated anal aggressiveness. It's rare for an artist to reinvent himself in his sixties, even, much less his eighties. He was like the Verdi of The Merry Wives of Windsor.

I know that Ruggero played a major role in your life, that you left him and not he you, but I fear you've overidentified with the treacherous White and are "whitewashing" the really infantile and destructive aspects of his personality. Let's face it: he was the original "bitchy queen." Just look how he egged on his famous French writer friends in their attacks on the hapless Butt Boy (who cooperated generously with me in my research and whom I found to be a thoroughly delightful and intelligent old man—unlike Ruggero I am attracted to my elders. Like wine they grow richer and more delicious with age. Just as Mozart's widow married his first biographer, my very own Substitute Teacher has taken a full professorship in my heart—no one could be his substitute after these ten years together. And of course I see why

Ruggero left the barren, bitter White for him). As Ruggero had declared to White in one of his hate-driven emails, "You want to be the center of every-one's attention."

Although Constance dismissed all of the biographer's objections as Freudian rubbish and as anti-White sentiments installed in him by his beloved, elderly Butt Boy, she did consider one of his points. Could she enter more into Edmund's and Ruggero's points of view? It didn't seem "scientific," as the French say even of things made up, but she thought she might as well please the unsuspecting reader with a close reading of their last confrontation, thoughts and all.

R uggero and the teacher let themselves in with Ruggero's key to Edmund's apartment. They were masked but calling out greetings cheerfully. They both rushed to wash their hands, the teacher in the closer bathroom and Ruggero in the kitchen. Their voices were slightly muffled until they took off their masks. They had brought the cold in with them on their coats. Edmund was seated behind his computer; the guests each swooped down to kiss him on one cheek. Ruggero smelled of citrus and was wearing a tight turtleneck that revealed every muscle of his torso and arms; a doctor could have conducted a complete physical from ten feet away without the patient ever disrobing. He was wearing beautiful navy blue slacks that were pulled tight across his famous ass. He often had severe lower-back pains; his old nanny had said once, "That's the price you pay for such a splendid *culo*." Everyone agreed it was splendid.

Edmund was "sweet" (tamed) but, though undemonstrative, his high color and his careless pat of the famous *culo* during their embrace showed that he was delighted. He told the teacher that he looked wonderful in his white shirt, which he'd unbuttoned down to the breastbone. "I've been working at it," he said with a smile. "I have to make some effort, don't I, since Ruggero is so perfect." The teacher smiled with bottom solidarity.

He was a handsome young man, taller than Ruggero, broad shouldered, someone who admitted to having been a short, fat preteen; now he might be what the French call a *faux maigre*, a misleadingly thin person who one could intuit was once fat and could easily fill out again; all the fat cells were dormant but eager to be awakened.

Ruggero often told Edmund how much the teacher loved him, Edmund, and certainly the teacher was always friendly, slightly respectful, and invariably even tempered (no moods, no cruel words about other people).

He had a Dudley Do-Right chin, a soft gaze (Ruggero would say "maternal"), a high forehead (he sprinkled his thinning hair with Rogaine). Michael said he was rather ordinary and if Ruggero had only waited a bit longer he could have done much better.

But aren't I better? Although Edmund was consumed with self-hatred, paradoxically he had more self-esteem. Once a psychiatrist had made Edmund look in the mirror and list everything he liked about himself and everything he disliked. The likes far outnumbered the dislikes, which surprised even Edmund. Ruggero's love had cast a spell over him, making him look on himself with favor. Now it was hard, so hard to accept the spell was broken and that the vows had been temporary. For no good reason Edmund continued to rate himself highly, at least intermittently. Edmund thought bitterly, You don't play with the heart of an eighty-year-old.

Ruggero, so restless, so efficient, had already opened the wine and started boiling the pasta water. He sat down for the antipasti Michael had set out, eating them hungrily (had he fasted again all day?). Ruggero discussed the pasta sauce of the day, a delicacy from Sicily that involved capers, fennel, and washed anchovies. He then excitedly recounted the latest episodes of *Golden Girls* they'd seen ("The characters never develop, they're types as in the *commedia dell'arte*"). Edmund had bought them clay heads of the Golden Girls planted with chia grass, perhaps an over-subtle suggestion of how disappointing Ruggero's new enthusiasm was.

Edmund could never hear the series mentioned without thinking of the happy couple watching it in bed (*avachis*, "sloppy, bovine" as the French would say). They also liked to smile at the transvestites on *Drag Race*. Of course Edmund was consumed with envy as when he heard of their car trips, their dinner parties in these COVID times with just two or three cute actors, their Facebook postings of their homemade haircuts. Now Edmund said something out of tune and Michael barked at him ferociously; Ruggero and the teacher exchanged complicitous glances (as if to say, "There they go again! I told you how hateful Michael could be to Edmund").

After the delicious dinner (Ruggero had brought the sides and Edmund had prepared Jamie Oliver's chicken in milk) they went back to the fireplace. Ruggero sat on the couch and the teacher stroked Ruggero's leg hopefully. A minute later the tireless Ruggero ("the energy bunny," as he credibly called himself) was up again in the kitchen rinsing the dishes and stacking them in the dishwasher despite Michael's protestations.

The teacher admired the Quimper nut bowl (blue, yellow, and green) which said Michel on it. "I bought it years ago in Paris when I first met Michael."

The teacher said, "I keep looking for one that says Ruggero."

"You could try Roger."

"Funnily enough, that's what he called himself when I first met him online."

"When was that, dear? The other day I heard you say your anniversary was in June."

Ruggero came back in from the kitchen and seemed alert.

"Yes, that was in June," the teacher said with a fond, complacent smile.

"That's strange," Edmund said, "Ruggero claimed he met you at the park in July."

Both guests leaned in and said, "We didn't have our second date until late July."

Edmund thought that must have been when Ruggero was buying so many new clothes and I'd guessed that he must have a new secret lover. "Oh, yes, when I was in Berlin." He thought if the teacher were wise he'd never go alone on a two-week trip and leave the faithless Ruggero alone.

Ruggero was frowning and making fire-dousing gestures with his hands, "We're all tired," he said. "This is the end of a long evening. It's not the right moment to discuss all this."

Edmund shot back, "And when would the right moment be, according to you?" Then he said to the teacher, "Did you realize we—"

"Overlapped? Yes, Ruggero told me that," and the teacher and Ruggero exchanged nods, Ruggero's more hesitant.

"And did it never occur to you that every time you kiss or caress Ruggero in front of me, it stabs me to the heart?"

The teacher looked genuinely grieved. "I had no idea. I'm terribly—"

"And," Edmund said, "you know he and I are still having sex?"

"He's lying, he's lying," Ruggero said, getting halfway out of his chair, looking at his boyfriend, probably studying his reactions.

The teacher's face crumpled in surprise and anguish. "No . . . no . . ." and he looked to Ruggero for guidance.

"We're leaving now!" They both rushed out the door.

"Why did you do that?" Michael asked.

"I was tired of these hypocritical adulterous scenes. I knew exactly what I was doing. I don't drink. I wasn't stoned." But in fact Edmund knew he'd just done something final, that he'd never see Ruggero again, and he wondered if he'd bargained for that.

Michael said, "I'm mortified."

"Mortified? What do you think that means?"

"Taken by surprise?"

"No, it means humiliated to death."

"That, too."

As they sat motionless in their chairs watching the dust from the explosion settle, Edmund said, "Well, that's over. He'll never speak to me again."

"No, he won't," Michael agreed and within two days Ruggero had mailed back his keys to their apartment and Edmund mailed back Ruggero's, attached as it always had been to a little silver turtle.

Constance thinks: I knew that the biographer had convinced his reluctant partner, the Substitute Teacher, to tape his reminiscences of Ruggero soon after the new couple met. I begged to be able to borrow the tape, which was a cornerstone of my research. The biographer confessed he was reluctant to share the tape, since he couldn't be sure how I would represent his companion; he admitted that the sound of his voice was sacred to him, especially late at night beside the fire with four or five good brandies. Since Titus Angelus (his real name, who'd never been a substitute teacher in his life, just one more of Edmund's withering monikers) was now surrendering to senility and made no more sense than a . . . two-year-old, to be precise, it was a pure delight to hear him when he was still articulate and precise and before those long-deferred fat cells had finally taken their revenge and made him as obese as Edmund himself. Edmund had died years before of a heart attack, appropriately slumped on the toilet like Elvis; Michael had scattered his ashes over the sliver of Central Park that still existed, unravaged by developers.

At last the biographer brought over the precious tape in a Hopi card case; he seemed as reluctant as he had been to confide his original pages on Ruggero (the ones the lawyer had nixed) and actually advanced the case toward me on my desktop and then pulled it back. I thought I might have to pounce on it during one of its close orbits, but finally he surrendered it almost indifferently beside a burning Kent in an ashtray as he stumbled off to the bathroom (I'd given him permission to smoke, thinking it might relax him). I'd secreted the tape in a drawer while he was absent and we never mentioned it again.

The biographer said: I interviewed Ruggero and he'd sworn Edmund and he had never had sex again after July 2019. Ruggero was adamant about that. I believed him and of course I believed my darling Titus. The only slightly discordant note was that whole avalanche of emails, which did seem contrafactual. Who would make all that up, especially the ones in slightly quirky Italianized English? All that S&M stuff? And then when I interviewed Michael, who seemed embarrassed by the whole issue, he told me reluctantly that Ruggero and Edmund spent hours in the bedroom behind closed doors and he could hear their shouts and whimpers. And that Ruggero kept a pile of "sex clothes" (briefs, t-shirts, athletic socks, jockstraps) under a discreet white towel. Ruggero said in any event Titus would never notice them during their communal dinners since he was the most "incurious boy" in the world. After their final rupture Edmund gave away all those clothes to someone they fit; the cleaning woman, whose sister worked for Ruggero, must have noticed that the chair was finally free. Edmund took two weeks before he gifted them, the way he'd hung on to the clothes of an earlier lover who'd died of AIDS. What if they'd come back, he'd asked himself, of the dead man and Ruggero? Edmund was a recognizable practitioner of magical thinking.

Of course I believed Titus and Ruggero and thought Michael was just covering for Edmund and Edmund was such a compulsive liar that he'd counterfeited the whole email correspondence.

Titus: I couldn't have been more shocked than I was when I read Edmund's hostile words about me. No one else ever found fault with my derrière; Ruggero used to sleep with his head cushioned on my buttocks. He and I would take turns rimming each other. He'd have me well lubricated with spit and gaping by the time he penetrated me with his "cunt wrecker," as I called it. He told me he'd never rimmed Edmund. It was all diaper rash and archaic blubber down there. Though he admitted Edmund's depraved anal kisses were the ones that had first awakened his rectal nerve endings.

I'd never seen Ruggero so angry as after that last night at Edmund's. As we rushed out, poor Michael looked stunned by Edmund's recklessness—though that one, Michael, was no picnic to live with either, I bet.

Ruggero grabbed the first taxi, whereas usually we walked the few blocks. I think he wanted to get back to our loft as soon as possible, hold me and reassure me. He could see I was traumatized. I who teach drama—*not* a substitute teacher but an adjunct in several prestigious Long Island colleges, the only white hired year after year despite being the wrong color, so diplomatic was I, so determined to cross racial barriers and, if I might add, so talented, though I graciously took early retirement, making room for a worthy minority—had never actually lived through such a dramatic moment. My family, in spite of our Italian

surname, were rather dour and undemonstrative Irish. My gay friends
and lady friends, though extravagantly affectionate, were *never* confron-
tational. Drama makes Americans giggle with embarrassment. Ruggero,
though Sicilian, was too aristocratic for such *scenette*. (I never learned
Italian much to my regret—Ruggero refused to teach me. I blame him.)

We watched *Golden Girls* in our bed that night; Ruggero lubricated
his middle finger and plugged my ass with it as we looked at the TV.
I found the contact pacifying. Ruggero laughed at the show. When I got
up to pee I threw Edmund's poisoned gift, the chia seed heads of the
Golden Girls, into the trash. "You did well," Ruggero said when I
reported my action to him. The character he liked the most was Sophia
Petrillo, the nasty, five-foot tall Sicilian mother. I got her autograph
while she was still alive. Which I kept in my "precious box."

Ruggero was always up early but the next day he slept in till seven
A.M. When I mentioned Edmund, he roared "We'll never say that bitch's
name again in this house." I knew he had emailed Edmund twice a day
and Skyped him every day at seven P.M. and I asked him two days later,
while we were watching *Schitt's Creek*—Ruggero loved Catherine
O'Hara, whom I never met, alas; I was so proud I'd weaned him away
from all those gloomy "classic" novels he used to read by someone called
Shasha(?) plus some ancient poet called Leopard(??) and plugged him
into North American pop culture, never so vibrant—if he missed his
daily chats with Edmund.

"That's a forbidden name in this household," he said grimly. "Just
imagine the savage things he'll write about us—luckily his star has
waned. No one reads him. And no, Ruggero never misses anyone."

"Not even me, sweetie?"

"Why? Are you about to leave me? Have you met some new top at
the gym—richer, smarter, more hung?"

I thought, not richer. "Of course not. I at least am faithful," I said
with an undue, reprehending emphasis on the *I*.

He forgave me (I think he was unsure how well I'd weathered that
last evening with Edmund), kissed me wordlessly. A moment later his
hand had pushed aside a panel of my Happy Face boxers and his finger
was comfortingly back in my ass (luckily I'd douched earlier). He

whisked me off on a road trip up the Hudson the very next weekend. We even saw some hot cadets near West Point. The lease had run out on our loft and we bought a nice A-frame next to a lake. I was afraid Ruggero would get bored.

Suddenly I was in a rage that Edmund had called me Butt Boy. My penis was small, but not as small as his, Ruggero assured me, and in my twenties I'd topped a few times, notably with that playwright, who had no complaints. And I'd always been extrasweet to poor fat, old Edmund, and he rewarded me by saying such nasty things about me. Jealous bitch, I guess. More pathetic, really.

Ruggero promised me that he'd never touched Edmund after that July 2019 (why would he? Ugh) and I believed him. I had to. He remained faithful to me until I eloped with that sexy, treacherous Virgilio I met at Crunch. Luckily, I'd already socked away lots and lots of "powder room money" by that time, and Virgilio wasn't able to wheedle it out of me for his gay sports bar. Then Virgilio went back to his native Panama with his new beau forming no inconsiderable part of his luggage. I met Edmund's biographer just before my looks finally gave out. I know Ruggero had suffered over dumping Edmund (no matter how thrilled he was to know me and live with me; he said I was the sweetest person, male or female, he'd ever known. I'm sure that's true, given his track record) and that if he could have borne sleeping with Edmund he would have, just as a compensatory award, but good-hearted Ruggero was revolted, as any blue-blooded homo would have been, by the whole disgusting package. And that horrible Michael saying Ruggero could have done better if he'd only shopped around more. Ruggero adored me and would often call me "his little boy" or his "wife." We considered having a child with a surrogate mother and Ruggero's sperm, natch, but then we thought we couldn't be bothered. We couldn't even adopt a stray dog during the height of the pandemic, they were that much in demand and we wanted to be free to travel.

CONSTANCE WROTE: EDMUND suffered horribly after the final break-up, but his sister the therapist patched him back together. She said that

Ruggero went into such rages if anyone challenged his character that he'd never come back. He was probably happy to be finally rid of Edmund. Ruggero like everyone wanted to be admired, not reproached. Moreover, she said, if Edmund got him back what would he have? Endless heartache. He'd already suffered for a year and a half. Nothing was more binding than random reinforcement—the pigeon is fed a pellet after the fifth peck and the seventh and the twenty-first. Ruggero was wonderful with Ed—radiant, loving, generous—only at random intervals. More typically he'd unzip his trousers, fish out his erection, pop it into Edmund's mouth, pull it out and say, "We'll get together later in the week," and never keep his promise. And yet he was someone who never forgot his obligations.

His sister told Edmund to hold out and not contact Ruggero for three weeks. There was no obsession, she swore, that could not be starved to death in three weeks. Five weeks later he was still looking at his email first thing (noon—COVID days) or at three in the morning (COVID nights). He'd ordered Bram Stoker's *Dracula* on Ruggero's recommendation *before* and it arrived *after;* now he'd never read it. A wonderful seat cushion arrived with no card; had Ruggero ordered it *before*? His sister's adopted son, Luca, had been so impressed with Ruggero that he was studying Italian on his own, and Edmund sent him a copy of Marcella Hazan's Italian cookbook; now, however, Edmund had no one to report this touching news to.

Each time he felt tempted to email Ruggero, he didn't want to give Ruggero an occasion for a fresh outburst. When he told his sister, Margaret, he'd received his house keys back from Ruggero without a note, she said, "It's better he didn't send a note, guess how wounding it would have been." Margaret had always respected Ruggero; she'd heard about his fits of anger but only from Eddie. With her he'd always been the Sicilian prince.

Edmund slept around with a few men. One of them, a kind, handsome young lawyer he'd met on SilverDaddies (the site for old men and their admirers), surprisingly told Edmund he was too old. "Wait! I'm too old even for SilverDaddies!? You give sixty to eighty as your range." He had sex with a very enthusiastic muscular middle-aged man but at last he put him off, weary of loveless sex. Maybe since he could no longer get hard or come he didn't really like sex. Ruggero had cynically thought Edmund was addicted to sex and that a big dick was his *nec plus ultra* in a partner, but in fact his only drug was Ruggero. He had hoped to die in Ruggero's arms, but that was absurd. No one knew in advance the moment of death, and it always occurred alone.

Edmund still thought it was so unfair that Ruggero had dropped him after all his promises of eternal love, but as Ruggero had said so reasonably, no one knows at the beginning of a love affair what he will feel at the end of it. Edmund had read a book in French about refined women who'd suffered from love year after year (it was called *Souffrir*); their habit of suffering seemed to have been a sign of their spirituality to the other women in their salons. He didn't think it was proof of sensitivity. Only stupidity (*bêtise*). He remembered how his best friend in Paris had said, when her cancer recurred, "*C'est bête!*" as if she or her body had done something foolish.

After communicating nearly every day for many moons with the same man, learning from him, sharing with him every thought (and all his recipes), it was so tempting to write him when he, Edmund, had just heard a beautiful piece, *Antiche danze ed arie*, by Respighi, a twentieth-century composer for whom Ruggero felt an improbable affection, maybe because he was Italian, despite the legend that the *Pines of Rome* had been Mussolini's favorite piece of music (not Respighi's fault).

IN THAT BLEAK COVID winter, Edmund seldom left the house. A big Tuscan biscuit jar painted with pomegranates he'd ordered for Ruggero's Christmas arrived, filled with sweets, and over the weeks of solitude he slowly ate the contents. He surrendered to the temptation of solitude. When an overly direct friend asked him why he bothered with lovers now that he was impotent, Edmund said, "Having a lover is like writing a novel. It ties your days together. It's a project."

Why had Edmund broken with Ruggero and revealed everything to Titus?

Before that evening he'd been rereading through his and Ruggero's old emails and had realized his every fight with him had been over

Titus's public demonstrations of affection and over the fact Ruggero had never told him to lay off. Ruggero wanted to bask in the sunny weather of his wives' affections and didn't want a single cloud to blot out the heat and light. Surely Edmund would get over this capricious objection, Ruggero must have reasoned. He's getting plenty on the side—the other day I must have fucked him for a good ten minutes without pausing once. He's Europeanized enough to grasp that the husband can visit the old wife's bed occasionally as long as the new wife never suspects. Once when Edmund started to discuss Ruggero's bigamy when they were alone, absolutely alone, Ruggero (who never wanted to be explicit unless it was absolutely necessary) had gone so far as to raise his index finger to his lips (s-h-h-h!). They'd already had several serious ruptures over this one point. Why hadn't Edmund learned his lesson? He couldn't even claim he was being publicly humiliated since he'd told all his friends that he and Ruggero were still lovers. They were all in on the giggly, naughty secret. It infuriated Edmund that don't-bother-me Ruggero didn't warn Titus. But as Michael pointed out, "Ruggero may have warned him, but he couldn't control Titus's behavior."

Edmund supposed he was what is known as a pushy bottom, passive technically but domineering in reality. That night it irked him to see Titus once again manhandling Ruggero. Edmund was outraged by Ruggero's indifference or cowardice and by Titus's unforgivable insensitivity. Even if you hadn't been warned, wouldn't you know better than to caress the wayward husband in front of the wife who'd just been dumped?

It was all so petty and spiteful. A shrink had once said to him, "Why do you clutter your head with all that vengeful garbage? You're supposed to be creative, right? Give your mind some room to think new, beautiful thoughts!"

Once Edmund had started out on that fateful course that last evening, he'd been irresistably drawn into the vortex.

And then maybe he preferred his solitude. Like all old people he liked to watch the news; the reported disasters assuaged him, made him feel less lonely. TV warmed up the room. He still had Ruggero's handprinted instructions as to how to access Netflix. He could leave those reruns of *Golden Girls* to those homosexuals who were genetically programmed, according to the queer scholar David M. Halperin, in *What Do Gay Men Want?*, to embrace them. Halperin had even written, "Who needs Edmund White when we have *Golden Girls?*"

"But what if I get sick?" Edmund said, meaning the virus.

Michael said, "I'd tell Ruggero right away, of course."

"He'd probably just hang up on you."

By chance Edmund looked at a diary he'd kept for a few months in 2015 long before he'd met Ruggero. On September 17 he'd written, "I like being alone in my bedroom and the radio tuned to a classical station. I've been with Michael twenty years and we're well-suited to each other—he's aloof and exquisitely tolerant, especially since we got married two years ago. He's singularly uninterested in other people's private lives. Strange in a novelist. I suppose he hears enough stories at his bar, the Barracuda, where he writes every day from four to nine. He calls it his 'office.' It and the karaoke bar in Key West are the settings of several of his funny stories."

Edmund had imagined from age forty on that his romantic life was over, but it had sputtered back to life again and again. His mother in her seventies had written in her memoir about her last adventure, the chapter called "Love at Last." The man, younger by twenty years, hadn't been that presentable, but he had made love to Edmund's ancient mother with her colostomy and her two mastectomies, her egomania and excessive drinking. When he abandoned her and moved without a forwarding address to, vaguely, "California," she had survived his desertion with her usual pluck. She invented good reasons for being "understanding." She thought of herself as fortunate for having found love at last.

Often Edmund thought he would hear Ruggero's deep voice on the phone saying, "I've been so bored without you, my little boy. I've had fun, I won't deny it, but I haven't written another word since we . . . we stopped, of course I play my concerts, tour and make recordings but I haven't sniffed out forgotten baroque composers with the same energy nor done another transcription, orchestra to harpsichord. We both know you're a terrible person, now unforgivably old, a complete traitor and liar, but I . . . miss you. I promised I would love you forever. And I have. Shall we give it another try?"

As a child Edmund had lived day in, day out with his mother's fantasy that her divorced and remarried husband would come back to her. Every time Edmund and Margaret spent weekends with their father and stepmother they were supposed to look for signs of his imminent return. He never did come back, nor did Ruggero.

CONSTANCE WRITES: I found this handwritten note, dated New York, January 2, 2018, in the White archives at Yale:

> *My dearest Edmund,*
> *You'll probably read this when you'll be back from Key West and I hope you've had a truly good time over there. Between now and the day you'll read this we'll have exchanged many emails but I've realized today I've never written you a "real" letter (you know by now that I'm quite an old-fashioned boy!) and it's now time to emend this and fill the gap. I'm writing lying in our bed, on your side, pretending I can feel the warmth of your body still registered in the mattress, in the bed sheets, the white bed spread, the blue quilted blanket. Ed, these days have been so wonderful! Every time I've been here with you I've "found" something new about myself and my feelings toward you, like a sort of journey that proceeds through different steps and grades. I can't forget the first time I walked through that doorstep and the first time I took my clothes off beside you and you said, "What a man!"—those words are engraved inside every cell of my body. But there are so many other "first-times," our first night at the opera, our first party together, our first visit to the Metropolitan Museum, our first visit to your Italian friend Carla and I could go on and on because even seeing you in the morning smiling at me, when I open the door and hearing your "Hey baby," all that feels like a first time every day, a new different emotion each time. I suppose I'm writing this to try to ignore the fact that I won't see you for some time and that this thought gives me an unspeakable fear. It's a pain I'd never experienced before, not just "missing" you but also missing my "me*

with you" *and not knowing when I'll have it again. Now I'm crying even though I'd promised myself that I wouldn't cry because we can only be happy one with the other. But I can't help that we've found each other—and it's been the most amazing, surprising, wonderful surprise of my whole life—but at the same time we're kept apart and we'll have to accept this. I've to tell you it's not an easy process for me and I know—from overthinking and brainy as I am—that it will take me time to accept the fact that we've met at a point in our lives when things are hard to change, if it's ever possible to change them. Against what most people would think, my struggle is to* see *our age gap, rather than trying* not *to see it! To me you're really my young boy, my wife and I am (I don't pretend I want to be) your big strong boy, your husband. So I must admit that I've to make an effort not to be too pushy or physically demanding when we're in bed since I become worried I could hurt you, I could tire your big, generous, loving but weak heart. I hope you forgive me for being so direct, possibly I pay for not having had an older lover ever before. My love for you is something I've never experienced before, an indescribable mixture of feelings entirely filtered by my brain—every single part of it—that concur to make you my absolute everything. Saying goodbye to you this morning I realized once more that my fear of losing you is so painful that I'd feel torn inside even only thinking of it for a second. You've become so important, so central in my life! I still wonder every day how this could have happened. I believe in some mysterious way I could "read" through your writings the way you needed to be loved in your most intimate inner self and I sensed in a totally irrational way that you could love me in return exactly how I longed to be. Then—fortunately!—I happen to have all you like in a young man! (without forgetting our best mutual friend, the reliable, diligent Dickie!) My darling, I hope when you'll be reading this letter we'll have settled a date to meet again, here in New York or anywhere else. I've to admit that this deep sense of division is not too easy to live with. I don't know if you've experienced something similar in the past—when I look deeply into your eyes I often wonder what kind of memories populate that wonderful head of yours and how I'd fit amongst them. Sometimes I feel I don't belong any longer to my own life or at least as it would have been up to last June. But at the same time can I honestly say that I belong to another life as the one I share with you, these—all too few—days we've spent together? I suppose I just have to cool down a bit and give myself—ourselves—time to all that's happened to my—our—lives in the last six months. Now I'm going to finish packing my stuff and then I'll go out for a walk up to lunch time. Thank you for* everything, *even though those words are really too little to express what I feel inside, the gratitude for your and Michael's hospitality, generosity, your enormous love, your gift of my* new life *since that day when I understood I was loving you. I AM your husband, I AM your man.* Never forget it! *I love you so much, so much,* too *much. Yours forever, Ruggero*

PS I haven't checked my spelling, forgive my mistakes! Love! ♥

CHAPTER II

Eleven years into her marriage with Jason and nearly two years into her "study" (*étude*) of Ruggero and Edmund, as the French call their biographies in order to sound less ponderous and less achingly boring than their Anglo-Saxon counterparts (an "American biography" was the promise of "doorstop" length and inconsequential thoroughness in France), it occurred to Constance to interview Ruggero himself. Would his old email address work (seniors seldom change their details). How old must Ruggero be now? Eighty-three or eighty-four? Where must he be living if he's alive (she felt he must be splendidly alive somewhere, perfectly dressed, highly amused, very likely in love)? Would he answer some questions about Edmund or was he still too bitter? For years he had rejected all bids for interviews and would say, as Nelson Algren had said of de Beauvoir, "Who? Who? Oh, you mean that slut, the one who opened our bedroom door and invited the press in to observe?"

Of course Constance had few real questions since she'd read the two men's entire email correspondence many times and the letters from friends and other fugitive writings in Edmund's archives and all the relevant publications. His reputation seemed to be on the ascent, despite most academics' aversion to the subject of homosexuality. She'd kept up with Ruggero's recordings though there hadn't been any in the last six years, nor did he still tour as far as she knew. Why would he bother? He had lots of money and enough international prizes to paper a big room. Time for pure pleasure (if he was still in good health—her instincts told her he probably was). If he wasn't, she was grateful that she wasn't the one who had to push the wheelchair.

She'd run into Ruggero's and Brunhilde's son Carlo once in Manhattan during a four-day shopping and theater trip. Carlo was blond but had the same baby-sheep curls as his father, though the wrong color. He was also fatter in the face than Ruggero had ever been (at least to her knowledge). His English was perfect except he had a slight South-of-Thames accent, which she imagined was considered chic among his age cohorts. He scarcely recognized Constance until she flagged his attention and reintroduced herself. He smiled with a yellow smile and pulled slightly apart, as if he remembered Constance was an enemy of the family's. Through him she learned Ruggero was living in Spain. She had only two questions to ask Ruggero: How did he feel about Edmund now—and what had happened to him, post-Edmund?

Constance composed an email:

I have the fondest memories of you. I don't think I knew what a "gentleman" was until I met you. Of course you're also a kind man, a very sexual man, a very faithful and attentive lover, the most cultured man I've ever had the good luck to know, a happy, even-tempered spirit (except Edmund was able to get under your skin, it seems, but I know that only from your and his emails); once you told him he was a slut and not a gentleman and you could never take him to Castelnuovo. You wrote, "You're not a slave but a slut, you're not a gentleman, and I'll never take you to Sicily." Edmund agreed he wasn't a gentleman, not in Ruggero's sense. He questioned what a "slut" could be in the twenty-first century. What did that mean?

The only thing that hurt him was your vow never to take him to Sicily. Edmund could just picture Titus queening his way on the flower-laden Castelnuovo balcony overlooking the village, downing bright red cocktails, though he couldn't speak Italian. You were never angry with Edmund until you left him for Titus and Edmund was so cross about Titus's open displays of affection. Do you think now it was a mistake to try to make things work with Edmund? You're so diplomatic, if anyone could have made it work, it would have been you.

My life has been quiet here in Pittsburgh, my marriage a reasonable success, my greatest joy my two children. My Marco, who is now ten, is very musical; he loves your recordings and is very impressed I once knew you (he plays the piano but wants his daddy to buy him a harpsichord). I told him the fingering, as you taught me, is completely different, but he likes the crisp, even-tempered tone and uniform volume as well as the nervous responsiveness of the action.

He's trans, something he never doubts in his for intérieur. He's immensely clever and has done his research. He insisted we let him have from his pediatrician monthly injections of gonadotropin-releasing hormone, GnRH, which stops puberty, prevents erections, and ends voice-deepening (which makes me think of your wonderful castrato character—but a less violent measure to obtain the same results).

It gives the boy time out to think whether he really wants the vaginoplasty and penile inversion. Some subjects of gender dysphoria reconcile themselves with their birth gender.

I tell you all this because I remember how much you like children, especially talented, musical children, and how you respond to their qualms (Luca and the prosciutto, which you told me about several times; the incident must have stuck with you). Also, I must confess that I sometimes fear Marco's dysphoria is Fate's revenge on me for all our polyamorous adventures.

Why did I leave you for Jason? Probably for the same reason you left Edmund: too old. I wanted to construct a life with a man my age and have children, just as you were drawn to Titus the Perfidious (you did get a good ten years out of him before he ran off with Virgilio). It's a relief to live with an age-equivalent, to be with someone who's not dragging behind him a heavy peacock-tail of memories, who's never been to Venice before and doesn't have his favorite palazzi to point out to you.

Although you could write moving letters and emails you were always reserved and undemonstrative in life (except in sex). With all my deep insecurities I suffered terribly from fear of abandonment. You wrote that you were torn up with jealousy and possessiveness, but I never saw that in the flesh; I guess it wasn't your style to sob or tremble. I couldn't help remembering that *your London shrink had told you that your greatest flaw was a fear of hurting other people. You certainly overcame that "flaw" with Edmund; you dropped him from one day to the next, and that made me so fearful that you'd do the same with me, that you'd become an expert, like your friend in Rome, in never doing anything that didn't bring you absolute pleasure in the moment, not even a coffee with an old uncle in Trastevere.*

She signed the email with the word *love* and three emoji hearts.

RUGGERO WROTE BACK:

How lovely to hear from you and to know you're safe and well. I'm sitting here in my eighty-third year at my little stone peasant house in the country-side of Provence, where I've lived for the last six years. I'm on the terrace looking at the cypresses towering over me on two sides—descendants, no doubt, of the very trees van Gogh painted so ecstatically. The madhouse where he was confined is just 300 meters away, still a sort of convent I suppose because I see nuns processing about within the cloisters and the odd peculiar-looking patient. The ratio nuns to loonies seems to be 2:1 as best I can guesstimate.

What a pleasure to write in English. With the years so many of my English and American correspondents have "passed away" as we say in English, or "disappeared," as the French say, as though with age we become highly mobile ghosts.

This is quite a large property and I have a good five minutes between the time a car starts to crunch in sight and mounts the gravel path up to my house, a delay I find propitious since it gives me a chance to divine the iden-tity of the drivers and prepare myself for the ensuing visit. At the foot of the hill there are olive trees and a swimming pool (really a bassin *for farm animals fed by icy water from a* source*). There are no animals anymore except my Irish setter, Cuchulain, and the rare gaggle of village teens who come out to enjoy the waters unless I shake my cane at them and shoo them off. Maybe I should let them stay. Some are very attractive.*

The light here goes from a bleached-out brilliance at noon that makes you squint to an evening intensity of color, blue blues and greens as green as Verdi's name. We have no flowers except springtime bougainvilleas and around the door lavender, which for some occult reason the locals say is not "real" lavender, which supposedly died out after the last world war. Though it smells the same: heavenly.

We have no air-conditioning but a copious wind blows up at eventide. In the heat of the day I take a long nap to the incessant buzz of those little bacchantes, the crickets, and my sheets are often wet and tangled after a feverish hour (my doctor, an English pederast in the village, tells me, with much ogling, that "men" my age should take two naps a day). I can only manage one; you recall how over-energized I've always been, which has helped me preserve my 762 mm waist (thirty inches to you!) despite a sweet tooth that by now has become a sugar tusk.

I live here with Adriano, the son of Edmund's great-nephew and his charming bright-eyed wife, Teresa. My mother's lover that Dutchman left me the mas in his will. I was completely—how do you say in English? I don't have a good dictionary here—taken aback? Taken up? by his generosity. Bouleversé. Sconvolto? We didn't even visit the house for the longest time, but then one day I packed up the "kids," as I call my young lovers, and the three of us drove all the way from Barcelona. We stopped along the way in a beautiful chateau et relais. We had such fun eating in the Second Empire dining room with its Nile green walls and white lattices tacked to the pilasters. You know that food in Spain is simple and honest if greasier and less "curated" than in Italy. But we had forgotten how elaborate service can be in France, with these great silver bells lifted by three or four waiters at once to reveal one kumquat with a sprig of fresh mint and a bruised slice of fennel "in its own juice," the whole rigmarole described by the head waiter, like grace said before a Protestant dinner. We laughed ourselves sick. The three of us are wildly compatible; at last I've stumbled on the happiness I sought all my life but which my perfectionism always kept at bay. Indulge me for a moment. It seems strange to rhapsodize over one beautiful woman to another (you) even more beautiful. But Teresa is a classic beauty with an endearing smile, sparkling eyes, features perfectly formed but slightly too small for her face. Her hair is black and lustrous and long without the least bit of curl. Her breasts are so sweet and generous, like her noble spirit. She can be fiery in defending her opinions (she is an expert in African cinema and organizes African film festivals all over the world, most recently in Telluride), but her default mood is sweet and, as they say in America, "supportive." She is writing her dissertation on Kayode Kasum, the Nigerian director, taking a close look at This Lady Called Life *starring Bisola Aiyeola. Kayode has visited us more than once in Barcelona. His Castilian is excellent since he has a degree from Saragossa in biblical arts.*

Years ago now I found Adriano and Teresa because I'd met his father once when I was touring and played at the magnificent Palau de la Música Catalana, that art nouveau masterpiece with its circular seating and pillars covered in bright, childish mosaics. When I called the father he said that he was about to go to their apartment in Sitges but that his son and fiancée would be delighted to spend the evening with me. I called Adriano and was immediately charmed by his Catalan-inflected Spanish. He gave me his address and said he'd make reservations at a nice Syrian restaurant just off the harbor.

I was delighted by my young companions. They knew from their grandmother that Edmund had once been a celebrated gay writer and that I'd been his lover. Halfway through the meal and the opening of a second bottle of rosé, they told me that though they were engaged and would soon be married, they weren't just another pair of dull normals. They said they were Communists and polyamorous.

"It all started because Teresa confessed to me that she was bisexual and had a girlfriend. Instead of being shocked I was intrigued as most men would be. Once I felt Teresa wasn't going to leave me—" Adriano looked over to her and she stroked his cheek, looked at him tenderly and leaned in for a kiss, though she shyly checked to see if I was watching and approved.

I did. I could see she was a bewitching young woman, assertive in the modern way but feminine in the delicious way we're no longer allowed to mention.

"—once I felt Teresa wasn't going to leave me," Adriano said, "I relaxed and became even more excited and interested. Teresa is so kind and beautiful—those are my words for her, 'kind and beautiful—' I tried to open

myself up to her completely. She and her girlfriend let me play with them, but then Teresa insisted I try it with a man. I was terrified. Spain as you know is a very macho culture, though it's changed over the years immensely. Now in Catalonia we have nearly as many same-sex marriages as hetero-sexual ones. I know that real homosexuals don't trust or like polyamorous people like us—"

"So did Teresa," I asked, "convince you to try a man?"

I should tell you that I was (am) mortally attracted to Adriano. As you know better than anyone, I dropped Edmund for the boring but cute Titus because Edmund was so ancient. I know it sounds theoretical and a bluff, but I always envied men who had loved Edmund when he was young and slender and muscular. Now the very version of Edmund I always wanted was sitting there looking at me—the same hair swept across his forehead, the same eyes, the eyebrows that made you think he was sad, the same chubby cheeks, the same thin lips, the same firm but unobtrusive chin.

Thank you for sending me that posthumous interview of Edmund where he calls me "the love of my life." Until I met Adriano (who I'm happy to say has a much larger cock than his great-uncle), I could scarcely bear to hear that name. Hearing him mentioned would make me sick. Thank God he's not published in Spain and his books are scarcely mentioned elsewhere, though they seem to be creeping back into view. Thanks to "scholars" like you. I hope your étude won't rehash the whole mess. From my point of view I fell in love with the wrong person. They say no one is as vengeful as a woman scorned, but you could add a bitchy queen to that list—far worse in fact because there is always something nurturing and forgiving in a woman. Edmund attacked me and poor Titus relentlessly (Titus in no way resembled Edmund's terrible caricature, purely the invention of a jealous bitch). It's not my fault that Edmund could never find a new lover. My biggest mistake was not to let him join Silvio in Rome. Edmund had already lived a full life. What if he'd died from COVID in Rome? At least he wouldn't have written that insane, obssesive, hate-filled book and his ashes would be scat-tered (if Silvio could be bothered) over the foro antico rather than what's left of Central Park.

Just thinking about Edmund again has challenged my hard-won inner peace. But here we are, my darling Teresa and my man, yes, that's right, my man, Adriano. And our daughter Christine. We don't know who the father is—Adriano or me. She's as pretty as her mother and as calm as Adriano, but she does have those telltale sheep curls. Just four years old. When we had guests the other day I could hear her saying, "This is the door to our house. My room is upstairs. Do you want to see it?" She was already as hospitable as any Sicilian.

You may be astonished to hear me call him "my man." You remember how indifferent I was to penis when we lived together. It was only ass for me (you'll recall how beautiful Colin's was and how ensorcellé I was by the idea of penetrating that boy, as fleet and as lithe as Mercury minus winged cap and winged sandals, but holding a caduceus, my giant staff. You'll be glad to know he's become a successful writer and is kept by a handsome man no older than he is).

When we would play as a threesome, I became more and more fascinated by Adriano's cock. I never sucked cock in the old days except in a perfunctory, polite way to show I had no taboos, usually to gain a youngster's confidence so I could turn him over. But with Adriano, maybe because I truly love him, I couldn't get enough of his cock (fortunately uncircumcised—he is Spanish after all). Sometimes Teresa and I would "service" him at the same time, each of us licking one side of his dick, taking time out only to kiss each other. One time while I was fucking Teresa, Adriano began to play with my hole, first licking it and then entering it gently with his rigid member. I almost swooned from the pleasure of being invaded by my young lover while I penetrated his wife (I wish he and I could both have married her, but we did celebrate our triune union in bed that night if not at the altar that afternoon).

I gasped from the outrageous pleasure of yielding to him. I realized that now the three of us truly were married. That evening we walked into the village enjoying the siesta stillness and the urban indolence.

ACKNOWLEDGMENTS

Thanks to Bill Clegg, Liese Mayer, Will Evans, Nadja Spiegelman, Yiyun Li, Quinn Roberts, Adrian Lopez Fleming, Isabella Romero Wiehls, Rick Whitaker, Elisabeth Ladenson, Alfred Corn, Philipp Stelzel, Chris Bollen, Nick Radel, Damon Galgut, Beatrice von Rezzori, Mark Bianco, and especially Michael Carroll.

A chapter of this book was published in LitHub. A few passages appeared in German in *Mein schwules Auge*.

A NOTE ON THE AUTHOR

EDMUND WHITE is the author of many novels, including *A Boy's Own Story*, *The Beautiful Room Is Empty*, *The Farewell Symphony*, *Our Young Man*, and *A Saint from Texas*. His nonfiction includes *City Boy*, *Inside a Pearl*, *The Unpunished Vice*, and other memoirs; *The Flâneur*, about Paris; and literary biographies and essays. He was named the 2018 winner of the PEN/Saul Bellow Award for Achievement in American Fiction and received the 2019 Medal for Distinguished Contribution to American Letters from the National Book Foundation.